MW00893470

Contents

HIGH PRAISE FOR BORNEO DAMMED

AARPP Magazine: *"...evoked memories that may or may not be my own, but at this point, who cares? I only wish the print were bigger."*

Toledo Times: *"haven't had so much fun since Billy the Mountain and his wife Ethel left town for Arizona."*

Men's Monthly: *"Totally turgid!"*

Sheboygan Gazette: *"how can you lose with a buxom dark-skinned Ceylonese lady-of-the-night who channels the Flying Nun? Eat your heart out Sally."*

Motorcycle Magazine: *"Roxanne, we love you (sorry about Lucille)."*

Entertainment: *"A light-handed but intensively scholarly work of great cultural importance that instructs while it entertains. A must read."*

Saginaw Daily: *"Goes well with Mrs. Wagner's pies."*

Readers Digestion: *"Soon to be available in condensed form."*

Timber Tree Press: *"Finally, a novelist who knows xylem. His biogeochemistry is impeccable."*

Hollywood Hits: *"Soon to be a major motion picture."*

Argassy: *"A man's man, even if he collects fruit and wears shorts."*

PREFACES

PUBLISHER'S PREFACE

On the basis of its literary quality and the important themes that it covers, Cypress Highlands Press (CHP) is pleased to publish Borneo Dammed. Based on our experience, readers interested in tracking down the author will have a hard go of it. In keeping with his/her interactions with the publishers of his/her previous books of poetry and plays, the author's identity was never revealed to us. Presumably to help reduce his/her traceability, all profits from the sale of this book go to a charity we are contractually disallowed from revealing. Our lawyers have warned that CHP may not be able to avoid litigation and prosecution for some of the salacious contents of Borneo Dammed, but in the interest of *les beaux artes*, we decided to publish this astounding book.

AUTHOR'S PREFACE

This is a work of fiction but Sarawak exists, as does Kuching, but they are not and never were exactly as depicted. For the purpose of this story, where hills were needed they miraculously appear, and realistic travel distances are disregarded when convenient. In contrast to the geographical liberties, efforts were made to assure that the history and biology are accurate. Fact checkers were not employed, and careful readers are sure to uncover numerous errors, some of which were knowingly retained to challenge those sorts of readers. A glossary and chronology are provided as appendices, but there are no footnotes to assist readers unsure of any of the more arcane references---that is why God invented Google. Any resemblance to people living or dead might be attributed to my lack of imagination, insufficiencies in my prose, or the fact that I don't give continental damn about offending people, alive or dead.

Chapter 1. ETHAN GOES TO TOWN

Excerpt from an aerogram from Ethan Yarrow in Kuching, Sarawak, to his parents in Chevy Chase, Maryland:

1 February 1971
Dear Mom and Dad,
I've been in Malaysia for only 4 months but I really feel at home. The people and the forest are fascinating, diverse as all get out, and mostly quite welcoming. I'm getting particularly close with the Iban man with whom I work. Of all the people here, Chinese, Indians, Malays, Bidayuhs, Melenau, and etc., the Iban are the easiest to befriend. I suspect that the approachability of Ibans derives from their sharing a history with Americans. Like us, they're newcomers to this mega-island, having arrived only a few centuries ago. Since then they slashed-and-burned, fought and pillaged their way across the landscape, much like we did in North America. They no longer take heads, but they're still quite aggressive in their manners. Unlike the Bidayuhs, they don't even get along with each other that well---their longhouses--the communal buildings the entire village occupies—grow just so much before one faction or another splits off and colonizes a new area and builds a new longhouse...I'm writing you from Kuching, which Mom wouldn't like but I find fascinating. Great food, overwhelming smells, lots of noise...

THUMP! THUMP! THUMP!
The deep rumblings of a massive single cylinder engine reverberated off the inside wall of the hilltop police station where it roused the three officers from their semi-slumber. They'd been sitting around under the overhead fan sipping tea through the hot hours of the equatorial afternoon and welcomed the divresion. It'd been another quiet early 1970's day in Kuching, a city of 70,000 on the north shore of the mega-island of Borneo in the Malaysian state of Sarawak.
They got up and sauntered out onto the porch. Looking down the road towards town they confirmed that the thumping was emitted by an vintage single-cylinder British motorcycle driven by a young American botanist, a regular visitor to the station.
On duty on that quiet early 1970's day in Kuching, a city of 70,000 on the north shore of the mega-island of Borneo in the Malaysian state of Sarawak, were a slight man of Chinese extraction, a big Tamil Indian, and the ranking officer, a paunchy young Malay. They hadn't seen the motorcycle rider for a few weeks and, although they wouldn't admit it, all looked forward to chatting with him.
The approaching rider was Ethan Yarrow, an American botanist doing his PhD research in Sarawak on the climbing palms that provide the rattan canes used to make furniture. The motorcycle, to which he

referred fondly as "Roxanne," was a 633 cc, single cylinder, side-valved "Big Four" Norton manufactured in '46, a year before the young man's birth. The bike was brought to Malaysia by a British soldier stationed in Kuching after the Japanese surrender.

Ethan's frequent visits to the police station were partially due to its hilltop location. Roxanne, a cantankerous beast of a machine, refused to be kick-started. Ethan's standard explanation for that reluctance was that to be kick-started was an affront to her dignity, a comment on which he refused to elaborate. Motorcycles of that vintage had magnetos, which powered their lights when the engine was running, but no battery and obviously no electric starter. Kick starting was made especially challenging by the massive compression in the single cylinder. To avoid having to enlist assistance jump-starting the 400-pound machine, Ethan tried to park her on hilltops. He sometimes wondered about the influence of that restriction on his social life insofar as it precluded visiting anyone who lived on flat ground or in valley bottoms.

In addition to the convenience conferred by its hilltop location, Ethan considered it wise to touch base regularly with the police who provided him with the permits required for travel into the hinterlands, locally known as the *ulus*, where he carried out his botanical explorations. He also enjoyed the friendly repartee with the now familiar trio and then the walk down through town to the riverside night market where he often took his evening meal.

Ethan pulled Roxanne around in front of the station and parked her where she cast a long shadow over the policemen's Honda 50s. Once he killed the engine, the principal sounds were from the swiftlets hawking insects overhead and the territorial calls of house geckos from inside the station. As he walked up to the steps to the porch, the Tamil man addressed him with his deep and heavily accented English, "Good evening professor. It looks like you've been missing some meals but Roxanne seems to be in fine fiddle. Was she happy to have you back from the *ulus*?"

"Why yes, thank you Officer Ramakrishnan, she does seem glad to have me home," Ethan answered politely in really bad Tamil and then continued in English. "And how's that little ragamuffin of yours?" he asked in reference to Ramakrishnan's 7-year old son and light-of-his life.

"He's driving his mother crazy, but shows potential as a batsman," he replied, beaming with pride. Ramakrishnan was the captain of the cricket team for which Ethan sometimes played. Other than Ethan, the team members were all of Indian descent—Gujaratis, Tamils, and Sikhs, most of whom worked for the government departments other than the military, which had its own team.

Ramakrishnan had lived in Kuching for several years and considered it home, but his family had known many homes over the previous decades. After many generations in the same village in India, their transience still seemed odd, but the family got caught up in the changing times. His father first came to Malaysia late in 1941 with the 7th Indian Battalion of the British Army, which he'd joined to escape from his village in the Indian state of Tamil Nadu. In that impoverished land, even the oldest of his brothers could look forward to inheriting next to nothing. After suffering from the demeaning status of an enlisted local in the British Army and in response to some of what he heard from Indian nationalists, he soon started to question the wisdom of fighting for the colonial overlords. Just two months after they arrived on the island of Penang, the Indian troops and their British officers were overrun by the Japanese. He then spent a month in a prisoner-of-war camp during which the Japanese guards treated the Indians markedly better than the British. That good treatment coupled with his captors convincing arguments for "Asia for the Asians" and the "Asian Co-Prosperity Scheme," he joined a large group of Indian soldiers who switched sides and agreed to fight for the Japanese against the long-nosed colonialists in Burma. It didn't take long in Burma to realize that the Japanese were more brutal than the British. In mid-1944 when his battalion was decimated by American bombers, he deserted and made his way overland back to the jungles and rubber plantations of northern Malaya. There he waited out the end of the war and then joined the newly constituted police force. A little more than two decades later, his son followed him into the police after finishing 5th form in a high school in the Malaysian state of Kedah near the Thai border. To secure a slight promotion, that son accepted what was considered a hardship assignment in Sarawak. The only hardship he experienced, which was being away from his parents, was relieved when his father retired from government service and the family was united in Kuching.

The next to speak up was Wong Swee Lee, a man of Hokkien Chinese descent whose family had been in Sarawak for centuries. His ancestors fled coastal China in the early 1700s in response to increasing repression by the Manchus who'd taken over the country. His people were merchants, and under that Ching Dynasty, anyone in business was suspect, especially the firms to which government representatives owed money. Soon after they arrived in Sarawak, antimony and then gold were discovered inland from Kuching near the town of Bau. His ancestors joined other Hokkien merchants in setting up shops to supply the miners, most of whom were Hakka speakers. There were ancient rivalries between Hokkien and Hakka people, who hailed from the same general region in China, but they mostly coexisted peacefully except in 1857 when Hakka miners attacked Kuching. That quickly suppressed rebellion was nominally against the White Rajahs of Borneo, but Hokkien merchants were also targeted.

The Wongs flourished financially under the Brooke Regime (1841-1946) and continued to thrive during the brief period of British rule after World War II. The tide turned against them in 1963 when Sarawak joined the new Federation of Malaysia. Due to incursions of politically powerful Malays from Kuala Lumpur and elsewhere in Peninsular Malaysia, their fortunes steadily diminished. Chinese business communities were long accustomed to contributing to the upkeep of inept governments, which they were adept at keeping at bay, but the Wongs and others were caught unawares by the Malay's lack of business-savvy. The government's many Chinese-restricting regulations were bad for all parties, the Malays included. To survive, and in keeping with their time-tested ability to adapt, many Chinese companies took on Malay partners, who served as ethnically appropriate figureheads but were given little power to damage the business, the workings of which they were often blissfully unaware. These 'Ali Baba' companies where proliferating with the 'Ali' being the Malay front man and the 'Baba' the Chinese in charge.

That Swee Lee was a police officer irked his father, a successful merchant, but Swee Lee was and always had been remarkably lazy, which suited him well for government service. Over the months that Ethan was in Sarawak, the two men became connected in numerous ways. Swee Lee referred to one of these connections when he said, "My sister's husband was asking about you the other day when I was up in *Sungei Lengkap* (Lengkap River). He wondered if you planned to visit again soon." Swee Lee's brother-in-law ran a small pottery factory just outside the fence surrounding the resettlement village where Hakka Chinese farmers had been relocated a few years earlier by the government. The official justification for this forced move into the internment camp was the concern that the farmers were providing the mostly Chinese "communist" insurgents with food and other sorts of support.

"My sister's family apparently enjoys reading with you," said Swee Ming, and then continued with a slight smile and teasing tone, "but professor, I've seen some of the pots you made and recommend you stick with your plants," and then laughed.

Ethan smiled at this derogatory comment about his admittedly limited skills as a potter, but then teased Swee Lee back by saying, "Okay, I agree, but I'm still learning. But I should also say that your young nephew Lim Boo, although a relative of yours, is sharp as a tack." They all laughed and Ramakrishnan patted Swee Lee amicably on the shoulder. Although that boy was only 13 years old, Ethan looked forward to their intellectual interchanges. The boy's father was also a great source of insights into local politics and history, which Ethan very much appreciated. Their routine was that Ethan would work at a pottery wheel, under the guidance of the boy's firm-handed grandmother, while Lim Boo and his father would discuss politics, history, and whatever they had recently read. They mostly read short stories and novels selected by Ethan from those he received via diplomatic pouch from his mother.

Swee Lee and Ramakrishnan appreciated that Ethan seemed genuinely interested in their families and that he made efforts to speak both Chinese and Tamil. That he was such a pleasant chap made them wonder about the strong suggestion they'd both received in private from none other than Cheong "Eddie" Hing Hong, one of most prominent Chinese businessmen in Kuching. Mr. Cheong had encouraged them both to do what they could to keep Ethan out of trouble. When he inquired about why they should look out for the young American's well-being and the sorts of trouble to which he was prone, the older man simply used the expression, *zhu-lian jiu-zu*, which literally means 'cousin nine-times removed,' and then was unwilling to elaborate.

Ethan then spoke to the Malay officer in his best Bahasa Malaysia, the official language of the new nation. "And good evening to you Captain Abdullah bin Mustafa. I was thinking about you a few evenings back while enjoying a lovely bowl of Ipoh-style curried *laksa*."

Abdullah, who was actually only a lieutenant and not a captain, wasn't yet sure of what to think of the American. Whereas his interactions with the young man were always pleasant, and he was impressed by the quality of his Malay language skills, he'd been warned about Ethan by his superior officer. His instructions were similar to those received by his fellow officers insofar as he was advised to keep an eye on him, but not in the protective or supportive sense. Although no specific accusations or allegations accompanied that advice, he figured that Ethan was suspected of falling into that nebulous class of "outside agitator" about which the Malay leaders of the country were so concerned. Their concerns were perhaps justified insofar as Malays from Peninsular Malaysia, all of whom were also Muslim, had essentially taken over the government of Sarawak where they constituted a small portion of the population. Abdullah's interpretation of his superior's instructions were confirmed the last time he was advised about Ethan. He was told to look for grounds for deportation, which were easy to find due to the far-reaching and vaguely defined police powers under the Internal Securities Act. That Act, which could not legally be discussed in public due to the country's tough anti-sedition laws, effectively stifled political dissent. Both laws were loathed by the non-Malays who constituted the majority of the Malaysian population and a super-majority in Sarawak. Ethan was amused that despite the legal prohibition on discussing those laws, the topic that dominated the private conversations among non-Malays was Article 153 of the Malaysian Social Contract, which bestowed on the *Bumiputra* (literally 'princes of the earth' and usually used in reference to ethnic Malay people but included other natives).

In regards to Ethan's teasing about having eaten his favorite food, Abdullah knew perfectly well that the young botanist had been in the *ulus* of the Third Division and nowhere near his home state of Perak in Peninsular Malaysia. He nevertheless went along with the joke and said, "I am indeed jealous and also fascinated that your Dayak buddies have mastered the art of cooking Ipoh *laksa*. Did you have it with or without palm grubs?"

Ethan laughed and responded, "I'm trying to cut down on grubs...wreaking havoc on my girlish figure," at which he stuck out his hip in a funny pose, "but if they're serving them fresh at the night market this evening, I might indulge myself."

While all four men were still chuckling, Ethan waved farewell and started walking down the hill into town on his way to the riverside market. Despite the air-cleaning late afternoon storm, when he reached the boundary fence around the police compound at the foot of the hill, he was hit with the first strong smell of the tropical city into which he was plunging. The pungent odors varied with the shifting breezes and ranged from the cloyingly sweet aroma of *ylang-ylang* (*Cananga odorata*) tree flowers, to the fetid odors of open sewers mixed together with the redolent emissions from the Kuching River at low tide. He smiled to himself when he thought what his mother would do if he told her that Kuching smelled like home, but he did indeed feel at home in Sarawak.

Ethan was well known in Kuching, appreciated for his friendliness, and easily spotted because he stood a head taller than most Malaysians. In photographs the young man was not particularly handsome, but in person his upright posture and the fluidity of his movements evoked the image of a Spanish matador, not an American botanist. That resemblance, according to Yarrow family legends, derived either from an escapee from the ill-fated Spanish Armada or from some Berber involved in the ancient Huberian-Iberian sea-trade. His mother joked that although his prominent Yarrow family nose somehow 'worked' on the face of a boy, as it did on his father and had on his grandfather, she would not envy a woman so endowed. Given that Yarrow families seemed to invariably spawn but one offspring per generation, and always a male, she was not aware of any females who had suffered that fate. As per usual, Ethan sported a batik shirt that was neat but obviously well washed and just a bit threadbare; that many of those washings involved beatings on river rocks was unlikely to be recognized by residents of this bustling third-world city.

On the outskirts of town Ethan approached Chan Motors, run by Bernie Chan, a widely respected if somewhat unconventional mechanic. His small shop was in a rickety wooden building with a rusted metal roof and sliding wooden doors that sagged on their hinges. Against the walls outside and on the peripheries of the shop inside, various machine parts were strewn around and amassed in piles, but the center of the shop was clear and occupied by a gleaming metal lathe. Ethan was a fairly adept mechanic, but he turned to Bernie when he needed advice, as did many other professional mechanics and machinists in Kuching. Many of Roxanne's parts were fabricated by Bernie on that metal lathe. With a sort of harmonic progression, the lathe was surrounded by concentric rings of increasingly obscure and grime-coated engine parts.

In addition to being a great mechanic, Bernie was widely known because, as the afternoon progressed, he slowly transformed himself into Bernice. By six, when he closed the shop, the Bernie-to-Bernice transformation was nearly complete—she would be dressed for the evening but with her hair up in curlers. It was a testament to the tolerance of the people in this multi-ethnic, multi-cultural, and multi-religion town that Bernie/Bernice was accepted as a fact-of-life and appreciated as source of local color. Sarawak was famous for its cultural tolerance; it was normal to see a Hindu temple next to a Muslim mosque, with a Christian church and a Buddhist shrine nearby. Socially, people of different ethnic and religious backgrounds also cohabited comfortably and the assembled multitudes offered a cuisine that rivaled Singapore in its diversity. That tolerance and diversity had recently started to be eroded by the influx of fairly strident and intolerant Malay people from Peninsular Malaysia. There was little Islamic fundamentalism; it was rare to see a Muslim woman with a veil, and burqa-wearers stopped traffic, but the Muslimization campaign was starting to cause social rifts. Also eroding the customary social tolerance were the many federal mandates, regulations, and quotas that favored Muslim Malays over other ethnic and religious groups.

Bernice did not make a particularly pretty woman, but was definitely striking in her heels and revealing attire— exactly what was being revealed was the subject of much idle curiosity. Having just spent the afternoon describing in botanical Latin the male and female genitalia (i.e., the flowers) of a species of palm that seemed to be new to science, Ethan smiled when he considered describing Bernie/Bernice in that dead language.

Learning Latin, a requirement for all plant taxonomists at the time, had been a drudgery for Ethan until he hit upon the idea of using it to write a pornographic short story. It was not his intention to circulate that silly story, but one of his classmates had it mimeographed and sent copies to their botanical colleagues, thereby securing for Ethan a somewhat notorious reputation among members of that generally chaste group of scientists.

As Ethan approached the shop he was thinking about Latin descriptors of flower parts and was distracted by a mynah singing its heart out on a branch up in a bedraggled sea almond tree. For these reasons he failed to see Bernice until she spoke in what she believed was a Bette Grable accent, "Hey handsome, going my way?" Before Ethan could respond, she continued, "I heard Roxanne go thumping by and hoped you'd stop in for a chat. I have so much to tell you," she continued almost breathlessly with a not very well executed Mae West impersonation.

Bernie/Bernice liked the young American, with whom he'd worked closely, but he too had been asked by Eddie Cheong to look out for Ethan's best interests. Bernie thought it best to not ask for an explanation for this request, especially after Eddie had employed that phrase *zhu-liam jiu-zu*, which suggested some sort of obscure familial relationship. Furthermore, he was inclined to do whatever Eddie asked because he, like many other Chinese merchants in Kuching, needed the Chair of the Hokkien Businessman's Association to help ward off the increasingly onerous demands of the newly elected city government officials.

Bernie/Bernice's fondness for Ethan first derived from the fact that he was more accepting than most of the other expats in Kuching. Their friendship was secured one afternoon while they worked together on Roxanne's drive train. Ethan was rambling on about his father being a musician and how he and his very 'interesting' friends threw such wild parties. Something about the way he described those parties and people caused Bernie to surmise that some of his father's friends were gay. That impression was confirmed when Ethan mentioned that some of his father's friends were victimized during Senator Joe McCarthy's 'Lavender Purges' of the 1950s.

"And you are the picture of loveliness, ready to break some hearts it would appear," Ethan said good-naturedly.

"You lie so sweetly, I think I'll believe you. But before you go off to trip the lights fantastic there really is something I need to tell you," Bernice said in a hushed tone that suggested she was bursting to reveal a great secret. "When I was down on the rockets the other evening," she said in reference to the flotilla of houseboats on the Kuching River that included many of the town's brothels, "I heard some really tough looking Malay chaps talking —ex-military by the looks of them, but gone to fat. I wouldn't have paid any attention, not my type, but then one of them mentioned you by name. Just then that silly black girl from Ceylon came in and they stopped talking and started gawking, but it sounded to me like someone in high places doesn't like you and that those men are out to cause you harm. I can hardly imagine why--you seem like such a sweet young man. In any case, perhaps you should watch your step a bit--I would be absolutely devastated if anything were to happen to you."

"Perhaps they're amateur botanists and want to consult with me about orchids or something," Ethan said, trying to make light of the warning, "some of those orchid fanciers are pretty rough characters."

"You can joke, but from what I heard happened later, they are really not nice fellows," Bernice explained.

"Why, what happened?" Ethan asked, "Now I am curious."

"Well, those nice Muslim boys were drinking a little too much brandy and started to get rough with some of the girls, which of course Miss Jasmine will not allow."

What Ethan had heard about this Jasmine character was confused and conflicting. He'd been told by different people who were presumably in-the-know that she was a respected stock broker and real estate tycoon, a courtesan to royalty, a hippie, a political advisor, and the Madam for all the whores in the floating city. She was also reportedly fluent in several dialects of Chinese, Japanese, English, Hindi, Tamil, Malay, and Russian. About her ethnic background and nationality there was no agreement whatsoever, but everyone did agree that she was a force to be reckoned with.

"So what happened? Did Miss Jasmine kick their butts?" Ethan asked.

"No, of course not you silly boy. Miss Jasmine does not involve herself in such sordid affairs. But the girls did take matters into their own hands in a most amusing fashion," Bernice continued, obviously enjoying the story. "One minute those bad boys were high and dry and harassing some of my favorite ladies-of-the-night and the next they were swimming in the ooze," she said with a laugh, "which must have been yucky because the tide was low at the time."

"I don't envy them their swim in the Kuching River, even at high tide. It reminds me too much of my mother's greasy gravy, but lumpier."

"But do let me give you the blow-by-blow description of what happened," Bernice insisted and then continued when Ethan gave her an encouraging nod. "I don't know which of the approaches to problem solving is most amusing."

"Do tell," Ethan responded.

"It's really too bad that you haven't met these girls yet," Bernice responded, "but when you do, beware of the Chinese doll...she's a blackbelt in *kung fu*. When she became exasperated by the fattest of the three thugs, she hiked up her dress, spun around, and caught him in the center of his chest with a kick that sent him flying into the drink."

"Yikes, she sounds dangerous," Ethan remarked.

"Ah so petite and sweet, but she does pack a wallop."

"And other pursuers, what were their fates?"

"Also long swims in that murky water. The tall one made the mistake of harassing an overly endowed Malay wench. He was on a gangplank between houseboats when he made a grab for her that she didn't appreciate so she swung around and sent him flying...hit him with both melons," Bernice laughed and then continued. "She watched him flounder for a while, and then threw him a rope, but it wasn't attached to anything, so he too was pulled downstream to the Malay village."

Laughing at the image, Ethan then asked, "And the third of my pursuers, how was it that he ended up swimming?"

"Sister Bertrille, who claims to be a member of the Daughters of Charity order, whacked him overboard with her wimple, which to be perfectly proper is actually a wing of her cornette. That rude man was apparently gazing down into the recesses of deeply plunging neckline of her habit and didn't see it coming," Bernice said, and laughed.

"Wait! Are you telling me that one of the ladies-of-the-night dresses up as a nun?"

"Yep, the Flying Nun to be exact, but with very different proportions and a quite different occupation," Bernice said and they both laughed.

"But how does she even know about the Flying Nun?" Ethan asked.

"Well sir, don't assume that here in this tropical backwater we're entirely unaware of cultural developments in the outside world," Bernice said in a pretend huff.

"My apologies, but I would hardly call the Flying Nun a cultural development," Ethan said laughing.

Bernice looked at him with feigned shock and then warned, "If you want to stay dry when we're down on the river you'd better not say anything bad about the Flying Nun or Sally Field for that matter. Our Sister Bertrille may be a buxom, dark-skinned, and big-bottomed Tamil girl, but she claims to be Sally's twin sister. Up until a few years ago she was Gidget, but she actually seems more comfortable as a vamped nun. She's seen all the episodes multiple times on pirated Betamax tapes. Right before she whacked the thug, for example, she quoted her favorite line."

"Pray tell me what it was, your revelations are most captivating," Ethan responded politely.

"*When lift plus thrust is greater than load plus drag, anything can fly,*" Bernice quoted and then continued. "In case you consider getting fresh with the good Sister, you should also know that the humidity was causing her wimple wings to wilt, so I reinforced them with 10-guage wire, so they really do pack a wallop."

"I'll be sure to be on my best behavior. But yes, let's make a date of it, now I'm more interested than ever to meet your friends and especially Miss Jasmine, the mystery lady about whom I keep hearing," Ethan said and then continued on his way towards the night market and dinner.

Bernice blew him a kiss and went back into her workshop to continue gussying herself up for an evening on the town.

As Ethan walked he thought about the three thugs mentioned by his mechanic friend. He was starting to realize that despite his efforts at keeping a low profile, as well as his long absences in the forest, there were powerful people in Sarawak who were very much aware of his presence. And although he had never spoken out about environmental issues or the government's disregard of the rights of local people, he suspected that his feelings about those topics were widely known. Seconds later, any glum thoughts were dispelled by a flock of low-flying swifts that swirled past him hawking insects.

After Chan Motors he walked by a series of open-fronted stores that occupied the ground floors of two-story colonial era wooden buildings. The upper floors were business offices and the headquarters of various Chinese business and social societies. The click-clack of mahjong tiles accompanied the street noises of cars, motorcycles, the bells of bicycles, and the cries of hawkers of various wares on display in pushcarts. As he walked he acknowledged the proprietors standing in doorways enjoying the slight breeze. He also smiled at the lounging shop girls, which caused more than a few them to flee inside tittering. Passing the open glass doors of the shiny new Bata Shoe Emporium he was hit by a blast of cold air from their cranked up air conditioner. That cool air reminded him of his planned evening ride up into the hills inland from Kuching, which made him worry about whether his weekly doses of chloroquine, which had so far protected him from malaria but also seemed to have diminished his night vision. He quickly disregarded that explanation in favor of blaming Roxanne's malfunctioning magneto and corroded headlamp.

On the corner just past the shoe store a young teenaged Chinese boy in a disheveled school uniform sat reading on a stool next to a pushcart. His cart featured a hand-cranked ice shaving machine and a Plexiglas box in which sliced pineapple and papaya, as well as skewered pieces of jackfruit were displayed. As Ethan approached the boy jumped up, put down his book, and busied himself with the fruit. By the time Ethan reached him, the boy had a slice of papaya ready for him in a small plastic bag, over which he held a slice of lime, ready to squeeze over the fruit.

With a big smile, the boy said in carefully enunciated English, "Good evening Professor, how are you today?"

"Just fine, Khoon Ming, how is school?" Ethan replied as he handed the boy a dime and accepted the lime-juice-anointed papaya. The fruit and conversation were part of a ritual they'd developed over the past months. After school and until sunset the boy took over the fruit cart so his mother could go home to attend to his younger siblings and cook dinner. She'd previously told Ethan that she would have preferred for Khoon Ming to go immediately home to do his homework, but since the boy's father died, they couldn't forgo the additional income, however modest. For the boy, conversing with a native English speaker was useful, but Ethan often went further than just pleasantries by asking him detailed questions about his school work. Ethan had been impressed by the boy since the first time they met and the boy asked him where he was from. When Ethan replied Madison, Wisconsin, this boy from Borneo astounded him by asking him whether Madison was closer to Beloit or Milwaukee.

After a few minutes with the young fruit vendor Ethan walked on, enjoying the papaya until his musings were interrupted by a greeting from the overly friendly Sikh proprietor of Kuching's best sporting goods store. In addition to selling badminton rackets and shuttles, soccer and cricket supplies, and beautifully woven *sepak-takraw* balls made from fine-stemmed rattan canes, the proprietor was also a travel agent. As if that weren't enough, Ethan had recently learned that the man earned most of his income as a bookie. He was also a great talker and would be happy to bend Ethan's ear for an hour, mostly about cricket, at which he often hinted at his former prowess, but Ethan managed to make it by the store with a wave and a shouted greeting.

Despite his hankering for a beer, Ethan then stopped to chat with the old Sumatran man who ran the best Padang-style restaurant in town. Ethan often took his lunch there when the food was fresh, but after those same dishes sat out on display all day in the tropical heat, he admitted that they were a lot less appealing. Ethan asked about the man's family and chit-chatted for a little while in his best Bahasa Indonesia, which wasn't quite up to the standard of even a moderately well-educated Indonesian but was nevertheless appreciated. Upon leaving, the man used his customary farewell in English of, "okey dokey," the origin of which always piqued Ethan's curiosity. In response, Ethan salaamed in a quite formal manner.

Without breaking stride, for he really did long for a cold beer after pounding away most of the day on his Olivetti, Ethan turned down a *roti canai* (fried unleavened bread served with curry or dahl) from a Tamil man with a pushcart. He next gave a high-five to a teenaged Hakka boy who was arranging his display of bootlegged cassette tapes on a cloth he'd placed on the sidewalk. At the next corner he dropped some coins in the cup of a Malay widow woman with a baby sitting in her customary spot on the curb. Although she had somewhat bedraggled spools of thread to sell, Ethan doubted she ever sold any. He briefly contemplated the fact that supporting beggars and widows was a central tenant of Islam, a religion about which he was determined to learn more.

Chapter 2. NIGHT MARKET WITH TALES OF ROXANNE

Excerpt from an aerogram from Ethan Yarrow in Kuching, Sarawak, to his parents in Chevy Chase, Maryland:

9 February 1971
Dear Mom and Dad,
...I admit that my relationship with Roxanne has its ups and downs. She can be lovely, fun, and thrilling, but some days it's is hard to get her going. I push as much as I can, but sometimes to no avail. She's only a year older me, but sometimes behaves like she's ancient...Ian won't have very much to do with her, but he's flourishing and already discovered several new species of rodents collected by his mentor, the famous "Two Bobs a Nod Harrisson."

When Ethan arrived at the night market, the process of converting a parking lot into a temporary food bazaar was mostly complete. The afternoon rain had washed most of the day's accumulation of trash into the open sewers that ran down to the river and the vendors were busily setting up their tables and chairs while others strung the multicolored lights that would provide illumination and a festive atmosphere.

Ethan was known by many of the vendors from whom he received and returned greetings. Those same vendors then turned to their young female assistants, Malay, Chinese, and Bidayuh alike, and scolded them about neglecting their work. The whispering provoked by Ethan's arrival was quickly replaced by furtive glances and reluctant sweeps of their brooms; they were obviously stung by being deprived of the opportunity to gossip about the notorious but fascinating young man who'd just arrived.

Ethan espied his friend Ian, an English mammologist, and sat down next to him at a round table in front of one of the stalls. He'd barely lifted his finger to place an order when he was delivered a liter bottle of Bintang beer and a glass by a young Chinese waitress who never made eye contact. In contrast to that demure Chinese woman, the similarly employed Bidayuh woman in the next stall was pouting directly at Ethan and obviously on the verge of scolding him for not patronizing her *tokay*'s (shop owner's) establishment.

Ethan and Ian occupied adjacent apartments in a government house in a complex on a small hill on the edge of town. The two apartments were carved out of a large wooden house perched up on stilts. It was built for the British District Officer during the brief colonial era after the Japanese occupation between the last of the Brooke Rajahs and independence.

Around the market the other early-to-arrive patrons had placed their orders and the cooking had commenced. The smells of both the city and the tidal river would soon be overwhelmed by those of frying garlic and *belachang*, a tangy mixture of fermented shrimp and chili peppers.

Before Ethan had taken even a sip of his beer Ian asked, "Why do you continue to tease your mother?"

"Oh, hi Ian, how have you been?" Ethan answered, avoiding the question, "I take it she called again?"

"Of course she called. You were due back a week ago and she was worried."

"That woman," Ethan said with feigned exasperation, "I keep reminding her that it's a jungle out there and transport is not always reliable."

"Actually, I believe that she really wanted to talk to me about Roxanne."

"My motorcycle?" Ethan said with some irony.

"You know perfectly well that your long-suffering mother has no idea that Roxanne is a noisy and unreliable death-trap of a machine"

"Shhhh, careful, Roxanne's so very sensitive, I hope she didn't hear you. But I really hope you didn't give our little secret away. I really do like teasing my mom; she deserves it. Whenever I do talk with her, all she does is prod me about settling down, getting married, and providing her with grandbabies to spoil."

"Well, she told me that you told her in a letter that Roxanne is fast and has trouble stopping."

"And that's the God's truth!"

"Ah well, you are mean. I do so like your mother, despite her scuttling your incipient relationship with my good friend Linda." After a moment's reflection he continued. "To my enduring shame, I continued to play along with your little Roxanne ruse."

In mentioning Linda, Ian referred back to a sunny spring afternoon when Ethan's mother was visiting her son at Oxford. At that time, Ian was finishing his PhD in mammology and Ethan was a Rhodes Scholar reading botany. They were both fellows at Oriel College but had become fast friends after Ethan had bested him in Real Tennis, an ancient European sport also known as *jeu de paume*. No one could believe that although that complicated sport was new to Ethan and Ian was a long-standing champion, he'd beaten the Englishman. Somehow the American had adjusted almost immediately to its arcane rules, nearly dead cork ball covered with woolen cloth, asymmetrical racket and court, sloping penthouse roof rolls, assorted hazards, and other oddities. The other factor that aided their friendship was that they were both outsiders at Oxford. As a Yank, Ethan was readily dismissed by the gentry that still prevailed. Although Ian was very British and quite accomplished, as the son of a coal miner from the Midlands, he could hardly claim to be high-born.

The Linda to whom Ian referred had mentioned to Ian that she wanted to meet his American friend. When Ethan's mother was in town visiting, he arranged an afternoon outing for the foursome to Blenheim

Castle. Ethan knew of Linda and found her attractive but was not aware that an impediment to their having any sort of serious relationship was the Englishwoman's belief that Americans were barbarians and dangerous to themselves and others. Linda figured that being out with Ethan along with his mother and her friend Ian would be a good way to get to know the American without taking any chances.

The afternoon was going swimmingly, the sun even appeared for a few minutes. By the time they'd enjoyed creamed scones in a charming tea house in the castle's formal garden, Linda had shed most of her misgivings about American men, or at least about Ethan. Meanwhile, Ethan's mother had decided that this English hussy was in no way appropriate for her darling son. She successfully hid her growing misgivings about the girl until the group paused on a stone bridge over the moat that surrounded the castle. As they all gazed down at a school of lazily swimming fish she said just loud enough for Linda to hear, "If we had some dynamite we could do some fishing." Judging from Linda's response, Ian realized that the comment about fishing, which he found hilarious, was enough to reconfirm her initial opinion of Americans.

The relationship that flourished after that afternoon was between Ian and Ethan's mother. Ethan had told her that Ian was gay, which didn't faze her in the slightest. Instead, Doris Yarrow found the young Englishman entirely delightful and he, in turn, was charmed by her. Over the next week, while Ethan studied and played ice hockey, Ian always seemed to find time to take her on various outings or just gossip for hours. For one thing, Doris was delighted that Ian looked out for her son. When both boys ended up in Sarawak, she would often call, presumably to talk with her son, but end up chatting with Ian in whose apartment the telephone resided.

"So what did you tell my mother?" Ethan asked in amused concern.

"I agreed that Roxanne is not good for you, that she's taking you to bad places, and that, furthermore, she's too old for you."

"Yikes, I bet she really glommed onto that last comment."

"She sure did....'exactly how old is Roxanne', she asked...she's 30 right? Anyway, that's what I told her. She was shocked by that information and asked what you were doing with an older woman."

"Roxanne, by the way, is only 25—a year older than I am," Ethan corrected with a big smile and then purposefully changed the subject. "How goes it at the Museum? Are you making sense of all those rats and bats?"

"Ah, I persist, but pray tell me about your trip," Ian responded, not willing to take Ethan's bait. "How were the ladies up in the *ulus*? I must admit that I respect you for your eclectic taste in females."

"For a guy who doesn't like girls, you certainly are fascinated by my sex life."

Ian wasn't alone in his interest in Ethan's adventures and in the social mores of the native peoples of Borneo in general. The latter topic had fascinated people around the world since the 1920s when Margaret Mead published her well-known first book, Coming of Age in Samoa. The mostly undeserved reputation for sexual lasciviousness of Dayaks, a catch-all name for all thc indigcnous people of Borneo, was enhanced under the White Rajahs of Sarawak, who discouraged their European employees from bringing European wives until they'd served at least ten years. This rule was particularly stringent under the first of the line, Rajah James Brooke who, to keep his young men in line, encouraged them to co-habit with local women. An advantage of this arrangement was that men with local mistresses learned local languages faster and were better at dealing with issues that required social insights and sensitivity. Those professional benefits were reflected in their native "wives" being referred to as "sleeping dictionaries." To the Iban and Bidayuh people, this was just one of the many strange customs of the European overlords whom they mostly tolerated.

"Sure I'm fascinated. While I'm sorting the skulls and pelts of long dead and little known mammals, you're out in the jungle cavorting with nubile young Bidayuh women."

"You have it all wrong. You let your imagination run away with you. For one thing, I was with Iban on this trip, and I was working. I actually came up with what I think is a new species of rattan."

"But there always seem to be women in your life, and I do so enjoy them vicariously."

"Fine, but in your twisted imagination, you should recognize that I'm providing a valuable social service," Ethan explained with exaggerated patience.

"Some service! For a manly man like you, it sounds more like you died and went to heaven!"

"But after trudging through the forest all day, sometimes all I want is a good night's sleep," Ethan mock complained.

"So tell me, what happened this time? Weren't you going to fend them off by sleeping in a hammock?"

"Ah, now that you mention it, that hammock strategy backfired big time--it was neatly the death of me," Ethan chuckled at the memory and then continued in response to an eager look from his friend. "It intrigues me that whereas no self-respecting Amazonian native would go anywhere without a hammock, or the wherewithal to make one, I have yet to see one here in Borneo."

"But why was the idea stupid?" Ian inquired with some impatience.

"Well it worked the first night. I strung the hammock in the usual room they give me at the end of the old portion of the longhouse and slept like a baby. The next day I was out in the forest with the Iban men all day, felling trees to plant hill rice. When I returned to the longhouse in the evening, totally knackered, I noticed that my things had been rearranged even more than usual. It never occurred to me that Singa and who-knows-who else played in my hammock---I should have unstrung it when I left in the morning. Sure enough, sometime in the middle of the night I was awoken by one of them crawling under the mosquito net and on top of me in the hammock."

"Then what happened and who was it?" Ian said with glee.

"I'm believe it was Singa, but because she couldn't use her typical entry route, I'm not completely sure. But in any case, what happened is that we nearly tore down the bloody longhouse. The ironwood beams and old rattan lashings were really tested by that crazy female. I felt like a small ship in a storm-tossed sea. Luckily the two adjacent rooms are used for storage and not sleeping. I just wonder how far the house swaying was transmitted. In any case, in the morning I woke up alone, as usual, and packed the hammock away."

Ian had finally stopped laughing and was about to respond, probably to ask for more details, but just then their friend Hazel stalked up to the table in her characteristically gruff manner. She abruptly sat down across from the two men and with no preamble, asked in an accusatory tone, "And what terrible sexual exploits is our morally reprehensible American colleague describing?"

Ian often commented that Hazel was more English than the Queen, but the two had been friends since childhood and were comfortable with each other. Amongst the socially conventional, it was convenient that most people mistakingly presumed that they were a couple. Although Hazel was trained as an accountant, she was a fanatical bird watcher and an ardent environmentalist. Her job in Kuching was to keep the books for a British conservation group that was supporting the establishment of protected areas. Although she never admitted it to herself or anyone else, she was starting to like Ethan and already respected his intellect and dedication even if she continued to disapprove of some aspects of his lifestyle.

Ian, calm and collected as always, responded, "Oh, he was just telling me about his new rattan species."

"I'm sure," Hazel said in a feigned huff.

"And don't you look lovely my dear," was Ethan's response, which Hazel acknowledged with a very expressive grunt that indicated her pretend annoyance. Even as a hardened lesbian, Hazel recognized some of Ethan's undeniable charms.

"But now for the big decisions of the day," Hazel charged on in her inimical fashion, "rice, bread or noodles? Fish or fowl? I had beef *rendang* for lunch, but I rather suspect it was *kerbau* (water buffalo) and not cow. Okay, we're ready to order," she said without asking the two men about their preferences. She then signaled the waitress hovering near their table. In keeping with local tradition, they would share several main courses. "Please bring us curried prawns, a pan of *kangkong belachang* (fried Chinese cabbage with garlic and shrimp paste), and a plate of chicken with black bean sauce."

"And rice," Ethan added unnecessarily, with a wink at the waitress.

The threesome was soon joined by a few other friends and the dinner passed with a lively discussion of new government-sponsored efforts to promote the establishment of oil palm plantations, the reasons for the apparent failure of the orangutan rehabilitation center to rehabilitate even a single of the too-intelligent-for-their-own-good orangutans, and the revealed shenanigans of some local politicians. In the relative cool of the evening after the party broke up, Ethan walked back up to the police station, jump-started Roxanne on the hill, and took her for a fast ride out the Bau Road to blow the carbon from both their cylinders.

Chapter 3. JUNGLE WITH JIKA

Excerpt from an aerogram from Ethan Yarrow in Kuching, Sarawak, to his parents in Chevy Chase, Maryland:

2 March 1971
Dear Mom and Dad,
Sorry for the gap between letters but I've been off in the ulus *and out of touch. I remain enchanted with the forest here—it's gothic and inspirational, far grander than those Amazonian tangles I used to favor. I feel so lucky to be able to spend so much time in cathedral-like groves and especially appreciate being out with Jika, my Iban guide/teacher/friend. He's fully a foot shorter than me, but bigger in every other way. Inky blue tattoos cover his body up to his chin, each with its own story---don't worry Mom, I'm not even tempted (and I remember your threat to get whatever tattoo I do). Several of his tattoos commemorated events when he was a resistance fighter with the Sarawak Rangers and that English polymath, Tom Harrisson. He showed me the Japanese heads he took, which are kept separate from those that confer more status. Don't worry about him taking my head— he's assured me that I'm too ugly for a trophy---then he laughed uproariously...he and the other Iban do like to laugh.*

After dining on the sticky and nearly tasteless sago paste they'd extracted from the stem of a palm, fish they'd caught in a net they'd fashioned from palm leaf fibers, and fresh fern fiddleheads, the two men relaxed around the embers of their cook-fire sucking the sweet flesh from seeds of *mata kuching* (eye of the cat fruit). Ethan reclined on the bark hammock he'd strung between two small trees while Jika squatted comfortably on the split bamboo platform on which they would both sleep. They were awaiting darkness, which descends quickly in the tropics, confident with their preparations for the night.

Just before arriving at their campsite after a long day of plant collecting, they found a *mata kuching* tree in full fruit beside the *jalan kancil* (trail of a mouse deer) Jika claimed they'd followed most of the day. They gathered all the fruit they could eat from clusters that emerged from near the base of the trunk. Ethan had seen cacao and other trees that bore fruits on their trunks, a habit known as cauliflory, but this was the first time he'd seen fruits produced so close to the ground.

On his first expedition with Jika, Ethan was surprised by the frequency with which they encountered trees that produced edible fruits growing near trails, and even near the less-than-trails they followed through what he presumed was pristine forest. The reason for this localized super-abundance of useful species gradually became clear while he became less convinced about the existence of any truly virgin forests. For one thing, whenever his Iban friend encountered a fruit tree encumbered by vines or crowded by less useful neighbors, he would stop to liberate it with a few deft swipes of his *parang* (a short and heavy-bladed machete). He also planted the seeds of any fruits they'd eaten before abandoning a camp site.

While Ethan's research concerned the taxonomy of climbing palms, he was becoming increasingly intrigued by the Iban sense of ownership. In regards to fruit trees, for example, he'd learned that those an Iban planted or tended within a day or two walk from their longhouse were claimed as personal property that was passed on to their children and from which no one else could collect fruit without permission. This concept of ownership was intriguing to Ethan insofar as Ibans didn't seem to apply the same concept to the land itself, a cultural trait that was fully exploited by land-grabbing Chinese, British, and, most recently, Malays.

"What do you figure eats *mata kuching* other than brave white hunters and savages of questionable nobility?" Ethan garbled with his mouth full of fruit. The edible portion of a *mata kuching* fruit is just the fleshy coat of the marble-sized seeds. After peeling off the leathery skin, the tart and flavorful flesh is typically sucked off one seed at a time, but Ethan preferred to fill his cheeks with them and then savor both the flavor and the texture of the smooth seeds.

Jika smirked at his young friend's ironic sense of humor and then responded, "Oh, I suppose the regulars, orangutans, gibbons, sun bears, and civets—I also once found *mata kuching* seeds in the scat of a leopard cat, but I believe the tree hopes its fruits are eaten by tortoises."

Ethan grunted amiably in response to yet another of Jika's intriguing natural history observations. It certainly was plausible—tortoises love fruit and can't climb to get them, so why not? He recalled that on one of their previous trips they'd encountered a large tortoise that Ethan figured would soon end up in their dinner pot. To his surprise, after they watched the ancient-looking reptile lumber down the trail for a few minutes, Jika squatted down in front of it, mumbled something to it, got up, and walked on leaving the animal unscathed. When Ethan later asked what had transpired, Jika explained that he had asked for the tortoise, to whom he was related, for its blessing.

The day they'd found the *mata kuching* fruit they'd climbed and descended several substantial hills, but both were accustomed to that physical regime and neither was very tired when they reached the place where they would camp. Their collections of palm samples were few, but the young scientist was pleased with their work and still impressed by the older man's uncanny ability to spot new species. During the months they'd worked together in the forest, their overall collection of palms and other species was substantial, with a few likely new to science.

As they sat in comfortable silence in the darkness under a closed canopy of tall trees, the air temperature suddenly dropped several degrees while fronds of understory palms around their camp simultaneously rustled and then stopped. When Ethan first experienced this temperature-drop-phenomenon he mistook the chill as a warning of an on-coming malaria-induced fever. After several similar early evening experiences, none of which were followed by fever, Ethan deduced that the effect was akin to cold air drainage down into mountain valleys. After sunset the air above the forest cools and increases in density. When that body of air is sufficiently heavy, it breaks through the canopy and plunges down into the understory. Over his months in Amazon, Ethan had never experienced this phenomenon, but then he remembered that those forests are much more dynamic and thus the canopy is structurally more heterogeneous than the dipterocarp forests of Borneo. In contrast to the closed canopy and open-understory dipterocarp forests that he was growing to love, those Amazonian forests were jungly tangles.

After a while, Jika commented, "I heard some Malay goons are after you."

"Ah, word travels fast. I'm not exactly sure what I did to annoy them, but it's troubling," Ethan responded.

"You didn't annoy them," Jika explained, "but their boss considers you an outside agitator."

"Who's their boss?"

"Paib," Jika responded.

"You mean Abdul Paib bin Mahmud, the Chief Minister's nephew and Deputy Minister?"

"Yep, one and the same, those Melenau bastards," Jika muttered with surprising vehemence for a usually even-keeled man.

Ethan knew that there was some traditional strife between the Iban and other ethnic groups in Sarawak, but he was only starting to understand how those conflicts were playing out. For one thing, unlike the Iban, most Melenau people were Muslims and could pass as Malays, which greatly increased their political base. Although a minority ethnic group in Sarawak, that alliance with other Muslims gained them access to substantial political power.

"Perhaps I'm missing something, but it sounds to me that these are people that you don't like very much."

"Ah but you are perceptive. I should have killed his uncle when I had a chance during the war—nasty collaborator that one. But young Paib seems smarter and even more dangerous. I suggest you steer clear of them both," Jika advised.

After a few minutes silence, Jika guffawed with laughter.

"What's so funny now? I have bad men after me and you're laughing."

"Sorry, I shouldn't make light of your situation. But I was going to say that you should try to fit in better, adopt some sort of camouflage so you don't attract so much attention," Jika explained.

"And what's so funny about that?" Ethan asked.

"You're so tall and that beak of yours is so large that the only place you would blend in would be in a herd of skinny tapirs," Jika explained, and then laughed again.

Ethan harrumphed at his friend's comment and then they both just listened to the night sounds of the forest. While they reclined comfortably on their flexible bamboo-slat beds, the fire burned down to ash-covered embers and then the darkness was complete, but not for long. As his eyes became accustomed to the dark, Ethan could see that the edges of every fallen leaf and twig were outlined by bioluminescent fungi. Only where their footsteps had broken the connecting threads was the spectral light not evident. He wondered if he could backtrack on the path they'd followed that day, just by seeing where the fungal hyphae had been ruptured.

After a few more minutes, Ethan's belief was reaffirmed that when out in nature, something miraculous always happens if you watch for long enough. He espied a pair of bright lights approaching their camp. Suspecting that Jika was watching the same thing, Ethan quipped "That look to you like a Land Rover or a Datsun?"

Jika laughed at the joke that dated back to one of first nights they'd spent together in forest many miles from the closest road. Despite having read about Bornean beetles that sported lights on either side of their carapace, Ethan had mistaken one for a distant automobile, which Jika wouldn't let him forget.

Even farther back, when they went on their first plant collecting expedition together, Ethan assumed that as a veteran tropical researcher, he was appropriately outfitted. His external framed Kelty backpack filled with everything he needed weighed about 45 pounds, which he could manage. After working in the forest with Jika for half a year, his kit was reduced to less than 20 pounds, not including the can of spirits they used to pickle the plant samples they stashed along the trail for later pickup. The can got lighter every day as they used the alcohol, which Ethan admitted was a blessing. He'd long since traded his fancy backpack for a simple one fashioned from split rattan canes by one of the women in Jika's longhouse. It had shoulder straps, but he more often used the padded crown strap that left his hands free. In it he carried a change of clothes, a sarong, a small mosquito net, however many chloroquine tablets he'd need for his weekly doses, several fish hooks and some monofilament line, a spoon, a roll of plastic, a ball of parachute cord he seldom used since learning which lianas served the same purposes, a small flashlight, and the US Army issue compass and Zippo lighter his father gave him when he first stated his jungle work. They employed the lighter daily whereas the compass remained unused, at least when Ethan was with Jika. In the way of foodstuffs he started each trip with a bag of salt, a half-kilo of dried fish, and a few days' supply of rice. For footwear he'd replaced his canvas and leather U.S. Army issue jungle boots with a pair of slip-on tennis shoes made from latex tapped from Brazilian rubber trees like the ones the Iban grew in plantations and tapped when they needed cash. Those shoes, which sold for just a few *ringgit* (1 *ringgit* = $0.25) and were jokingly known as "Adidas *Kampong*" (village Adidas), were familiar footwear for jungle workers, rubber tappers, and other rural poor people; Ethan was one of the few Europeans to wear them. Unlike the boots, the rubber shoes didn't get wet and weighed almost nothing. Inside his *Adidas Kampong* and tied with a drawstring just beneath his knee, Ethan wore leech socks. Although they didn't provide complete protection from the blood suckers that abounded on the forest floor and dropped down on passerbys from low branches, they reduced the carnage. On his hip, Ethan strung a wooden sheath that enclosed a small *parang,* the heavy-bladed local bush knife favored by forest people in Asia. He'd soon add to his kit a short-barreled blowpipe fashioned by Jika from Bornean ironwood, but initially he left the hunting to his more able companion.

Ethan's *parang* had been a special gift from Jika after their first expedition. On that trip Ethan carried a long-bladed machete of the sort he'd used in Cuba when he joined a sugarcane cutting Vinceremos Brigade of revolutionaries from Madison. That sort of tool was great for giant grasses, but not as versatile as the much smaller *parang* that Jika had given him. Over the months since, Ethan had come to realize just how special that *parang* was while remaining mystified about why Jika had presented it to him. First of all, unlike most local *parangs*, which were made from truck leaf springs, this one was fashioned from the much higher-quality steel from the bar of a chainsaw. It was hard to sharpen but retained its edge much longer than the softer leaf spring metal. The particular chainsaw bar from which this *parang* was fashioned was special because it was from the saw that cut the tree that fell and killed Jika's elder son when he worked in a Japanese timber concession near Miri. Ethan had learned this portion of the *parang*'s story from the same old women who made his backpack, not from Jika himself. But Jika did proudly explain the significance of the matching wooden sheath and handle, both of which he'd carved from a plank of teak he'd found submerged in the mud on the bottom of the Skerang River. Back in 1841, that particular site witnessed an epic battle between James Brooke, the first White Rajah of Sarawak and his Iban allies from the Second Division against renegade Iban from the Third Division. Given that teak is not native to Borneo but is widely used in shipbuilding, Jika reasoned that the plank was from of one of Brooke's boats that sunk during the battle.

Jika's family had resided in and around Sarawak's Second Division for nearly 10 generations, about which he knew a remarkable amount. Stories of great grandparents back to the great grandparents of great grandparents, were still told while families sat around in the semi-darkness on the verandah of their longhouse after evening meals. The Iban valued these oral histories highly and also valued the capacity to retain and relate them well. Jika himself was not a renowned raconteur, at least not by Iban standards, but he'd related many of his family stories to Ethan as they waited for sleep to overtake them while bivouacked in the forest. While he didn't boast, he could trace his ancestry back to the Iban warriors who sided with James Brooke back in the 1840s. That connection, which was widely known, meant that he had to be careful when working in the Third Division lest he reawaken historical antagonisms.

Jika's kit was even sparser than Ethan's except that he carried an ironwood blowpipe that was about as tall as he was, as well as a bamboo-and-rattan sheath for the poison-tipped darts and wadding. He too sported a woven rattan basket on his back and wore *Adidas Kampong*, but with shorts and no socks. His *parang* was even smaller than the one he gave Ethan, but shared the same genesis.

Ethan and Jika were equipped similarly, but Ethan was frequently impressed by the older man's impressive economy of motion. Whether swinging a *parang* or simply stepping over a log, Jika moved like a dancer, expending no more energy than needed.

On botanical expeditions in the Amazon and field courses in Costa Rica, Ethan surprised people when, with the first raindrops, he'd pull from his pack a folding umbrella. He'd learned that in the heat and humidity of tropical forests, raincoats are worthless—you got just as wet from sweat as from the rain. In contrast, other than in thick brush, an umbrella worked perfectly. On their first joint expedition when Ethan pulled out his umbrella, Jika just smiled and with a few deft chops of his machete, fashioned a palm frond umbrella that was twice as large and equally effective. After that, Ethan reserved his umbrella for city use.

Whereas Ethan was very much Jika's student when it came to jungle craft, Ethan's hammock-making prowess still made Jika smile. When they were out on their first collecting trip, that simple craft had started Jika on the path towards respecting the young man's woods skills. Hammocks are not unknown in Borneo, but for some reason they remain very much a Latin American form of appropriate technology. Ethan could fashion a workable hammock from the bark of a tree sapling in just under a minute—but it was not just any species of sapling, it had to be a member of the basswood family, so named for the long bast fibers in their bark. He'd find a suitable sapling, reach up and cut the crown off overhead, lop it off at the ground, beat the bark with the flat of his *parang* or against a tree, and then peel off the bark as you would take a sock off inside out. Then he'd gently separate the long fibers, tie a length of parachute cord to each end, string it between two trees, and make himself comfortable. With only a sarong to keep himself warm at night, Ethan chose not to overnight in hammocks, but they were more comfortable than chairs or the forest floor for sitting around in the evenings. In contrast, Jika was comfortable squatting on his haunches for hours on end.

The next day was much like the previous, and when they arrived where they would camp for the night, they set about preparing for the evening without even speaking. They first worked together with their *parangs* to clear a small area in the understory. With the fronds of understory palms gathered together into brooms, they'd sweep the sparse leaf litter down to the mineral soil, and then set the palm leaves aside to fashion a quick roof in case it rained. Jika then constructed a sleeping platform for them both from split bamboo lashed with strips of rattan, over which he framed but did not cover a roof. When bamboo was scarce or leeches were numerous, they'd floor their sleeping platform with the bark of a latex-producing tree species, sticky-side down. While Jika built, Ethan collected the small amount of firewood they'd use to cook their evening meal. Meanwhile Jika's dog, which Ethan had nicknamed Guapo, Spanish for "handsome" because of his protuberant ribs, torn ears, and many scars, silently ran in increasingly large circles around the camp, searching for signs of game.

After the ten or so minutes it took them to set up camp, Jika headed off with his blowpipe on the heels of his trusty dog. Dusk and dawn were the best times to hunt because as the nocturnal animals replaced the diurnal both were disoriented and more susceptible to a well-aimed poison dart. Along a game trail that was not perceptible to Jika but quite evident to Guapo, Jika set a few wire snares that they'd collect in the morning, empty or not. Given how few animals Ethan ever saw, he was impressed by how often the Jika-Guapo team hunts were successful. If their prey was larger than a jungle rat, squirrel, or mousedeer that the three could eat at one sitting, they'd stay put for a day to give Jika a chance to salt and smoke the meat. Ethan never minded these interruptions of their regular schedule because they allowed him time to explore nearby areas more thoroughly and recover from their often arduous pace, plus the jerky was always appreciated as a complement to their usually meagre fair.

While Jika and Guapo hunted, Ethan collected edible fern fiddleheads and a palm heart, and made himself a hammock. After dropping the vegetables at the campsite, he headed off to the stream to take a quick splash bath and wash out his still sweaty shirt. Refreshed, he took out a hook and a length of monofilament and fished for a few minutes until it was time to return to the camp. The fish he caught were small but would be appreciated since they were near the end of their trip and had run out of supplies, which was why they were eating palm sago mixed with anything edible they caught or collected.

When they returned to camp after less than an hour of foraging, Ethan had a string of fish, none of which more than three inches long, and a discarded glass jar he'd found near the stream. Jika and Guapo returned without meat but carrying two pointed wooden stakes with their ends painted yellow.

Jika looked at Ethan's string of tiny fish and jokingly asked, "Did they put up much of a fight?"

Ethan responded in kind, "And you and your silly dog," at which point he glanced down at the dog who assumed a guilty look, with his ears back and his tail between his leg, "have exactly what to contribute to the pot?" It was unusual but not unprecedented that Jika's hunt would fail, but they soon realized that one reason for this particular failure was that the area had been hunted out.

Jika held up the stake and quipped "perhaps if we had some spices," he said with a glint in his eye, "we could make these into a soup," and then continued in a very serious tone, "a line of these runs up to the ridgetops on both sides of the stream."

Ethan looked at Jika with consternation and then held up the discarded jar he'd found. "There's a fairly recent campsite just upstream with trash strewn about. I believe this once contained Vegemite, so at least one of the campers was an Aussie—they're the only ones who can stomach this wretched stuff," he said while making a wry face about the strong-flavored, brewers' yeast-based spread. "It looks like they were here for a while, which might explain why you and your miserable mutt came back empty-handed," to which Guapo flapped his tail as if he appreciated the vindication.

Jika thought for a minute and then said, "I heard about a group of miners in Kapit who planned to come up this way. The people in Long Berawan will know what's going on, but these are bad signs and I'm worried. We can make it to Long Berawan tomorrow if we climb up onto the ridge and follow it for a few clicks before dropping down to the Balui River just above the rapids. Then if we're lucky, someone will be fishing in a boat will give us a lift but even if we have to walk, we should be there in time for dinner. Oh, but now I remember, you know that walk and those rapids intimately," Jika said with a chuckle.

The plan that Jika proposed would require cutting their trip short by a day or two, and after making the suggestion, Jika worried that he had presumed too much. Although he thought of Ethan as his nephew and not his boss, it was easy for him to overlook the fact that he was actually only a paid guide and that Ethan was the boss and these were the young man's expeditions. Ethan had never "pulled rank" on the older man, whom he regarded as his teacher and friend, but Jika had done his best to avoid any cause for him to do so. Now he feared he'd overstepped the unstated bounds of their relationship. His concern lasted only a few heartbeats because Ethan almost immediately responded, "Yes, by all means. We have plenty of specimens and these signs are indeed worrisome." He then added with a smile, "and I'm not looking forward to your curried stake dinner."

While talking they'd prepared dinner so as to be finished before darkness fell. In the absence of rice they settled for the palm sago they'd extracted the day before. That gelatinous tapioca actually went well with the fish Ethan caught and the chopped heart of one of the palms from which they had collected a specimen, which was bitter to Ethan's palate but quite edible.

The next morning they were up and out of the camp well before full light. The trek up to and along the quartzite ridge was much longer than either anticipated due to a large landslide they had to circumvent. The vegetation on the ridge itself was sparse and the going was easy, but the soil was course and severely drained, which meant that there was no water. On the way up they'd quenched their thirst from water vines--it never ceased to amaze Ethan that so much delicious water would pour out of a few feet of vine stem, if cut first above and then below. Water vines didn't grow on the thin quartzite-derived soil on the narrow ridge, so they resorted to drinking water from pitcher plants, which grew in abundance. To prevent ingesting the partially digested carcasses of the insects that were the remains of the plants' nitrogen-rich prey, Jika showed him how to strain the water through shredded fibers they collected from the bases of palm leaves. Despite his raging thirst, Ethan had to admit that the flavor of pitcher plant water left a lot to be desired. He looked forward to really quenching his thirst when they reached the river.

They walked along the ridge for a few hours on a fairly well established trail. The going was easy, but the sun was hot. Ethan was walking in front while Guapo ranged more widely with his nose to the ground. As he walked along quietly, without warning, the small dog launched himself at Ethan from the side, knocking him to the ground and nearly off the narrow ridge. He fell into a shrub with stiff branches that tore his trousers and scratched his arms. As he struggled to extract himself and remove the dog, who had fallen on top of him, Jika came up to investigate the commotion. He looked down at Ethan to check that he was okay, and then inspected the trail ahead. While Ethan continued to curse the dog, Jika patted Guapo affectionately on the head, which caused Ethan to switch his diatribe from dog to owner.

When Ethan was finally back on his feet, with a hand from Jika, and was about to describe what he was going to do to Guapo, the older man pointed up the trail. There, not more than two strides ahead, was the largest king cobra Ethan had ever seen, fully coiled and ready to strike. Now that he realized why the dog had attacked him, Ethan started to apologize, but Guapo, with seeming understanding, flapped his tail in response to Ethan's glance. Then, without comment, Jika took out his parang and cleared a path around the snake, which both men recognized as a magnificent beast.

After finally dropping down off the ridge, they realized that there wouldn't be enough daylight to make it to Long Berawan so they made camp near a spring that emerged from the hillside. They slaked their thirsts and then set about making camp. Jika returned with a large arboreal termite nest through which he'd inserted a flexible rattan cane to serve as a handle. He'd present that treat to the communal flock of chickens at Long Berawan. The nest looked like a charcoal black beach ball, but weighed considerably more. The thin papery covering and its denser tunnel-ridden contents all consisted of plant material masticated and molded by the tiny termites. In this species, the heads of the soldier caste individuals had cone-like extensions from which they exuded a sticky substance that was apparently effective in entangling the legs of attacking ants, their nemesis.

Tired after their arduous hike, the two men built a quick camp, ate leftover sago with chopped palm heart for dinner, and retired early. After just a few hours of exhausted sleep, Ethan was awoken by a terrible ripping noise from a few feet away. He started to sit up abruptly while reaching around for his flashlight when Jika's hand on his chest caused him to lay back down, still breathing hard in fright.

A skunk-like smell had awoken Jika a few minutes earlier, before the racket began in earnest. He'd used Ethan's flashlight to verify the identity of the noisemaker, whose smell he'd recognized.

With the weak illumination of the flashlight's beam filtered through Jika's fingers, they watched as a *pangolin* (scaly anteater) tore into his termite nest with its powerful claws. As Jika slowly spread his fingers to illuminate the subject more brightly, they could see that the *pangolin* was carrying a baby on her back, just at the base of the tail. This was the first time Ethan had watched a *pangolin* at work, and he was fascinated by the power of an animal generally considered to be harmless. After a few more minutes, the *pangolin* wandered off having destroyed only half the nest.

After contemplating what he had seen, with a concerned voice, Ethan asked, "Did we scare it off?"

"Why would you think that?"

"Because it ate only half the termites," was Ethan's seemingly reasonable response.

"Oh, *pangolins* don't over-harvest—they're not like timber companies. They know that if they leave some of the termites behind, and especially the queen, the nest will be repaired and ready for another feeding in just a few months."

The two men laid quietly in the dark for a while before Jika inquired, "You didn't smell it?"

"No, at least not at first."

Jika considered his answer for a few seconds, then asked, "So what exactly do you do with that big snout?"

In response, Ethan lashed out to smack his friend, but his mosquito net stopped him so he settled for hissing, "savage," at which they both chuckled and fell back to sleep.

After trekking for a few hours the next morning, they finally reached the Balui River, the appearance of which caused the two men shock and dismay. What was previously a clear-running stream was now brown with mud and choked with debris. Ethan wondered if there'd been a flash flood that dislodged a lot of sediment, but then espied a sawn log that had escaped from a raft that was presumably destined for the sawmill in Belaga. Ethan got to know the river well on his first visit to Long Berawan some six months before. At that time it was running high and he spent two days in a motorized dugout beating his way up to Long Berawan. At that time, there was no logging in the upper stretches of the river above the rapids, but that situation had apparently changed.

On that first trip upriver, Ethan recalled that when the boats reached the rapids, which were some distance downstream from where he and Jika had intercepted the river, the boats had to be unloaded, and then manually hauled up over the rapids. As Ethan joined a dozen Iban on the ropes, he felt the rhythm and then naturally started to sing the halyard shanty "Clementine." He was pleasantly surprised when many of the other pullers joined in, with only minor changes in the tune but lyrics that, over time, had devolved from English to nonsense syllables with little resemblance to the original ballad. None of the Iban realized that they were singing about a miner's daughter who wore number nine shoes made from herring boxes and drowned tragically, but it was definitely the same song. Once they were above the falls and back in the boat, they demanded that Ethan continue to sing and translate the words for them, which amused them all.

The down-river trip to which Jika had jokingly referred, was in reference to Ethan's ill-fated attempt to raft bamboo canes down from Long Berawan to the market in Belaga. It was a longhouse tradition that whenever groups of young men had the urge to get away, the river was especially inviting, or they wanted some cash, they'd float bamboo down to Belaga to sell. The venture was more for fun than profit, and that fun started the day before with the construction of elaborate rafts from bamboo canes 20 feet long and fully six inches in diameter. The goal was to use as many canes as possible but to construct river-worthy rafts on which they could negotiate the rapids.

The Long Berawan Iban were overjoyed when Ethan asked if he could join them on a rafting expedition. They warned him that the river level had dropped so the rapids would be booming, but Ethan assured them with exaggerated bravado that he was more than up for the challenge. His first big mistake was to turn down their offers of split rattan for lashing and instead use his precious parachute cord. Later, when they offered him other assistance with his raft he declined and provoked his friends by adding, "Perhaps I can show you something about raft-making, American style—mine will be based on scientific principles and modern engineering techniques not your unschooled village approach."

The Iban considered his behavior and attitude hysterically funny, and continued to comment on his scientific approach right up until the launching early the next morning.

As the rafters helped each other to carry, slide, lug, and heave their heavy but buoyant crafts into the river, the rest of the villagers watched from the overlooking bluff. Ethan's was the last raft to be put in the water, and when he climbed on and sat regally on the top tier of canes, the assembled villagers cheered wildly. He waved to them like the Queen of England while the other rafters sounded their good-natured derision.

The first few hours of the trip were slow and steady, with the rafters having only to pole occasionally to keep their unwieldy crafts in the center of the river. Ethan admitted to himself that his raft was challenging to handle and consequently he was generally at the rear of the flotilla of a dozen crafts. But as he floated high and dry on a raft of unique design, even the Iban were ready to admit that perhaps his engineering had components to emulate. That was before they hit the rapids in which his engineering would be sorely tested.

The rafters could smell and hear the rapids long before the first white water could be seen. As they approached, Ethan judged that the rapids were no more than Grade 2 or 3. He figured that with his experience whitewater rafting and kayaking, he'd be fine. They'd all tied up above the rapids to give each raft the chance to shoot down on its own. As he watched, Ethan was impressed by the grace with which the men guided their rafts through the boulder-strewn rapids. When it was finally his turn and his raft began to accelerate, his heart did likewise, a feeling that he relished. He moved towards the bow to be better placed to deploy his pole. He easily avoided the first few exposed rocks and momentarily harbored the impression that he'd figured out how to maneuver the cumbersome craft. That impression was fleeting because, when the raft simultaneously plunged into a pool and he pushed off a rock, the next thing he knew he was swimming through the rapids amidst a tangle of bamboo canes only partially connected by threatening lengths of parachute cord. He quickly gathered a few canes in his arms for flotation and continued to fly down the rapids submerged half the time and bouncing off boulders at every turn. After what seemed like an hour but was no more than a minute, he was ejected into the relatively calm water below the rapids.

Even over the booming of the rapids he could hear his Iban friends hooting and hollering with glee. They were looking down on him from the vantage point to which each had climbed after successfully negotiating the white water. Ethan's clothes were shredded and he was cut and bruised but not hurt badly, so he stood in the shallows, gave them a victory sign, and bowed from the waist like a great performer, which provoked even more good-natured laughter.

After a bite to eat and numerous retellings and technical analyses of Ethan's debacle, they collected most of the bamboo from his raft, lashed it onto the others, and bid him adieu for his long walk back to the village. Along the way, Ethan fabricated a story about what happened that would contrast so markedly with both the truth and the Ibans' embellished account of his misadventure that the difference between the stories would provide the longhouse residents an additional source of amusement for many years.

Now, only a few months later, that river looked completely different. Ethan indicated the sawn log to Jika, who had already seen it, and nodded sadly before they both started up a fairly well trodden trail along the river to Long Berawan.

As they approached the longhouse, they could first hear roosters crowing, then dogs barking, and then the deep whirring of ornamental windmills attached up in the treetops. The latter were constructed from sections of bamboo about 10 feet long and notched to catch the wind. They emitted a deep pulsating sound that the Iban told him repelled *hantus* (ghosts). Their final approach was heralded by a pack of yipping dogs that ran out to greet them—they swarmed around Guapo in a menacingly way that would have worried Ethan had not he seen the little dog in action before.

To remind the assorted canines of Long Berawan who was top dog, Guapo immediately singled out the biggest and most ferocious-acting male. The two dogs squared off, and although his adversary was nearly twice his size, within seconds the big dog was on his back with Guapo's teeth clamped on his throat. Ethan had watched carefully, but in the blur of dog he'd failed to see how his little friend had managed. Once the big dog realized he'd been bested, he relaxed, Guapo released him, and a round of friendly butt sniffing and tail wagging ensued until they ran off in a happy yipping pack.

Warned by the dogs, a dozen children emerged from the river where they'd spent the afternoon frolicking like otters. Iban children are given a great deal of freedom, which they celebrate raucously. The Protestant missionaries condemned the Iban for spoiling their children, but Ethan considered their upbringing close to ideal—at least they never lacked for indulgent affection from the extended family that constituted the longhouse. When the children recognized the two visitors, they rushed towards them gleefully. As they swarmed around, the youngest grasped the men's' legs while the rest vied for attention in other ways. After the initial flurry, the group made its way up the bank to the longhouse where some women were already preparing food for the hungry travelers. Although they had stopped to eat the leftovers from the previous evening's meal, which they'd wrapped in taro-like leaves, they were both famished.

Ethan was happy to be so well-accepted in the Iban longhouses but was unaware of a fundamental reason for that reaction. Iban are famous for their hospitality, but they treated him more like family than as an esteemed guest. They even seemed surprised by how little he knew about Iban history or his own family for that matter. What all the Iban knew from the first time they saw him was that Ethan was a close blood relative of Ribut, the famous Iban warrior. That same warrior was Jika's foster father and protector; they'd fought together in the resistance during the Japanese occupation. It therefore seemed perfectly natural that Jika and Ethan travelled together. Ribut, a much storied warrior, had passed away a few years prior to Ethan's arrival in Sarawak, but his daughter Juus was his spitting image and Ethan's too.

This familial connection first became known to the Iban when Jika first met Ethan in the herbarium in Kuching. Jika was busily identifying dried-and-pressed plant collections when the Chief Conservator walked in with a young European man in tow. After introducing Ethan as a botany student from America, he asked Jika if he'd be willing to help the visitor with his plant collections.

Jika was startled when he looked up from the sample he was inspecting and saw Ethan's face. One look and he knew that this young man was somehow related to his foster father. That prominent nose and high forehead were dead giveaways. When the Conservator mentioned that Ethan's family name was Yarrow, any lingering doubts he had about the relationship were gone. Jika quickly figured out that Ethan's grandfather, Storm Yarrow, was Ribut's father. When it became clear that Ethan was completely unaware of his relatives in Sarawak, Jika and the other Iban felt that it wasn't their role to inform him.

Jika agreed to help Ethan and the two planned to go on their first expedition the next week. A few days later they met at a dry goods store where they'd purchase provisions for their expedition. Ethan was surprised when an elderly Chinese man, presumably the *tokay*, who'd been dozing in a chair near the cash register, sat up abruptly when he walked into the store with Jika. With a shocked look on his face, he blurted out what to Ethan sounded like 'Frankie,' which was his father's nickname. Jika immediately responded to the man in what sounded like a mixture of Hokkien and Iban, the only word of which Ethan understood was *rebut,* which means storm in both Iban and Malay. That his grandfather's name was Storm did not cross his mind at the time.

Ethan didn't remember Grandfather Storm very well because he'd died when he was still a little boy. Nevertheless, when he first arrived in Southeast Asia and smelled clove cigarettes, he thought of his Grandfather immediately.

After that short interchange, Jika and the Chinese man, with whom seemed to be well acquainted, rushed off together into an office. Ethan was confused by this behavior, but so much was new to him in Sarawak that he let it slide and continued to peruse the shelves of canned fish and other foodstuffs.

After about ten minutes, Jika and the proprietor emerged from the office and came over to Ethan. In a rather formal manner, Jika introduced Mr. Cheong Hing Hong to Ethan in the amalgam of Malay and Iban languages in which they generally conversed. While they shook hands, Mr. Cheong said with a distinctly American accent, "Please call me Eddie, and if there is anything I can do for you, don't hesitate to ask." Ethan was somewhat taken aback by this interchange, which was also noted with alarm by several eavesdropping store workers. Those employees had never seen their boss be so gracious to anyone, let alone a European. But what really concerned them was that they'd wrongly assumed that the old man spoke no English, which immediately made them worry about what they might have said in his presence.

After arranging to have the purchased supplies delivered to the government boat dock in time for their departure, Jika and Ethan headed back to the herbarium. While walking Ethan asked, "Is Mr. Cheong a friend of yours?"

Jika hesitated for a few seconds and then responded, "Yes, we've been friends for a long time." After a pause he continued. "A year or so after the war Eddie came to Sarawak, originally to Kapit where he ran a trading post. At that time I'd just left the Sarawak Rangers and was also a trader of sorts, or at least an accumulator of non-timber forest products. Eddie became my agent, and we went into the export business together."

"What did you sell?" Ethan asked.

"Mostly *dammar* (tree resin used in perfume, incense, and other products), *gahuru* (fungus-infected heartwood of *Aquilaria malaccensis*, also known as agarwood), edible birds' nests, *tengkawan* (Bornean Illipe nuts, seeds of a native tree from which an oil is extracted), and rattan canes. We tried marketing rubber, but the jungle rubber produced by my people is of lower quality than from the big plantations, and we couldn't compete."

After a minute or so, Jika continued. "After a few years, Eddie did well enough in Kapit to move to Kuching and open that store and now a dozen more. I really have no idea how many businesses he owns, but he's a rich and powerful man." After pausing for a few seconds he continued, "And a good ally. Our families are actually very much intertwined."

Chapter 4. TROUBLE BREWING IN LONG BERAWAN

Excerpt from an aerogram from Ethan Yarrow in Kuching, Sarawak, to his parents in Chevy Chase, Maryland:

23 March 1971
Dear Mom and Dad,
I've been out in the ulus again with Jika. We explored the Iran
Mountains (remind me to find out how they got that name) and ended
up in Long Berawan after one of those legendary "shortcuts" that
reduced us to drinking pitcher plant water, which is really yucky. The
conditions in and around the longhouse have deteriorated since my visit
only a few months back, and the people are a bit dispirited. But some of
the young lads and I had some fun with heavy equipment, and I tried
my best to promote the budding relationship between my friend Adam
from Iowa and Pinai, a lovely young Iban woman—Adam is
remarkably shy and upstanding, even for an Iowan, which confuses
Pinai—Iban are not at all like Lutherans, which is probably why I find
them so refreshing.

After Jika and Ethan had taken splash baths and washed out their clothes in the only stream that still ran clear near Long Berawan, they changed into sarongs and sat down on the verandah to eat. They were hungry but also eager to find out from the longhouse residents what had been going on in the vicinity. In addition to the appalling state of the river, the longhouse showed many other signs of deterioration. Most alarming was that the longhouse's elaborate bamboo plumbing system was not operating. That marvel of indigenous engineering was formerly one of the pleasures of Long Berawan—through hundreds of interlinked canes with joints sealed with resin, it delivered fresh water right to the longhouse from a spring about a mile away. Ethan also espied what he presumed was the remains of their jury-rigged mini-hydro generator and, right next to it, the television that had hypnotized so many longhouse residents. He was looking forward to hearing night sounds and not the raucous laughter of Ellie Mae Clampett or the grunts and groans of professional wrestling. He smiled when he wondered about the outcome of the planned matchup between BoBo Brazil and Dick the Bruiser, and then shuddered when he considered the consequences of receiving one of BoBo's signature CocoNut Headbutts. He'd often been tempted to point out that the matches were all carefully choreographed, but held back because he too enjoyed the suspension of disbelief and certainly wouldn't want anyone to make such a claim about the Stanley Cup.

The longhouse residents were eager to share their news, but they also looked forward to hearing about the outside world. After eating their fills of rice with fish and plenty of stewed manioc leaves, the latter prepared especially for Ethan, the villagers clustered around the two visitors with their plentiful children playing on the outer periphery. As was typical of the Iban, most of the young men were off working in logging concessions, on off-shore oil rigs, or on ships. They usually returned to their longhouses about once per year, generally for the annual rice festival. After a decade or more when their wanderlust was sated, they'd return to the wives they'd married and the children they'd sired on their previous visits.

Before the talking began in earnest, each adult took out the accoutrements needed to prepare betel nut for their after-dinner chew. Ethan had come to enjoy the slight buzz of betel nut, but he only indulged when at a longhouse. In a somewhat unusual change in the seating protocol, the matriarch of the house, Ibu Jati, came and sat directly in front of the visitors—she clearly had some important matter she wanted to discuss and her advanced age and the power that she radiated lifted her above many established conventions. It was Ibu Jati who prepared a betel nut chew for Ethan with an elegance that rivaled a Japanese tea ceremony. She picked from her kit a choice nut and a perfect leaf, shaved off slivers from the palm nut with what might have been a solid silver shear made for the purpose, spread lime on the leaf, folded it all together with origami-like precision, and handed it to Ethan with lowered eyes to show respect for the young visitor.

Ethan popped the packet in his mouth and, while contentedly chewing, marveled at the brightness and whiteness of the light from the carbide lamp hanging from a rafter above the group. He was unfamiliar with that technology when he first arrived in Sarawak, but now almost preferred the light of its ignited acetylene to incandescent bulbs—it was certainly preferable to burning dammar, which was the fallback option. For him there was still magic in the idea that water dropping on a rock-like chunk of calcium carbide was producing the brightly burning gas, even if the swamp smell could be a bit off-putting.

Even Ibu Jati was not above the tradition that, before transacting any business, there was time for social gossip and news from the outside world which, for them, extended downriver to Belaga and Kapit, over to Kuching, but not much farther. Ethan and Jika answered their questions as well as they could, bringing much appreciated news of family members they had encountered in their travels, and some juicy gossip that mostly involved the incompetence of the Malays who ran the government of a state in which Iban people were in the majority. For the sake of politeness, they held off mentioning their concerns about the river, the dysfunctional plumbing, or the other signs of deterioration around the longhouse.

Finally, after nearly an hour of chatter, Ibu Jati broke the ice by saying to the visitors "I suppose you've noticed that things haven't been going well here of late."

When Jika and Ethan nodded sympathetically, she continued, "I'm sorry to have to tell you, but this is the work of that worm of a *Tuai Rumah* (village head), the man who was supposed to be looking out for our collective best interests," she said with vehemence and punctuated with a copious and emphatic spit of red betel juice.

Jika had noticed the man's absence and had some inkling of what had happened, but nevertheless asked, "And where's the *Tuai Rumah* now."

"Probably in Singapore spending the money he got from the loggers and miners," Ibu Jati replied in anger.

With this subject broached, many other longhouse residents lamented vociferously about the dirty deals their leader had made. "They're cutting down our fruit trees, even the durians," said one, which everyone else acknowledged. "They totally smashed our bamboo plumbing system," said another. "The river is a mess, as I'm sure you've seen," added a young woman who continued, "Now we have to fetch clean water with buckets from the only stream that's still clean." Another woman chimed in, "And we worry that a runaway log from one of their rafts is going to hurt one of the children." "And don't even think about fishing," said one of the old men, "even the fish eagles have left."

The comments and condemnations came so rapidly that it took a while for Ethan to piece together the sad story. Eventually it became clear that the *Tuai Rumah* had signed an agreement and accepted a cash payment from the loggers without consulting the other longhouse residents, his wife included. Jika had previously expressed concerns about this man's leadership abilities, but his earlier transgressions were relatively minor and there were plenty of strong characters, including Ibu Jati, to keep the longhouse functioning. Overall, the current conditions were quite bleak. River fish was a major source of protein and the villagers made money every year when the durians were in fruit. The major physical improvements in the longhouse came from the proceeds of sales of fallen seeds from the *tengkawang* nut trees that they tended in groves and as scattered trees throughout the forest. Unfortunately for the villagers, *tengkawang* and *durian* timber also make good veneer for plywood.

When Jika enquired about the camp and survey stakes he and Ethan found, the villagers confirmed that a group of miners had passed through a few months previously. They said that the miners had gone away, apparently not having found any gold or antimony or whatever it was that they were seeking. They'd stopped at Long Berawan on their way back to Belaga and met with the *Tuai Rumah* alone, but they suspected that not even their disreputable leader knew what they'd been up to.

Although Ethan was still dutifully collecting and describing rattan palms, he found himself increasingly interested in exactly this sort of land rights issue, especially as related to the indigenous people of Sarawak. Two other comments related to the land around the longhouse piqued Ethan's curiosity. One villager mentioned that when a representative of the logging company was angrily accused of allowing their fruit trees to be felled, he responded that the longhouse was going to be moved anyway, so why did they care. A seemingly related comment was from Ibu Jati, who reported that several of the Foochow pepper and rubber farmers, who for generations had occupied land claimed by the

Iban along the Balui River, were moving out and had even offered to sell the land that wasn't theirs back to the Iban. Ethan wanted to pursue these issues, but he was getting tired and decided to bookmark them for future discussion.

When he could no longer keep his eyes open, Ethan finally went off to the room they had allocated him, but not before both he and Jika promised to go out with the villagers the next day to appraise the situation. Tired as he was, he didn't expect an uninterrupted night of sleep and, sure enough, two or so hours after retiring he had a visitor.

Ethan was awoken by someone, obviously a woman, sitting down next to him on his sleeping mat. Still half asleep, he moved over to give her room and, in what he considered a polite and gentlemanly manner, put his arm loosely around her waist. He suspected that his visitor was Pinai, which was confirmed when she finally spoke.

"I don't think that Adam really cares about me," she lamented without a preamble but in a whisper.

"Oh Pinai, don't be silly, he's crazy about you," Ethan assured. Adam Lyskowski was a Peace Corps volunteer who helped farmers with technological challenges throughout the region. A Lutheran farm boy from Iowa, Adam could fix almost anything, and cobbled together the most ingenious machines, from methane-powered generators to windmills using nothing more than junk. The romance between Adam and Pinai had been underway for months, but was apparently not progressing as quickly as the young Iban woman hoped.

"So why won't he touch me? We hold hands sometimes, but he even seems reluctant to do that if anyone is around. Does he have a problem with women like your friend Ian?" Pinai asked in dismay.

Ethan was a bit surprised that Ian's sexual proclivities where known even out here in the *ulus*, but the reach and speed of the jungle telegraph never ceased to amaze him. Furthermore, Pinai worked off-and-on in both Kapit and Kuching, so she was somewhat familiar with the ways of the world.

After collecting his wits, Ethan reassured Pinai by saying, "I'm sure that Adam is a red blooded male of the species, but you know all that stuff the Protestant missionaries told you about the benefits of abstinence? Well, Adam believes it. And on your wedding night, to which I am sure Adam pines, you should be as virginal as he is, if you know what's good for you."

The explanation for Adam's avoidance of intimacy was so completely alien to her that she was not completely convinced, so she continued to explore the topic in her own inimical fashion. While they chatted in the dark, she took Ethan's hand and put it on her bare breast, her sarong having somehow slipped down, and then asked, "But is it normal for a man to not respond to this sort of encouragement?"

Ethan squirmed around a bit in response to this provocation, which revealed to Pinai that she had elicited what she considered the appropriate response from a healthy male. Instants later, and before Ethan could respond to what he realized was a rather rhetorical question, she had straddled him and both their sarongs were somehow no longer an impediment to their love-making.

When Ethan woke in the pre-dawn to the sounds of longhouse residents stirring, he was alone, fully rested, and ready to investigate the goings-on in the area. After eating some rice and fish, he headed out in the cool of the early morning. He walked through various fallows of different ages and fields in which rice, corn, and cassava were the principal crops. His destination was the forest on the far side of their hill rice fields where many of their fruit trees grew and the loggers had reportedly invaded.

Instead of growing fruit trees in geometrically precise plantations, the Iban gradually enriched natural forest with useful native species. The untrained visitor might mistake these forest gardens for old-growth forest, but the representation of useful species was far higher than what would occur naturally. In addition to *durian, mangosteeen, mata kuching,* and other fruit trees, there were abundant trees of a species that produces both valuable resin, called *dammar*, and winged nuts from which an oil is extracted that can be used both for cooking and in the manufacture of perfume. Whereas the durians and other fleshy fruited trees produced harvestable crops annually, these *tengkawang* (Illipe nut) trees produced seeds in vast quantities but at irregular intervals of several years. This phenomenon is common among temperate zone oaks, but like so many ecological phenomena, mast fruiting episodes in Southeast Asia are exaggerated to a hard-to-imagine extreme. During a mast event that might last just a few months, he had read that there is so much fruit that orangutans and bearded pigs both double in size, and virtually all fruit and seed-eating animals reproduce abundantly. For the Iban, a windfall of *tengkawang* nuts represents a major influx of cash into the community, and everyone participates in their collection.

Ethan, accompanied by some young boys from the longhouse, walked for a while along the skid trails opened by the loggers' bulldozers. While he was accustomed to seeing bad logging practices, Ethan kept noticing that many trees much smaller than the minimum legal diameter had been harvested. Loggers were allowed to cut such trees only in areas being converted into oil palm plantations or other sorts of tree farms, but Long Berawan seemed far too remote to warrant that sort of investment.

The loggers' incursions suddenly stopped in the middle of a large stand of *tengkawang* trees, some of which were felled but not extracted. Having surveyed the damage, he and the boys wound their way back to their family gardens, where they joined in with the weeding and other chores. Jika was apparently off with some of the other villagers preparing a shipment of *dammar* for which Eddie Cheong had found a buyer and arranging for *tengkawang* nuts to be harvested, if the expected mast event actually occurred.

When they were all back at the longhouse, Ethan described to Jika what he'd seen. That the loggers were breaking the law was not unusual, but they both agreed the number and brazenness of the infractions far exceeded the norm. They also agreed to help the villagers compose a formal letter of complaint to forestry authorities in both Kapit and Kuching. They knew the longhouse was entitled to compensation for the fruit and nut trees that had been killed, and the residents wanted to reassert their claims to the forest around their longhouse. Ethan decided to spend the next day in the active logging area, trying to glean information from the loggers themselves.

After a good night's sleep that was interrupted only briefly by a not-so-talkative Pinai, he was ready to head out to the logging site. It was not yet full light as he walked the length of the longhouse on the springy bamboo floor of the open verandah. None of the 22 bamboo-and-bark doors he passed was yet open, but he could hear families stirring inside and the pigs were grunting and rooting underneath. He'd told no one of his planned outing, but as he prepared to climb down on the notched log that served as the longhouse's stairway, Ibu Jati emerged from the darkness and handed him a leaf-wrapped packet of glutinous rice. Then, with smiles in her eyes but without speaking, she managed to tease him about having weak knees after his night's activities.

As he walked to the logging site, Ethan again recognized that little went on in the longhouse that wasn't known to at least Ibu Jati if not everyone else. Given the efficiency of the jungle telegraph and the Ibans' love of gossip, that knowledge was most likely widely shared. While at one time in his life that transparency might have worried, him, Ethan reassured himself that it was fortunate that he was such an upstanding citizen and beyond reproach, a joke about himself that served to improve his already good mood.

When he arrived where the workers were actively felling trees and yarding logs with bulldozers, he waited on the side of their main skid trail until he was noticed. The logging crew's initial surprise at encountering a European in the middle of the forest was quickly put to rest when Ethan explained that he was a botanist out collecting plant specimens—for some reason that made sense to them. He'd heard them shouting to each other in Bahasa Indonesia, so he addressed them in his best approximation of that language. He continued by asking whether it would be okay for him to collect samples from the crowns of the trees they were felling.

It quickly became apparent that the leader of the harvesting crew, which included the feller, dozer driver, and their two assistants, was the dark-skinned, curly headed, heavily built man who wielded the chainsaw. As they chatted together he held his massive Stihl 060 chainsaw with a 36 inch bar over his shoulder like it was a plastic toy. The Indonesian he spoke in a deep rumbling voice was better than Ethan's, but was clearly not his first language. He considered Ethan's request and then responded that it would be best for him to check with the logging block supervisor, a Filipino man who was most likely to be found sleeping in his truck on the road that ran along the ridge above them. When they all laughed at his comment, the atmosphere eased and they decided that Ethan's appearance was enough of an excuse to take a break. One of them wondered out loud if the supervisor would come down to investigate when he didn't hear the dozer or chainsaw, and then they all laughed again, their supervisor being famous for his laziness.

Fast friends, the men explained that they were all Indonesians but from various parts of that archipelago nation. Their leader was Timorese, two were Bugis from the Celebes, and the other was a Dayak from across the border in West Kalimantan. They'd all been hired by a Chinese subcontractor to work for three years in the logging concession. They were annoyed that their passports had been taken away, reportedly for safe-keeping, but were otherwise fairly contented with their jobs. The feller's assistant, who seemed to be only 16 or so years old, had worked for a while in an oil palm plantation, which he said was terrible, so he was happy to be logging. From what they said, Ethan surmised that they were all illegally in Malaysia, which was common. When he asked if any Iban were employed by the company, they reported that most of the forest workers were Indonesian, with only one Iban from up near Brunei and no locals.

When the crew went back to work Ethan clambered around in the crown zones of felling gaps looking for orchids, other epiphytes, and anything else he might find in flower or fruit. Epiphytes were much scarcer in Bornean trees than in the Amazon, but he found some nice ones, which he carefully packed in his rattan tote bag. He also found a few canopy vines in flower, which would be much appreciated in the herbarium in Kuching.

After collecting for an hour or so, Ethan bid adieu to the crew and climbed up the muddy skid trail to the ridge. The slope was so steep that the loggers had to use the blade of the dozer to cut switchbacks across the hillside. After traversing several times, he noticed that one clear path led directly down a slope too steep for a bulldozer to negotiate. It took him a while to figure out the cause of that swath of plowed-down forest that extended from near the ridgetop to the bottom of the valley. Next to the skid trail near the top was the stump of a gigantic Bornean ironwood tree that was felled directly down the slope. Standing on that stump, Ethan could see that after that tree hit the ground it didn't stop moving but instead continued to slide down the hill, leaving downed trees in its wake until its branches were stripped off and it came to a rest at the bottom of a ravine where it was likely to remain. The thought of all that destruction, and for nothing, made Ethan both angry and sad, but anger took the upper hand when he remembered that ironwood was on the list of protected species, reserved only for use by local villagers.

By the time he reached the ridge-top logging road and espied the logging block supervisor napping in the cab of his Toyota Hi-Lux 4-wheel drive pickup, he'd calmed himself down. To keep from startling the man, he made some noise as he approached. The man nevertheless awoke with a start and addressed him gruffly in English. Ethan's immediate response, which endeared him to the man instantly, was "Ah, I am so happy to hear my native language."

The man hailed from the Philippines from whence he was recruited by the logging company as a forest engineer. It was not clear why he'd been demoted to the job of block supervisor, but Ethan suspected it had something to do with his apparent lack of a work ethic.

After explaining why he was there and even taking out his permit for the man to inspect, the fellow was satisfied. He was actually happy for the company and the chance to speak English. Slowly, over the next two hours, the man revealed quite a bit about the logging operation. Ethan was happy to let him talk, without having to ask many questions. It also became clear that the man was not fully informed about any long-term plans for the logging concession. They discussed and then dismissed the idea that his bosses planned to convert the area into an oil palm plantation—too remote to be profitable, they decided. Based on frequent visits by Australian miners to the main camp, the block supervisor was convinced that the intention was to deforest the area and then mine it, but he wasn't sure whether it was for gold, antimony, coal, or bauxite. One reason he provided for this conclusion was that he was told to not worry about abiding by the government-specified minimum cutting diameters, which sounded to him like no one expected to log this area again. He also pointed out that due to the remoteness of the area, and the fact that they could only raft out logs when the river was high, it wasn't clear that the concessionaire was making much of a profit.

There was a moment of tenseness when Ethan revealed that he was staying at Long Berawan and had seen where some of the Iban's fruit and nut tree had been felled. After Ethan clarified that he was a neutral observer, the man explained that he'd sent his crews into that area under the explicit instructions of his boss. He then became more animated when he revealed that they'd only stopped harvesting timber near the longhouse after some old toothless and tattooed guy with dangling earlobes shot a blowgun dart into the neck of one of his tractor drivers. Apparently the dart was not poisoned, but they got the message. Ethan successfully suppressed a chuckle and had immediate suspicions about the identity of the perpetrator, whom he'd be sure to congratulate.

As he walked back to Long Berawan after his day with the loggers, Ethan realized that any action in response to a formal letter of complaint to the authorities, which was unlikely, would still take at least many weeks, so he formulated an alternative approach to interfering with the logging operations. Although it had been a long day and he was tired, when he got back to the longhouse he invited a half-dozen teenaged boys to meet him down at the riverside after dinner for a secret mission. Without explaining to anyone exactly the nature of the planned clandestine activities, he asked Pinai to melt blocks of palm sugar in boiling water and to pack the resulting syrup in stoppered gourds. Each gourd was equipped with a shoulder strap fashioned from *meranti* bark for hands-free transport. He told the boys, all of whom were excited to be singled out by their American friend, to wear dark clothes and to bring flashlights, if they had them.

When the group of boys assembled at dusk, Ethan explained that their mission was to use the syrup to disable the bulldozers and other heavy equipment that was wreaking havoc on their forest. As they nearly danced around in anticipation, he heightened the excitement even more by getting them to smear their faces with dark mud. He paired them off and asked Ravalda, with whom he had spent time in the forest before, to lead their way. For his own partner he chose Rentap, the youngest and smallest of the boys. Ethan had heard some grumbling about this boy being invited to participate, but he'd seen him in action before and knew that he was quite capable of living up to the reputation of the famous Iban warrior who was his namesake.

They followed familiar paths through their fields and forest gardens and then, before reaching the active logging area, they doused their lights and proceeded with just moonlight. Walking along the skid trails was fairly easy and they reached the first of the machines without incident and, Ethan was confident, without detection. The capacity of the boys to move quietly through the forest was quite impressive. The smoothness of the operation being carried out by young teenagers made Ethan reflect on the fact that they were probably living out an Iban war ritual about which he was clueless.

From that first bulldozer, the paired boys split off in the directions indicated by Ethan. He and Rentap took some time to find their machine and then struggled to remove the cap from the fuel tank of the monstrous D-7 Caterpillar bulldozer. They were concentrating on the task at hand when suddenly they were caught in the beam of a flashlight. Blinded by the light, they both dove off the far side of the dozer and landed flat out with a big splat in the deep mud churned by the machine. As they struggled to extract themselves, they heard the sounds of poorly suppressed laughter. Sure enough, a few seconds later a couple of the older boys who had finished their jobs quickly rounded the machine and revealed themselves while continuing to laugh for the most part silently, and gesticulating with glee at their prostrate friends.

Ethan had been sorely frightened by the encounter, which ignited a flash of anger, but quickly realized that no harm was intended. He also realized that it must have looked really funny to watch them leap off the bulldozer. Soon he and his young compatriot were chuckling along with the others as they scrambled back onto the machine to finish the job.

On their walk back to the longhouse, the farther they got from the logging area the louder was the laughter and celebration. To avoid an unwanted encounter with a riverine crocodile, one of which they knew lurked around the longhouse at night, they washed off in a small stream before returning triumphantly to their families. They'd all sworn to not reveal the nature of their mission, but Ethan was sure that the story would soon make the rounds. He was also certain that the part of the adventure that would break the silence was their having witnessed an American trying to fly.

Chapter 5. EASY DAY TURNING POTS

Excerpt from an aerogram from Ethan Yarrow in Kuching, Sarawak, to his parents in Chevy Chase, Maryland:

3 April 1971
Dear Mom and Dad,
Tomorrow I head up into the hills inland from Kuching to visit the Wong family. They run a pottery factory where I'm learning to throw pots. If it doesn't work out in botany, I want to have a fallback career option (just kidding!). The Wong's are fascinating, and their place borders a compound set up by SALCRA, Sarawak Land Consolidation and Rehabilitation Authority—looks more like a concentration camp for Hakka people.

Ethan looked forward to his visits to the Wong family home/factory/farm. He spent his days there chatting with Lim Boo, a teenager with a remarkable intellect, while churning out a series of misshapen bowls and plates on one of their pottery wheels. He also enjoyed the frequent interruptions with tea and luscious food. Given that someone would always clean and wax polish Roxanne while he was otherwise engaged, he suspected that she enjoyed the visits as well.

The Wong place was a few hours up the Kuching-Serian Road in the rolling hills near the border with West Kalimantan. Along the way there he passed several military checkpoints, vestiges of the 1963-1966 "Confrontasi" with Indonesia during which President Sukarno of Indonesia made a feeble attempt to take over Sarawak, which he called North Kalimantan. As per usual, at each checkpoint Ethan was lazily waved through with hardly a glance from the uniformed sentries, most of whom seemed to always be napping. After a leisurely drive Ethan turned off the tarmac and wound his way through secondary forest on a dirt track. The young forest opened occasionally where there were patches of bright green alang-alang (*Imperata cylindrica*) grassland where the topsoil was damaged by heavy machinery and the vegetation repeatedly burned. The terrain was also pocked with water-filled depressions that were the legacies of long-since suspended tin mining activities. At the crest of a narrow ridge, he paused to gaze down on the lush and diverse landscape the Wong's had created. That verdant scene contrasted starkly with what was just beyond the Wong place and inside the fence that surrounded the Sungei Lengkap Resettlement Camp. That fence enclosed rows of identical, small, tin-roofed houses provided by the government for the mostly Hakka farmers who, a few years before, had been forcibly evicted from their farms. Ethan reflected that at midday those houses must be ovens because they were surrounded by hard-packed red earth with hardly a tree left standing. In contrast, the Wong land was well shaded and every square inch seemed to be in some sort of production.

Ethan was told that the official justification for the forced move of the Chinese farmers into the internment camp was concern that they'd supply food to Communist insurgents. Based on what he'd learned about the so-called Emergency and the Communist insurgents who reputedly threatened the young nation of Malaysia, he was somewhat dubious about the severity of the threat. Comments from Jika and others also made him question the official accounts of the political leanings of the insurgents and their numbers. Jika had once intimated that the few dozen men who continued to employ guerilla tactics were mostly Chinese who were active members of the resistance against the Japanese during the occupation. After the war, these freedom fighters were disappointed when rather than establish a free, independent, democratic state, Rajah Charles Vyner Brooke ceded Sarawak to the British. Their frustrations grew when, after finally gaining independence in July of 1963, Sarawak joined the Federation of Malaysia in September of that same year. They perceived that Sarawak had become a colony of Kuala Lumpur-based Malaysian government. They were also incensed by the increasingly onerous restrictions on Sarawakian Chinese, even those whose families had been in Borneo for hundreds of years.

The Emergency increasingly seemed to Ethan as a convenient excuse employed by the government for a wide variety of restrictions on civil liberties, particularly those of the ethnic Chinese. While the politics were obscured by anti-sedition laws and a government-controlled press, it was clear that the politically powerful Malays from Peninsular Malaysia had used the presumed Emergency to grab farmland abandoned by the incarcerated Hakka farmers. On that land they, or more likely their foreign business associates, were now busily establishing rubber estates and African oil palm plantations.

The Wong family, which had escaped incarceration because they were Hokkien and well-connected politically, had established their farm, earthenware pottery factory, and home on the sloping banks of one of the larger of the water-filled mine pits. Ethan could see from the ridge that the surface of the pond was nearly completely covered by water hyacinth. Even from the distance, Ethan could see the bright purple and yellow flowers of that peculiar plant, but had to imagine the many fish living underneath. Near the center of the pond, which covered about an acre, was a small wooden house accessed by a rickety boardwalk. When on a previous visit Ethan learned the function of that little building, he took some clay and fashioned a crescent moon to hang on the door. When asked why the moon was the symbol of an outhouse, he had no explanation to offer, but they were nevertheless happy to adorn the door with his creation. Stretching back from the bank of the pond were two long buildings, one covered with palm thatch that housed the pottery wheels and the other with rusting metal roofing that protected a wood-fired kiln. The pond-side opening in the kiln allowed entry of breezes blowing across the water, which flamed the fires inside the sloping earthen oven. Behind the two factory buildings on top of the hill was a rambling wooden house set atop short stilts and surrounded by mango trees. On the far side of the pond from the buildings where the slope was more gradual, a patch of bright green leaves emerging from the water indicated where the family was growing water chestnuts. In slightly shallower water they'd planted sago palms, which initially surprised Ethan because he assumed that only Melenau people were adept at extracting the edible starch from their stems. About a quarter of the way around the pond was a low, ramshackle building in a fenced-in area where the soil was obviously churned. From his distance, Ethan couldn't make out the many mud-covered hogs that lived happily inside that fence. He now knew that it was the hogs that were expert at sago starch extraction; they made quick work of split sections of the succulent stems. Those well-fed hogs were also supplied with water hyacinth plants harvested from the surface of the pond, chopped, and boiled. They had to share any table scraps and excess fish from the pond with the chickens that lived next door. Other than those structures, the property was covered by vegetable gardens and fruit trees, all of which were mulched with water hyacinth and fertilized with chicken and pig manure.

After enjoying the breeze for a few minutes, Ethan motored down into the Wong complex and parked Roxanne in the shade of a mango tree amidst a pack of yipping dogs, none of which was very threatening. Although he had not warned the Wongs of his visit, they were clearly awaiting his arrival and the welcoming rituals swiftly began. Those rituals included many inquiries about his family's health, his work, and life in the big city as well as *dim sum* with tea; Ethan found the steamed dishes delicious, and was generous with his compliments. With the rituals of greeting completed, Lim Boo took out the mimeographed copy of the story that Ethan had sent for him to read and the young American sat down at the pottery wheel at which he'd work while they talked.

Whenever Ethan first sat down on the low stone bench of the kick-powered pottery wheel, he reflected on the wisdom of generations that went into its design. While it was initially hard as the rock from which it was constructed and extremely uncomfortable, over the hours that he'd spend sitting on it, the bench would somehow seem to mold to his shape, whereas the opposite was clearly the case. The transition of acute discomfort to complete comfort reminded him of the pillows provided to opium smokers, which were blocks of wood or occasionally of finely crafted porcelain. They too were initially uncomfortable but then turned out to be the perfect shape and texture for propping up one's head while travelling in an opium daze.

While the informal lessons, which were conducted in English, were intended for Lim Boo, other family members never seemed to be out of earshot. Ethan's assumption that they were not following their discussion was belied early-on when the grandmother interjected a penetrating question about one of the stories, which she addressed to her grandson in Hokkien.

As Ethan patted a lump of wet clay in the center of wheel, Wong Tick Mee, Lim Boo's father, asked, "And what sort of torture do you have planned for my son today?" This question, which he asked in a good-natured manner, referred to Ethan's surprising method for helping his son relate to the Jack London story, "To Build a Fire." Midway through their discussion of that story a few weeks back, when Ethan felt that the boy was missing its essence, he had him submerge his hands in ice water for as long as he could stand.

They all chuckled at that memory and then Ethan asked, "How did you like the reading for this session?" He'd asked him to read one of his old favorites, "The Sound of Thunder" by Ray Bradbury. He hoped the story would resonate with Lim Boo, who was about the same age as Ethan was when he first read it, but he was still often surprised when cultural differences resulted in entirely different reactions to the same story. "I hope it was a quick read."

"It would've been a 'quick read,' as you say, but after my father and I both read it, Grandma demanded that I translate it for her into Hokkien," Lim Boo responded and smiled at his doting grandmother, who averted her gaze in a way that somehow signaled approval.

That old woman was striving to help Ethan learn to throw a decent pot. As the others chatted, she guided his hands.

"How did that go?" Ethan asked.

"Not bad, but some of the passages were really hard to translate. Then she scolded me because I mistakenly used some Mandarin words instead of Hokkien. Grandmother seems to still resent the people she refers to as barbarians from the north."

"I wonder what your grandmother thinks of the 'butterfly effect?'" Ethan asked in reference to the story's portrayal of infinite spatial and temporal interconnectedness.

In "The Sound of Thunder," time travelling big-game hunters are transported from the year 2055 back to the late Cretaceous where they are permitted to shoot a *Tyrannosaurus rex*. To avoid changing the course of history, scouts from the Time Safari Company first made sure that the beast was seconds from dying anyway. Contrary to their plan, an exceedingly rich and otherwise despicable coward by the name of Eckels panicked when he saw the dinosaur, jumped off the elevated pathway, and squashed a butterfly. Upon return to the present, the time travelers discover that the results of the recent presidential election had changed and the fascist candidate had won. The sensitive dependence of complex phenomenon was recognized earlier by meteorologists who suggest that the trajectories of a hurricane might be determined by the flap of a

45

butterfly wing on the opposite side of the planet, but Bradbury's 1952 story is nevertheless often credited as the source of the "butterfly effect" phrase.

"She said it sounded like Confucianism. And then she mentioned *zhu-lian jiu-zu*, do you know that phrase?"

"I've heard the phrase and understand the individual words, but perhaps not the concept."

"It refers to cousins who are nine-times removed," the boy explained.

"With that degree of separation, you and I might be related," said Ethan.

That offhand comment caused Lim Boo's father to look up with interest from his tinkering with the bearings of one of the other pottery wheels he'd dismantled as the boys talked. Grandma Wong was also apparently following their conversation, because she too responded, but with a long series of comments and questions in Hokkien that the boy translated for Ethan.

"Grandmother seems to think that you don't know much about Confucianism," to which Ethan nodded that she was correct.

"Don't ask me what it mean," Lim Boo continued, "but she told me to tell you her favorite aphorism from Confucius."

"Okay," Ethan replied, "lay it on me."

"Never give a sword to a man who can't dance."

Ethan thought for a minute then said, "Yikes, I'll have to think about that one." He then smiled to himself when he remembered one of his own favorite sayings from a fellow named Zippy, who was rapidly becoming his favorite guru: 'Frivolity is a stern task-maker.' He considered mentioning it to Lim Boo and his grandmother, but decided against it.

After a pause, Lim Boo continued. "And my grandmother thinks you know shockingly little about your family," with which Ethan also had to concur.

After a few rebellious teen years, Ethan had again become very close with his parents. He nevertheless continued to grapple with the fact that on both sides of the family, but particularly the Yarrows, they were as close to being American aristocrats as was imaginable. He therefore resisted any efforts to educate him about his upper class patronage, and resented that he might have been admitted to Harvard as a 'legacy' that stretched back generations. He wanted to think of himself as a "self-made man," but strong family ties made such an objective unobtainable.

"She wants you to understand that Confucius teaches us about connectedness. Connectedness between generations, which is why ancestors are so venerated in our religion, but also other sorts of connections that need to be kept in mind when we act."

After another long harangue by the grandmother, Lim Boo apologized for having trouble following his grandmother's comments because they were so liberally sprinkled with ancient aphorisms and expressions. When he looked to his father for assistance, the man looked away as if to say, 'sorry kid, you're on your own.' Lim Boo then translated her comments for Ethan while obviously struggling to make sense of them himself. "She wants you to know that your family is forgiven, and added that for 'long-noses,' sorry, but that's the phrase she used, you've always had your hearts in the right place."

Ethan gave the grandmother and Lim Boo a questioning looks, and asked for some explanation. After the boy chatted with his grandmother for a while, he reported that, "She's adamant that forgiveness doesn't remove blame. She also won't clarify whether she's referring to your family or westerners in general." Lim Boo considered his words for a moment and then continued. "But she did say that one of those long noses convinced one of her ancestors to establish a plantation of gambier (*Uncaria gambier*) just before its market crashed."

Lim Boo then took a minute to figure out how to translate what his Grandmother said next, which was fortunate for Ethan because he needed the time to process what she'd said about gambier. He knew that the leaves of a related species of liana in the Amazon known as *uña de gato* (cat's claw) were famous as a tonic for waning sexual prowess in men, but didn't know that the Asian species were sometimes still used in the same way. But a more important gap in his knowledge was that until the end of the 19th Century, there was a huge market in Europe and China for the leaves and twigs of 'white catechu' for tanning leather. Those plants were grown on trellises in small plantations scattered around Southeast Asia until an industrial alternative was discovered and the market crashed.

Lim Boo then continued. "Grandmother then mentioned the conscription of Chinese men for railroad work in your country—when was that, 100 years ago?" Lim Boo asked and then continued after Ethan nodded, fascinated with this history of Sino-American relations. "Apparently she lost both her grandfathers to that venture, in which she suggested your ancestors were involved. She also mentioned how certain long-nosed Anglican priests couldn't leave the local girls alone and were also much involved in the opium trade, which was a disaster for her people."

After a moment of joint reflection, Lim Boo and Ethan agreed to being flummoxed by much of which the old woman had said. They also agreed to investigating aspects of her story and then talking about it again.

Ethan's pottery wheel had stopped while he listened to this extraordinary tale, but he gave it a kick and resumed inexpertly shaping his bowl.

After he worked for a while, Grandma Wong spoke again to her grandson who then translated. "I think she said that our great grandfathers crossed paths somewhere. Sorry, she's using lots of unusual expressions that I don't quite understand, and when I asked for clarification, she refused and said that she'd already revealed too much. Oh, and she's annoyed with me about not being fluent in Hokkien." After a pause he continued. "I had no idea that my Grandma is such a terrible gossip, and have no idea about the truth of what she's saying."

Grandma Wong gave her grandson a stern look and then asked Ethan directly, in carefully enunciated Hokkien, "Did you ever think about the fact that in your father's family, they only produce one child per generation, and always a son?"

Ethan understood the question, but didn't understand how she had come by that information, so he just nodded his affirmation.

"And did you know that the same is true for the Cheong family."

"As in Eddie and Tommy Cheong?"

"Yes."

"But what does the Cheong family have to do with the price of beans?" Ethan asked in his broken Hokkien, and then had to explain the expression to Lim Boo in English who then translated it for his grandmother.

Any chance that Grandma Wong would provide explanations for her enigmatic questions and comments evaporated as she left the men in the pottery barn and made her way up to the house from which soon emanated the enticing smells of lunch.

When it also became clear that Lim Boo couldn't answer Ethan's question, Tick Mee, his father, tried to explain. "The Cheong and Wong families have been linked for many generations," he said and then hesitated before continuing. "The Cheongs have always been merchants while my family has always worked with clay, but not like this," he said with a sweep of his hand around the rather humble establishment that produced flowerpots and other utilitarian earthenware items. "Before we were forced out of China by the Manchus, our factory produced fine porcelain—'bone China' your people called it because it was so white and hard and almost translucent. One of my ancestors mistakingly showed that Wedgewood chap how to make it; before that he'd only made terra cotta pots like these. In any case, the Cheongs were our main distributors."

Ethan apologized for his ignorance but had to confirm that the Manchus took over China 400 years ago, which he assumed to mean that the Wong's had been in Sarawak for almost that long. He was well aware that some Sarawak Chinese had deep roots in the country, but that seemed extraordinary. He wanted to ask more, but they were called to lunch and the conversation went back to considerations of The Sound of Thunder from a very Chinese perspective.

As he motored back to Kuching in the afternoon, Ethan reflected on the day's conversations. When he considered how really little he knew about his family, he promised himself that when he returned home to Maryland, he'd drag out the family bible and ask his father to explain the entries. But then he reflected that his father too seemed to resist the dynastic tendencies of some establishment families in the States. Ethan also remembered that while his father was always cordial with Grandpa Storm, their relationship was apparently still strained by the latter's unwillingness to support his father's desire to pursue a career in music. That his father failed to follow in his father's footsteps into the import-export business was also a bone of contention.

He drove along for a while longer, enjoying the breeze and the steady thumping of Roxanne's giant piston, but then remembered a snippet of conversation he'd overheard when he was still a small boy. He remembered that he was sitting behind the swinging door in their kitchen, sucking the blueberry filling out of a jelly donut surreptitiously supplied to him by Grandpa Storm. His father and grandfather were sitting at the kitchen table chatting over coffee. His father was home from work because he was just recovering from an attack of malaria, a disease he'd caught in Florida before being shipped off to the China-Burma-India Theatre in 1943 to join the Flying Tigers, which had just been incorporated into the US 14th Army Air Corps,

At the time the conversation between the two men meant little to him, but now it made him wonder about his family's business ties to Asia, and to Borneo in particular. For some reason, Grandpa Storm was relating how in the years immediately before the US entered World War I, he had refused to sell *gutta percha* (latex of *Palaquium gutta* trees) to the Germans, who needed it to insulate telegraph cables. When Grandfather Storm said that his own father, Miles, would've rolled over in his grave if he knew that his son had missed such a great business opportunity, Ethan gave himself away by laughing at the thought of an old man rolling over. Discovered with his face smeared blueberry jam and powdered with sugar, he was turned over to his mother for a scrubbing by the two chuckling men, the elder of whom failed to appear guilty for being the donut provider.

After Ethan parked his motorcycle and turned off the engine, she continued to sputter. Listening to her dieseling caused him to forget about his family and wonder whether Roxanne's condition was due to bad gas. He'd run her hot for two hours, which should have burned off any carbon in her cylinder. Or perhaps it was because she was hot. Something else to ask Bernie.

Chapter 6. WORDS FOR JUNGLE

Excerpt from an aerogram from Ethan Yarrow in Kuching, Sarawak, to his parents in Chevy Chase, Maryland:

20 April 1971
Dear Mom and Dad,
Thanks for the books—I've read them all, some for the third time, and now run my own lending library. Meanwhile, I'm struggling to describe the jungle in my dissertation and can now consult my betters for inspiration-- Tarzan, Rima, Mowgli and the rest of them. Incredible how few words Burroughs needed to invoke the jungle of Tarzan: "From a great mass of impenetrable foliage a few yards away emerged Tarzan of the Apes"—that's it, nothing more, but enough to inspire generations of readers.... Ian's helping me with my writing, or at least listening to me complain about it. My Olivetti is getting a lot of use. Oh, an unexpected benefit of your sending me the books via diplomatic pouch (not sure how you manage that trick!) is that the American Consul, who is a little twerp, is insanely curious about the contents of the packages. He's miffed that a lowly grad student seems to have influence—in addition to being a twerp, he's prone to bouts of jealousy...don't worry Mom, I treat him with undeserved respect...

"Good morning, or rather, good afternoon?" Ian said as he sat on the edge of the bed and handed Ethan a steaming cup of coffee. "I heard you pounding away half the night and, based on the wreckage around your typewriter," he continued with a gesture to the cascade of crumpled paper that seemed to flow from the Olivetti and across the floor, "it appears that in your war with words, you lost."

"You're right on that score, but thanks for the java," Ethan said, blowing across the top of the mug and taking a sip. "I'm trying to write a study site description and am having a deuced of a time describing the forest here. Everything I write fails to convey at all what it's actually like."

"Knowing you, I expect that the problem is that you're not happy with the standard 'canopy trees of 30-40 meters, emergents to 70 meters, dipterocarps dominate, nutrient-poor soils' and so forth," Ian opined in a droning voice.

"Exactly. It's way more than that, but when I try to capture the forest's essence, I fail miserably"

Ian contemplated his friend's challenge for a minute, looked at the stack of books on his bureau, and then suggested brightly, "Why not take a cue from your betters?" When Ethan's look revealed that he did not understand what he was suggesting, Ian explained. "Why not see how really good writers approached your challenge. Thanks to your mother, we have this wonderful collection of jungle books—perhaps you could use them for inspiration rather than just your puerile pleasure. Take Hudson's <u>Green Mansions</u>, for starters," he suggested and walked over to a stack of books, "and what about this tome," he said, holding up a much-thumbed copy of <u>The Naked and the Dead</u>. "I remember reading that in midwinter back at college, remember the intense cold in that bloody place?" he asked in reference to the frigid rooms they shared at Oriel College when they were both at Oxford. "I ended up in a sweat, but can't recall exactly what he wrote about the jungle. And what about those silly stories by your unapologetically American Edgar Rice Burroughs," he said with fake derision, having avidly read all 28 books in the Tarzan series, "which I do believe have had an undue influence on your character. How did that noble, British I might add, king of the jungle describe it?"

Ethan laughed at the Tarzan quip but recognized the wisdom in his friend's suggestion. As Ian got up to go back to work at the Sarawak Museum, Ethan said seriously, "Thanks for that suggestion," and then added with a smile, "You aren't just another pretty face."

In response to that comment, Ian pranced out of the room swaying his hips like a floosy, which made Ethan laugh again, but then contemplated his friend's suggestion. As Ian disappeared out the door, Ethan shouted, "How about banana leaf tonight for a change?"

When Ethan joined Ian at the Indian restaurant that evening, he was carrying a satchel of books and wearing a smile on his face. Almost immediately after he sat down, the proprietor came over with banana leaves draped over his arm and was proceeding to slap them down on the table in front of the two men when Ian interrupted him, "Give us a few minutes please Thamarajin, but please bring me a mango lassi." He looked over at Ethan and asked, "one for you as well?" Ethan nodded and the proprietor left to fill their order.

"What a wonderful afternoon, for which I have you to thank," Ethan reported, pulling a bedraggled copy of <u>Tarzan of the Apes</u> from his bag and waving it at his friend. "I didn't write a word, but now I'm inspired. You won't believe the jungle descriptions I found, some of them are positively lurid, which I know you'll enjoy."

"It turns out that the only writers whose portrayals of tropical forests are unkind, as it were, are the ones who actually spent time in the tropics. Take Stanley, for example, his impressions of Congo Basin forests captured in <u>Through the Dark Continent</u> (1878) couldn't contrast more markedly with my own. For him it was a *'region of horrors...a place where it was difficult to accustom myself to its gloom and its pallid solitude. I could find no comfort for the inner man nor solace for the spirit.'* And thanks for reminding me of <u>The Naked and the Dead</u> (1948). When I pulled it out I remembered my father mentioning that he and Mailer were in the same class at Harvard ...didn't have much good to say about his singing voice and made some disparaging comment about the author being a camp cook in the Philippines during the war, but he agreed that his writing really can raise a sweat." Without waiting for encouragement, Ethan continued. "Get this: '...the jungle offered far more resistance than the Japanese...In the heart of the forest the trees grew almost a hundred yards high, their lowest limbs sprouting out two hundred feet from the ground...Beneath them...a choked assortment of vines...wild banana trees...brush and shrubs squeezed against each other, raised their burdened leaves to the doubtful light that filtered through, sucking for air, and food like snakes at the bottom of a pit...Everything was damp and hot as though the jungle were an immense collection of oily rags growing hotter and hotter under the dark stifling vaults of a huge warehouse. Heat licked at everything, and the foliage, responding, grew to prodigious sizes....' Yikes, beautiful stuff, I definitely need to work that word 'prodigious' into my thesis."

Ethan was on a roll, enjoying himself thoroughly, and plowed on. "And what do you make of this one from O. Henry's Cabbages and Kings (1904), 'T'was a sort of camp in a damp gorge full of wildness and melancholies...The trees was all sky-scrapers, the underbrush was full of needles and pins; ...ye stood knee-deep in the rotten water and grabbled roots...surrounded by a rangin' forest full of disreputable beasts...waiting to devour ye. The sun strikes hard, and melts the marrow in your bones. Ye get similar to the lettuce-eaters the poetry books speaks about...Tis a land, as the poet says, Where it always seems to be after dinner.' Now what the heck does that mean? After dinner? Lettuce eaters? What am I missing?"

Without waiting for a reply he continued. "And what about this from Peter Mathieson's <u>At Play in the Fields of the Lord</u> (1965) 'In the dark tunnels of the rain forest the dim light was greenish. Strange shapes caught at his feet, and creepers scraped him; putrescent smells choked his nostrils with the density of sprayed liquid...a cathedral of Satan where all prayer was abomination, a place without a sky, a stench of death, vast somber naves and clerestories, the lost cries of savage birds...,' powerful but not at all like the forests I know. But later you'll have to remind me of the difference between a nave and a clerestory."

"Sorry for boring you," Ethan said and looked up at his friend, who didn't seem the least bored, "but let me read you just two more, both from Conrad—this one in <u>Almayer's Folly</u> (1895): 'In the midst [of giant trees] merciless creepers clung to the big trunks in cable-like coils, leaped from tree to tree, hung in festoons from the lower boughs, and, sending slender tendrils on high to seek out the smallest branches, carried death to their victims in an exulting riot of silent destruction.' Or try this from <u>Heart of Darkness</u> (1902): 'it was like a weary pilgrimage amongst hints for nightmares...back to the earliest beginnings of the world, when vegetation rioted on earth and the big *trees were kings....the heavy, mute smell of the wilderness—that seemed to draw him to its pitiless breast by the awakening of forgotten and brutal instincts, by the memory of gratified and monstrous passions.'* Yikes, that man could write."

"Not to inflame your jealousy, but I should point out that English wasn't Jozef Korzeniowski's first language," Ian reported and then laughed at his friend's pretend scowl.

Resuming his exposition, Ethan continued, "It turns out that the writers whose descriptions I find most appealing spent no time whatsoever in the Torrid Zone. Try this one, for example, by Phillip Gosse, one of your very English country vicars—it makes me think of that painting by Henri Rousseau, the one with the lady reclining on a settee in the midst of fantastic plants—Rousseau also never made it past the Jardin des Plantes in Paris, by the way. But this is from Gosse's The Romance of Natural History (1860) *'Solemn are the primeval labyrinths of giant trees, tangled with ten thousand creepers, and roofed with lofty arches of light foliage, diversified with masses of glorious blossom of all rich hues; ...the gigantic scale of life strongly excited astonishment...'* Now that prose is going to be hard to beat," Ethan opined. Then, without waiting for a response said almost to himself, "I wonder if I could get away with 'romance' in the title of my dissertation?"

Just as he pronounced the word romance, their friend Hazel sat down and interjected, "If you ask my opinion...," at which point Ian interrupted her.

"Did you ask her opinion?" he asked Ethan.

"No, did you?" Ethan responded quickly.

"Nope, but I'm sure we are going to hear it anyway. Have at it old girl," Ian said with a smile.

"It pains me that we are countrymen," she retorted in a feigned huff. With Hazel it was often hard to know when she was serious and when she was poking fun at herself, but it was always hard to detect her growing fondness for the two men. Turning her back on Ian to the extent possible sitting on the same side of a round table, she addressed Ethan with the warning tone of a grade school teacher, "I do believe that you, my young American friend, are being led down the road to perdition by this English reprobate," she said with a rude gesture at Ian. "And I rather suspect that you are both going to get in trouble for your ill-conceived and sophomoric 'flounder' campaign, and now you want to work 'romance' into the title of what I presume will be a serious scientific treatise. And how is it coming, if you don't mind my asking," she said, changing the subject and her tone, all without taking a breath.

At the mention of 'flounder,' the two men both laughed. Over too many pints of Scrumpy at the Eagle and Claw pub back in Oxford they had pledged to use that word in whatever they published. So far, with five articles between them, they'd managed to honor the pact for which Hazel showed such disdain.

"For that eloquent string on *non sequiturs* you deserve a mango *lassi*," Ian said.

"I thank you for the *lassi*, which is less than I deserve for putting up with you two testosterone poisoned louts, but I'm famished and need to eat," Hazel gushed. She too was on one of her 'rolls,' so the two men just sat back and listened to her rant, happy to be taken for a ride. As she spoke, Ethan put his books away and signaled the proprietor that they were ready to eat.

With a flourish the man came over, spread a banana leaf in front of each of them and started to ladle out the various dishes. All three ordered *dosai* (a fried, crepe-like sourdough bread), *kuzhamba* (spicy vegetable stew), and *aviyal* (stewed vegetables with buttermilk gravy).

When Ian asked for additional *rasam* (a spicy but sweet tamarind stew) and *oorukai* (pickled limes with ginger), Hazel commented "Ah, sounds like you are trying to etch away a difficult day with spices," which elicited a chuckle from her two friends.

As they commenced eating, Hazel complained in her most amusing way. "I spent the entire day holed up in my miserable cubicle at the National Parks office trying to make sense of a spreadsheet submitted by that *Alam Liar* group we're funding. Such an ungodly mess, I wonder how they ever managed to cobble together a credible proposal."

Taking opportunity of the gap in Hazel's diatribe, Ian briefly explained what they'd been talking about, and then commented to Ethan, "I find it interesting that you go for the romantic depictions whereas my impressions fall closer to the brutality of mercilessly tangled labyrinths than to your Elysian fields. I should note that it's been more than a month since our 'pleasant jaunt' through the forest, of which I am reminded every time I scratch one of my leech bites. And why is it that I got chewed and you suffered nary a bite?" Ian asked in exasperation.

"Blood type, I believe," was Ethan's response. "I'm A and you, my tasty friend, are B, isn't that right?"

Ian affirmed his blood type with a nod but then said, "But do you really think that makes a difference?"

Ethan smiled and suggested with a leading tone, "We could do an experiment."

"Not on your life," Ian responded in a huff, and then turning to Hazel and continuing on with his rant, "And did I mention the food on that journey? No, well there wasn't much and what they had was terrible."

"If you were hungry, you would've eaten what was offered," Ethan retorted.

Ian reflected on that comment for a minute, and then turned to Hazel for confirmation of what he thought to be reasonable dietary restrictions, "But you and Jika eat almost anything and seem to be nibbling nearly constantly. Hardly an hour went by when you didn't find something to eat along the track that would be generous to call a path. I didn't mind the palm grubs, they were actually pretty good, but the termite wings stuck in my teeth, the fiddle heads were bitter as hell, and some of those fruits were so acidic they could be used to remove paint—and I saw you eating other things that you didn't even offer me, for which I probably owe you thanks. But overall, I remained half-starved for most of the trip."

Hazel nodded encouragement while Ethan laughed and then said, "Your unfair and unjustified complaints notwithstanding, you are welcome to join us. Next week we're going up into the Hose Mountains and make our way down to Long Berawan. Care to join?"

"What," Ian responded in a horrified voice, "so you and Jika can play Beat the Reaper again at my expense?" Looking at Hazel he explained. "On our last little walk in the woods I was bitten or stung by something on my back---it hurt like hell but I didn't see what it was. Instead of helping me, these two clowns gleefully speculated whether it was a snake or a wasp, a centipede or a deadly spider. Meanwhile I suffered," he ended with a pout and a sniffle.

"Does that mean you're not coming?"

"Sorry old chap, as much as I would like to, I won't be able to join you. I found an opportunity to volunteer for unnecessary dental surgery, and that seems like too good an opportunity to miss," Ian said in the voice of an Oxford don, at which they all laughed and continued to enjoy their meal.

When they finished, the proprietor himself once again returned to their table to clear off the banana leaves and ask with his deep rumbling voice, "And now my friends, can I offer you something sweet?"

Ethan and Ian were both full, but after Hazel ordered the *payasam* (sweet rice/wheat/tapioca pudding also known as *kheer*), Ian succumbed and went for the *kesari* (a sweet dish made from wheat and colored with saffron) and Ethan held out for his regular, a small bowl of *glabjams* (fried balls of milk solids, spices, and flour floating in a sugar sauce).

As the proprietor was clearing the table, Ethan asked, "Has Arjun been in? I haven't seen him for a while and I'm missing his column in the Borneo Post.

The mention of the newspaper reporter caused the proprietor to freeze momentarily, look around to see if they could be overheard, and then reply quietly, "Haven't you heard? He was arrested and then deported a few weeks back."

"Yikes," Hazel burst out, "is he okay?"

"Yes, thankfully. I heard from his cousin, you know Pranav, the big fellow at JKR (*Jabatan Kerja Raya*, the public works department), that he's safely back in Petalying Jaya, a bit bruised but nothing broken."

The three Westerners were sorely vexed by this news. They enjoyed Arjun's company; he was sharp-witted and very droll. They were also alarmed at the government's growing crackdown on reporters, even in laid-back Sarawak.

"But what did he do?" asked the irrepressible and somewhat naïve Englishwoman.

In an even more guarded whisper, the proprietor explained. "I don't know the details, but apparently that story he wrote about the threatened destruction of Fairy Caves by a cement company annoyed someone in power, most likely the Chief Minister or one of his cronies."

"But isn't that cave a sacred place for Hindus?" Hazel asked.

"It certainly is, but little difference that makes to the government," the proprietor replied in disgust.

The trio commiserated with the proprietor for a few minutes, settled their bill, and then left the shop. As they were strolling across town in the relative cool of the evening, Ian said, "Well that explains that."

"What?" asked his two friends simultaneously.

"Why my boss suggested that I might want to study the bats in one of the small side caverns in the limestone formation that contains Fairy Cave. He said that Harrisson had once told him that he suspected the presence of new species there. I now suspect that in his guarded manner, the Museum director is looking for ways to keep the cement company at bay."

"Doubly interesting," Ethan then said, "because my boss also suggested that Jika and I explore that area for new species." After a few seconds of reflection he added, "I find it particularly intriguing that he suggested we take Ahmad bin Mustafa along. He's the new botany graduate from Kuala Lumpur--doesn't know much, but he's enthusiastic."

"But what are they going to do with all that cement," Hazel asked, disregarding the musings of her two friends.

"No idea," Ian responded, "but it's a good question."

The trio walked along quietly until they were roused from their thoughts by the passing of a Honda 50 with four passengers. After a brief consultation, they agreed that four was not the record.

Chapter 7. OPIUM DEN ESCAPE WITH PILLOW

Excerpt from an aerogram from Ethan Yarrow in Kuching, Sarawak, to his parents in Chevy Chase, Maryland:

5 May 1971
Dear Mom and Dad,
...My relationship with Antonio, that young orphan I mentioned, is a source of great happiness. He's not yet two and talks in complete sentences complete with perfect punctuation, but I can't yet make sense of any of his words. He's a happy soul with a tremendous concentration span. I've given him toys--trucks and such--but he destroys them and goes back to playing with sticks. The facility where he lives is about an hour from Kuching, so I don't get to see him as often as I like, but when we're together we have a blast.

A refreshing breeze worked its way up the meanders of the Sarawak River from the South China Sea. Along the way it picked up the redolence of mangroves and nypa palm swamps at low tide, but those smells were sweet compared to those of the city's open sewers and belching diesel engines. A torrential late afternoon rain had swept through town and both muted the odors and moderated the temperature, changes appreciated by all. Along the riverside, evening food bazaar vendors were assembling their stalls in what an hour before was a packed parking lot. The cooks set up their mobile kitchens while their assistants swept in front of the stalls and arranged metal tables and folding chairs for the soon-to-arrive patrons. The strings of colored lights that surrounded and crisscrossed the bazaar were brightening against the rapidly darkening sky as the charcoal stoves for cooking *satay* (meat on skewers, eaten with spicy peanut sauce) were ignited.

Ethan was among the first patrons to arrive. As usual, he sported a batik shirt and dark pants, but his face was a bit bedraggled. He acknowledged the various vendors as he strode across the bazaar, but then plopped down in a chair, ordered a Bintang beer, and awaited the arrival of his friends.

As the smells of the city and river were being overwhelmed by the even more pungent aromas of frying garlic and *belachang*, Ethan's friend Ian arrived and was presented by the Chinese waitress with a glass and a bottle of Tiger beer. Although the two friends admitted that Tiger and Bintang were pretty much indistinguishable and both were lame excuses for beer, they were consistent in their choices.

Ian examined his friend closely, quaffed his beer, and then asked the question he'd stored up all day. "What do you remember about last night?" After a pause he continued. "I'm frankly glad that you look at least slightly worse for the wear."

Ethan pondered the question for a minute and then responded, "I'm having trouble reconstructing exactly what happened last night, but I remember pleasantly floating a few feet above the ground in one of those downtown dens of inequity. All was well and then, suddenly, it was dark, uncomfortable, and hot. That reaction to opium was new to me, but I flowed with it until I found myself being rudely manhandled. At that point my arms were pinned and I must have struggled because one of my captors said, *Nakarum nirutta ninkal patukappaka ullana* and then something like *oru kalutai irukkai kutatu*," Ethan recalled in a somewhat dreamy voice.

"Help me Mr. Polyglot," Ian asked, "what, pray tell, does that mean?"

"Translating loosely from some rather rough Tamil, it means 'stop moving and you will be safe' and then 'don't be a donkey,' but perhaps I don't have that completely right. In any case, I did what he said. The next thing I knew I was on our front lawn looking up into your ugly mug."

"My goodness, you really are a piece of work. You don't remember anything else?" Ian asked in exasperation. "We figured you'd been denning from your oblivious state and the fact that you had grasped in your arms like a rugby ball a well-warn block of wood that we deduced is one of your beloved opium den pillows."

"Ah, yes, that's what it is, beautiful, no? But really sorry you had to take care of me," Ethan told his friend with genuine remorse.

"The little you remember explains a lot," Ian continued, "but here's some more of the sordid story. Hazel and I were sitting on the porch drinking tea when a car screeched to a stop in front of the house. Two men jumped out of what looked like an old Mercedes taxi, hustled quickly around to the boot, picked up a large object that turned out to be you, and tossed it not-so-gently onto the lawn. It was too dark to see who they were or what they had dropped, so I ran down to investigate. They sped off before I could make out the plate number. You, my friend, were pretty whacked out, but seemed to have suffered only minor injuries. We got you on your feet, at which point you explained, in a quite lucid voice, that you had finally mastered self-levitation and wished to be allowed to float up to your apartment. We finally got you into your room, and stabilized, if that's the proper term for a person in your state, and I went off to town to figure out what happened."

"Really sorry my man, I didn't intend to be a bother," Ethan said apologetically.

"No apology necessary, at least to me," Ian responded, "but you might want to thank Hazel for mothering you."

"I certainly will," Ethan responded, "especially since it sometimes seems like Hazel can barely stand being around me."

"Oh, don't worry about Hazel, she likes you well enough, but you do stress her."

"Stress?" Ethan asked, "Why's that?"

"A bit difficult to explain," Ian responded, "but perhaps you'll get the point if I tell you, in strictest secrecy of course, what she once said about you."

When Ethan signaled that his lips were sealed, Ian explained. "One day as Hazel and I watched you run off to kick a ball around with some young children she said that you were to a lesbian what bacon is to a vegetarian."

Ethan contemplated that explanation for a minute and then said, "Okay, not sure I fully understand, but thanks for the insight."

They sat together quietly for a few minutes and then returned to the opium den escapade. "Now that I can put two and two together, I wonder if one of my captors was my Indian buddy from the police station."

"That's exactly who I think it was," Ian agreed, "at least from what I've been able to deduce. But this story is complicated, and I'm only beginning to piece it together."

"So what do you know?"

"Well, it turns out that the row of shanties that houses your beloved den sits on some pretty pricey real estate on which your friend Paib has his eye."

Ethan's Iban friends were initially pleased that Sarawakian natives had risen to power in the government, but soon realized that Paib and his extended family were ruthless characters hell-bent on taking over the state. They were doing so with the blessing of the United Malays National Organization (UMNO), the political party that controlled the federal government.

"Although the property is owned by Eddie Cheong, of whom the government generally steers clear, Paib had the opium den and the rest of the other less-than-above board establishments in that block raided last night. The raiders included both military and local police, many not in uniform. Your Tamil police buddy must have been in the vanguard, and when he saw you he must have acted fast to spirit you away before the rough-housing and arrests started. I heard that the pokey is currently spilling over with the reprobates with whom you consort along with a dozen or so innocent Hokkien shopkeepers. Needless to say, if you'd been caught, the consequences would not have been pretty. I understand from Fatimah that the powers-that-be are looking for some excuse to throw your bum out of the country."

"Yikes, that was a close one, I do need to be more careful."

"Yep, I believe that would be a good idea. You should also probably find some way to thank your guardian angel. And frankly, I can't believe you are still visiting opium dens after what happened last time."

"Now wait right there," Ethan corrected, "I recall my last opium den visit with great fondness, and I have that beautiful blue and white porcelain pillow to prove it."

"Pillow aside, your friend Pamela told me that it was a very painful experience," noted Ian with a glint in his eye.

Pamela Wilson was one of Ethan's ex-girlfriends. Her work for USAID sometimes brought her to the region. They'd briefly renewed their relationship when both attended an international ethnobotanical conference in Penang Island off Peninsular Malaysia. Back when Ethan was finishing his undergraduate degree in botany at Harvard, Pam was working on her Ph.D. on tropical food crops through the Ethnobotany Institute. When she invited him to serve as her field assistant in Amazonian Venezuela, Ethan readily agreed. Despite their difference in age, they became easy friends and worked together well. Ethan helped her collect and preserve samples for her genetic analyses but had plenty of time to carry out research for his senior thesis on the local uses of the *piassaba* palm (*Leopoldinia piassaba*). When they became lovers, their lives under what were otherwise harsh conditions improved immensely. In that border area across the river from Colombia and upriver from Brazil, the food was monotonous and bland, biting insects partitioned both day and night so one species or another was always available to bite or sting, and the local people were mostly hostile and wary. All of those hardships were of little consequence when the pleasures of a shared hammock awaited them every evening and some afternoons. The other high point of their months on the Rio Negro, at least for Ethan, were afternoon paddles in a dugout canoe through the flooded forests. It was relatively rainless when they were in San Carlos de Rio Negro, but heavy rains downstream near Manaus backed up the river and flooded the forest to depths of up to 20 feet. Under those conditions, fishing was bad because the fish were scattered throughout the flooded forests eating fruit, worms, and such, but it was a marvelous experience to paddle through the lower canopy. Ethan particularly enjoyed swimming through the forest underwater—it was almost like being able to fly through the totally submerged understory in which the trees were in full leaf.

When Ethan and Pam returned to Boston they remained together as a couple, but the relationship was strained by both professional and personal challenges. For one thing, Pam became increasingly dependent on Ethan's ability to interpret data and became jealous of the fluency of his writing. He was more than generous with his time, helped her with lab work, which he loathed, and extensively edited whatever she managed to write, but it irked her that her former student had transitioned into her teacher. Her aggravation intensified when, as she still struggled with the first chapter of her dissertation, Ethan finished his senior thesis and published it in a prestigious botanical journal. That he had accomplished so much while lettering in ice hockey and spending lots of time with his young friends, annoyed her to the screaming point, and scream she did, on more than one occasion.

When Ethan graduated and went off to spend a year at Oxford as a Rhodes Scholar, he was glad to escape from their increasingly strained relationship. In contrast, Pam was less than happy about his leaving. While she was often upset with Ethan, she often admitted to herself that much of that frustration sprang from jealousy, against which she disappointed herself by failing to guard.

Over the years since they split up, Pam had still not finished her PhD but she took a position with USAID to run their new campaign against slash-and-burn farming. Although she was glad for the job, she still carried a chip on her shoulder about her failure as an academic. Meanwhile, Ethan flourished during his year in the UK, enrolled for a PhD at the University of Wisconsin in Madison, completed his course work, and received a substantial research grant to study the evolution of climbing palms in Sarawak.

For her job as with USAID, Pamela visited Sarawak fairly frequently. While Ethan mostly managed to avoid her by fleeing to the forest on often hastily arranged expeditions, it was natural that during her visits she would often dine with Ian, Hazel, and the rest of the expat regulars. To Ian she had opened her heart, which was common for people who spent time with him.

"What exactly did she tell you?" Ethan asked and then continued without waiting for an answer. "As I recall, she particularly enjoyed the train trip from Penang down to Singapore," he said with a glint in his eyes.

"She didn't say much other than that she was so sore afterwards that she could hardly walk—I pressed her for an explanation but none was forthcoming, so now it's your chance to provide the gory details. It's the least you can do after what you put me through last night."

Ethan burst out laughing and then said, while still chuckling, "I can well believe she was sore. Let me try to reconstruct what happened, but remember that we were both higher than hoot owls. The conference we attended was dreadfully dull, so we skipped out a bit early. We decided that before hopping on the train to Singapore we'd treat ourselves. We spent a few hours in an upscale opium den, from which I absconded with the porcelain pillow. Somehow we made it to the train station in Butterworth, pawing each other the entire way. Once set up in our private sleeping compartment, we took full advantage of our time together. I've never had that reaction to opium before; fucked like bunnies for hours. No not bunnies, some sort of sea creatures--are porpoises like bunnies?" Ethan asked his mammologist friend, laughed, and continued without waiting for an answer. "For some reason we both felt like we were swimming through warm syrup in which there was no gravity. We finally passed out somewhere south of Kuala Lumpur. As we approached the station in Singapore, even in that small space we had trouble finding our clothes and then in dressing ourselves. We must have made a peculiar sartorial statement when we walked from the station to the Methodist Guest House off Orchard Road." Ethan laughed again and then continued, reflectively. "I can't understand why she'd complain about that rather memorable trip. But I must admit that she still scares me and I'm glad to be shut of her."

The friends sat quietly sipping their beer until Hazel appeared. After she sat down and Ethan apologized for the previous night, her only response was to say severely, "You don't have the sense that God gave geese. Fortunately, you mostly seem to be a danger to yourself. One of these days you're going to get caught." After a minute of nursing the beer she'd been served, she continued on an entirely different topic.

That she'd change the subject came as a surprise to Ian, given that the previous night their friend had been rudely delivered in a jute sack, stoned out of his mind. It struck both Ethan and Ian odd that Hazel seemed to have taken that event in stride, but obviously had another axe to grind. "I'm more concerned about your interference with efforts to reintroduce orphaned orangutans into the wild."

That comment, which came out of the blue, caused Ethan to gaze at her with incomprehension so she elaborated. "I visited the Orangutan Rehabilitation Center earlier this week and the director told me that your visits there are terribly disruptive."

Mostly due to the illegal pet trade, the numbers of confiscated young orangutans grew as their habitat shrank. One of the environmental groups that Hazel's organization funded was dedicated to reintroducing the often abused animals back into the wild. They ran a facility in which orangutans free-ranged in the forest, but were provided supplemental food until they could forage on their own. The idea was to wean them gradually off free bananas.

"What?" Ethan sputtered, "I thought that my visits were appreciated."

"Yes, exactly, appreciated, but far too much."

"What do you mean?" Ethan asked, obviously exasperated by the accusation.

"Well for example, that young male you spoil so terribly."

"Antonio?"

"Yes, him. After your visits he goes into sulks that last for days," Hazel explained. She admitted to herself that her feelings about this situation were conflicted, but the concerns were real. She too adored the orangutans and would have spoiled them even more than Ethan, if given the chance, but for some reason they always acted wary of her. Even Antonio seemed to avoid her; he certainly didn't spend his time on her head or riding around on her foot as he did with Ethan. She was also aware that even without Ethan's well-intended interference, all efforts to fully rehabilitate orangutans were failing, presumably because they were too smart to voluntarily forgo regular meals.

The threesome sat contemplating this sorry situation for a few minutes until Ian said, "And now I understand something your mother wrote me about." In addition to irregular phone calls, Ian kept up a regular correspondence with Doris Yarrow. "Have you really led her to believe that Antonio's human?"

"He is, nearly," Ethan said defensively.

Ian smiled at this friend's subterfuge but also shook his head in condemnation.

"But what did she say?" Ethan asked.

"She noted that you have no experience with retarded children and that hopes you aren't getting too close. She's already worried about your relationship with Roxanne, and now she's concerned about Antonio too. I don't know why you make that woman suffer so," Ian replied and then laughed in a conspiratory manner.

Hazel had been sitting quietly but fuming about the jist of their interchange. No longer able to repress her censure, as their food was served she burst out, "Can you imagine what it was like to raise that monster?" she said with a withering glance at Ethan, "and now you both prolong her suffering. You should be ashamed of yourselves."

In response to her attack, Ethan and Ian both looked a bit sheepish, but they couldn't hide the smiles in their eyes. Ethan broke the silence by raising his beer and offering a toast, "To my long-suffering mother."

Chapter 8. WACKY WEDNESDAY READING CIRCLE

Excerpt from an aerogram from Ethan Yarrow in Kuching, Sarawak, to his parents in Chevy Chase, Maryland:

10 June 1971
Dear Mom and Dad,
The evening class I offer for local students preparing for their college entrance exams is going better now that more of them are speaking up. The other night the debate got animated—seems like I touched a nerve when I broached the topic of pharmaceutical companies cashing in on local medicinal plant knowledge. My struggling playwright friend Joe Weldman will be happy when I tell him that we read his play about the pharmacological potency of Madagascar periwinkle, but I'll not relay some of the comments about it from the more critical students...

"Good evening class," Ethan said in a formal manner to the group of young Malaysians—Indians, Chinese, a few Malays, and one Iban-- assembled in a meeting room in the Sarawak Museum for their regular reading group meeting. His smile revealed that with that salutation he was gently teasing them. He worked hard to break down the teacher-student divide with which they had grown accustomed throughout their schooling. That formal and very traditional interchange was therefore in jest.

"Good evening Professor Ethan," was their polite if not quite synchronous response.

In preparation for the 2-hour long Wednesday evening sessions, all participants read the same short story, book chapter, or play that they would then discuss. The discussions were generally very serious and the students strove to rise to the challenges posed by their teacher. Despite that seriousness, the group ended up referring to itself as the "Wacky Wednesday Reading Group," named after one of Ethan's favorite children's books.

Most Wacky Wednesday attendees were finishing 6th Form and preparing for their university entry exams. They appreciated the extra tutoring, especially from a native English speaker. Due to Ethan's expeditions that kept him out of Kuching for weeks at a time, their meetings were sporadic but much anticipated. Even after a dozen sessions, the very diligent and often overly earnest students still sometimes struggled with Ethan's American accent and unconventional teaching methods. Given that many aspired to studying outside of Malaysia, preferably in the UK, USA, or Australia, they recognized that this cultural exposure would be advantageous even if it was sometimes uncomfortable.

"I trust that you found the reading for this evening at least somewhat provocative?" Ethan asked the group and then continued, not expecting an immediate answer. "Now if you would be so kind as to share your impressions."

The assigned reading was a play written by a friend from Boston. In the play a Malagasy teen has to decide whether to reveal to a representative of a European pharmaceutical company the identity of a plant species used to prepare a medicinal unguent used as a traditional medicine in his grandmother's village. While sorely tempted by the offer of a motorbike and a trip to the capital, his conscience tells him to not comply with the request. The plant in question was the rosy periwinkle, *Catharanthus roseus*, extracts from which later proved to be effective in combating childhood leukemia, Hodgkin's disease, and several other cancers. Shareholders of the pharmaceutical company that extracted and then synthesized alkaloids from that species became wealthy while the villagers whose knowledge led to its discovery and could thus justifiable claim intellectual property rights benefited not at all. The play was set at a time before the plant's identity had been revealed to outsiders. Ethan selected the play because it was short, which made copying cheaper, and because it dealt with a topic close to his own heart. He also hoped the theme would resonate with his students, many of whom had rural backgrounds and all of whom were familiar with traditional herbal remedies. His final motivation for assigning this script was that he wanted to use it to inform a debate about a local plant he thought had commercial potential.

Ethan forced himself to wait for the students to respond. A painful silence enveloped the room as he counted slowly to 10, but he was confident that eventually someone would speak up. It was always this way, but he knew that once the conversation started, it would be auto-catalytic.

After what seemed like an interminable delay, he prodded again. "Oh, my apologies, perhaps you did not understand my question. *Que piensas sobre nuestro cuento?*" but still the students all stared down at their copies of the play. "*Quesque tu pense de cette histoire? Hatway, hinktay histay torysay?*" In response to that final prod in Pig Latin, a couple of students laughed and Veronica finally responded.

"I thought the boy in the story was too simply portrayed. I couldn't picture him in my mind, which made it hard to empathize with him," she said in the beautiful Queen's English she generally employed in class. What she actually sounded like when she wasn't affecting an accent puzzled Ethan, because he'd heard her sound American, Australian, South Indian, Chinese, and even Malay, depending on the topic and situation.

Ethan was pleased when Tommy Cheong saved him from having to respond. The success of a discussion-format class depended entirely on the preparation and then the participation of group members. In this group, Tommy, Veronica, and Pagik were the most dependable. Based on outward appearances, the three teenagers couldn't be more different but Ethan had seen them coming and going from class together and so knew they were friends. Tommy was the grandson of Eddie Cheong, the Hokkien *tokay* who ran the store where Ethan purchased provisions for his expeditions. Pagik was the second son of Jika, Ethan's own teacher, friend, and field companion. Ethan knew nothing about Veronica's background, but recognized that she was extremely bright. She often looked Eurasian, but then would shift her guise and seem pure Chinese one minute and Malay the next. The three would often contest each other's opinions, seemingly taking great delight in their arguments. It amused Ethan that it didn't seem to bother them in the slightest if, over the course of a single session, they switched sides on a topic. Veronica even seemed to take particular pleasure in contesting Ethan's opinions, which she did with considerable charm.

"With due respect, Miss Veronica, but I must disagree," Tommy interjected in an amusingly formal manner. "I was impressed with how the playwright presented him so clearly with so few words. And remember that this is a play intended to be performed, so the audience will be able to see the fellow in the flesh," Tommy continued with more confidence than he often displayed.

This interchange right off a page in an Archie comic made Ethan wonder if that was where Veronica got her name. In any event, it was sufficient to spur the other students to share their opinions. The class went merrily on for almost an hour, with much lively discussion. Ethan only occasionally had to steer the conversation and overall was pleased that every one of the twelve students contributed something. For this he had to thank Veronica, Tommy, and Pagik—a few classes back he'd taken them aside and explained his pedagogical goal of one hundred percent participation. They turned out to be masters at getting their classmates to speak up, even those who were less-than-comfortable with their English.

As hoped, the discussion revolved around the issue of intellectual property rights. Ethan provoked them by coming to the defense of the pharmaceutical company. He pointed out that to get a new drug on the market, the firms first needed to invest millions of dollars in extraction, purification, and testing. He went on to encourage the students to keep in mind that more often than not, the presumed cure turned out to be ineffective or to have adverse side effects.

After the first hour when the group stopped for its accustomed break, Ethan announced that he was providing refreshments. His friend Isa had supplied him with a package of Oreos purloined from her American employer and Ethan announced that he wanted everyone to try a mystery drink that would be the topic of the second portion of the class.

As he laid out the cookies on a plate and prepared the special drink Ethan explained. "To explore the ethical and financial issues broached in the play, which I should tell you was written by a friend of mine—don't worry, I won't tell him what you said," he jokingly added while looking straight at Veronica, "I want to introduce you to what I expect to be a new drink sensation. I also want to provide you with an investment opportunity." As he spoke he pulled a small, palm-like plant from his satchel. "As you know, I'm a botanist and aspire to a career as a faculty member at some prestigious university where I can preach plants. The problem is that faculty salaries are inadequate to satisfy my considerable material needs." When he said this some of the students smiled, knowing that he was a very frugal fellow and was unlikely to aspire to great wealth. "I believe I hold in my hand," he said, displaying the plant, "the key to my future financial success and yours too if you choose to get in on the ground floor of this marketing venture. I also want to warn you that we will use the next hour of tonight's session to hone your debating skills—more about that in a minute."

Ethan's plant looked like a palm seedling with a rosette of long, strap-shaped leaves, but closer inspection revealed large yellow flowers and clusters of small white fruits. "If you mistook this plant for a palm, don't feel bad, I did too, to my great embarrassment. I actually planted one in the palm section of the Botanical Garden," he chuckled at his own mistake. From the time he dug up the plant on one of their first expeditions, Jika was aware of his mistake but chose to not say anything. After the mis-identification was revealed, he still insisted that Ethan's non-palm be left in the palm garden, probably so that he could continue to tease Ethan. "Now I know that it isn't a palm at all, but *Curculigo orchioides*, a member of the Hypoxidaceae family—its common name is *lembah*." At least a few of the students recognized the plant, but everyone watched quietly as Ethan pulled one pea-sized fruit from the cluster. With his pocket knife he sliced a tiny piece off the fruit and dropped it into in a pitcher of water that he then stirred. "I learned about this plant from an Iban friend of mine."

"While we wait for the infusion to develop, let me tell you a bit about the multi-million dollar artificial sweetener industry. Most of you've heard of saccharin, which is marketed globally as 'Sweet'n Low,' but did you know that it's made from coal tar and that its off-putting chemical name is benzoic sulfnide? And did you know that recent studies with rats indicate that it's carcinogenic?" He hesitated for effect and then continued, "As people get more concerned about being over-weight, diabetes becomes more common, and demand for non-fattening sweeteners grows, don't you think there will be a market for a natural artificial sweetener instead of one derived from carcinogenic tar? Here I have for you a totally natural, fruit-based alternative that is totally safe and inexpensive to produce."

With that introduction, Ethan poured *lembah*-water into small cups, which the students then took with some hesitation. "Please, trust me and try it, I think you will be pleasantly surprised."

When the students tentatively took small sips they were overwhelmed by its sweetness. As they continued to sip the drink and munch on the Oreos, which were also new to most of them, Ethan elaborated. "These *lembah* fruits contain a taste-modifying protein that is 200 times sweeter than sugar. Saccharin, in contrast is 400 times sweeter but I already pointed out its down-sides. And there are potentially therapeutic benefits from this plant that we haven't even begun to explore," he continued with enthusiasm.

While they were still sipping their drinks Ethan divided the class into two teams for the debate. One team was to defend his right to sell the concept to an international food conglomerate that would then commercialize it. The other team was assigned to defend the intellectual property rights of the Iban people who introduced him to it. Each team would be given 10 minutes to assemble their arguments, which they would then have 5 minutes to present. After the formal presentations, there would be time for cross questioning.

The ensuing debate was far more heated than anticipated, which pleased Ethan. The Iban defenders made an impassioned plea for protection of intellectual property rights and even came up with several examples of how those rights had been trampled in the past. The advocates for commercialization by an outside company undercut their opponents' case by outlining a scheme in which 25% of the profits would accrue to the Iban once the costs of product development, testing, and marketing were covered. To his surprise, after just 10 minutes the team defending the local community's rights had formed their own corporation, decided to contract out the chemical testing, and come up with a marketing scheme for a product they planned to call 'Jungle Sweetness.' When Ethan asked about how much he could be expected to be paid for his efforts, Veronica, dazzling in her role as the Jungle Sweetness Corporation's lawyer and spokesperson, shocked everyone by making it clear that Ethan could be expected to be paid exactly nothing, thank you very much.

When everyone stopped laughing at her bombastic statement and Ethan's vociferous response, he complemented them for their efforts and then warned them about some potentially negative consequences of financial success in the commercialization of a natural product. He explained that it can be socially disruptive when there are large influxes of money into communities unaccustomed to wealth. As an example, he described a village in Ecuador that was torn apart by disagreements about how their new-found ecotourism profits should be distributed among community members. He then pointed out that if *lembah* did become a successful product, it would be hard to keep wealthy companies from growing it themselves, thereby cutting out the Iban.

After some further discussion it was time to end the session so Ethan said, "For next week we'll read 'To Build a Fire,' a short story by Jack London, an American author who wrote such legendary books as White Fang and The Call of the Wild. Thanks again to Rajit for providing us all with copies of a story I hope you enjoy," he said with a nod to the young Indian student who, by some means or another about which Ethan had never enquired, provided the copies without charge. "Please note that this was London's first published work. It finally appeared in 1902 in a magazine called 'The Youth's Companion,' but we're going to read the 1908 version from 'The Century Magazine.' I should note that London finally got this story published after it was rejected no less than 43 times. I offer that footnote particularly for the benefit of the aspiring authors among you—do not be disheartened by rejections, but keep trying. After all, what you'll read is perhaps the most often re-published short story ever."

When Ethan arrived back at his apartment his friend Isa was there, as he hoped and expected. He noticed that, as usual, she'd straightened up his things and was pleased to see evidence that she'd also been reading the manuscript he'd left next to his typewriter. She was also, as usual, grumpy about her job as *au pair* in the home of the American Counsel.

Isa was the younger sister of Singa with whom she grew up in the Iban village of Long Awan, where the latter still lived most of the time. Singa was widowed after a very short marriage to Jika's eldest son and still lived in the longhouse whereas Isa had remained single and lived in Kuching. Ethan was fascinated by both of them as they apparently were with him.

"It's terrible what you have to put up with," Ethan commiserated. "Those Americans should be happy to have you. Perhaps a foot massage would help?"

Isa grumbled an unconvinced response but then with apparent reluctance, she stretched out on Ethan's bed. While Ethan massaged her feet, starting with her toes, she continued to complain about men in general and then more emphatically about the American Consul, his wife, and their teenaged son about whom she revealed a startling amount.

"I can't believe how much television that woman watches," she said in reference to the Consul's wife. "And that rotten son of theirs takes his father's copies of Playboy into the bathroom at least three times per day. Wouldn't you say that is an excessive amount of masturbation? Doesn't it cause blindness?" she asked in rapid succession without expecting responses. "And why do American men prefer women with excessively large breasts? Is that why you prefer Singa to me?"

Isa knew she shared Ethan with her older sister who, among her other virtues, had larger breasts. While neither of the women were possessive about the young American, and therefore not prone to jealously, she was fascinated by this strange breast fetish. Her opinion was reinforced by movies she'd watched with the Consul's wife, plus the magazines she found stashed in her ward's room. That American men chose mates on the basis of the size of their mammaries seemed ridiculous, and reinforced her general disdain for men, especially Americans.

The sisters were physically quite different, Isa being more willowy, but shared their disdain for adult males. Singa didn't think much of men in general whereas Isa's aversion was mostly American. Ethan's surprise about the apparent lack of jealously of his two lovers was partially explained when Singa described her short stint in Europe with a former Dutch boyfriend. That experience was enough to convince both Singa and Isa that going home to the West with Ethan was not an option that either would consider, so they just enjoyed him.

That question caught Ethan unaware, but then she continued with her complaining without expecting an answer. "And today the little rat hid his mother's tranquilizers, which made her frantic. Lucky for the old cow, her son is not very imaginative even in his bad behavior and I had no trouble finding them. I must admit that I took guilty pleasure in not returning them to her right away. I should be ashamed about letting her suffer, but I'm not."

In response to this revelation about the apparent Valium dependence of the Consul's wife, Ethan started to sing quietly, which was a common response when something she mentioned in her diatribes reminded him of a song. Isa didn't slow her down a bit in lamenting the hardships of her governess job, but she did listen with one ear as he sang, *"Kids are different today, I hear every mother say, mother needs something today to calm her down, and though she's not really ill, there's a little yellow pill, she goes running for the shelter of a mother's little helper..."* That phrase "mother's little helper" was one she wanted to use and wanted to ask Ethan about the source, but by then he was massaging above her knees and it was getting increasingly difficult to concentrate.

By the time Ethan reached her thighs, Isa's laments about her employers' many foibles were mixed with quiet moans. By mid-thigh she was breathing hard and starting to thrash around. When he reached her upper thighs she suddenly, in one fluid motion, slipped out of her sarong and pulled the already naked Ethan down on top of her.

Afterwards, as they laid comfortably in each other's arms, Ethan asked, "I can't figure out why you put up with me. You've pointed out at various times that I smell bad, behave poorly, speak Iban like a moron, and have a gigantic nose."

Isa responded sleepily, "Because you're hung like a goat!"

Ethan laughed in response to this rude statement, especially coming from a woman who, most of the time, was rather demure. "Shocking my dear, where do you learn such language?"

"From those terrible novels the old cow reads. Want me to nip you one?"

Still laughing, Ethan replied, "no thanks, my taste in literature is a bit more high-brow than that, but I do like the cover pictures."

That response provoked Isa to smack him lightly but then she reported, with some derision, that none of the books had covers because they were torn off by the Consul's wife. This interchange had caused Isa to wake up, so she sat up and continued to gossip. "And did you hear what the girls down on the rockets do to the Consul?" she said in reference to the floating brothels down on the river.

"Heavens no. You know that I would never frequent such establishments," replied Ethan, which caused Isa to determine his sincerity by looking at his face in the moonlight streaming in through the window as Ethan continued. "And I'm frankly shocked that you consort with such women," he said in mock horror.

"What sort of women?" Isa asked with an edge in her voice and then continued without awaiting a response. "You shouldn't be so close-minded," Isa said in defense of the prostitutes and then continued with her story after huffing a bit.

"The Consul is a frequent client, which of course is a secret, at least to his wife. But what's amusing is that despite having visited a half-dozen times, he's still never even touched any of the girls."

"Now that is strange," Ethan commented, "why would he go there if he didn't want to do a lot more than just touch them?"

"Well that's the funny part. The girls have figured out ways to stimulate him from afar to the point that he comes without being touched."

"Poor man, that must be terrible," Ethan commiserated somewhat seriously. He really detested the Consul, whom he considered a bully and a bore, but as a male, he empathized about the likely embarrassment of extremely premature ejaculation.

Isa was less concerned about male sensitivities, especially given that the male was the Consul. "The girls have made a sport of it. They're competing to see who can make him come the fastest. So far the one called 'Sister Bertrille of the Daughters of Charity' is winning," she said in reference to the whore who dressed as a nun. "Her record is less than 3 minutes," she said and laughed. "But in his defense, he reportedly does pay them anyway, and handsomely. But now you've woken me up.

Perhaps you need to massage my feet again," she said coyly. Looking down boldly at his erection, she then continued. "It appears that you are again up to the task."

"Madam, it will be my pleasure, but perhaps I can skip the feet this time and start up a bit further, I'm thinking thigh ward," Ethan responded and commenced again with the pleasant process.

While lounging alone in bed the next morning, Ethan stretched luxuriously and savored the smell of frying bacon coming from his small kitchen. He enjoyed the young Iban woman in bed and out, but the ritual of her cooking him monstrous breakfasts on Thursday mornings was an added bonus. That the food she prepared with such a flourish was from the storeroom of her odious boss made it even better. After a few minutes he put on his sarong, walked out to the kitchen, and announced, "I think I can answer your question now."

Isa looked over her shoulder, smiled, and responded, "What question my love?"

"Why I'm attracted to you," Ethan reminded her of one theme of their regular pillow chats—or rather, Isa's monologues.

Isa turned back to her cooking but when Ethan stated his answer in the single word, "bacon," she spun rapidly around and sprang at him with her spatula raised in the attack. Laughing uproariously, Ethan pinned her arms to her sides to avoid being struck, but the inertia of her assault with a kitchen utensil caused them both to tumble to the floor. Within seconds of landing in each other's arms, they were making fast-and-furious love, which fairly shocked them both.

The lovers were disentangling themselves when neighbor Ian waltzed in unannounced, stepped over their entwined bodies, picked up the spatula, and flipped the bacon that hadn't yet burned. Then he turned around, gazed wide-eyed at the lovers on the floor and muttered without explanation, "So much for the Grover Cleveland effect." After saying that, he stood erect, switched to the strident voice of a preacher, and proclaimed, "Fallen angels, rise my children and behold. I am here to deliver you from sin lest the fires of Hell consume us all—or at least the bacon." He then continued in his normal voice, "And what a waste to overcook such lovely morsels of meat. Mind if I stay for breakfast?"

Ian was a regular guest for these Thursday morning breakfasts, and he came and went from Ethan's apartment as if it was his own. Nevertheless, even Ethan was a bit embarrassed to have been caught on the floor *in flagrante delicto*. Smiling at Isa, who was also looking a bit sheepish, he simply explained to his friend, "We fell."

"I can see that," Ian replied with a broad grin. He too had come to like Isa more and more especially as her penetrating intellect and sharp wit emerged. The two would often join forces in their condemnation of all things American, which delighted them both and didn't bother Ethan in the slightest. That she would share with both what she overheard at the house of the American Consul was entertaining and sometimes useful in their efforts to maneuver around the various bureaucratic obstacles confronting expats in Malaysia.

Ian then continued. "Isa, I've noticed that bacon is a common theme for these wonderful breakfasts you whip up for my reprehensible neighbor. Is there more to this pattern than meets the eye?"

Isa gave Ethan a furious glance but couldn't help smile when she said in an accusatory tone, "He," she paused and threatened Ethan with the spatula she'd recovered from Ian, "likes bacon." After another slight pause she continued, "and since you asked, it's generally advisable for marriageable men in this part of the world to eat pork at least once per week to keep the Malay girls at bay," she said in reference to Islam's ban on pork.

In response to this comment the men laughed and Ian reminded her, "You don't have to worry about me on that score my dear."

"Don't be too sure of that Doctor Ian, you're big, rich, and look like Dean Martin. I know some girls who have their sights on you even if they are aware of your, well, um," she searched for the right word then decided on "preferences," she said with a smile.

Ethan followed up by saying, "And I for one only like Iban girls," in response to which he was again threatened with the spatula.

After a minute Ian said to Ethan with a conspiratory tone, "From what I hear, the biggest threat to your sovereignty isn't a Malay or Iban girl but that Bidayuh wench Riska." He'd spoken to Ethan but Isa was paying close attention and he continued, now speaking to her. "Perhaps you have some Bidayuh repellent?"

Isa was more aware of the situation with Riska than even Ian, the great gossip. She wanted to protect Ethan, but didn't want to sound jealous, so she considered what she should say in response to Ian's jesting provocation. "The problem isn't Riska," she explained, "it's her mother—she's convinced that Ethan would be a good catch for her darling daughter."

Ethan laughed at Isa's use of idiomatic American English and mock scolded, "You're watching too much television—since when am I a 'catch'?"

"Well you are, at least in her estimation. I think you need to stay away from her."

"That's going to be difficult since I have to pass by their longhouse at least once a month when I go to check my trees," Ethan responded in reference to a research project he had underway in a forest on the far side of the longhouse where Riska lived with her mother, siblings, cousins, and others.

For a while the trio ate quietly. Isa had a bowl of rice with vegetables while the men dug with gusto into rashers of bacon and eggs. Isa had previously prepared them blueberry pancakes with bacon, cheese omelets with bacon, and oatmeal with a side of bacon, but she noted that the little round steaks wrapped in bacon evoked the most enthusiastic response from the two men of whom she was so fond.

While eating Ethan thought about this remarkable young woman. He was scheming about ways she could get the formal training appropriate for her considerable linguistic and mathematical skills. For her part, Isa was simply looking forward to a day alone in the apartment and away from the American family she contended with the other six days of the week. She'd start by straightening up Ethan's things, because she liked doing so, especially since that task included reading the most recent and dependably weekly aerograms from his mother and any other mail he'd received. After that, she'd sit at his desk and read the manuscripts on which he'd been working. She skipped over the ones about palms but read carefully whatever he wrote about land-use practices, ethnic politics, rural economics, and other aspects of life in Sarawak.

After Ethan left for work at the herbarium, Ian and Isa remained chatting for another hour. Ian was fascinated by the young woman, not attracted to her physically, but increasingly aware of her intellect. Their conversations had evolved over the months from standard "village talk" about mundane topics to analyses of complex cultural and political issues. Most of the Sarawakians with whom he interacted were Chinese and Malays, both of which tend to be very guarded in what they say; it was refreshing to interact with this straight-talking Iban. He'd started to lend her books and articles, which she devoured. She would often then comment on their contents from a world-view so different from his own that it would often take him days to process what she'd said.

Ian finally dragged himself away from the kitchen table when he was sufficiently nagged by the realization that Ethan was hoping that Isa would read and comment on his most recent manuscript. He'd espied a considerable stack of them sitting next to his neighbors faithful Olivetti. He'd been lulled to sleep several times over the previous weeks by Ethan typing. He was intrigued by the evolution of his friend's research from botany to politics, and shared his concerns about the blatant infringements of the land rights of the indigenous people.

"Sorry that I must leave you now," Ian said to Isa, "but the dead rats at the Sarawak Museum await my attention and I've already occupied enough of your time."

"Always a pleasure Doctor Ian, and please give my fond regards to your beloved rats," Isa responded with a smile. She was amused that Ian spent his days working with the skins and skeletons of dead animals. In his defense, Ian's work involved the taxonomy of those animals, and the specimens he was trying to classify, assemble, and otherwise curate were mostly collected by the Museum's former director, none other than his predecessor at the Sarawak Museum, "Two-Bobs a Nod" Harrisson.

Ian had to admit that he idolized Tom Harrisson, a man he'd met in person several times back in Oxford. One of the ties he had with Isa was that when she was a little girl, Harrisson was a frequent visitor to Long Awan. The ostensible reason for these visits were professional, trapping rats and the like, but he also spent a great deal of time talking with the Iban men he'd befriended during the Japanese occupation when they fought together in the resistance. He'd tell anyone who would listen that his Iban collaborators were the most effective jungle fighters ever imagined. The "Two Bobs a Nod" sobriquet derived from the rumor, which he would neither confirm nor deny, that he paid the Iban for any Japanese heads they took. Whether or not that rumor was true, the temporary resumption of head-taking, which had been outlawed by James Brooke, the first "White Rajah of Sarawak," struck terror in the hearts of the occupation forces. Apparently many Japanese believe that a body should be buried intact for successful passage to the afterlife. He'd asked Isa about the business of head-hunting and she was quite emphatic that what happened during the war was quite different from the ceremonial practice of *ngayau*. She explained that while it was an effective way to keep the Japanese from penetrating very far from the relative safety of the towns, it conferred very little prestige on the head taker. She also pointed out, in a way that made Ian unsure of what she actually believed, that the Japanese heads were useless for divination, conferred little power on the head-taker, and really just collected dust in the headhouses.

After Ian finally left, Isa set about her self-assigned tasks around Ethan's apartment. When she first started to read Ethan's manuscripts, she'd been careful to leave no indication of having seen them. While she tried to arrange the papers just as she found them, she often revealed what she'd read in their night-time conversations. After dealing all week long with a young teenaged American boy and his demanding and really boring American parents, by Wednesday night she was intellectually starved. She also appreciated that Ethan always seemed to take her so seriously. As an attractive young woman in Sarawak, especially as an Iban, it was rare to have a man even listen to her. When Ethan finally fell asleep, which was to be expected after working all day, teaching in the evening, and then their vigorous love-making, she was not at all offended and would curl up next to him and sleep as well.

Ethan was well aware that she was reading everything in his apartment and was not offended in the slightest. She'd revealed the attention she was paying to his "life in Sarawak" manuscripts by her out-of-the-blue questions or comments about a topic about which Ethan had recently written, perhaps an Iban farming technique or a linguistic difference between Malay and Iban. He also realized that he couldn't find a better fact checker. After being circumspect for a few weeks and with just a few words of encouragement from Ethan, she'd started scribbling marginalia on the manuscripts. As the weeks went by, her comments became more-and-more detailed and, to Ethan, more-and-more useful. He responded by leaving larger margins. While they never openly acknowledged this arrangement, Ethan had also started to include comments and questions to her in what he was writing. Sometimes he would insert something intended solely to tease or amuse her and that had nothing to do with the topic. These provocations were also never mentioned, but over the months Ethan came to depend on her insights to such an extent that he thought that when and if he published any of these manuscripts, she deserved co-authorship.

Chapter 9. CONSULATE DINNER WITH WARNING

Excerpt from an aerogram from Ethan Yarrow in Kuching, Sarawak, to his parents in Chevy Chase, Maryland:

6 July 1971
Dear Mom and Dad,
I spent a most informative 4th of July at the home of the American Consul here in Kuching. The expression, "the sins of the father...haunt...," came to mind when the Consul warned me to curb my too liberal leanings that are beginning to annoy some Malaysian officials. It appears that Dad's permanent record in international politics hasn't been entirely expunged. At the heart of the matter is the government's designs on the Iban's land. I know that the Chief Minister and his cronies plan to plant African oil palm everywhere they can, but I actually expect something more devious and destructive is afoot...

"Sprucing up for the big Fourth of July to-do at the Consul's I see," Ian said after strolling into Ethan's apartment unannounced, as was his custom.

Ethan grunted acknowledgement, not at all surprised his friend knew his destination. He admired the effectiveness of Ian's social network—he always knew an amazing amount about the social comings and goings of the movers and shakers in Kuching. His knowledge derived mostly from Fatimah, his busy-body Malay maid, but he also had a surprising number of other confidants. Although he was tall, movie-star handsome, and could be frightfully English, people of all sorts were almost immediately comfortable in his presence. Ethan was shocked at how rapidly people were willing to provide Ian with the most intimate details of their lives, but had to admit that he was one of those people.

Ethan's suspicion that Fatimah was the source of information about his plans was confirmed when Ian continued. "Fatimah couldn't wait to tell me that the Consul invited both the Changs and the Pongs—imagine having Teocheos and Hokkiens at the same social gathering—and those families in particular," at which he made a tisking sound with this tongue in condemnation of the social *faux pas* that was unfolding. "One might hope for fireworks, but there's unlikely to be more than a slow burn given the propensity of these people to avoid confrontations—disappointing, but should nevertheless be interesting to watch. I'm sure they'll all be there because both their firms are vying for that big undersea cable contract and they probably assume that the Consul has some influence. As I understand it," Ian continued in a manner that indicated that he was aware that he was being a terrible gossip, "Johnny Chang swindled the Pongs on that offshore drilling deal last year. Word is that they haven't spoken since and that there have been some unsavory interactions between their minions," he added without elaboration.

Ethan didn't take the bait or otherwise seem to be listening, but Ian was accustomed to his friend's behavior, wasn't offended, and continued to chatter by commenting brightly. "That's a pretty shirt. Is it silk?"

"Not sure, it does feel silky. It was a present from my boss's wife. She seems to have taken on the mission of rendering me presentable."

"An admirable mission for Madam Lee, and I do like her taste, but why do you insist on wearing those yucky black pants?" Ian asked with feigned exasperation.

"You know very well why," Ethan reminded his friend. "Riding Roxanne with anything but black below the knee is a recipe for disaster---likely end up black anyway."

Ian was especially careful to say nothing to offend his friend's motorcycle, which Ethan treated more like a lover than a large miserable mass of metal. While amused by this relationship, he was also fully aware that Roxanne was a death trap—far too much horsepower with insufficient braking power. Those deficiencies, which he knew Ethan shared, caused him considerable concern.

"I should also tell you that Fatimah is again upset with you for buying vegetables in the market from that Chinese woman and not from her Malay friend. She insists that you're being terribly overcharged."

"She's right," Ethan responded, "I'm being over-charged, but it's worth it. That Chinese woman is friendly, young, and cute whereas Fatimah's friend is a nasty fat old hag."

"Yikes, a shocking comment from a man famous for finding something lovely about every woman he meets! " Ian responded in mock horror. "Well, I'm not about to tell my housekeeper what you said or she'll put bamboo hairs in my boxer shorts," Ian said and laughed. He referred to the irritating hairs on the leaf sheaths of some bamboos, which constituted just one of many weapons in the reputed arsenals of spurned or otherwise offended Malay women.

"You know what's odd?" Ethan continued, still musing about the Chinese vegetable vendor. "She can't seem to help herself from over-charging me, but a few weeks back she invited me to her son's birthday party, which turned out to be an incredibly sumptuous feast. What I ate was undoubtedly worth ten times her questionable profits from what she sells me."

Ian nodded in reflection about Ethan's observation and then said with a laugh in his voice, "All the more impressive that you forgive her, given that I hear she's still teasing you about *susu ayam* (chicken milk)." He looked at Ethan, hoping for a reaction. When there wasn't one, he continued in a more direct manner. "I've only heard that story second hand, perhaps the horse's mouth might reveal what actually transpired."

"Okay, I'll tell you what happened---given your frequent abuses use of the Malay language, I'm sure you'll understand," Ethan responded with a fake grimace and then continued. "When I first arrived here in Kuching and had only mastered a few words of Malay, I went to the market to buy food. That was the first time I tried to negotiate with her, and in what turned into a pattern, she got the best end of the deal. In any case, I'd managed to buy the produce I needed but then thought it would nice to have some milk. I wasn't sure what sorts of milk they might have for sale—cow, goat, buffalo, or whatever-- so I tried to clarify the source but switched the word for chicken with the one for cow and said 'Saya mahu beli susu ayam' [I want to buy chicken milk]. Without cracking a smile, she responded in her schoolbook Malay that she'd only just run out of chicken milk, and then, without asking me, she shouted out something to the other venders in Hokkien. My Chinese was worse than it is now, but I distinctly heard the phrase *susu ayam*. After various vendors shouted back at her, she turned to me and said in beautiful Queen's English, "I believe that if you come back tomorrow, several of us will be happy to sell you chicken milk," at which she struggled to hide her mirth while the other market ladies made no such effort at discretion. To this day, I am the chicken milk man."

Ian chuckled for a few minutes and then abruptly changed the subject. "And do you know who else is going to celebrate our nations' divorce?" When Ethan looked up with concern, he continued. "None other than your favorite USAID rep....drum roll please...the famous Pamela Wilson."

Ethan's face dropped in dismay at this information, which Ian anticipated, knowing as he did about the rocky history of his friend's relationship with Pam. Ethan responded with a very descriptive "argh," and then in an effort to make lemonade from the lemon he'd been handed said, "Perhaps we'll have the chance to talk about her 'Alternatives to Slash and Burn' project. I'm increasingly convinced that Iban farming is a drop in the bucket compared to logging and, even worse, the massive conversion of forests to African oil palm plantations. The last time I flew to Miri I could see that the extent of deforestation is already mind blowing. I think that for anyone concerned about the fates of forests here in Sarawak, swidden agriculture is a red herring."

"It does seem like the oil palm boys are throwing a lot of money around here in Kuching," Ian affirmed, "and the Forestry Department is losing land at a rapid clip as logging areas are re-gazetted for plantation agriculture. So much for the 'permanent' forest estate. Your boss is doing what he can to maintain his domain, but he nevertheless seems to be losing ground."

"I'm also worried about what Australian geologists are doing up along the Balui River. It's curious that we didn't find any placer mines or bore holes, but lots of survey lines up and down the hills. I want to talk with you about that some other time, but now Roxanne and I need to fly up to what is likely to be a fiasco of a 4th of July." At that, Ethan walked out singing his favorite stanza of the Star Spangled Banner, the one that features rockets and bombs.

Although the nature of the invitation left him little choice about attending, Ethan was sort of looking forward to the affair at the Consul's lavish house in the hills above the city because he needed the Consul to approve his visa extension. He was also curious to check on some of Isa's gossip. She'd told him, for example, that the Consul had secured his post by donating a pile of money to Nixon's presidential campaign. She then gleefully pointed out that the money he used he'd gotten from his father and hadn't earned on his own. She also suggested that the Consul might know something about the goings on in Ulu Balui. He wondered for a minute why she hadn't warned him about Pamela, but then realized that she might not know about his connection with this particular American visitor.

As Ethan motored up to the house, he was surprised by the absence of cars parked near the house. He pulled into the garage and parked Roxanne between the Consul's boat-like 1968 Pontiac Bonneville convertible and his new Chevy Impala, both imported at US taxpayers' expense. After pulling Roxanne up on her stand and asking her politely to be on her best behavior, he went to the front and rang the doorbell, wondering if he'd mistaken the starting time of the party.

When Abdul, one of the Consul's smartly dressed young Malay servants, opened the door, Ethan quickly asked whether he was early, but the young man reassured that he was expected and on time. "The Tuan is waiting for you by the pool," he said. Before stepping over the threshold Ethan stopped to take off his shoes, but the young man stopped him by saying, "No need, you're in America now." Ethan put his shoes back on and then was led through the carpeted house and onto the patio where the Consul was standing with Pam with no other guests evident.

When he saw Ethan, the Consul came over in an overly friendly manner and said in a flurry, "Welcome to my humble abode, please make yourself comfortable, I believe you know Dr. Wilson."

Ethan couldn't keep himself from flashing a look at Pamela when he heard her addressed as "Dr." because he knew that she still suffered terribly from not having finished her degree. Not letting on just how well they knew each other, Ethan said, "Nice to see you again Dr. Wilson. I hope you are doing well." He turned back to his host and said, "It appears that I've arrived early—my apologies."

"No need to apologize my young man, I hoped you' come early so we could chat privately before the rest of the guests arrive. But before that, can I offer you a drink? I'm sure you miss American beer—I can offer you a Ballantine, Miller, or even an Iron City—pick your poison."

Smiling as if his dream had come true, Ethan asked for a Miller and then quipped, "The Champaign of bottled beer." While the Consul went over to the bar to fetch the beer, Pam grabbed Ethan's arm, drew him a bit farther away, and whispered hurriedly, "He knows you were in SDS and even that you went to Cuba with the Venceremos Brigade, but seems more concerned about your father being a commie. Didn't you tell me that he was called before a Loyalty and Security Commission back in the 50s? He also mentioned that you've been interfering with the government's development plan for Ulu Balui. What the hell have you been doing to get yourself in such hot water?"

"What?" Ethan responded in alarm, "All I've been doing is collecting plants. And why am I being scrutinized? And you've met my father—he's a patriot and you know it. But since you mentioned the Balui, did he say what the government has planned?" he asked in a rush before the Consul returned with his beer.

Pam had met his parents briefly when they came to Boston for Ethan's graduation. She was charmed by his father, with whom she mostly discussed politics and music, so she knew very well that he was not a communist sympathizer. His father, who was an easy man to like and seemed to find something good about everyone he met, was taken by Pamela's intellect and appreciated her good looks. His mother, in contrast, was not at all impressed, which she made abundantly clear when they were departing and she whispered to her darling son, "Check out her ankles." His mother believed that a woman's future shape could be judged in her youth by the thickness of her ankles. She then muttered "cradle robber" under her breath. Ethan of course realized that no woman was ever going to meet his mother's standards, but he considered that comment a low blow even for his ferociously defensive mother.

Frank Yarrow was indeed a patriot, a World War II veteran decorated with a Purple Heart and a Distinguished Service Medal. He'd spent the war years in the India-Burma-India Theatre and had seen plenty of action. Despite his sacrifices for his country, he was victimized during the Red Scare of the 1950s. Ethan didn't understand it at the time, but in 1955 when his dad was called to testify before the House Committee on Un-American Activities, their lives were about to change. The interest of Senator McCarthy and cronies in his dad was provoked by a letter he'd written soon after the Armistice to an Army acquaintance who had landed a job with the State Department.

The letter sent by Frank Yarrow to Dean Rusk described conditions in China under the Kuomintang. He knew that Rusk was at least somewhat aware of the situation since he'd visited Kunming. Rusk would later become Secretary of State under President Kennedy, but when Ethan's father wrote him late in 1946, he was just another de-commissioned G.I. with a low-level government job. What Ethan's father didn't know was that Rusk was struggling to get ahead without apparent regard for the people whose lives he ruined on the way. The offending letter was based on Frank's three years as accountant for the Lend-Lease Program of the Assam-Kunming Branch of the 'India-China Ferry.' It was his responsibility to assure that the shipments of jeeps, weapons, ammunition, C-rations, and other supplies flown 'over the hump' in lumbering DC-3s and C-46 transport planes by the 'Flying Tigers' actually got into the hands of Chinese soldiers who were fighting the Japanese. On the basis of nearly daily interchanges with representatives of the Chinese Nationalist Army, he had plenty of evidence for his claim that Generalissimo Chiang Kai-shek was a crook. Based on more personal interactions with some of his henchmen, about which Ethan had never heard details, his father also knew that the supreme warlord he referred to as 'Chancre Jack' was also a thug. His father never had much good to say about Mao Tse Tung either, whom he called 'Moose Dung,' but his condemnation of the Generalissimo was scathing. As well-informed and well-intended as that letter was, it ended up costing him his job with the Government Accountability Office. Ethan's father wasn't the only of the so-called China Hands who lost government jobs during the McCarthy-led purges. So many people with first-hand experience in China were forced out of the government during the Red Scares of McCarthyism that when conflicts in Indochina escalated, there was almost no one that knew China or spoke Chinese. Ethan's father insisted that the Vietnam War could have been avoided if the State Department hadn't lost most of its experienced staff to the Communist purges. His father was also one of the few people Ethan knew who ever mentioned the "Lavender Purge" of reputed homosexuals that accompanied the "Red Purge" of alleged communists. Many of his musician friends had suffered because of questions about their sexuality, which enraged his father even more than his own fate at the hands of the same witch hunters. McCarthyism had long since run its course and Ethan's father had started a very successful accounting firm just outside of Washington, D.C., but his name was apparently still in the books as a communist sympathizer. Ethan continued whispering to Pam in an exasperated tone, "And why did he tell you all this? Doesn't he know about our history?"

"He seems unaware of our 'history,' as you call it, but seems to assume that I'm CIA and here to weed out pinko scum," she whispered as the Consul came towards them smiling.

"Glad to see you young people getting better acquainted. I'm sure that the little matter we have to discuss can be settled quickly, and then we can enjoy our beer, or should I say beers?" He joked casually but in a manner that made both Pam and Ethan uncomfortable. He then addressed Ethan in a tone that seemed almost theatrical.

"I'm sorry to report that it has come to my attention that you've been seen interacting with some local characters about whom our host country officials have some serious misgivings-- of a political nature. As you know, Malaysians are concerned about communists in their midst. Their anti-sedition laws may seem a bit strict, but this is a young nation and has already been threatened from both inside and out."

The Consul looked at Ethan for confirmation that he was being heard, but then continued without waiting for a response. "As visitors from the U.S. of A., I feel that it is our responsibility to set shining examples of the benefits of democracy and free trade. We need to champion our way of life and the living examples of Captain America and the Green Lantern."

At the mention of the Green Lantern, Ethan couldn't help but quickly glance over to Pam, but she just shrugged her shoulders. The Consul didn't notice their brief nonverbal interchange because he was staring off into the great blue yonder and gesticulating as he thought appropriate for a great orator.

Like an increasing number of Americans, Ethan was confused about communism but adamantly opposed to the escalating war in Vietnam. He was unaware that he'd so far avoided trouble with his draft board because it was gerrymandered to protect rich white boys from his wealthy suburb.

His district reached out to include the poverty stricken city of Bethesda where there were plenty of draft-aged young men who, if not enthusiastic about serving, were unlikely to resist conscription with the help of doctors and lawyers. After graduating from college, during which he had a student deferment, the Board had therefore granted Ethan an exemption on the basis of his research being in the nation's interest. As a graduate of a Quaker school and the son of a high-ranking Mason and a member of the Daughters of the American Revolution, the draft board members probably also recognized that he would most likely be more trouble than he was worth anyway.

While in Madison, Ethan participated in the anti-war movement, joined SDS (Students for a Democratic Society), and was an active member of the Green Lantern Food Coop. It was at the Green Lantern that the most radical students met to plan demonstrations and other anti-government activities. The Green Lantern had been raided by police several times, but Ethan always managed to escape, once by hiding in the grease spattered fume hood over their still-hot commercial-size stove. The idea that his association with the Green Lantern might be known by the Consul was especially disconcerting. He was glad that the Consul hadn't mentioned his father's alleged communist leanings because he wasn't sure that he could resist denying that accusation vociferously, which would have not been politically wise.

After a deep breath, Ethan thanked the Consul for his advice and assured him that he would be very careful avoid unsavory characters. At the same time, he wondered which of his friends fit that category.

"Just one more bit of fatherly advice," the short and paunchy Consul said to the tall and lean young man with all the pomposity he could muster. "Stay well away from the Balui River, wherever that is. And with that we will consider the matter settled, and can now celebrate the birth of our nation by drinking and eating our fill," which the Consul obviously did frequently.

Ethan wanted to contemplate the Consul's comment about Ulu Balui and what he'd observed in Long Berawan, but other guests arrived and Ethan got caught up making the social rounds. He was acquainted with some of the attendees and knew about many of the others, thanks to Ian's gossip. A few guests sought him out to thank him for helping their teenaged children prepare for their Cambridge exams, which they considered the major benefit of the Wacky Wednesday Reading Group.

The Consul's party, which was painful for both Ethan and most of the other guests, exceeded even Ethan's expectations for excess and poor taste—the Consul seemed to go out of his way to reinforce many bad stereotypes about Americans. The food served, for example, was pure American, with absolutely no attempt to accommodate local preferences and religious strictures. Ethan was sure that most of the fixings had been flown in from a military commissary somewhere in the region—you certainly couldn't buy the American cheese, Jimmy Dean Pork Sausages, and Ballantine beer anywhere locally. The Consul ostentatiously played the role of American *paterfamilias* by personally manning the gas-fired barbecue grill, or at least he flipped the burgers and hotdogs that his servants otherwise handled. He also served sweet New York wine, to which Ethan switched after a half-can of Budweiser just to be sure that he didn't drink too much. Throughout the affair, Rudy, the Consul's massive male Labrador retriever, tried to make friends with everyone present, including the Muslims who were horrified that they might have to touch a dog other than with their feet.

While Ethan actually enjoyed the food, he was amused to observe how cleverly the other guests avoided eating anything other than crackers. The Malays of course wouldn't eat anything cooked because it wasn't Halal—the Consul was actually cooking pork sausages on the same grill as the burgers that he assured everyone were 100% pure American beef, which of course rendered them unacceptable to the handful of Hindus in attendance. If not for Ethan and a Sikh fellow and his wife, the platters of assorted cheeses would have gone untouched. Ethan had previously asked several Chinese friends why they wouldn't eat cheese and was informed that its manufacture involved worms, which disgusted them, an ironic response given their dietary diversity.

While he was wickedly amused at the Consul's expense, Ethan actually felt a little bad for his clueless countryman—he really was making a real effort to feed and entertain his guests. Hopefully, Ethan thought, the guests had anticipated the fare to be offered and ate their rice before coming—that was certainly what they would do immediately upon returning home. The main beneficiary of the Consul's largess was Rudy. The big dog happily scarfed all the burgers, sausages, and bits of cheese that frequently but discreetly fell from the guests' plates.

Throughout the affair the Changs managed to avoid the Pongs, as Pam seemed to avoid Ethan. He finally managed to get her aside to discuss their shared goal of protecting tropical forests from rampant destruction. He wanted to describe all the clearing he'd seen for oil palm plantations and ask her about the mining he suspected were being planned for the Ulu Balui area. Fortunately, before they said much, his friend Isa, who was waitressing, caught his eye to warn him that their conversation was being overheard by some of the other guests. Ethan and Pamela could have sauntered out further into the garden to continue their discussion, but Pamela saw the exchange of looks and jumped to the conclusion, this time correct, that his relationship with the young Iban servant was more than Platonic. As she stormed off in what for Ethan was her typical jealous huff, she muttered something about tigers and spots.

Finally, after what seemed like hours, guests started to leave and Ethan figured he could slip out. The house was fortunately perched on a hilltop, which meant that he could coast Roxanne away quietly before jump-starting her when out of earshot. While his intention was to get away clean, a nasty surprise awaited him in the garage.

Roxanne was parked where he left her between the Chevy and the Pontiac, but while the party was underway, she had what Ethan always referred to as an "accident." Instead of pure white concrete, the floor under her was puddled with 30-weight crankcase oil. She often leaked, but he did not expect her to do so this time because he'd recently replaced all her oil seals. The fleeting thought passed his mind that she was annoyed about being parked between the two thuggish American cars. The damage was done, so he quietly pushed her off her stand, gave a slight push, and coasted down the hill alternately feeling embarrassed and amused about the mess she'd left.

Chapter 10. LOVESICK LEE CHAI CHI

Excerpt from an aerogram from Ethan Yarrow in Kuching, Sarawak, to his parents in Chevy Chase, Maryland:

1 August 1971
Dear Mom and Dad,
Given your misgivings about my choices of mates to date, you'll be amused to hear that I have been forced into the role of "marriage counselor" for a young Peace Corps volunteer I met upriver, a Lutheran farm boy from Iowa. His intended, with whom I believe he occasionally holds hands, is a much worldlier Iban girl who is frustrated about the slow pace of development of their relationship. He's SO incredibly serious and SO naïve that I can hardly keep from laughing out loud—Dad, your Puritan ancestors would be proud of him...

"Howdy Ethan, how's Roxanne," Adam asked as Ethan approached him at his regular table at Ah Ming's coffee shop on the main and pretty much the only street in the river town of Kapit. Adam had been waiting for a bit more than an hour, watching the boat traffic. He'd expected Ethan to arrive by river taxi, but recognized the plane that flew overhead and deduced that his friend had once again managed to catch a lift from the missionaries. Given Ethan's reputation, which Adam mostly discounted as baseless rumors, he was surprised that the missionaries would have anything to do with him. But to the only slightly younger but much less experienced fellow American, Ethan was a never-ending source of surprises.

Just the sound of Adam's Midwestern drawl made Ethan smile. He was fond of this young Peace Corps Volunteer, and respected him for his industriousness and the ease with which he interacted with locals. "Lee Chai Chi, so nice to see you and so nice of you to ask about Roxanne. She's just fine, taking a bit of a holiday at home while I spend some time in the forest. What's the news from your family?"

Adam's family name, Lyskowski, had been misunderstood more than once as Lee Chai Chi, and Ethan had adopted that as a nickname for his friend.

The Iowan smiled at his Chinese moniker and then said, "I just got a letter from my parents. After putting my older brothers and sisters and then me through college, they finally took a vacation--their first ever." With that, Adam stopped his explanation, worried that he was boring his world-wise friend.

"Go on," Ethan encouraged, "how did it go?"

"Terrible, they had a terrible time," Adam responded and then continued in an upbeat voice, "which is really great!"

"What? They had a terrible time and you're happy about it?"

"Sure," he said and then hesitated again, still worried about being boring. In response to an encouraging expression from Ethan, he continued. "I told you that I'm the youngest of four kids, right, and that money was always tight? My parents scrimped and saved to raise us, but as I approached graduation, they started preparing for a long-awaited vacation. For my father, that preparation involved building what is perhaps the most beautiful camper top for the back of half-ton pickup you've ever seen, and probably one of the heaviest. Just before I left for Malaysia, we loaded it onto the truck for a trial run." With that, Adam stopped talking and, with a slight smile, stirred his drink.

"And then?" Ethan had to ask. Having lived in the Midwest for a while, Ethan appreciated the region's story-telling traditions, which included this characteristic reticence.

Adam then explained as he chuckled a bit, "When we pulled the rig out of the barn and tried to steer it around the chicken coop, the front wheels hardly responded--they were all but off the ground. That discovery cost my father a few weeks' work, but by replacing the two-by-fours with two-by-twos, and some other modifications, he got the camper down to manageable weight."

After another long delay he continued. "Finally, last month, they drove off on their long-awaited holiday, leaving my oldest brother in charge of the farm."

"Where'd they go?"

"Florida."

"In July?" Ethan asked aghast.

"Sure, that's when rich Iowans go on vacation."

"But Florida in July?" Ethan exclaimed in dismay. "They must have been toasted."

"More like par boiled," Adam clarified. "They were so miserable they cut their vacation short."

After a minute of reflection, Ethan asked, "So, exactly why is that a happy story?"

"Well, when they got back to the farm they declared that vacations weren't all that great and that they certainly hadn't been missing much," Adam explained.

As Ethan reflected on his friend's story, it crossed his mind that while he often struggled to come to grips with aspects of the cultures of Borneo, you didn't have to cross an ocean to run into such differences.

The two sat quietly for a while, and then Ethan continued, "And how are your girls?" Ethan asked, referring to the small herd of cows under Adam's charge.

"Oh, I guess you haven't heard, I gave them to Rajatharan."

"You what?" Ethan asked in surprise. While he had recognized from the start that it was a hair-brained idea of some bureaucrat in Brussels to give cows to the Iban so that they would keep cattle instead of slashing-and-burning forest to plant hill rice, he also knew that farm-boy Adam had grown fond of the cows.

"Yea, you heard right, I gave them to Rajatharan. He will take way better care of them than the Iban. Like you suggested months ago, the Iban don't know one end of a cow from the other. The girls will be much better off with a cow-loving Hindu than that bunch of headhunters. Plus, I get all the milk and dung that I want for free."

Coming from almost anyone else, Ethan would have taken offence at the "headhunter" comment, but he knew that Adam was very much a part of Iban longhouse life. He also suspected that Adam was awaiting him with hopes of asking for advice about his relationship with Pinai, the Iban girl from Long Berawan with whom he was smitten. Adam was probably also hoping for a valve for the methane generator he was assembling from assorted spare parts, but the young lovely was occupying more and more of his thoughts. Given that Pinai was also fond of Adam, all would be well but the young fellow was hopelessly shy and afraid to proceed. Ethan knew that Pinai was more of a raptor than a dove, which is what her name means in Iban, but very likeable and desperately awaiting Adam's next move.

Adam was the ideal Peace Corps Volunteer and a classic Polish, Lutheran, farm-boy from Iowa. Back home he'd participated in nearly every Future Farmers of America and 4-H activity his little town offered, and could plow, milk, and fix almost anything with moving parts. In contrast to his mechanical prowess, he was lacking in social skills, especially when it came to relations with the opposite sex. Ethan was pretty sure that he was a virgin, and nearly sure that he'd never had a serious girlfriend. In addition to being socially awkward and easily flustered, he was very tall, very thin, and very white—Iban girls, and not just Pinai, went out of their way to tease him, just to see him blush. He also had blue eyes, which most local people found shocking.

Ethan was the only person in Sarawak with whom Adam was at all comfortable discussing his feelings. That intimacy between the two men, which was unexpected given the vast differences in their characters, was partially based on Adam's taking at face value something that Ethan had said about formerly having been plagued by shyness, a comment actually made as a joke.

"All this talk about cows reminds me, here's your fart-trapper valve," Ethan said and handed Adam a package from his rattan tote sack.

Adam unwrapped the package, inspected the valve from various angles, and then, as a slight blush passed over his face he responded, "It's perfect. How much do I owe you?"

"Consider it a gift from me to the methane gods...I just hope you don't blow yourself sky high."

"But how'd you get it?" Adam asked, having failed to obtain one himself.

Ethan hesitated for a minute, considering how he'd obtained the valve, then responded, "I suggest you don't look a gift horse in the mouth, especially not this one. But when you come to Kuching, I'll introduce you to Roxanne's mechanic, perhaps he'll tell you." Ethan in fact didn't know where or how Bernie had acquired the valve, but suspected that somewhere in Kuching someone had a gas leak. That approach to machine part acquisition had worked before—the Mercedes diesel truck generator at the core of the mini-hydro electrical plant that Adam ran with bamboo-piped water from the hills behind Long Berawan was likewise supplied by Bernie, no questions asked.

The two friends sat quietly for a while as Ethan drank his thick bitter coffee and Adam a Horlicks on ice. They comfortably watched the comings and goings along the Batang Rajang River. Adam obviously wanted to ask Ethan for advice about Pinai, but was extremely hesitant, and Ethan was giving him plenty of time to reveal what was on his mind.

Finally, impatient to start the conversation about Pinai that he knew was coming, Ethan asked "Have you been back up to Long Berawan recently to visit Pinai?"

"Sadly no, but this valve gives me a good excuse for making the trip," Adam responded and the continued quietly, "I'll just disregard the fact that Jim Engelwood, my boss at Peace Corps, told me to stay out of Ulu Kapit in general, and the Balui River in particular. Any idea what that directive is all about?" Adam asked.

"No, but I'm really starting to wonder what plans are afoot," Ethan responded, I too was warned to stay out of Ulu Balui."

"By whom?" Adam asked.

"Most recently by the American Consul but before that by none other than the Director of Forestry," Ethan responded and then continued. "After my last visit back in March I gave him the protest letter from Long Berawan and told him a little bit about what I saw the loggers doing. He listened and said he would investigate. But then a few weeks later, without mentioning the logging, he warned me out of that area, almost apologetically. When I asked for an explanation, he hemmed and hawed a bit and then said that he had been told that 'undesirables' were working in the area."

"I am sorry to hear that," Adam replied and then said, "for a while there I actually thought that the letter you delivered had an effect."

"What gave you that impression?" Ethan asked.

"Because the logging stopped, at least for a while," Adam explained.

Ethan smiled to think that their palm sugar syrup had actually worked, but then simply said, "I really doubt that interruption in their work had anything to do with the Ibans' complaints," without offering any further explanation. He wasn't sure whether Adam had heard about what he and the Iban boys had done to the bulldozers and worried that his mechanically inclined friend would feel sorry for the machines.

Desperate to get back to the matter that weighed so heavily on his heart, Adam changed the subject abruptly by saying, "I wanted to thank you, by the way, for bringing Pinai down with you after your last trip to Long Berawan. We got to spend some nice time together. Sorry I missed you—when you passed through town briefly I was downriver working on a new irrigation system for Long Morum. But I heard you once again lucked out and caught a missionary flight back to Kuching."

"Yep, the gods once again smiled on me. I wouldn't mind the water taxi ride so much if they didn't screen really bad Kung Fu movies at full blast for the entire trip. I like a good Bruce Lee movie as much as the next guy, but the grade D Kung Fu films they show are really awful, as you well know. Often instead of subjecting myself to the gore and guts, I stay topside, but that isn't such a nice option when it's raining," Ethan explained. "Plus, I was anxious to get back to Kuching to deliver the protest letter from Long Berawan."

Ethan waited for Adam to continue talking about his sweetheart, which he finally did by asking, "Did Pinai mention me?"

"She sure did," Ethan said encouragingly, "she's crazy about you. I'm wondering when you plan to pop the question?" which caused Adam to blush and stammer incoherently.

While he watched with some amusement while Adam struggled to compose himself, Ethan thought about the life that he and Pinai might have together after Adam terminated his Peace Corps service. Were Adam planning to return to his family farm in his little town in Iowa, Ethan would certainly not have condoned their marriage. The grim life for a Bornean woman in the West had been amply described by him by his friend Singa, who'd spent several grim months with a beau in the Netherlands. When that very nice fellow brought his lovely young lady friend home to Europe, their relationship didn't stand a chance. In response to the cold climate and what she considered cold people, plus the loneliness of being away from her family and the bland food, she was soon on a plane back to Borneo.

Adam, the youngest son of a small farm owner, had no intention of returning home. Instead, with only a few months remaining of his Peace Corps contract, he was already negotiating for a job with Heifer International, a newly formed non-governmental organization that provided farm animals and associated support to people in developing countries. He'd applied for a position they had open in Madagascar. Given the cultural ties between Southeast Asia and Madagascar, an appointment in that struggling island nation would be good for both Pinai and Adam. For one thing, the Malagash language shared many words and structures with Malay and Iban, and they would likely make the linguistic transition quickly. By Ethan's estimation, if Heifer International had even an inkling of Adam's abilities, he'd get the job in a heartbeat.

Adam finally calmed down enough to rather sheepishly ask, "Do you really think she'll accept?"

"Absolutely," Ethan responded enthusiastically, "no question about it, go for it buddy!"

Chapter 11. A WORK DAY IN KUCHING

Excerpt from an aerogram from Ethan Yarrow in Kuching, Sarawak, to his parents in Chevy Chase, Maryland:

20 August 1971
Dear Mom and Dad,
I spent the week in the herbarium, which was restful and productive. My palm work is progressing, but I increasingly find my attention drawn to the plight of the natives. Although they outnumber the Malays, most of whom arrived recently from the peninsula, the locals lack political power. The status of the Chinese Malaysians, some of whom have been here for generations, is even more precarious, but they don't lack in cultural resilience and economic power. I'll certainly finish my revision of this one genus of rattans, but I'm now writing mostly about I call 'political economy.' I'm learning a lot and staying out of trouble, mostly...

Ethan was sitting at a workbench by a window in the Forest Department Herbarium studying a climbing palm specimen he'd collected. He was concentrating hard at using the 'camera lucida' on a dissecting microscope to make a detailed drawing of its male flowers. He also had a pad of foolscap paper on which he was making notes about the flowers in Latin, the language in which new plant species are still described.

After standing behind him for a few minutes watching him draw, Hong Tuck Liew, one of the herbarium assistants with whom Ethan worked closely, made himself known by asking "Is that your new species of *Calamus*?"

"Ah, Tuck Liew, yes it is. Lovely, wouldn't you say?" Ethan replied.

"Looks like a tangled mess of nasty spines to me," was Tuck Liew's response. "I still don't understand your fascination with lawyer vines," he continued, using one of the derogatory names for rattan palms. The name was apt insofar as it was hard to free oneself once they got their hooks in you. "But are you sure it's new?"

"Yep, I just got confirmation from Dransfield at Kew Gardens--it's new to science. *Calamaus jikaensis*—not sure that Jika will appreciate having a wait-a-minute vine named after him, but he was the one who found it, and he can be prickly at times, wouldn't you say?"

"You shouldn't talk about our *guru* that way," Tuck Liew jokingly scolded, "but I have to agree. He does have some lawyer-like tendencies." They were both Jika's students, and liked and respected the man immensely, but in both their cultures, no one was above ribbing.

"You wouldn't believe how hard we worked to get this sucker down from the canopy," Ethan continued. "Usually the two of us together can pull them down, but this one had its hooks set in too many places and we ended up having to climb three different trees to cut branches to free it. Jika must be 20 years my senior, but damn he can climb. While I climbed one of the smaller trees, he was up and down two of the other big ones. Then we both suffered from the stings of the blasted ants that live in these swollen leaf sheaths," he said and pointed at one of them on the sample he was studying. "The soldier ants in this species bang their heads against the walls of these chambers as a warning, and then come swarming out, stingers at the ready. The sheaths seem to amplify the sound—they make quite a racket."

"How'd you deal with them?" Tuck Liew asked, secretly thankful that he was seldom expected to go out into the forest.

"Take a sniff," he said, "smell the smoke?" When Tuck Liew did so and nodded, Ethan continued. "When we held the samples over a fire, the ants bailed out and made it possible to handle the fresh plant samples."

"But you still had to deal with all those nasty spines," Tuck Liew commented and then continued. "And now I suppose you have to describe it in Latin?"

"I'm working on that description now. Once I nail these male flowers, I should be pretty much finished," Ethan said with relief. "Fortunately, my Latin is coming back to me. It appears that the pornographic story I wrote serves to keep that dead language alive."

"Almost makes me want to learn Latin," Tuck Liew teased, "but I'll pass."

Tuck Liew was a good herbarium botanist, but preferred his samples dried, pressed, and indoors rather than fresh and out in the field. Unfortunately, after nearly a decade as a civil servant during which he'd been passed over for promotion several times, he'd lost much of his motivation. The two nevertheless got along well, and Ethan appreciated Tuck Liew's willingness to share his rather seditious opinions about Malaysian politics, especially in regards to the poor treatment the government meted out to its Chinese citizens. Tuck Liew also provided Ethan access to members of the Chinese community who would otherwise have been out of reach.

"I'm about done here," Ethan reported and then asked, "Might you be willing to accompany me to town for tea and a stop at the pharmacist's?"

"Tea I'll take, if you're treating, but I am not sure I should take you back to the pharmacist. Didn't you threaten him with a grisly death?" Tuck Liew asked in mock horror.

"Oh, that reminds me, I should carry out my threat and throttle the old bastard," Ethan said in similarly feigned rage.

"But I thought that the ointment he provided did the trick," Tuck Liew questioned, hardly able to hide his smile.

"Well, it did cure my crotch rot," Ethan explained, "but took several layers of skin with it. I was in such pain that I took to driving Roxanne around at night with my sarong open on her handlebars so the wind cooled the family jewels."

With a bark of laughter, Tuck Liew said, "I heard that didn't end well. Appanah's girls apparently got an eyeful. I wonder if they'll ever be the same?"

Dismayed that the story of his midnight encounter with his neighbor's daughters was already in Kuching's gossip mill, Ethan took a deep breath and reflected on the fact that it really was a small town, and chock full of people with nothing better to do than gossip about silly foreigners. Then, laughing along with his friend, he continued his reflection. "They nearly blinded me with a monster of a torch. What were they doing walking around in the middle of the night anyway?"

"At least now people must be reconsidering the conclusions about you based on your near escape from their ferocious water buffalo," Tuck Liew said and then laughed even more uproariously. He was referring to Ethan's widely discussed encounter with what was actually a very tame creature soon after he'd arrived in Kuching.

Ethan had been out for a morning stroll through the neighborhoods downhill from his apartment when he turned a corner and confronted a huge water buffalo with a rack of horns an arm-span across. To Ethan it was obvious that the beast had murder in its eyes, so he walked slowly backwards to give the animal room, talking softly all the while in an effort to calm it. Not watching where he was going he made the mistake of backing himself into a corner between a house and a flooded rice paddy. Although he was dressed for work, he was about to launch himself into the mud to escape being gored to death. Just at that moment, Appanah's youngest daughter, dressed in a yellow sari and jingling as she walked from the many gold bracelets on her arms, walked up, gently took the buffalo by the nose, and led her away. As they walked off, to Ethan's great relief and embarrassment, she explained to him that Petunia spoke only Tamil. That story, much elaborated and embellished, had quickly made the rounds in town, to the great amusement of all.

After he stopped laughing, Tuck Liew said, "Well okay, I'll go with you for tea, but you need to promise to not carry out your threat. Dr. Wang is a respected pharmacist and a very old man—it would not be proper from him to be accosted by a long-nosed barbarian." After a pause for effect he continued, "Today's Tuesday, so let's go to the Indian shop and get *idli* with coconut curry. And before you offer me a ride, I thank you very much but I will drive myself...it's taken me weeks to recover from my last ride on that terrible machine of yours—I can't figure out how you haven't killed yourself already."

Dietary diversity is one of the great pleasures of working in Malaysia. Sometimes when Ethan had been on an expedition and subsisting on scanty field rations for too long, he'd find himself planning his meals for the first week back in Kuching. Over those seven days, which would involve twenty-eight meals including teas, he would be sure to eat both south and north Indian foods—he particularly favored the various breads of which he preferred *puris* and *chapatis*. Other meals would be dedicated to the many sorts of Chinese cuisine. Included on at least a daily basis would be various curries from around the region, and of course his favorite, water buffalo *rendang* made with plenty of coconut milk and lemongrass, served with glutinous rice.

With that the two men headed off to town, tall and thin Ethan on Roxanne alongside short and fat Tuck Liew on his Honda 50. After stretched tea (black tea with condensed milk that is poured rapidly back-and-forth between two glasses to raise a froth) and *idli* served on banana leaves at one of the Indian shops in town, they walked down the street to the Chinese pharmacy. The ancient pharmacist had his back to them when they walked into his open-fronted shop, but when he turned and saw Ethan, he panicked and ducked behind the counter. Ethan's laugh stopped his flight, but the old man still sought assurance from Tuck Liew that the young American hadn't come to carry out his threat. Ethan's Cantonese was still rudimentary, but he heard Tuck Lee say something about the Indian girls who surprised him in the dark of night. Whatever Tuck Liew said caused Dr. Wang to smile and then let out a high-pitched cackle before resuming his serious and very professional demeanor.

"Wait a second," Ethan asked, "did you tell him the crotch-rot on motorcycle story?"

"No, not me," Tuck Liew responded, holding his hands up and sounding offended, "he'd heard it already. I was just confirming that your technique, combined with his salve, did the trick."

"I should throttle you both," Ethan stated in a huff, but then laughed along with them.

While the trio calmed down, Ethan's eyes wandered around the apothecary. From floor to ceiling, one wall consisted of a beautiful wooden cabinet of tiny drawers. The other walls had shelves that held hundreds of vials, jars, and other containers, all of which contained the pharmacist's stock-in-trade. He knew, because he'd asked, that the medicinal substances for sale included powdered sun bear gall stones, sea horses, flying squirrel feces, pangolin scales, toad secretions, and unimaginable other strange things reputed to cure every disease known and many yet to be described.

In his quest for non-timber forest products that might provide income sources for the Iban, Ethan was in the habit of bringing to the pharmacist samples in which he thought there might be commercial interest. It was no surprise to anyone when he reached into his satchel and brought out several small packages fashioned from folded leaves. As he laid them out on the glass counter and opened them one-by-one, Ethan explained that they were collections he'd made in Ulu Balui. The pharmacist inspected the contents carefully and then asked questions about each of them. Ethan was impressed that by sight, smell, and in two cases, taste, the pharmacist was able to identify all the samples. Out of the collection, he was most interested in the fruit valves from a tree in the citrus family. All around the world, dried fruits of various species in the same genus (*Zanthoxylum*) are used as a spice (e.g., Szechuan pepper) or refined into an essential oil and used to treat various skin, oral, and spiritual ailments. Ethan was familiar with the genus from back in Maryland where it was known as "toothache tree," but before coming to Asia he was unaware of its many uses. The specimens he'd collected were particularly spicy, with a strong peppery taste and a rich floral aroma.

In reference to those fruit valves the pharmacist said, "Please leave these with me for further analysis. I might be able to find a market for them, but let me see."

Ethan nodded in agreement but then asked the pharmacist to consider the dried fruits of *lembah*, the plant he'd used with his Wacky Wednesday Reading Group. He was hoping to find a market outlet for this product, which could be collected in great quantities near Long Berawan. In response to his prodding, the pharmacist reluctantly touched a piece to his tongue, but then quickly washed out his mouth with tea. The pharmacist knew *lembah* well as a treatment for various ailments, from pleurisy to gout, but he prepared his medicinal tinctures from its roots, not its fruits, hence he was not fully aware of its exaggerated sweetness. Ethan was pleased to have revealed something new to the pharmacist but was then disappointed when the man showed no interest. When Ethan asked him to explain what seemed to him to be a peculiar reaction, the pharmacist explained that for a Chinese medicine to be effective it had to be bitter or otherwise unpleasant tasting; he had no use for a sweet potion. When prodded further, the pharmacist revealed that he actually was already aware of *lembah*'s saccharine-like effect. He explained that while the Bornean species that Ethan collected is powerfully sweet, it contains only a low concentration of curculigoside, the phenolic compound that is of most pharmacological interest.

With all the graciousness he could muster, Ethan thanked Dr. Wang for his consideration and promised to be back with more samples after his next trip. He and Tuck Liew then returned to the herbarium for the remainder of the work day.

Chapter 12. LIFE IN LONG AWAN

Excerpt from an aerogram from Ethan Yarrow in Kuching, Sarawak, to his parents in Chevy Chase, Maryland:

6 September 1971
Dear Mom and Dad,
I'm heading back up to my friend Jika's longhouse next week. They're preparing to plant hill rice and can use some help. I find it mildly amusing that I will be helping with their slashing-and-burning, a process that Pam Wilson (remember her?) is dedicated to eradicating. I know it's destructive, but seeing the HUGE clearings for oil palm plantations that are springing up all over the place, an acre or two for subsistence farming doesn't seem like a major environmental threat. Long Awan is such an idyllic place for me these days, especially after witnessing what is happening at Long Berawan and elsewhere. The government's complete disregard for the rights of the indigenous people is really alarming—they just put a group of Penan people in prison for blocking a logging road being cut through one of their cemeteries...

Although Jika earned enough working for the Forest Department to buy all the food he and his family might need, as a male Iban he felt obliged to plant at least an acre of hill rice. Planting and harvesting rice were a central component of Iban society and religion. They farmed a few small areas of flooded rice paddies in the valley bottom, but most of their production was on hillsides. Ethan had accompanied him to Long Awan to collect rattans but also to help with the preparation of the fields. The villagers assisted one another with the heavy tasks of forest clearing, later with the planting, and finally with the harvest and threshing. For several years the first task was facilitated by the availability in the longhouse of a chainsaw, but it had thrown a rod and was out of commission, which made the presence of another axe-man appreciated.

Ethan had plenty of experience with axes, but not of the sort employed by the Iban. Instead of a stiff wooden handle, Iban axe handles were made from flexible rattan canes, and were half again longer than a standard axe in the West. After a few days of practice, he finally mastered the art of tree felling with a flexible-handled axe and realized that the extra acceleration that derived from the whippy rattan cane handle really helped when felling huge hard-wooded trees.

As instructed by Jika, Ethan had been working on a cluster of trees towards the top end of what was being converted into a steeply sloped field. He'd deeply notched more than a dozen mid-sized trees, but left them standing and vulnerable. When he started on the large kingpin tree at the top of the hill, Jika and the other men came over to watch. As was common among the Iban, they made a game of the work, wagering heavily on the outcome. In this case, they were mostly betting on how many trees would be pulled down by the kingpin when Ethan finally felled it.

While Ethan chipped away at the big tree, the other men wandered around in the patch of partially cut trees, inspecting and commenting on both the notches and the extent to which the trees' crowns were interconnected with lianas. Satisfied with their observations they assembled to place their bets just upslope from where Ethan continued to slowly but steadily chop.

As Ethan worked, they badgered him in a good-natured manner. One said, "I believe he's trying to pester that tree so much that it will finally fall to avoid his incessant banging."

"Did anyone mention to our young friend that axe sharpening is allowed?" added another.

"Didn't I hear from the ladies that our friend here is good with his tool?" which was an obvious double entendre that got even Ethan laughing.

Ethan rested for a minute and then demanded with feigned seriousness, "I will appreciate your silence, can't you see that there's a master axeman at work?" which caused them to laugh even more uproariously.

The predicted number of notched trees that would be pulled down by the kingpin ranged from three to thirteen, but for Ethan, more would be better. A large number would enhance his reputation whereas a small number would provide his friends yet another reason to tease him. In addition to being an effective work-reducing approach to forest clearing, bowling with big trees was exciting to witness.

After nearly an hour of steady chopping, the tree, which was a few feet thick, finally started to topple. To make sure it fell with speed, Ethan made a few well-placed chops before jumping out of the way and joining the men as they watched the forest falling. When the carnage finally ceased, the count was nine, which was respectable but far from a record. The Iban men were nonetheless impressed, and congratulated Ethan while they settled their bets and derided both the winners and the losers.

Tired after a long day of heavy work, the men made their way down to their temporary streamside camp, collected their meagre possessions, and then walked back to their longhouse a few kilometers away. While engaged in tree felling they bivouacked near their fields, but now that the trees were on the ground drying, they were happy to be returning to their wives, children, and better food. They would return to their field-side camps with their entire families for the burning and planting, and then again a few months later to protect the ripening grain from wildlife and then to harvest. Ethan was sorry that he was unlikely to be back for the planting. He was intrigued to see exactly how the Iban farmers distributed the dozen or more varieties of rice they planted each year. He knew that a sacred variety was planted in the center of each field, but where they planted the various other strains of black, sticky, long, and short-grain varieties was a mystery to him.

They arrived back at Long Awan in time to bathe in the river and then sit down to a big meal. After eating, everyone sat around trading stories for a while before heading off to bed. Ethan was provided a room at the end of the old portion of the longhouse where tools were stored and visitors accommodated. Like the Dayaks, he slept on a mat woven from *pandan* (screw pine) leaves, but unlike his hosts, he always burned strips of *medang* (trees in the Lauraceae) bark to keep the mosquitoes at bay. He carried a mosquito net, but preferred to burn the bark because, at least early in the evening, it was hot inside a mosquito net.

Even though he had been awoken from a deep sleep, there was no mistaking Singa's signature entry into his sleeping quarters. He smiled as her swinging breasts and silky hair brushed against his cheeks and then gasped as she suddenly dove like a seal after a fish, right under his sarong. She would then lift her head joyfully with his rapidly growing fish in her mouth. Having captured her primary target, she lowered herself onto Ethan's mouth, which he received with pleasure. Making love with Singa, which Ethan enjoyed immensely, would often take unpredictable and sometimes dangerous turns, but always started the same way. Afterwards they would lie entwined and chat until they both fell asleep, but somehow Ethan always woke in the morning refreshed and alone. He had no idea about how the Iban women communicated with each other, but noted that on the nights when Singa joined him they were never disturbed. He chuckled when he recollected the underwear-on-the-doorknob signal he used with roommates in the dorm back in his college days.

After love-making that night, as they lay enjoying each other's company, Ethan finally spoke up. "I had the most amusing experience when I returned to Kuching after my last visit with you."

Singa made an encouraging sound so he continued, "I looked in a mirror."

Singa laughed and asked, "And what did you see my funny-looking white boy?"

"Exactly that, a white guy with an *enggang pauh* (hornbill's beak) and a furry face," which caused Singa to laugh more. One of her attractions for Ethan was that laugh, which reminded him of water rushing over rounded rocks in a flowing stream. His reference to his own nose as a beak reflected a comment made by one of the old Iban women on his first visit to Long Awan. When he was asked to perform the hornbill dance during one of their many festivals, she pointed out that his beak was so big that he didn't need the traditional mask. The ensuing hilarity caused by that remark was shared by all and had become one of the lovers' inside jokes. To be fair, at least by European standards, Ethan's nose might only warrant being called prominent, but it definitely distinguished him from the Iban.

"No, seriously, after a few weeks without looking in a mirror or seeing any of my countrymen, I had somehow slipped into thinking that I looked like everyone else and blended in."

Singa laughed again but then said, "Sorry for laughing, but I do understand. A few times during my dreadful stay in Holland I managed to delude myself into thinking that I was a tall blond Dutch lady," and she laughed again. "Then I'd be shocked when my reflection revealed that I was still a short, dark-skinned and black-haired Iban. No wonder everyone stared at me," she ended with just a trace of rancor. She and Ethan had spoken before about the efforts she'd made to lighten her skin when she was young and to otherwise try to conform to a very narrow European standard of feminine beauty. She'd since accepted her own appearance, which was quite striking, and Ethan had made abundantly clear that he considered her a beautiful woman.

After a while they fell asleep in each other's arms, but when Ethan woke in the morning he was alone and well rested. While bathing, Ethan heard the melodious duet of Bornean gibbons coming from the ridge behind the longhouse. He was always pleased to hear them sing, but particularly so because his open schedule for the next day would allow him to enjoy one of the other pleasures of being in Long Awan, which was to spend time with this family of gibbons. Through repeated exposure to people who did not harass them, the gibbons were acclimated to the bipedal terrestrial beasts they looked down on from their lofty perches in the treetops. Ethan promised himself that he would spend the next morning with them. He spent the day pressing his specimens and writing up his notes with the dubious assistance of a swarm of youngsters. He spent another wonderful night with Singa, but before dawn the next morning he was climbing up to where on the ridge he'd heard the last duet of the evening.

After ascending for a little less than an hour, he smelled fermenting fruit and followed his nose (and flashlight beam) to a large strangler fig tree from which the last of the night's bats were messily feeding and dropping fruit. Figs are fed on by a wide diversity of bats, birds, and primates, including gibbons, so Ethan figured that it was a good bet that the family of gibbons would visit soon after sunrise. He climbed up a steep pitch of ground just above the fig tree, found a place from which he could peer laterally into the crown, swept away the leaf litter with a handful of palm fronds, turned off his flashlight, and sat down to await the coming day.

Although large fig trees are not common in most Bornean forests, when one is in fruit it draws animals from far and wide. Ethan had once followed this same family of gibbons for a mile or so when they made a bee-line to a fig on which the fruits had only that day ripened. From the ten thousand canopy trees in their two square mile territory, they somehow seemed to know exactly when that particular tree would provide them a meal.

As Ethan peered into the crown of the fig against a slightly lightening sky, he could see that the tree was indeed swarming with bats, none as large as a flying fox, but impressive in their numbers. He'd earlier found himself thinking about the ancient movie theatre at home in Maryland, then realized that it was the smell of buttered popcorn that elicited that memory. After just a few seconds, his *binturong* (bearcat, a large omnivorous civet) suspicions were confirmed when he saw the silhouette of a large one clambering down from the crown. Only a few minutes later he was startled when an animal twice the size of any flying squirrel he'd ever seen leapt out of the fig tree and glided over his head. It took him a minute to realize that it was a *colugo* (flying lemur), which surprised him because he'd read that they ate leaves and tree gums, not fruit. He supposed that even a colugo couldn't pass up a ripe fig, but made note that he should mention this observation to his mammologist friend Ian.

Ethan had guessed right—as dawn broke he realized that when he looked out into the valley through the branches of the dipterocarp tree adjacent to the fig, he could make out the silhouette of a sitting gibbon. That they hadn't slept in the fig tree itself made sense to Ethan after witnessing some of the all-night party that the tree had hosted. An arm-span away from one gibbon sitting upright he could see the other adult draped over the horizontal branch on its back with its arms and legs hanging down. Dawn comes quickly on the equator and after only a few more minutes in nearly complete daylight, he could distinguish a third individual, obviously a youngster, standing on the branch and hugging the sitting adult from behind. They were grooming each other but the young one was apparently getting bored and starting to move around in what seemed like a playful manner. The mother, for it became clear that he was watching a mother and babe, tried to hug her young ward but he slipped out of her grasp. An instant later, having apparently realized that he was free, he dashed down the branch and stepped directly on the belly of his recumbent and presumably sleeping father.

In watching primates, or any animal for that matter, it's easy to overly anthropomorphize their behaviors, but Ethan was completely convinced that the father was fake sleeping and was totally prepared for his son's attack. In any case, before the young gibbon had taken another step, his father had grabbed him by the leg, swung him down below the branch, and tossed him back into the waiting arms of his mother. Ethan had audibly gasped when he saw the baby flying through the air, but the gibbons ignored him and seemed to take the acrobatics in stride.

With that bit of rough-housing the family was fully awake and ready for the dawn chorus before heading off into the fig tree for breakfast. Later in the day and especially before turning in for the night they'd seek out fruits rich in fats that are slower to digest, but as a breakfast food for gibbons, figs are apparently hard to beat.

While the music of the gibbon's duet washed over him where he sat not a stone's throw away and at nearly the same height, Ethan felt blessed. It might be, as the ethologists surmised, that they were calling to defend their territory against the incursions of other gibbons, but it was also clear that they rather enjoyed themselves in the process. He could see that the male and female were calling back and forth to each other as well as broadcasting their location to the world around them. And with the aid of their distensible throat sacs, even the deep rumbling hoots of the female didn't seem to require much exertion.

The morning song was becoming intermittent when the family lazily brachiated its way towards breakfast. Whenever the branches were spaced apart more than an arm span, the baby crawled onto the back or the front of one of the parents, but otherwise he swung hand-over-hand on his own. Ethan realized that he really had no basis on which to conclude that the young one was male, it was just something about its antics that led him to that conclusion. In either case, he wanted to put their graceful and seemingly effortless movements through the canopy to music.

Ethan had been so intent on watching the family awake that he hadn't noticed that the fig was already full of hungry patrons. He'd heard the pair of rhinoceros hornbills fly in—it was hard to miss the whishing of wind through their wings and raucous calls—but there were dozens of other species of birds munching away as well as a pair of Prevost's squirrels. All that eating made Ethan recognize his own hunger, so after watching for a while more he started back down the hill to the longhouse.

He walked under the fruiting fig tree, which caused some fluttering above his head, but the feast continued mostly unabated. As Ethan reached down to pick up a few freshly fallen fig to eat himself, he startled a mouse deer who ran off just a few meters before turning around to gaze at the human interloper. As he chewed the slightly sweet package of seeds, he wondered how many dead fig wasps he was eating, and whether they were of any importance to the protein intake of the animals he'd been watching as well as the bats and other nocturnal frugivores he'd missed the night before.

Ethan's tally of wasps in each of the figs he popped into his mouth started with the carcasses of two or three long-since deceased pollen-laden females who had found their way to this tree from another one perhaps kilometers away. That such small beasts could fly so far was amazing, but strangler figs were rare in the area and the nearest fig tree in flower was certainly not close by. After the females made their way to the tree, they searched around for a fig that had not yet been pollinated. Once found, they worked their way inside through the overlapping scales at the summit of the round inflorescence, losing their wings in the process. Once inside, they groped around in the dark, pollinated a few dozen flowers, and oviposited in a few dozen others. A few months later a single seed would be produced by each of the former while a fig wasp would hatch from each of the later. The wingless and grub-like males would emerge into the darkness in the middle of the still hard fruit before the elegantly winged females, some of whom were their sisters. Ethan had read that the males didn't always wait for the females to fully emerge before impregnating them, but in any case, once they served their reproductive function, the males would be left behind in the fruit while the inseminated females chewed and wiggled their way out into the light. Before emerging the females went around gathering pollen from the male flowers clustered around the exit. Within no more than a day or two, they would repeat this process at some other fig tree, which they would locate in some mysterious manner. Meanwhile, as soon as the females opened the exit route, the wall of the fig would soften and sweeten and become somebody's breakfast.

His wasp tally was up to several dozen, but rather than be disgusted, Ethan felt a bit ashamed that he was unlikely to disperse the seeds he'd eaten effectively. He expected that the hard little seeds would make it through his gastrointestinal track unscathed and ready to germinate. But these seeds were from strangler figs, which start their lives as epiphytes perched high up in the canopy. From those lofty perches perhaps several decades later, roots from a lucky few would make it down to the ground, which would speed their growth rate considerably. The roots that grew down the trunk of the host tree would then fuse, and the anastomosing grid of thickening fig roots would form a woody straitjacket around the host's trunk. Deprived of the ability to grow in diameter and replace its non-functional vessels, the host would die, eventually decay, and leave a hollow cylinder composed of fused fig roots up which it was fun to climb, if you don't mind the bats that share the interior space. Unless Ethan climbed high up into the canopy, which he wasn't planning to do, and defecated at the base of a lofty branch, which seem awkward, the seeds in his gut were now among the living dead. He reconciled himself with this fate by thinking about all the other animals that were feeding on the tree that are more effective seed dispersers. The bigger challenge, he then remembered, was to keep the forest, and particularly the big trees, standing. That goal was becoming increasingly difficult to attain as African oil palm cultivation became more lucrative and more and more forests were converted into plantations.

Chapter 13. VESPAS VICTORIOUS

Excerpt from anaerogram from Ethan Yarrow in Kuching, Sarawak, to his parents in Chevy Chase, Maryland:

5 October 1971
Dear Mom and Dad,
I had some fun this week with a group of local boys. We raced motor scooters, of all things. I didn't win, but had a blast racing through the streets of Kuching. Don't worry Mom, it was a legally sanctioned race. And Dad, I'm sorry to admit that I was riding an Italian scooter. There actually was an ancient Cushman Airborne in the race, like the ones they parachuted into Europe during the War, but I was mounted on a Vespa...Enrico Piaggio, your favorite Italian fighter plane engineer, would have been proud of my showing but perhaps annoyed by its modifications for the race.

"Nice view, eh?" Ian asked Hazel as they both looked over the city of Kuching from the rooftop club atop the newly opened Hilton Hotel.

"That it is," responded Hazel, "but how did you wangle an invitation and why didn't you tell me that it would be such a swank affair?"

"You look lovely my dear, but when we stepped out of the elevator, I too was surprised. Who would've thought a motor scooter race would attract so much attention from the well-to-do?" He gazed around and the crowd and then continued. "When I stopped in Cheong's store the other day, the old man went out of his way to invite me, and you're my date."

Ian and Hazel were the only westerners in a group of about fifty mostly middle-aged Chinese people mingling around the pool, sipping drinks from the bar. Everyone was comfortably but elegantly dressed, with men in fancy batik shirts and the women in stylish dresses, but the casual nature of the gathering was reinforced by the bathing suit-clad children frolicking in the small pool, all closely monitored by their nannies. Shade was provided by trees in ornate planters and large beach umbrellas.

Most of the attendees were wealthy Chinese merchants and Hilton Club members, many accompanied by their much younger looking wives. There were timber barons and mining company executives, now the poorly disguised power behind the new *Bumiputra*-owned companies created in response to directives from Kuala Lumpur that required Malay leadership of private sector firms. The few Malays present were mostly high-ranking government officials who looked uncomfortable and probably felt obliged to be present.

Less than a block away and 15 stories below hundreds of motor scooters jockeyed for position near the starting line for the 10 km race. Even from the rooftop, the noise of the two-stroke engines was impressive, but nothing like it was down on the ground amidst the machines. On the platform erected at the starting line, the Mayor was giving his welcome speech. Ian and Hazel couldn't hear what he was saying, but suspected that people nearby couldn't either.

The Mayor still had a year to serve in his first term but nevertheless used every opportunity to emphasize why he should be re-elected. His more immediate objective was to instill in the assembled racers the importance of safety, fair play, and respect for private property. After he harangued both the riders and spectators with warnings of dire penalties for lawbreakers, he realized that he might as well save his breath. He was also realizing that he had not assigned enough officers for crowd control. He could have gotten help from the army, but was reluctant to ask them for favors because of the latent costs involved. In the past, he'd ended up repaying them several-fold in favors, some of which pushed the bounds of even his low personal standards for good governance.

A few months prior to race-day when a group of prominent Chinese businessmen came to his office to request permission to hold the race again, he had no idea that it would grow to be such a large affair. The previous year's race was modest in comparison, with mostly local riders and only scattered spectators. A few of the race's sponsors had supported the Mayor in his previous campaign, and he knew he'd need their political and financial support in the future, so he acquiesced without even suggesting the need for a gratuity. When he later realized that the promoters were likely to make a lot of money on this race, he regretted his uncharacteristic failure to request compensation for his trouble. They would make their money not from entry fees, which were modest, but from the percentages they would claim from all the bets wagered, at least those of which they were aware. Betting was illegal but so culturally embedded that it was unstoppable. He'd heard rumors of some massive bets on this race, and knew that even more would be wagered after it started and the odds changed by the minute.

As of an hour before the starting time, nearly 300 racers had registered for the Second Annual Kuching Motor Scooter Race. The Mayor was dismayed to see that crowds jammed the sidewalks for as far as he could see, and every window in the buildings lining the street seemed to have at least one head hanging out. He'd also learned that this was no longer a local affair; racers had arrived from Singapore, Kota Kinabalu, and Kuala Lumpur. Clearly the competition would be fierce and the stakes correspondingly large.

Back atop the Hilton, Ian and Hazel had settled into some comfortable chairs in the shade of a large potted palm from which they could look down on the race and surreptitiously observe the other guests. They divided their attention between the increasingly frenetic movements below them and the more urbane social interactions taking place among club members and visitors. While the adults on the roof maintained their gentility, it was obvious that financial transactions of some sort were taking place at a rapid clip. And every time the elevator door opened, many people turned to see who would emerge. Often a young man would step out, look around, locate the man who was presumably his patron, quickly dash over to his side, whisper in his ear, and then leave.

Hazel was perplexed by the behavior on the rooftop and asked Ian, "Do you have any idea what's going on up here?"

Ian chuckled and then explained. "I too was mystified at first, but then I realized that many of these people are betting on the race that looks about to start," he added as he looked over the parapet. "I suspect that the fellows who arrive in the elevator, to whom everyone seems to pay undue attention, are delivering messages about the racers and their machines. Based on that information, the odds probably change. I would love to know how much is being wagered, but I suspect that it's well above our pay grades."

Just then, Eddie Cheong came over to speak with Ian and Hazel. "Dr. Ian, I'm glad you could come. And this must be Miss Hazel, about whom I've heard so much. Welcome. I trust you are both enjoying the festivities?"

Eddie Cheong was retired but still held the reigns of Kuching's Chinese-dominated business community. Although he'd officially turned the running of his various enterprises over to his son Billy, it was hard for him to not interfere with the running of the diversity of firms he'd worked so hard to build. Although this interference was occasionally annoying, his son knew that the family's success in the rapidly changing world of a newly independent Malaysia depended to a large degree on Eddie Cheong's network of connections, both friendly and antagonistic. Some of those connections dated back several generations and spanned from Sarawak to Canton, to England and India, and across the Pacific to the USA and Canada.

"Yes we are, thank you. The view from up here is splendid and the breeze is a blessing. By the way, how's your grandson doing, I don't see him here." Ian knew from Ethan that Tommy Cheong was Eddie's pride and joy. He also knew that the young teenaged boy was struggling with his family about the line of study he was to pursue if he secured a place in a university in Malaysia or, the option he would prefer, Australia. He was an exceptional student, but the government had imposed limits on the number of ethnic Chinese who could attend university, even to study abroad with family funds. While he leaned towards biology, his father was adamant that he study either business or law, so as to be prepared to run the family's businesses. Surprisingly, Grandfather Eddie encouraged Tommy's interest in nature.

"Thomas is fine, thank you. He does enjoy the Wednesday Evening Reading Group that your friend Ethan runs. I'm not sure I approve of all the stuff they read, but the practice for his O levels is wonderful," Eddie responded and then added, "but I do hope he doesn't develop a dreadful American accent like mine." Most people in town, including many of his employees, didn't know that Mr. Cheong spoke English at all, while those who did wondered about the genesis of his New York City accent and frequent use of out-moded phrases.

After gazing over the assembled racers, Eddie continued, "A few of my friends wondered if you'd like to bet on the race?" and then looked at Hazel and added politely. "You are also invited to play if you wish."

Ian responded for them both by commenting that, "With so many contenders, we'd have no idea about who is likely to win."

"Ah yes," responded Cheong with a slight smile, "but you needn't restrict yourself to winners and losers. You could, for example, bet on how many of those scooters will not make it to the starting line. Or, if you are more grizzly in your fancies, you might wager how many will crash after crossing the line, or even how many will end up in the Kuching River."

This information was a revelation to Ian and Hazel. Having never witnessed a scooter race, they couldn't imagine how even one scooter would end up in the river. What would soon be revealed was that the coming race would resemble the chariot race scene from Ben Hur combined with a Roller Derby match on steroids and with considerably more horsepower.

The race was to start and finish at the line below them near the center of town. It was to be a "gang start" with the hundreds of registered scooters, mostly driven by amateurs, starting at once. In professional races the competitors are sorted so the fastest are in the front of the pack and hence not encumbered by the slower racers. In this case, where a particular scooter was located relative to the starting line was not organized but rather was a function of luck, timing, and aggressiveness of the riders as they jockeyed for favorable positions.

Another factor that Eddie Cheong didn't mention and that wasn't obvious to many spectators, even some who were wagering bets, is that this was not a race in which it was every man for himself. Rivalries among clans, language and ethnic groups, and neighborhoods were to be played out as the scooters raced down city streets, along the river, up into the nearby hills, and back into town. Now in the minutes before the race started, these teams of riders made great efforts to assemble themselves so as to effectively execute the strategies they'd worked out in advance, and to take collective advantage of any opportunities that might emerge during the race.

"Thank you Mr. Cheong, but I think we'll just watch this time. We do wish you well if you are wagering yourself," Ian responded.

"If you lack for anything, just give me a nod," Eddie said and then looked up as an obviously important family emerged regally from the elevator. "Ah, and now we are to be graced by the presence of our future Chief Minister and his young lovelies."

The newcomer was Paib, an up-and-coming Melenau politician, his tall Lithuanian wife, and their stunningly beautiful teenaged daughter, Jamilah. Behind them came a Chinese amah carrying Suleiman, their baby boy. Like most Melenau, Paib was Muslim, but so was his wife due to her Tatar ethnic roots—their religion connected them with the United Malay National Party (UMNO). Paib's remarkable rise in wealth and power since returning in 1959 after taking his law degree in Australia, was due to this connection as well as to his cunning and ruthlessness. His uncle, Abdul Rahman, was the current Chief Minister, and Paib was expected to replace him with UMNO's blessings.

Before excusing himself and walking away Eddie Cheong whispered to Ian and Hazel, "As environmentalists, I suggest you steer clear of that man," he said indicating Paib, "he does not care about nature and he's not one to take prisoners."

Ian and Hazel were not terribly surprised by the information, but they were shocked that Eddie Cheong was the one to warn them.

Less than a decade after independence, relationships between nature groups and the Malaysian government were cordial, but tensions were growing as the pace of development accelerated. The established environmental groups were still mostly spearheaded by expats, with an increasing number of locals joining the ranks. Protests in Sarawak against the extraordinary rate of logging were attracting some attention internationally, particularly in the name of indigenous rights, but confrontations were rare due in part to cultural sensitivities. Many of the confrontations that did occur were not reported in the government-controlled press.

Eddie Cheong joined a group of men in animated conversation with a wizened old man who had recently joined them on the roof. Ian assumed that the man had delivered new information of relevance to the outcome of the race. Meanwhile, as the Paib family continued to make their rounds of salutations, everyone seemed to track their progress and had big smiles ready to greet them. Most were aware that one of Paib's many companies owned and operated the Hilton.

The assembled scooters massed in the street below represented a wide range of brands and ages. Vespas predominated, but there were also quite a few Lambrettas, a handful of Bajaj Chetaks from India, and a few Cushmans, some of which dated back to the immediate post-war years. To register for the race, the rider needed a helmet, the scooter needed functional brakes, and the engine displacement could be no more than 200 cubic centimeters. All the riders had helmets, many of which were for motorcycles, but there were also cricket batting helmets, pith helmets, rugby ear guards, and a few homemade jobs. As for the engine specifications, given that the people at the registration desks had no way of confirming them, many of the registered scooters exceeded the limit on horsepower by substantial margins. And as for brakes, after being badgered by the riders, the race officials decided to disregard that requirement as an undue encumbrance.

Lack of brakes endangered the riders, but a bigger threat was exploding engines. To increase horsepower, many scooter owners bored out their cylinders until they were paper-thin and installed over-sized pistons. To reduce weight, riders removed the cowlings that protect the engines of standard-issue motor scooters.

Next up on the podium was the race official who carried the chequered flag neatly rolled up under his arm. Before waving that flag he intended to explain the ground rules to the riders, which his secretary had neatly typed on a piece of paper he fluttered before the microphone. As he dutifully read through his list he was aware that virtually no one could hear him. He also realized that whatever he said, it was going to be a no-holds-barred race.

While the official was reading out the rules, a commotion commenced at the back of the pack. Towering over the other riders was a man garbed in skin-tight black leather from head to foot, with a black helmet and deeply shaded visor that rendered his face invisible. He was astride a huge black motorcycle poorly disguised as a motor scooter, complete with a Vespa cowling cobbled onto its massive frame. Although the racers were tightly packed, the biker-in-black powered his way towards the front of the pack.

Up on the roof where the spectators were awaiting the start of the race, everyone watched spellbound as the biker-in-black bullied his way to the starting line. Like all the other riders, he wore an official number over his leathers—how he'd passed even the cursory inspection of race officials was the topic of much speculation amongst the spectators, with some already crying foul as they saw the prospects for their bets crumble.

Hazel leaned over to Ian and whispered, "I hope the man-in-black isn't who I think it is. I thought you said Ethan was spending the day working on his dissertation?"

Laughing at the suspicion, which he shared, Ian responded, "My God, will you check out that butt." He paused in response to a slashing look of disapproval from Hazel, and then continued, "If that's him, Roxanne is certainly looking svelte today...but no, that can't be Ethan...he distinctly mentioned that he was going to work on his research. But look, what's going on now?"

As everyone watched, the official, perhaps clued by rumblings of the crowd or the throbbing from the poorly disguised motorcycle, looked up from his notes, quickly assessed the situation, climbed down from the podium, and walked over to rider number 69, the biker-in-black. No one could possibly have heard what he said, but his frantic gestures were abundantly clear. Seemingly with reluctance, the biker-in-black pulled ahead out of the pack, drove up onto the crowded sidewalk, and parked his machine among the stunned spectators who stepped back to give him room.

Anyone who could see the starting line now had their eyes glued on this recent development. The now dismounted biker-in-black looked around, spotted a young fellow sitting on a scooter on the sidelines—not a racer but a spectator. In front of stunned on-lookers, he walked over to the boy, lifted him bodily from the scooter and then, while holding the scooter's owner at arm's length, tore off its engine cover, which he handed to the awestruck youth, got on, kicked-started the scooter, and drove back into the front of the pack. The boy protested vigorously but to no avail as he was held back by several men. His struggle was quickly disregarded as all eyes were drawn to the race official, who had climbed back onto the podium and unfurled the chequered flag.

From the rooftop Eddie Cheong watched the events unfold with amusement but was quickly besieged by colleagues who wanted to wager for or against the man-in-black. Alone among them Eddie knew that the scooter the rider-in-black appeared to have stolen was a 1970 Vespa Rally that had been bored, stroked, and otherwise modified by Bernie Chan. He also knew that the boy from whom the scooter had been taken was his grandson and the rider was indeed Ethan. It had cost him several hundred *ringgit* in bribes to get Ethan officially registered on Roxanne and quite a bit more to modify the Vespa. The leather suit that Ethan was wearing had been custom-made by his tailor in Hong Kong, the expense of which was increased when it had to be adjusted to accommodate Ethan's very un-Chinese buttocks. Despite all these expenses, he expected to recoup that amount and much more even after paying Ethan and Tommy their agreed upon shares. He knew that the young American would probably have raced for free, and certainly for the leathers alone, but he always made a point to treat Ethan Yarrow fairly.

Eddie knew that Ethan's scooter was fast and that he was a competent driver, but had no illusions about him actually winning the race—his size was against him, for one thing, and he wasn't sure he had the killer instinct needed to deal with some of the crazies in the race. He was therefore impressed when Ethan successfully pushed his way towards the front of the throng without resorting to driving through the crowd on the sidewalk. He did expect Ethan to finish the race, and to place in the top 20 if not the top 10. His likelihood of finishing was enhanced by the fact that by keeping his participation in the race and sponsorship secret, none of the gangs of riders had targeted him in advance for elimination. He would certainly become a target as he raced with the lead bikes, but Eddie Cheong figured that a former ice hockey player would be able to hold his own when the elbows started flying.

When the flag came down the sound of 300 totally revved two-cycle scooter engines was overwhelming, even up on the roof a block away. The first few dozen scooters came off the line with their front wheels high in the air but three lost control and flipped, which caused a massive pile up behind them, with several other scooters down. The front wheels of the remaining leaders hit the ground almost simultaneously after about two hundred yards, at which point they were up to nearly 60 miles per hour in first gear. When they popped into second gear, most did wheelies again but settled down to the ground more quickly. To anyone knowledgeable about motor scooter transmissions, this behavior made clear that their stock issue, belt-driven, continuously variable transmissions had been replaced by chain-driven motorcycle transmissions.

Behind the starting line further pandemonium ensued as the effect of the flipped scooters reverberated to the back of the pack. Several unrelated crashes resulted in a dozen downed scooters. Several had stalled out and failed to restart, but most were eventually righted and made their way across the starting line and onto the race course with the leaders already far ahead.

On the rooftop some bets were already being settled while everyone watched as the lead scooters passed from view down the river road. Cheong was happy that the rider-in-black was among the leaders. Others noticed that as well, which stimulated a new flurry of bets. Cheong took many of those bets as well, betting both for and against his own rider. He was still confident that Ethan would finish the race but also remained convinced that he would not win.

Meanwhile, down on river road, a rider on a souped-up Lambretta mistakenly decided to play rough with Ethan. They had been jostling for position for several minutes as they approached a curve. He'd purposefully bumped into Ethan several times, once almost pinching him into the curb, which would've been disastrous. Although they were travelling at nearly 100 miles per hour, it did not appear that anyone was going to slow down for the curve. The rider pestering Ethan was on the outside of the curve next to the river and about half a length behind. He didn't expect Ethan to decelerate quickly and certainly did not expect to hip checked so forcefully. The next thing he knew, he and his scooter had parted company with the ground and were sailing out into the Kuching River. That same bend in the river would welcome three more scooters before the pack passed, which Mr. Cheong had predicted precisely. With his winnings from the river, he'd already recouped his expenses for the scooter, leather suit, and then some.

There was another pileup but no more scooters in the river when the main pack of racers reached the rockets. Several of the ladies-of-the-night had roused themselves early and arranged themselves in their exceedingly provocative regalia along the roadside above their houseboats. As they cheered the riders on, their ample distractions were more than enough to cause several to veer from their chosen paths, which resulted in a maelstrom about which people would talk for years. Ethan slowed a bit to enjoy the display of femininity but was near the head of the pack and unaware of the pandemonium that ensued behind him. He similarly avoided the ruckus caused by youths with bottle rockets and other fireworks, but later heard that the effect was stunning even to the perpetrators.

As the lead group reached the hills on the outskirts of Kuching where the wealthy people lived, Ethan's size started to take its toll. That he weighed nearly twice as much as some of the other riders was obviously a disadvantage. As he dropped from the fourth spot back to sixth, he also had to admit that some of the riders were extremely skilled. He hadn't spent much time on motor scooters, preferring instead big bikes like Roxanne, and it was obvious that the leaders knew their machines and how to ride them.

As the leaders approached the finish line, two broke down at almost the same time, their cylinder walls apparently not able to take the pressure. When another veered off the road and out of the race, Ethan rose in the ranks and felt like he actually had a shot at winning. That hope was dashed when he was overtaken by three identical Lambrettas driven by identically clad drivers. Ethan didn't see what happened a minute later when they approached the finish line, but he would have been impressed.

On the roof when the front runners came into view, new bets flew as odds changed by the second. At about city block from the finish line on a straight stretch of wide road, the three Lambrettas were a few lengths behind the two first scooters. Those two were neck-and-neck but spread across the road seemingly to avoid each other. Suddenly, the riders on the two outside Lambrettas grabbed the jacket sleeves of the rider in the middle and hurled him forward. This technique was familiar to roller derby fans, but not expected in a motor scooter race. The extra momentum catapulted the central rider in front of the two leaders and across the finish line.

Ethan ended up in 6th place, about which he was thrilled and so was Mr. Cheong who had wagered that he would finish in the top 10. Of the 295 scooters that started the race, 207 crossed the finish line, with the last one limping across nearly 10 minutes after the first.

As the accounts were being settled on the roof and elsewhere in the city, many spectators hoped that the biker-in-black would reveal himself but, as agreed beforehand, that was not to be. Immediately after crossing the finish line, Ethan had driven his scooter into Chan Motors, changed out of his leathers, and gone to fetch Roxanne from where he'd left her on the sidewalk. In the heat of the race while no one was looking, Tommy had removed Roxanne's disguise. After the race, if anyone noticed Ethan driving away on the motorcycle, they didn't connect him with the biker-in-black. Ethan calmly drove home for his afternoon siesta as the storm clouds moved in from the South China Sea.

Just after sundown a few hours later, Ethan joined Hazel, Ian, and some other friends at the food stalls at the night market. As per usual, he had parked Roxanne up at the Police station, but only the Lieutenant was there and he was not in a chatty mood, having been on crowd control duty all day. As he approached their regular table, his ebullient mood was confirmed when he announced that the evening meal was his treat. Even before sitting down, he signaled to Orpa, an Iban girl who was one of his favorite waitresses, to serve them a half dozen large bottles of Bintang.

Everyone at the table had watched the race, and before Ethan arrived they'd been gossiping about the mystery rider. Ian was the first to speak and asked "What's the occasion?"

To which Ethan replied, "I want to share my winnings from the race today!"

Hazel then asked, "So you indeed were the biker-in-black," to which Ethan nodded assent. She then continued, "But you didn't win!"

"Hey, I came in sixth, that's worth something isn't it?"

"Not enough to pay for dinner, I would expect," Hazel responded tartly. Her relationship with Ethan amused everyone—while she secretly adored the young American, she refused to acknowledge in public that he had any redeeming qualities, and took every opportunity to put him in his place. For his part, Ethan enjoyed the repartee, and never ceased to enjoying teasing her.

"Not unless you account for my splitting the pot with my sponsor, and that he bet on me finishing in the top 10, not to win. He also had bets pay off for the number of scooters that ended up in the river and the number of crashes. We would've won even more but even Eddie Cheong was unaware that those Teochew boys would pull that roller derby trick on their Lambretas—now that must have been something to see."

Ian then asked for confirmation, "So, old man Cheong was your sponsor?"

"Yep, and his grandson Tommy was the one who hatched the plot, I just played along—didn't you notice that he was the one from whom I grabbed the scooter?"

"No, we couldn't see his face from atop the Hilton, but he certainly acted upset," Ian noted. "And I suppose the men who restrained him were part of the charade as well," to which Ethan nodded.

These admissions sparked substantial hubbub at their table of ten, around the adjacent table of eavesdroppers, and then around all the other footstall tables in the night market. It wouldn't be long before the whole town knew the story, which would likely result in the settlement of even more bets.

"It is not at all clear to me why Eddie Cheong puts up with you," Ian commented and then continued, "but now I understand why he invited me up to the Hilton Club...he didn't want me to talk you out of that crazy stunt." And with Ethan's revelations, he also understood the peculiar interaction he observed between Eddie Cheong and his son Billie, who was apparently unaware of the charade and was complaining vociferously about the biker-in-black.

Ethan contemplated Ian's question about Eddie Cheong's increasingly apparent efforts on his behalf—he too wondered why the old man seemed to take such a personal interest in him. He wasn't outwardly friendly, at least not in an American way, but he did seem to take an interest in his life. He finally figured that it was because his grandson Tommy was a regular Wacky Wednesday attendee.

"I hope that you and Dame Hazel had a smashing good time up with there with the swells while I risked life and limb for the cause," Ethan responded jokingly in his faux-Oxford accent before diving into his dinner of *kangkong belachan* with strips of braised water buffalo meat over rice.

With chopsticks elevated over his meal, Ian responded in the same fashion. "Yes, it went swimmingly," to which Hazel made a very expressive tisk-tisk sound with her tongue. Ian then remembered that he needed to pass the warning about Paib to Ethan, but this was certainly not the place for that sort of sensitive communication.

Chapter 14. MEDICINE WOMAN PROVES HER PROWESS

Excerpt from an aerogram from Ethan Yarrow in Kuching, Sarawak, to his parents in Chevy Chase, Maryland:

31 October 1971
Dear Mom and Dad,
Last week up in Long Awan I met a well-known medicine woman from whom I hoped to learn about plants (but she had other plans)...I ended up being pretty soundly humiliated, which everyone in the longhouse enjoyed. She kept asking me about you, Dad, and your family—in some cases, her questions seemed curiously informed and she was merely seeking confirmation of what she already knew. Her probing made me realize how little I know about your time in China, Dad, so get some stories ready for when I get home.

The morning mist was slowly burning away as a group of men sat chatting at one end of the open verandah of a 55-door Iban longhouse while a group of women did the same at the other end. All had breakfasted, bathed in the river, and were starting to celebrate a holiday the exact nature of which still eluded Ethan. The Iban calendar was marked by so many holidays that it was hard to keep track. They were also prone to suspend working in response to various signs, usually communicated by birds. This propensity did little to enamor them to employers, such as those running logging operations. For example, their beliefs in bird augury were such that if on their way out of camps to a felling area a bird called to the right of the trail, they'd refuse to work. Employers of Iban may have despaired at the frequency with which they were absent, but their culture prized leisure and not efficiency. While they were capable of prodigious quantities of work, their capacity for what seemed like sloth was also impressive. Having just returned from a rather rigorous 10-day plant-collecting trip with Jika, Ethan was happily looking forward to a day of leisure, which was reportedly the way this particular holiday was to be celebrated. The only activity to which Ethan aspired, other than a long afternoon nap during which, in contrast to the previous night, he hoped to not be disturbed, was to interview an ancient medicine woman visiting from a longhouse in Ulu Baleh, which is nestled up against the Hose Mountains. Ibu Luni was regionally famous for her knowledge of plants and Ethan had many questions for her.

As was often the case, much of the men's conversation concerned the strange ways of animals. To these hunters, knowing all they could about animals was critical to their ability to put food on the dinner table or, in their case, on the floor mat around which Iban families ate. The theme of this morning's conversation was a bit odd insofar as it was about the

South American tapir, an animal that they were unlikely to ever encounter. When they were off in the jungle, Ethan had told Jika about the curious preference of tapirs to defecate in water, something he'd learned about the hard way, complete with intestinal distress. Ethan was impressed that although he and Jika had only arrived at dusk the previous evening, all the men seemed to have already heard the story. This peculiar natural history observation had inspired considerable curiosity when shared with the other men in the longhouse.

Ethan confirmed the tapir story and provided some more graphic details, which everyone appreciated. After sitting quietly for a few minutes in contemplation, Malang quipped, "Perhaps those aren't American tapirs, but really Melenau tapirs," to which the rest of the men erupted in laughter. Deriding the Melenau people who lived along the coast was a long-standing tradition among the Iban. That tradition had taken on new vigor as the logging concession of a Melenau logging baron and politician encroached further and further into territory that Iban claimed but for which they had no formal title. That the Melenau were Muslims gave them natural ties with the Malay political party based in Peninsular Malaysia but whose tentacles were extending rapidly into Sarawak. Many of the Iban's jokes about the Melenau related to the latter's reliance on palm sago as their staple food, whereas the Iban preferred rice or even cassava. Iban considered sago a food of last resort. The Iban were also amused by the Melenau's construction of floating outhouses, which was the basis for the joke about Melenau tapirs.

After the laughter subsided, Kalang, perhaps the oldest man present, said, "I followed a tapir once for an afternoon but never saw it crap in a creek," which elicited more laughter from the men but made Ethan sit bolt upright.

Tapir fossils were known from Borneo from as recently as the last global glacial advance when the island was connected to Peninsular Malaysia, Java, and Sumatra to form the now divided Sundaland, but believed to be long-since extinct. It was unlikely that Kalang was mistaken in his identification given that, unlike the uniformly grey American tapir, Malaysian tapirs are black in front and pure white on their hindquarters. Their long and flexible noses and large feet, with four toes in front and three in back, also distinguish them from other beasts.

Ethan curiosity about this claim was heightened by the frequency with which the Iban compared him to a tapir, on account of his comparatively prominent nose. If tapirs had really been extinct for thousands of years, why did that species figure so prominently in their stories?

When Ethan asked Kalang for some details, the old man thought for a while and then started his story. "I was just a young boy at the time, and out hunting with my father. We were nestled above the saltlick in Ulu Akabau waiting for mousedeer or whatever—it was mid-afternoon and we didn't expect any action until dusk. Suddenly, from out the bush, a tapir emerged, calm as can be. My father and I just looked at each other and then watched that great animal enjoy the lick. After about 15 minutes he had sated himself, and it was a male, by the way," he said in such a way as to elicit guffaws from the crowd, then continued. "We followed him until it was too dark to continue. He must have covered nearly 10 km in less than two hours, but never seemed to be hurrying. Strangely enough, he went in a straight line...didn't follow the creeks or ridges or anything."

These embellishments on a story that everyone, other than Ethan had heard a dozen times before, served to stimulate more discussion among the men. Ethan was about to interject a question when a young boy gestured for him to come. The boy was young enough to move seamlessly between the societies of women and men, and was charged with informing Ethan that Ibu Luni was ready to speak with him.

Jika once referred to Ibu Luni as a "witch doctor," but with none of the negative connotations of that term. She was regionally renowned for her knowledge of plants, and Ethan had been hoping for months to interview her and now he had his chance. The other men were well aware of Ethan's interest in Ibu Luni and expected the upcoming interaction to be a great source of amusement, at least for them but probably not for Ethan. In a close-knit community that lives mostly disconnected with the outside world, without electricity, radios, or many books, there is plenty of time for gossip, an undertaking at which the Iban excelled. The activities of nearly everyone in the 50-plus family longhouse were carefully monitored, with observations shared during the long evening chats when there was nothing better to do.

As he got up to join the women and meet the Ibu Luni, the men started to tease him. The general theme of their merriment, which surprised Ethan, was that he was in danger of an unspecified nature. When he enquired about what sort of threat he faced, many of them grabbed their crotches and rolled backwards in gleeful mock pain while laughing uproariously.

Ethan watched their antics for a minute or so but then asked one of the calmer men for an explanation. What that man said about the beauty and sexual prowess of the woman he was about to meet by no means matched the old crone he saw sitting regally among the other women. He had glimpsed her before and noted that she seemed well into her 70s and hardly seemed like a "man-eater." Like other men raised by ferocious mothers, he was already wary of women alone and especially by groups of them, so he naturally approached cautiously. Sitting on woven *pandan* mats on the split bamboo floor, the group of about thirty were stratified by age, with the medicine woman and older women in the center and the young girls on the periphery. Ethan was pleased that the one exception was that his friend Singa sat just to the right of Ibu Luni, who was looking down into her lap while weaving something from fine plant fibers. Ethan worried that his fluency in Iban was unlikely to be sufficient if the old lady started to use too many colloquialisms with which he was unfamiliar, but Singa could help them communicate. Singa's position in the group also reflected her status as medicine woman-in-training, already a well-respected midwife, and the likely inheritor of Ibu Luni's role in their community. Singa's knowledge of medicinal plants would also help if Ethan had the hoped for opportunity to explore this topic in detail with the older and more experienced woman.

Ethan's interests in the Iban's pharmacopeia were far ranging, but he was particularly intrigued by their approach to contraception. Once she was confident about Ethan's motives, Singa had shared what she knew, but there were interactions among the plant components and specified sequences that the tinctures had to be imbibed and applied that were beyond her understanding.

Ethan carefully wended his way through the group of seated women, bent over at the waist with his hand before his feet to show respect. A few seconds after he sat down in front of Ibu Luni, she looked up at him square in the face, her eyes widened in seeming surprise, and she emitted an audible gasp, which caused some of the women to look at her with concern on their faces. While continuing to stare directly into his face as if mesmerized, she took a deep breath, reached out and gently touched his leg, whispered something inaudible, and then went silent. After a few more seconds, she took a deep breath, shook herself slightly, and gave Ethan a smile that from a younger woman he was sure would have been devastating.

Ethan was both startled and confused by this little interchange. He was accustomed to eliciting stares when first encountering an Iban, and had even inured himself to their frequent comments about his ugliness. He had to remind himself that in the society of Iban, he was the odd one. The older Iban still followed the tradition of filing their teeth flat by rubbing them with silica-rich leaves of the water vine, their noses were nearly flat, they were covered with tattoos, and the earlobes of the oldest women hung down to almost their shoulders, stretched by earrings of substantial heft. Given their appearance, he had to accept that it was natural for them to make fun of his monkey-sharp teeth, white skin, and his relatively large nose. But this reaction by Ibu Luni was different—it seemed to be one of recognition, not horror.

Singa was also unsure of what had just transpired, but she knew much more about Ethan's family than Ethan himself. She also knew her social obligations in this meeting, which she proceeded to fulfill by formally introducing Ethan to Ibu Luni. She then explained who Ethan was and mentioned his interest in plants, all of which the medicine woman undoubtedly already knew. When she mentioned that he was spending a lot of time in the forest with Jika, Ibu Luni nodded as if she approved of that relationship.

While Singa was speaking, Ibu Luni continued to inspect Ethan. When the formal introduction was over, she asked Ethan a series of questions about his family, which was typical of the Iban and therefore not surprising. She started by asking about his family name, as if that would help place him in her cosmology.

After he explained that the name Yarrow related to the plant that Achilles, the mythical Greek warrior, carried into battle as a wound treatment, she nodded in such a way that Ethan was not sure she meant to indicate that the story made sense or that she'd heard it before. She then asked, "And do you come from a family of warriors?"

"I'm not a warrior, but my father fought in the Second World War. Now he's an accountant and plays the piano."

"Where did he fight?" Ibu Luni then asked.

"My father never talked much about the war," Ethan explained, which caused her to frown, "but I know that he was in China, in a place called Kunming." She seemed interested, so he continued. "He was in charge of turning over supplies to Chang Kai Shek and his Kuomintang so they could fight the Japanese." He though that this would not mean anything to Ibu Luni or anyone else present, but they still seemed to want more details, as if they knew part of the story and wanted to hear the rest. When he mentioned that his father flew back and forth over the high mountains between India and China, at least the older women nodded, seemingly in comprehension. This was more than he usually told people about his father's war experiences and Ethan thought that Ibu Luni would now be satisfied, but she continued to probe.

"Was he wounded?" she wanted to know.

"Yes," Ethan replied, and then recalled the little he knew of that family story. "He was in the Flying Tigers, which is odd because he hates to fly and never seemed to me like much of a tiger. He was trained as a radio operator, probably because he's a musician, certainly not because he's mechanically inclined," Ethan jibed. "Fortunately for him, the Army mostly had him on the ground working as the accountant for this Lend-Lease program from which the Chinese were thieving. But one day towards the end of the war, he was ordered to action at the last minute. I remember he said that when he did have to fly, he made it a practice to sit on his thick accounting book from college because the metal seat in the C-40 got so cold when they were up over the Himalaya. But that one time he didn't have time to grab his book and, sure enough, on the way back from India, when they were flying over Burma, he took some flak from an anti-aircraft gun through the seat and into his bum."

That account of the wounding, the few times he'd heard it told by his father, generally elicited laughter, but these Iban women were dead serious about the incident, about which they chattered among themselves. When they settled down, Ethan continued.

"The plane was disabled, but they made it out of Japanese-held territory and ditched it in a rice paddy. I know that crash landing must have been awful, especially for my wounded father, but he never elaborated. I do know that the flight crew, or what was left of them, met up with some aborigines, from the Nalga Tribe I believe, who helped them to safety. He didn't say much about the Nalgas, who have a reputation for," Ethan almost said head hunting, but after missing a beat, said, "ferocity, but did mention them with fondness sometimes."

With this telling of what he knew about his father's time in Burma, Ethan finally understood the really dark humor behind why his father would always say, 'sorry friend' before sitting down on a bar stool covered in with the faux leather material marketed as 'naugahyde.'

After a slight pause, Ibu Luni asked, "But was he badly injured?" She was obviously enthralled by the story.

"Yes, I guess he was, but as I told you, he never elaborated much. To this day, whenever it gets cold he jokingly complains about the metal in his butt...I guess the surgeons couldn't remove all the shrapnel. My Godfather, his good buddy, used to tease him that he was wounded while escaping from a whore house," which elicited a ripple of laughs among the women as his unusual word choice was explained. "I also remember that on several occasions when my father and I were on an outing in the forest and there were mosquitoes, he would say that it reminded him of Burma. Oh, and another thing," Ethan continued, having himself just put two-and-two together, "when I returned to my parent's home after six months in the Amazon, I'd lost a bunch of weight---my mother was beside herself with concern. Later I heard him reassuring her by saying that I had 20 pounds more flesh on my bones than he did after his 'sojourn in the jungles of Burma,' which is how he referred to it."

"Then what happened?" Ibu Luni asked, again with a tone that suggested that what she wanted was confirmation of a story that she already knew—he was reminded that when telling stories to very young children, it really didn't seem to matter if they'd heard them before.

Ethan wanted to ask Luni about medicinal plants, and was growing frustrated by her co-opting the conversation with all these questions about his family, but he accepted that this was the way of the Iban and continued. "He did say that when he got back to Kunming, he was in pretty bad shape, which I suspect was an understatement. They operated on him there, as well as they could, and gave him plenty of morphine, which kept the pain at bay but then became its own problem." Ethan reflected for a minute, dredging back memories of conversations heard or over-heard as a child. "Apparently, a Chinese friend of his was not happy with the conditions in the Army's hospital, and took my father to his house to recover. He would always laugh about this friend, who must have been his local counterpart in the Lend-Lease work...said he was a crook, but had a wonderful family. He would sometimes tease my mother by speaking reverently about someone he called 'Jade Flower,', whom I believe was his friend's older sister...I think she was the one who helped put my father back together as he was convalescing. Now I remember something else. One time when he was warning me about the dangers of drugs, he mentioned that during the war he had to deal with a morphine addiction. Oh, and my mother would act jealous of this 'Jade Flower' character, but I think she was just glad that there was someone to take care of my dad."

When Ethan mentioned the Chinese woman, he saw Ibu Luni make quick eye contact with another ancient Iban woman, in response to which they both smiled. He wrongly assumed that they were just considering the healing power of women. He was therefore surprised when Ibu Luni didn't ask about his mother, but instead inquired, "And your grandfather, was he a warrior too?"

Ethan realized that if he wanted to extract botanical information from the medicine woman, he would have to first satisfy her curiosity about his family, so he continued. "I didn't know my grandfather very well, he died when I was only 5 or so, but he used to tell stories about being in the jungle, I think somewhere in this part of the world."

"What was his name?" Ibu Luni asked.

"Storm," Ethan replied in English and then added, "which means 'Ribut' in Iban."

When he said the word "Ribut" the women all responded, the older ones in the center of the group by just nodding, but most of the younger ones towards the back by whispering to each other as if this information had special meaning. Ethan assumed it was because the name Storm is unusual, even to Americans, so he explained "He got that name because he was born when his father was supposed to have been passing around the Cape of Good Hope, at the bottom of Africa, on a trading ship, a clipper, bound for the Orient. Antarctic storms are supposed to be especially ferocious down there."

"This Storm fellow, was he a warrior too?" asked Ibu Luni.

"No, I don't think so, he was a commodity trader; he got rich importing rubber from Brazil then *gutta percha* from Malaysia, lost all that money during the depression in the late 1920s, but then made much of it back during the war. I remember that my father would sometimes only half kiddingly call him a war profiteer," to which Ibu Luni shook her head with disapproval, so Ethan changed the topic. "He was full of stories about places where he'd travelled. I also remember that he really liked spicy food."

"Did he have a big family?" Ibu Luni asked, "Do you have many uncles and aunts?"

"No, my father, like me, was an only child," Ethan responded, which elicited a slight smile from the woman, which surprised him.

"And with how many children is Tuan Yarrow blessed?"

After Ethan responded that he had none, Ibu Luni contemplated this information for perhaps a minute with downturned eyes before looking up and asking him a question. She employed an extremely idiomatic phrase with which Ethan had to struggle to translate but that was immediately understood by all the women sitting around listening. That phrase might best be translated as, 'you don't have but know how to make?' By the time Ethan figured out what she'd asked, the women were in hysterics. Ethan watched with a mixture of awe, embarrassment, and then distress as one after another, including his friend Singa, shrieked with irrepressible glee.

Ethan's consternation about the mirthful melee was partially due to his not really knowing how many of these women were among the nocturnal visitors to the small converted storeroom he occupied when visiting the longhouse. Singa was a regular, and he enjoyed their boisterous love-making, but given the complete darkness in his room, he wasn't sure just how many of these women were laughing because they knew the answer to the posed question from very personal experience. Although he was not a frequent blusher, he could feel the blood rushing to his cheeks, which served to provoke even more laughter—even Ibu Luni smiled broadly in triumph.

It took a few minutes for the women to calm themselves, and Ethan could finally feel the blush leaving his cheeks, but the medicine woman was apparently not yet finished tormenting him. While he was looking elsewhere, she reached over and started to lift his sarong, seemingly to get a glimpse of his male equipment. Ethan of course stopped her and sputtered something, but Ibu Luni just looked at him with a mischievous smile on her deeply lined face. Meanwhile, her act caused another round of hilarity among the women, some of whom had not recovered fully from the first.

Through the pandemonium, as Ethan suffered, Ibu Luni sat demurely with an amused look on her face. While the women pulled themselves together again, Ethan decided that if he did get a chance to ask any questions, he would steer clear of contraception. But before he could ask his first question, which was to be about the use of *lembah* fruit as an artificial sweetener, the old woman said, "All this talking has made me hungry. Perhaps we can take a walk tomorrow morning and discuss some plants." With that she started to get up and Ethan did likewise, with the giggles following him as he traversed the length of the longhouse back to the gathering of men. He'd definitely not succeeded in directing the interview the way he'd intended, but instead bore the brunt of her good-natured teasing.

Although the Iban men at the other end of the verandah always made it a point to disregard the goings on at the other end of the verandah, the shrieks of laughter from the women had drawn their full attention. They had no way of knowing what had transpired, but they figured that Ibu Luni had been true to form at Ethan's expense. When Ethan re-joined them they were all trying to hide their smiles so as to not cause the young man more anguish. Finally, the old man Malang said simply, "It seems like the man-eater struck again."

Ethan nodded and then, laughing at his own fate, responded simply, "She is indeed a tigress."

In response to this comment, the men all laughed good-naturedly. They half-hoped that Ethan would tell them what had happened but, failing that, they knew they could extract the full story from their wives and sisters.

Ethan had no intention of telling how the old woman had teased him, but he was curious to explore the peculiar reaction to his mentioning of his grandfather so he asked, "Does *ribut* mean anything in Iban other than 'storm'? I ask because of the peculiar reaction of Ibu Luni and the other women to my mention of my grandfather Storm, which translates as *ribut*."

In reaction to this question the men looked at each other, seemingly to see who would respond. Finally, Kalang answered: "Yes, in Iban *ribut* means storm, but as in *Bahasa Orang Puteh* (white people language), we also use it as a person's name. There was a famous Iban warrior by the name of Ribut, but Jika's the one to tell you about him—owes him his life, or so the story goes."

At this, all eyes turned to Jika. After a moment's pause, he started his account by confirming that Ribut had indeed saved his life. The story was familiar to everyone but Ethan, but it was a favorite of theirs so they all sat back to listen.

Jika began by explaining, "It was early in the season of the southwest monsoon in 1945. I was out on a patrol with Ribut and two other Iban men from the First Division. I was only 15 at the time, but already big..."

To Ethan's surprise, the old man Kalang interrupted Jika with a hoot of laughter and then said, "Jika, big? Please! You were never big," which caused all the other men to laugh.

This sort of derogatory banter was one of the reasons Ethan was drawn to the society of Iban. In interactions with most Chinese and Malays, in contrast, one had to be exceedingly careful to avoid causing the loss of what was usually translated as "face" or self-esteem but connoted more than either. The importance of saving face was reflected in an expression Ethan learned in a course on oriental religions he took as an undergraduate student: *ren hou lian, shu hou pi*, which translates 'men can't live without face, trees can't live without bark.' As the Iban men continued to tease each other, Ethan reflected on the fact that while Iban people undoubtedly cared about face, that state seemed to be enhanced by their ability to absorb insults, at least those made by friends. He also wondered again whether the shared histories of invasion and conquest of both Iban and American people could explain their similarities in character.

As the conversation resumed, Ethan reflected on the fact that Jika was indeed a small man, even for an Iban. Although he looked up to the man in many ways, he stood more than a full head taller. As Jika smiled in acknowledgement of the comments, Kalang continued, "Ribut, now he was big, but you've always been more of a mouse deer with the spirit of a tiger."

"Okay, point well made" Jika conceded, laughing along with the rest, and Ribut was a big man—nearly as big as the professor here, and equally ugly," he chided Ethan. "For you young men who, unfortunately, never had the chance to meet my protector, there was something about Ribut that everyone noticed other than his size. I'm not sure how to explain it—kind of like he was his name—he had a wild streak that was awe-inspiring. The Professor here has plenty of *kuasa* (force, power)," he said, gesturing to Ethan, "but with Ribut it was something else, something latent but nevertheless evident; he seemed invulnerable. Only once in my life did I see the full manifestation of that something, and it was terrible to behold. That was on the afternoon he saved my life. But wait, I'm getting ahead of myself. Let me explain for Ethan here that after the Japanese killed my mother and father in 1942, it was mostly Ribut who raised me, with some help from Ibu Luni. I'd been joining him on patrols for a few months, and I cherished that time with him."

"We'd been tracking a squad of Japanese soldiers up river from Kapit. Isn't it ironic that they'd been sent out on a special patrol to pursue us, which they believed to be an elite troop of 50 well-armed head-hunters with mystical powers! After we'd led them far into the forest and were pretty sure they were lost, we turned the tables and had them running scared. After about a week their squad of twenty was down to six and all in bad shape physically and worse shape psychologically. It might sound cruel to you now, but we amused ourselves sometimes by tossing sticks into the undergrowth, just to watch them frantically fire off their guns."

"We too were running out of provisions, it was late in the afternoon, and it was clearly time to finish them off and head home. We'd encircled their miserable camp and were closing in for the kill but were not yet all in position. One of the Japanese soldiers must have eaten some rotten sushi," Jika joked, "because he came crashing out into a patch of palms where I was hiding and dropped his trousers right next to my head. He didn't see me, but when he let loose an awful stream not a foot from my face, I must have made a sound. In any case, before I could do anything, he jumped up and shouted before I silenced him. When his comrades heard him and saw me, they started shooting wildly and one of them managed to hit me in the shoulder, which spun me around and knocked me down—it was like getting punched, really hard."

"When I looked up, five Japanese soldiers were standing around me looking at me with blood lust in their eyes. I was sure I was a goner, and that death at their hands would not be pleasant."

"It's hard to describe what happened next, but all of a sudden, Ribut was there like the wrath of God screaming at the top of his lungs" he said, now speaking directly to Ethan. "Do you remember when we were clearing the forest for my rice field a few months back? Remember what it was like when you felled the big tree into that patch of smaller trees that were all laced together with vines?"

Ethan recalled that experience quite well. When he finally felled the 'kingpin' tree and it pulled down its notched neighbors, the pandemonium that ensued was awe-inspiring, which was exactly the image that Jika wanted to evoke.

"It was too fast for me to tell you exactly what happened, but I know he shot one, then his gun must have jammed because he stabbed another with it...no bayonet mind you, with the damn barrel. Then he went to work with his parang while the dwindling huddle of soldiers blasted away with their guns, luckily not hitting either of us; it was over in seconds. By the time our friends came running up, the soldiers were all very dead. Ribut was terrifying, even to me, and I was the one he was saving," Jika related, and then shook his head as if he still found the spectacle unsettling. "It was only then that I realized that I hurt like hell and must have passed out from lack of blood. The next thing I knew, it was a day later and I was looking up into the face of Ibu Luni, the Man-Eater you just encountered." At that memory he smiled and added, "And I assure you that back then she was even prettier than she is today, but just as formidable."

Chapter 15. FETCHING ROXANNE'S YOUNGER SISTER

Excerpt from an aerogram from Ethan Yarrow in Kuching, Sarawak, to his parents in Chevy Chase, Maryland:

22 November 1971
Dear Mom and Dad,
I just sailed from Bintului to Kuching with a group of delightful local seamen on a dhow-like ketch called a pinisi. Okay, it was really a decrepit junk crewed by Bugis pirates, but good people at heart. They taught me some innovative sailing techniques and I taught them a few rather naughty halyard shanties. Those songs really help when raising a sail made from woven strips of pandan leaf; damn thing weighs a ton. But my reason for sailing wasn't recreational but more a family matter. I brought Roxanne's sister Lucille back with me to Kuching. She'd been abandoned and was in poor shape, but I'm sure that with some tender loving care, we'll get her going again...

After his morning bath in a nearby creek and a light breakfast of leftover rice and fresh fern fiddleheads, Ethan left Jika and his dog Guapo in the forest outside of Sebuah. They'd walked overland from Belaga, to which his compatriot planned to return after he finished some business in the town. Jika also needed to finish processing the bearded pig he'd darted the previous day.

Ethan was fascinated by the technique Jika used to hunt that bearded pig. He and Guapo knew that there was a small herd around, but had been unable to get close enough to shoot with his blowgun. That day Jika left Guapo with Ethan in the camp, about which the former was not pleased, and went off into the forest himself armed with a bag full of stones he'd collected from the stream bed. After a few hours of sitting silently on a small knoll above a swampy patch in which there were plentiful pig signs, he smelled them coming. Instead of remaining quiet, he started to throw the stones in ways that maximized the noise they made as they fell to the ground. Suspecting that what they were hearing was the sounds of fruit being dropped by a troop of macaques feeding up in the canopy, the herd drifted towards where Jika sat with his blowgun ready. His aim was true, and a young male squeaked when he felt the dart enter his neck. At that point, Jika jumped up from his hiding place shouting and waving his arms, which caused the herd to stampede off into the forest. The dart poison he used was strong enough to take down even a large boar, but to accelerate its effect on the smaller animal, he needed it to panic to increase its heart rate. He had no trouble tracking the stampeding herd, and after less than an hour, he caught up with the darted animal. By late afternoon he was back in camp with the pig carcass draped over his shoulders. They all ate very well that night, but Guapo outdid himself to the point that he was unstable on his feet.

The next morning when Ethan headed into Sebuah, in addition to carrying three large bundles of alcohol-soaked plant samples wrapped in plastic, he was carrying strips of dried and salted mousedeer jerky from a successful hunt earlier in the week. He figured that the meat would be good for his upcoming sail from Bintulu to Kuching. He had arranged to have Lucille, a 1948 model single-cylindered Norton, crated up and shipped to Kuching on a coastal trading ship but he wanted to personally accompany the cargo.

Ethan had not yet seen Lucille, but had heard from the mechanic friend of Bernie Chan that she was in terrible shape. He expected that they'd never get her running again, but that she'd be a good source of spare parts for Roxanne.

Lucille's crate would eventually be used to carry Roxanne, boxes of rattan specimens, and Ethan's few other belongings when he eventually returned to the States. He expected to continue to do field work in Sarawak for another year, but took Lucille's surprise appearance to prepare in advance for his departure. In keeping with an old family tradition, he had the crate constructed carefully from beautiful wood that he'd use at home to make furniture. In this case, the wood was *merbau* (*Intsia palembanica*), a deep red heavy hardwood that the timber merchants had trouble selling.

On the mostly unpaved road from Sebuah to the coastal town of Bintulu, Ethan hitched a ride on a truck with a mill-bound load of logs. While they bumped along for several hours, he was dismayed to see the recent destruction along the road. Near Sebuah the forest had obviously been logged hard, perhaps more than once, apparently in anticipation of clearing. As they travelled towards Bintulu the clearings got larger until, for the last two hours of their trip, both sides of the road were deforested as far as he could see and the forest replaced by row after row of African oil palms. Every half hour or so they would pass through a forlorn little village of wooden houses on the banks of a stream. Near the houses were a few fruit trees and some vegetable gardens, with sago palms in the wet spots, but otherwise little forest had been spared conversion. The presence of sago palms indicated that they were Melenau villages. Ethan wondered why even the Melenau people hadn't been able to retain more of their land given that the Chief Minister and many of his cronies were members of that relatively small tribe.

It was hard to converse over the roaring of the engine, and the driver had to concentrate to avoid the many large potholes. Finally, when they stopped to buy some *mangosteens* in a roadside stand, Ethan learned that the driver was from Long Seridan, an Iban village near the Brunei border. He had been working for the timber concession for several years, but had only recently been elevated to the job of truck driver. When he learned that Ethan was friends with Jika, of whom he'd heard, he opened up completely as if they were old friends.

The company for which he worked was as an example of the government's successful campaign to promote business development among the *Bumiputra*. When Ethan asked about his boss the man laughed and explained that although nominally owned by a Malay man from Kuala Lumpur, the 'Ali Baba' company's real owner was a Cantonese Chinese and the logging subcontractor was a local Foochow Chinese. When Ethan asked about the sustainability of the logging operations, his new friend was initially confused but then explained that the owners had no intention of staying in the logging business. Instead, they were using the profits from the sale of the timber to pay for clearing what remained of the forest to prepare the land for oil palm.

As they sat in the shade of a tree eating *mangosteens,* Ethan remarked that some of the logs on the fully loaded truck looked under-sized. Although the ends of each log carried several stamps and paint marks, several were clearly below what he knew to be the minimum cutting diameter. He wondered whether the driver would be fined when they approach Bintulu and passed a checking station run by the Forest Department. Again the driver was initially confused by the line of questioning, but then with a laugh he employed an expression in Iban that might best be translated, 'were you born yesterday?'

Sure enough, not half hour later the driver pulled over at a little wooden hut on the roadside that prominently displayed a somewhat tattered Malaysian flag with the symbol of the Forest Department stenciled on the wall. As the dust settled, a somewhat rotund man in a disheveled Forest Department uniform waddled out of the hut in which he'd obviously been napping. He nodded to the driver and glanced at Ethan with curiosity before walking around to the back of the truck for a cursory inspection of the tags on the logs. On a clipboard he ostentatiously carried as a symbol of officialdom, he wrote something before coming back over to the driver, from whom he received a sealed envelope. With that, Ethan and the driver climbed back into the cab for the last bit of their trip to the sawmill on the outskirts of Bintulu.

"How much did that cost, if you don't mind me asking?"

"Oh, he's a cheap one. Only 50 *ringgit* (about $15 US)," the driver replied without hesitation. From his perspective, this charge was normal and expected.

Given that a daily wage from the Forest Department was somewhat less than that amount and figuring that a dozen or more trucks passing every day, Ethan calculated that the man was doing a good side business. What he didn't realize was that more than half of that sum, which had been negotiated in advance, would go to his immediate supervisor, who would then have to share a portion with his boss. The logging concession owner accepted these payments as just another cost of doing business. He only complained when the governmental officials changed, which would lead to re-negotiation of the completely unofficial fees.

"Do you know for how much the logs we're carrying are worth?" Ethan asked, not at all sure that the driver would know the answer. Numeracy varied tremendously among Iban, but this man was obviously quite adept.

"Let's see," the driver mused, "we're carrying about 50 cubic meters, and a cubic meter sells for 50 dollars, so that's, what, 2500 U.S. dollars, right?"

Ethan was surprised by the driver's knowledge but even more so by the sale price reported, which was less than half the going market price. When he pointed out the discrepancy to the driver, the response was a variation on the 'born yesterday' phrase followed by further explanation.

"Sure, on the open market these logs would sell for $120 per cubic meter—hell, it probably cost them more than $50 per cubic meter to harvest."

"So?"

"Okay, let me explain. First of all, we're carrying 50 cubic meters but the manifest says it's only 25. The logger pays royalties on a volume basis, so that under-declaration makes sense, right?"

After Ethan nodded he continued. "He also pays a tax on profits, so keeping his profits down also makes sense."

"Sure, but why sell the logs so cheaply?" Ethan asked.

"Well, the Chinese guy who really owns the logging operation also owns the sawmill, so he's basically selling the logs to himself," he explained. "So why charge himself the fair market price for the logs?"

That explanation gave Ethan plenty to think about as they approached Bintulu and the road deteriorated further. That deterioration resulted from recent developments in the region that included paving of the major roads at least to the outskirts of town. For a few months after paving, road conditions were great, but then the potholes started to appear. Apparently the road contractor had failed to appropriately prepare the roadbed and then skimped on concrete. The result was that only a year after paving the potholes were sparser than in the dirt road but sharper-edged, deeper, and thus more treacherous.

In the two years since oil and natural gas were discovered near Bintulu, the influx of money and people had caused a building boom and major population influx into what was formerly a sleepy fishing village. Olfactory evidence of this development was clear long before reaching the limits of what was now a small city. Buildings were going up, but the government was slow to install proper sewage systems, and garbage often went uncollected.

When the road approached the Kemena River, along which it ran for the last few miles into the city, factories started appearing. First was a palm oil refinery in the final stages of construction; it would soon be processing fruit from the soon to be extensive plantations, the oldest of which were coming into production. Next were three sawmills, two of which had recently been upgraded to also produce veneer. Some of the wood to feed those mills was from managed forest, but the lion's share came from areas being deforested to make way for oil palm.

As the driver slowed to pull into the second sawmill Ethan jumped down and walked the rest of the way into town. Along the way he passed a gigantic and gaudy new mosque being built with government money, a new government office complex that was also under construction, a somewhat dilapidated wooden church of unclear denomination, various roadside food stalls, wooden village houses being engulfed by new concrete blocks of shops, and finally the bustling town center where the streets were choked with cars, trucks belching diesel smoke, pushcarts, and motorcycles. He was directed to the carpentry shop where his crate was being assembled.

The workshop was just off the main street in a dilapidated wooden building surrounded by wooden furniture in various stages of completion and teeming with workers, most of whom were using hand tools. Near the center of the open-fronted shop was the large wooden crate of rich red wood that Ethan had ordered. As he ran his hand over the carefully morticed joints, he was impressed by the work. Before the shop owner could complain about not having charged enough to make the crate, Ethan deflected the conversation by complimenting the handiwork and then commenting, "Nice wood, eh?"

"That *merbau* is hard as a rock," the carpenter responded. "When you wrote that you wanted it drilled and screwed I thought you were crazy, but no one could drive a nail into that wood. But why would anyone want such a heavy crate?"

"Well, sir," Ethan responded, "I'm not as dumb as I look," which caused the carpenter to look up and smile. "I'm going to use this crate to ship my belongings back to the States, and then use the wood to make some really pretty furniture."

"Ah," said the carpenter, "so there's a method in your madness. It will be ready to go in just a few minutes. Want me to get my boys to load it on the truck?"

"Sure, that would be great. And after it's loaded, it would help if one of them stayed to screw down the top."

A few minutes later they headed to the motorcycle shop where Lucille had been discovered, which was only a few blocks away. With the help of two junior carpenters, apparently sons or nephews of the owner, she was quickly loaded. Ethan added his packaged rattan specimens before they set the top of the crate in place and screwed it down. As they drove through town to the quay, the loaded truck drew plenty of stares. There was no passenger seat in the cab so Ethan rode in back with the crate and two young men who were happy to take a ride and avoid work.

To make it to dockside they had to negotiate their way through a crowded riverside market. The truck and driver were recognized, so their progress was not completely impeded. The tall European in jungle clothes, a small backpack woven from rattan, and a blowpipe drew not only stares but also many catcalls from the women hawking fruit, vegetables, meat, and fish, both fresh and dried.

Most of the Malay, Melenau, and Bugis women selling their wares sat on woven mats on the ground while small children clambered about, but there were also a few wooden stalls with Chinese proprietresses. The market was roughly arranged into sections, with mostly fruit sold in one area and fish in another. In the midday sun, the colors were brilliant, from the deep hues of the various fruits to glistening fish to the often mismatched but always brightly colored garments of the women.

The loaded truck wound its way slowly through the throngs of market people. When they finally made it to the riverside where a wide diversity of sailing and motorized ships were moored, the comments from the fishmongers, most of whom were Bugis women, became quite ribald.

"Hey girls, check out the pole on that one," one of the older women said in reference to Ethan's blowpipe but clearly meaning something else.

"It's long, but so so skinny," another one added with a gleeful shiver.

"Yikes, but it certainly looks stiff," said another.

"I wonder if he knows how to use it?" commented an ancient crone with a cackle.

After Ethan jumped down, the women continued in that vein, enjoying themselves immensely, incorrectly assuming that Ethan couldn't understand their patois of market Malay, Iban, and Bugisan. Indeed he missed some words, but the gist of their comments was clear. After listening for a while to their banter, Ethan smiled and made his comprehension clear by commenting back, "Ah but ladies, I assure you it gets much larger when I'm excited. Too bad that all the fish around here are long past their prime and the fruits are over-ripe."

It took a few seconds for the women in earshot to first accept that he was speaking to them in more-or-less the same language and then to understand what he'd said, but then they erupted in laughter. As his response was transmitted from one stall to the next, translated into various languages and probably embellished, a wave of laughter broke slowly across the market.

As the truck backed up to the loading platform and a jury-rigged crane made ready to load the crate, Ethan bought fruit and other supplies for what he expected to be a three-day voyage to Kuching. He caused more of a ruckus by innocently fondling a mango offered to him by an ancient Bugis woman, and by his provocative insistence that he was only interested in melons that were large but firm.

When the crane was finally operational, Ethan watched with trepidation as his precious cargo was hoisted up, swung over the water, and dropped rather roughly onto a space made clear near the bow of one of the older ships, a wooden one with a dhow-like hull and two masts. Realizing that he was to spend the next few days on that worn-out looking vessel, he took a deep breath and jumped aboard only to be greeted with hostile stares by the barefoot crew of a half dozen rough-looking characters. He introduced himself to the man who made evident that he was the captain, who immediately complained about Ethan being late and delaying their departure. Given that the afternoon breezes from the southwest monsoon had only just started and the tide had only just turned, Ethan recognized that this was a bogus complaint, but he nonetheless apologized. After ordering the crew to shove off, the captain retired to his cabin and the bustle of getting underway commenced.

The ship was a ketch-rigged hybrid between a Chinese junk and a Portuguese schooner constructed entirely of wood. Both the bow and stern were raised, there was a pair of aft-rudders, and a small cabin amidships. The deck was piled high with cargo that included wooden crates with unknown contents, sacks of what was evidently dried fish, and reeking stacks of rubber rolled out into mats. On one side of the cabin there was a pile of rattan canes that, from their smell, had been boiled in old crankcase oil. Through an open cargo hatch Ethan could see gunnysacks of coffee, pepper, and copra, along with tins of crackers. Atop the other cargo were several carefully stowed bolts of cloth that, on closer inspection, were of beautiful hand-woven silk, a specialty product from South Sulawesi from whence the ship hailed. With all that cargo it was no surprise that the heavily loaded lateen-rigged craft rode low in the water with only a few feet of freeboard.

As the ship swung out into the current, the crew struggled to raise the mainsail. Seeing an open spot in the line of men hauling on the halyard, he joined them as they heaved the heavy rope that was wound once around a wooden capstan. As they rhythmically pulled to raise the heavy canvas sail, Ethan noticed that other than grunts of exertion, the men were neither singing nor chanting to help them with their work. After a few more pulls, Ethan commenced to sing 'What do we do with a drunken sailor' in his deep baritone.

After listening for a few stanzas, several of the older crewmembers joined in the song. They obviously knew the tune, but the words they used little resembled those of the traditional English halyard shanty. Ethan was reminded instantly of his experience on the Balui River with the Iban. With a few more pulls, more of the sailors joined in the refrain, mimicking as well as they could the words that Ethan was using. Later he would be asked by one of the literate crew to write out all the stanzas. The pirates to a man listened with great interest as he translated the words with help from the youngest of the crew, who seemed quite gifted at languages. When they responded with glee to the stanzas about kissing the captain's daughter in the morning, Ethan added a few even more bawdy new ones of his own, composed on the spot.

The only singer who seemed to know many of the traditional words was a very old man who sat motionless in the shade of the cabin. The thin, shriveled, and much-tattooed man dressed in baggy trousers and a singlet that was once probably white, sat on a coil of rope. He evidently was not expected to contribute to the work on deck and was respectfully ignored by the crew. When Ethan looked over at him, the man gave him a thumbs-up sign and a nearly toothless smile. Ethan wondered whether he was the father of the captain, the ship's owner, or most likely an ancient sailor that they allowed to remain although no longer able to work.

With the frayed and much-patched mainsail raised and the wind stiffening, the crew turned its attention to the foresail. While the mainsail was a patchwork of canvas with bamboo battens, the much smaller foresail was nearly as heavy because it was made from woven *pandan* leaves covered with some sort of shellac. Ethan had read about such sails, but had incorrectly assumed that they were no longer in use.

Having worked together and been entertained with his shanty, Ethan was already more accepted by the crew. Ethan, in turn, started to differentiate the individual sailors. While he realized that they were indeed a motley bunch of pirates, with scars and tattoos covering most of their remaining body parts, they were friendlier than they first appeared. Such had been his experience many times before, but he was nevertheless chagrined that he had once again made assumptions about people's characters from their appearance.

The one exception to the generally rough appearance of the crew was a young boy of no more than thirteen. If he hadn't been shirtless, it would have been hard to determine his gender. His hair was long and tied up atop his head, and his clothes, which were somewhat tattered, were obviously of a high quality. While he participated in the work on deck, the men seemed to pay him deference.

With the sails in place, it was that young boy who showed him around the ship. While they wended their way around the deck, which was crowded with cargo, Ethan was struck by his gracefulness. He was also pleased that the boy was happy to answer all his questions and to offer additional information about the ship and its crew, always with a slight smile on his face and a twinkle in his eye.

After seeing the clutter on deck and peeking into the cabin, from which the captain had still not emerged, Ethan decided that the best place to sleep would be atop Lucille's crate in the bow. With the boy's help, he rigged an awning over his crate as protection from both sun and rain. In addition to being elevated above the deck where he would be out of the way of the sailors, he had seen signs of rats, which he would prefer to avoid. Being in the bow had the distinct advantage of being upwind from the rather pungent smells emanating from the hold and elsewhere.

After being underway for about an hour, they left the *nypa* palm and mangrove-lined river and started to weave their way through the exposed mudbanks out into the open water of the South China Sea. Perhaps in response to the switch from land to sea smells, the captain emerged from his cabin. With a brief glance up at the sails, he strode purposefully over to the ship's compass, peered down at it, and then ordered the helmsman to change course slightly. Ethan had previously noted that compass as seeming entirely out of place on that really junked up junk. It stood nearly waist high in a beautiful teak frame with lots of shiny brass fittings. As he watched the captain peer down at that lovely device, Ethan wondered how such a fine instrument ended up on a coastal trader manned by Bugis. He also wondered why the captain was paying the compass so much attention given that they were still close to shore in the estuary.

Curiosity compelled Ethan to jump down from his crate to ask the Captain about the history of the compass. Instead of responding to what seemed like a reasonable question, the Captain puffed himself up and made it clear that the compass was his pride-and-joy and that under no circumstances should Ethan touch it. By the volume of his voice and the scowl he gave his crew, he made clear that the warning extended to them as well.

Over the following hours it was revealed that it was the Captain's habit to frequently and ostentatiously consult that compass, even though they seldom sailed out of sight of land and obviously navigated by dead reckoning. The captain nevertheless insisted that he was the only one capable of reading the compass and interpreting its mysterious messages.

After stomping around the deck for a while and bellowing various orders to his crew, the Captain again retired to his cabin. The crew, for their part, mostly ignored the Captain's orders and kept about their business of sailing the ship. In the Captain's absence, Ethan took advantage of the opportunity to inspect the compass more closely.

When he looked down at the compass, Ethan immediately noticed that the needle was clearly pointing towards the west. A quick inspection of the near vicinity revealed the reason. Instead of pointing towards the magnetic north, the needle seemed to be drawn towards a dysfunctional but massive metal bilge pump that sat on the deck nearby. To be sure, Ethan slid the pump a few feet and, sure enough, the needle followed it. Fascinated by his discovery, Ethan asked two of crew members who were loitering nearby watching him to lug the pump all the way around the compass. He and some of the other sailors watched with interest as the needle followed the pump, as expected.

Unbeknownst to Ethan and the crew members involved, their activities were observed from the shadows of his cabin by the Captain. Before they'd fully circumnavigated the compass, the Captain was on them, with a roar of rage at their trespass.

That outburst terrified the crew, who were struck dumb by his unexpected appearance. After a few seconds of complete and very uncomfortable silence, the old man sitting nearby burst out in raucous laughter. He'd been fully aware of the Captain's charade and took great glee in its revelation. The privileged position of that old man was made apparent by the Captain's reaction. After scowling at the men, who were straining to keep from laughing, he shook his fist at Ethan and then chuckled along with them.

When the crew settled down, the Captain barked out a few apparently unnecessary orders that elicited the usual lack of reaction and retired again to his cabin. As he passed by Ethan he mumbled under his breath in a slightly threatening tone that the young white man should watch his step.

After they'd sailed on for a few hours and the sun was sinking towards the horizon, Ethan went over to join the old man who had beckoned him from the shade of the cabin.

"'I enjoyed watching you get the best of the old crones in the market," the old man said with a conspiratory cackle as Ethan was sitting down. "They'll be gossiping about you for quite a while."

"Yikes, they are a tough bunch," Ethan said in obvious admiration.

"Our first line of defense they are," the man explained.

"How's that?" Ethan asked.

"Well, if you think they gave you a hard time, you should see what they do to port inspectors," he said and cackled again. "Sometimes those ladies harass those young men in uniform to the point that they turn around and flee back to their offices without having set foot on board. And even if they do successfully run their gauntlet, by the time they get on board, we've had the chance to sort out our papers and lower over the side whatever we don't want them to see."

The Bugis-manned sailing ships that had plied the coasts of Malaysia, the Philippines, and Indonesia for centuries were traditionally involved in both legitimate and contraband trade. Of late, the contraband consisted mostly of tobacco products and alcohol on which stamp duties had not been paid, small quantities of panned gold and gemstones smuggled out of mining areas, and pirated cassettes.

They sat together in comfortable silence for a while, listening to the Captain once again haranguing the crew.

"Don't worry about him," the old man said in reference to the Captain, and then used an expression in mostly Malay that might be translated as, 'his bark is worse than his bite.'

"Your son?" Ethan asked.

"No grandson, or at least the son of the daughter of my wife," the man responded with his characteristic cackle.

"Your ship?" was Ethan's next question.

"At this point, that is less clear," he responded and then continued, "but I am their safe passage."

"Sorry sir, but I don't quite understand."

"I'm the keeper of the papers."

"Sorry, but I still don't follow," Ethan responded apologetically.

The old man then reached inside his baggy shirt and extracted an oil cloth packet. With some drama he then opened it to reveal a bunch of passports and various folded sheets of paper.

"Passports?" Ethan asked.

"Yes and other important documents," he answered and then continued. "Consider what we can do when out at sea and government agents approach in one of their motor launches. First of all, we need to know their nationality."

When Ethan looked at him with curiosity, he explained further. "We worry about our crew being forcibly conscripted. Right now, for example, the Philippines needs sailors. If we make a mistake and show them our Filipino passports, we'll lose half the crew. And then there are the customs boys who want to inspect our cargo and squeeze us for payments. For them, I have these," the man said and held up several somewhat yellowed pieces of paper. "If we're stopped here in Malaysia and I show the officers this letter, they leave us alone—don't even expect a bribe," the man explained with pride and handed Ethan the freshest looking of what turned out to be rather surprising set of official letters of safe passage.

Ethan carefully opened the single page, which was a letter typed on monogramed stationary and addressed to Erna Yassin. The old man confirmed that was his name and Ethan continued to scan the letter. He quickly noted that it was prominently signed by Colonel Sultan Sir Ismail Al-Khalidi Ibni Al-Marhum Major General Sultan Sir Ibrahim Al-Masyhur KBE, CMG, Sultan of Johore. Together with a lot of formalities characteristic of official correspondence in Malay, the letter stated quite emphatically that the bearer, Erna Yassin, as well as his ship and crew, were under the Sultan's personal protection.

"Yikes," remarked Ethan, "impressive! Might I ask how you obtained such a letter?"

"Family connection," the man replied. "The Sultan may act like a Malay, but his roots are Bugis. We're distant cousins, actually, on my mother's side." The old man thought for a minute and then decided to continue with his explanation. "And then there was the time after the war when his son Ismail went out into the world to sow some wild oats, and needed to be rescued. But in all honesty I must report that at the time he didn't appreciate being dragged out of that Batavian brothel nor in being delivered back to his irate father."

Ethan's surprise about the old man's high-level connections was in part due to his ignorance about the history of the Bugis people. He was not aware, for example, that several of the sultans in Peninsular Malaysia were of Bugis origin, as was the vice president of Indonesia and many other high-ranking governmental officials around the region. His assumptions about the Bugis were based on his interactions with really rough bunches of merchants, sailors, and an occasional forest concession worker. Had he known about the ancient Bugisan Empire, he might not have been so prejudiced.

"And are those others also 'safe passage' letters?" Ethan couldn't keep himself from asking, but then immediately felt like he'd overstepped the bounds of courtesy with his direct question.

Not the slightest bit perturbed, the old man affirmed that surmise with a nod of his head and then offered Ethan the other two letters. The first, from Rajah Vyner Brooke (the last White Rajah of Sarawak), commended Erna Yassin for his heroism and stated that he and his crew were under the Rajah's protection. When Ethan glanced up from the letter with a questioning look on his face, the man explained that the Rajah was commending him for rescuing a British pilot and his crew from drowning. The plane had crashed after a bombing run on the Japanese airstrip in Miri. The third letter was in Japanese, but the old man explained that it said the same thing, for the same reason and then laughed. After a minute he explained that they had indeed rescued some drowning Japanese sailors whose ship had gone down. What amused him was that, whereas the Japanese assumed that their ship had been sunken by an allied submarine, it was the Bugis that had launched the fatal torpedo.

After watching the sun set with the old man, with whom Ethan was now entirely fascinated, the two went amidships to eat the evening meal. If any of the crew members were still hesitant about the young American, those feelings were allayed when he shared the mousedeer jerky that he and Jika had smoked. The Captain deigned to accept a piece, but still grumbled at Ethan.

As they stood together at the rail enjoying the cool breeze after eating, Ethan asked Erna Yassin about the young boy. His curiosity had been piqued when he noticed that the boy graciously accepted the mousedeer meat he was offered, but then passed it to one of the other crew.

"He's *Bissu*, and I think he'll be a powerful one," Erna explained and then continued when Ethan expressed no comprehension of what that meant. "Not like you and me, way more important. Let's say you're having trouble with a bad *djin*. A *Bissu* can help you with that problem."

"But I assumed you're all Muslims."

"We are, at least when we're on land," Erna replied with his familiar cackle, "but as long as Sharia laws are not broken, we follow our own traditions."

For the Bugis people, Ethan would later learn, those traditions included the recognition of not just two genders, male and female, but five—*bissu, makkunrai, oroane, calabai, and calalai*. They also believed that for the collective good, the five genders all must co-exist harmoniously. The *bissu* are gender transcendents whose intermediate condition gives them the power to function as go-betweens—between heaven and earth, between men and their wives, and between arguing neighbors. Their connection with the *batin* (inner or spirit) world made them essential for the continued smooth functioning of society.

"But why is he on board?"

"For life experience, but this will be his last voyage. Soon he'll return to his village to practice his craft. While still young, *Bissu* are free to wander with the likes of us—such experiences are good for them, gives them a better idea of the *zaher* (outer world) with which you and I have to contend."

The two men sat in comfortable silence for quite a while, watching bursts of phosphorescence in the wake of the ship, and grabbing the occasional flying fish that landed near them on the deck. After a while, Ethan asked Erna, "Why are we running without lights."

From the darkness, Erna responded simply, "Better to see than to be seen."

After they retired, Ethan spent most of the night comfortably asleep atop his crate with any biting insects kept at bay by the breeze. He was roused near dawn by what sounded like voices coming from over the water. Finally he convinced himself that there were indeed voices and that they emanated from far behind the ship. When he sat up he could see two small lights bouncing along a few hundred yards back in the ship's wake. He jumped down to the deck and made his way to the stern in the wan light of a crescent moon and joined two crew members at the rail.

When he asked one of the sailors for an explanation he was told that a seine net of some fishermen had apparently been snared by one of the ship's rudders. When he enquired about coming about and freeing the net, one of the sailors invited him to wake the Captain to explain the situation, and then laughed nervously.

With the coming dawn, Ethan watched with a helpless feeling as the small boats of the fishermen were dragged towards Kuching at the speed of a few knots. The fishermen were shouting and waving their arms, but to no avail.

When it was nearly full light, the captain stomped grumpily on deck, assessed the situation, and ordered the crew to turn up into the wind to stop the ship so they could deal with the tangle. His manner conveyed more than his usual annoyance, so the men were quick to respond. As the junk slowed the two Melenau fisherman in small wooden *sampans* used the net to pull themselves hand-over-hard towards the now stationary ship. As they approached, they were complaining vociferously about damage done to their net and the inconvenience of having been towed so far from their village.

The challenge of freeing the net from the rudder became clear as the sailors revealed that none were willing to carry out what seemed to Ethan to be a simple task. Even the fishermen, whose net was at risk, were not diving into the water to deal with the problem. Finally, Ethan became frustrated by the stalemate, took off his shirt, and dove in. He quickly untangled the snarled net and then started to swim around, enjoying the water. When it became apparent that the Captain was anxious to get underway, he clambered back on deck with the help of several of the crew.

Later in the morning when he was again chatting with Erna Yassin, he asked why it was such a big deal to untangle the fishermen's net. The old man verified Ethan's suspicion that none of the crew, and probably neither of the fishermen, could swim, at least not well. He then clarified that all could at least stay afloat for a while, but that when a ship went down, which he'd experienced several times, there were always plenty of objects on which to float. Reminiscing, he describe with a laugh the day he spent with his arms around a plastic mannequin he found floating after the ship on which he was a crew went down off the coast of Mindanao. As he related the story, chuckling the whole time, he slipped more-and-more into Bugisan, which Ethan had trouble following. It was only later, after he had a chance to reflect on their conversation, that Ethan realized that the man had said that the mannequin compared very favorably with his first wife in most ways but especially insofar that she wasn't a nag.

That evening they anchored in the estuary at the mouth of the Igan River. Both banks were lined with mangrove trees with prop roots that made it look like they were walking out into the water. Dangling from the branches were two-foot long, cigar-shaped seedlings that germinate while still attached to the tree. When fully developed, the seedlings fall into the water and are carried by currents. Those few that are successful get stranded on a mudflat, take root, and grow up into another tree.

Ethan was surprised that they were stopping for the night given that sailing conditions were still good. When he asked one of the younger sailors, he explained that in the morning they would take on a load of *nypa* palm leaves to be sold in Kuching for roof thatching. He then added without explanation, "Tonight you are in for a treat."

After dinner the crew sat on deck watching night fall. When it was full dark, the moon not having yet risen, Ethan was startled when the forest lining the riverbanks pulsed with light bright enough to read. After a minute or so of darkness, the forest would again alight and daylight momentarily returned. Ethan had read about these synchronous flashing fireflies, but the spectacle exceeded his expectations. He watched in fascination from the deck and then from atop his crate until he finally fell asleep.

When he awoke just after dawn the next morning he saw in the distance what he mistook for a family of otters frolicking in the water. After he walked to the stern for a better look, he could see that they were proboscis monkeys, not otters. The animals did not seem at all alarmed by the presence of the sailboat, and even let the in-coming tide draw them closer.

The Captain joined Ethan at the rail watching the monkeys swimming around and playing. He then indicated that he'd forgiven Ethan for the compass episode by innocently asking him whether they were relatives. That question elicited howls of laughter from the nearby crew, several of whom jumped around imitating monkeys.

The Captain's question was motivated by the protuberant noses of the monkeys, particularly the adult males. That feature had earned them the local name of *monyet belandar*, the Dutch monkey.

Ethan feigned offense, but then laughed along with the Captain and crew as they all watched the animals in fascination.

The large family of monkeys made their way across the river, climbed into the crowns of the mangrove trees, and started to eat the young leaves. At about the same time the junk was approached from the opposite direction by a flotilla of *sampans*. Each of the small wooden boats was stacked with piles of tightly bound palm leaves. Each leaf was woven into an eight-foot long roofing panel. After the fronds were loaded there was hardly a place on deck to walk.

While awaiting the turning of the tide and re-commencement of their voyage, Ethan reclined on his crate and watched the mudskippers (gobies) that populated the river edge mudbanks. He was still enthralled by protuberant-eyed tree-climbing fish that spent so much of their time out of the water. Their antics, presumably inspired by territorial instincts, were also amusing.

Finally they got underway and after another day and night's sail, they arrived at a public dock on the Kuching River on the outskirts of town. After his crate was off-loaded, Ethan arranged to have it transported to Chan Motors and headed home for a shower with fresh water and a bite to eat that wasn't rice with dried fish or mousedeer jerky. It was Sunday, and his cricket team had a game, so after cleaning up and eating, he put on his uniform and rode Roxanne over to the *padang* (field) in the center of town.

When he arrived the 20-20 game was already underway and he joined his team on the pitch. After a few overs, Ethan was called to bowl, which he did with his usual flair and failure. His cricket prowess, what little he could muster, built on his earlier success as a baseball pitcher. He was nevertheless prone to bowling wides and highs that frustrated wicket keepers and cost his team runs. In his favor, his unconventional approach to bowling baffled batters, at least initially, but today the wickets stood for far too long and his fielders had to work harder than was their want.

When a new bowler was called in to replace him, Ethan joined his friend Ian who was sitting comfortably in the shade of a wide-crowned *angsana* tree on the edge of the *padang*. Without a preamble or bothering to ask Ethan about his recent trip, Ian asked, seemingly out-of-the-blue, "Why do you tease your mother so unmercifully?"

"What do you mean?" Ethan asked and then recognized the import of his question. "Oh no, did she call you again?"

"Oh, sorry, did I not mention that she called last week when you were out in the *ulus* chasing Iban girls or whatever it is that you do out there."

"I was collecting data for my dissertation, if you don't mind," Ethan replied with false huffiness, "but what did she want other than to check on her baby?"

"She asked about Roxanne's sister Lucille, the one you rescued from Bintulu and now plan to rehabilitate."

"Oh, that, I suppose I do like to string her along."

"What exactly did you tell her? Your Mum seems to think that you're now saddled with a hopeless case who is riddled with various rots and is otherwise dysfunctional."

"That is all true, right? Lucille is indeed a mess—perhaps more of an organ donor than a functional motorcycle," Ethan responded and then added, "but whatever you think, you have to give me credit for never lying to my mother."

"I know that you don't lie, and neither do I, but she's already worried about your relationship with Roxanne, to whom she seems to have taken a distinct dislike. Now she thinks that you have to contend with her meltdown of a sister."

Ethan responded by trying to change the subject a bit. "Lucille may be a wreck, but did I tell you that her front sprockets are in really good shape...and I think I now have a spare magneto that is probably no better than Roxanne's, but worth a try. Happy to show you when we go back up the hill. I've converted the spare bedroom into a workshop in which I can dismantle her."

"Thanks, but spare me your Pleistocene mechanics," Ian responded and then continued on the previous topic. "While I endeavor to conceal your little secrets without lying outright, I must say it's challenging when she asks a direct question. This time she wanted to know why you sailed and didn't fly from Bintulu back to Kuching when you fetched Lucille. All I could think to say was that Lucille was in no shape to fly, which seemed to mollify her. If that's okay with you, now I want to hear about your adventure. I admit to deriving guilty but very vicarious pleasure from your exploits."

"There's a lot to tell, but lest I forget, I enjoyed my first success as a blowgun hunter."

"What'd you get?" Ian asked with enthusiasm.

"A rat," Ethan responded, "a big fat jungle rat. I shot it right out of the canopy—you would have been impressed."

"And where's my specimen?"

"Woops," Ethan apologized. "We ate it."

"You ate the pelt?" Ian asked in shock.

"I didn't, but Guapo did."

"What sort of dog eats rat fur?"

"A hungry one, I suppose," Ethan responded with a shake of his head.

The friends spent the rest of the afternoon sitting in the shade and continuing to catch up on gossip. As Ethan anticipated, Ian was particularly interested in the five genders recognized by the Bugis, but was also thrilled with his accounts of frolicking proboscis monkeys and synchronous flashing fireflies. When the cricket game ended they joined the team for a beer at the club to celebrate their magnificent loss and then headed to the night market for dinner.

Chapter 16. CANOPY WALKING

Excerpt from an aerogram from Ethan Yarrow in Kuching, Sarawak, to his parents in Chevy Chase, Maryland:

15 December 1971
Dear Mom and Dad,
One treat in Borneo is strolling through the canopy on a walkway constructed by British medical researchers. Of course I only use the facility for research purposes—tracking the flowering and fruiting of canopy trees and vines—but it's really an excuse for spending time up in the "leafy cloudland." I otherwise spend my time gazing up into the canopy from the ground feeling like some kind of seafloor invertebrate. Although recording my data would really only take an hour, I usually spend much of the day bird and monkey watching, and of course taking a nap. The last time I was there I woke up to find myself in the middle of a mixed flock of birds—I lost track at 15 species. I do still wish I could fly, but don't worry Dad, I long ago learned my lesson about launching myself from high places...

Once per month Ethan made his way to Long Mongkos, a Bidayuh village about 60 miles inland from Kuching near the Kalimantan border. For his first few monthly visits he stayed overnight in the longhouse, but since becoming aware of his friend Riska's desire, or at least the desire of her mother that their relationship be sanctified by marriage, he restricted himself to day trips. He liked Riska well enough to not wish on her the sort of life he could provide in America, far from her tightly knit network of family and friends. He even worried about his own return to the States when he would have to complete, revise, and defend a dissertation very different from the one initially approved by his advisory committee.

Whenever he thought about defending his research in front of a panel of senior professors, most of whom he didn't know personally, even calm, cool, and collected Ethan Yarrow suffered some angst. Among academics, even at the ultra-liberal University of Wisconsin, he'd caused a ruckus when he changed the topic of his dissertation from palm taxonomy to the land-rights of the Iban. That change had required aerograms being sent back and forth from Sarawak to arrange for a change in departments and all but one member of his advisory committee. That sort of mid-course switch in direction was almost unheard of, but after his new principal advisor read the detailed outlines of several of Ethan's chapters she, with the help of the really senior professor who remained on the committee, somehow made it happen.

The canopy walkway consisted of boards laid on horizontal aluminum ladders suspended by ropes from a pair of heavy cables anchored to the ground near the ridgetop at one end and to a huge Bornean ironwood tree rooted down in the valley at the other. Intermediate supports were provided by emergent trees along the nearly 500-foot span of the canopy bridge. The walkway was constructed by researchers from the British Army's Tropical Medicine Research Unit, with plentiful help from local tree climbers and suspended bridge makers. The research carried out by the Army doctors was on canopy animals as vectors for scrub typhus and other communicable diseases. After Ethan had censused the trees and canopy lianas (woody vines) for two months, the Army doctors removed the caged chickens along the walkway that they used to sample for mosquito-vectored parasites. Ethan was glad that study had ended because their nearly constant clucking was both distracting and distressing. With the chickens gone, he could enjoy the choruses of native animals, which changed throughout the day, with major shifts at dawn and dusk.

Sleeping on the walkway was a source of great pleasure to the young biologist. Up in the canopy there was a nearly constant breeze in which the walkway swayed. Whether it was an afternoon nap in the shade of an emergent tree or an overnight stay on one of the platforms, waking in the crowns of trees was an experience hard to replicate. These reprieves from life on the ground Ethan enjoyed alone, after having once made the mistake of inviting his friend Riska to join him. Rather than romantic, their night together in the canopy was nearly sleepless because the young lady woke him repeatedly when she was disturbed by events as minor as the nearly silent passing of a slow loris and the gentle rattle of the scales of an ambling pangolin.

The quality of construction of the canopy walkway reflected both modern technology and traditional knowledge. Bidayuh are widely recognized for the quality of their crafts, but the Long Mongkos people were particularly famous for the hanging bridges they constructed over the ravines that surrounded their village in the Penrissen Mountains. Along the mile walk from the end of the road where he parked Roxanne to the longhouse, Ethan had marveled at the quality of the construction of one bridge in particular of the several he traversed. Its total span was well more than 150 feet, which was about half of the drop down from the middle to the surging stream below. The bridge was constructed entirely from materials collected in the forest, principally rattan and bamboo, but as Ethan became more familiar with the Bornean flora, he noticed special uses for other species of lianas as well as the incorporation of hardwoods in some critical places.

The canopy walkway was another mile past the village, but before walking the final stretch, Ethan would always stop for tea and a chat with the ladies of the longhouse and play with the children, for whom he often brought little presents. On his way back, he would typically stop for a late lunch and to talk with the men who, by that time, had returned from their fields, forest, or wherever they spent their workday.

After he climbed up the notched log that provided access to the verandah of the longhouse, he encountered a group of women sitting in their accustomed spot cooking while they wove mats from long *pandan* (screw pine) leaves cut into narrow strips. After admiring their handiwork, Ethan went over to smell the stew they had brewing and then asked his customary question "What's for lunch?"

While still laughing, one of the women said, "You're lucky today, we're making curry for lunch, but it isn't ready yet. If you're hungry, grab some rice from that other pot before you sit and tell us what's new in the world."

Ethan thanked them for their gracious invitation and then sat with them to gossip for a few minutes. He was relieved that Riska was visiting a cousin further in the interior, but her mother Orpa nevertheless made sure to sing her daughter's praises. And then, as sort of an afterthought, she said, "Three Malay fellows were here earlier in the week. They said they were friends of yours and that they wanted to see the sky walk."

"That's odd," Ethan replied, "I can't imagine who they were or why they'd be interested in the canopy walkway. What did they look like?"

"Big, ugly, and mean looking," Orpa responded. "I figured they were up to something so I asked my son Bawi to guide them but also to figure out what they were up to before delivering them to the walkway. He took them by way of the old rubber plantation on the far side of the rice fields west of here."

"But that isn't the way to the walkway," Ethan pointed out.

"Exactly," was the woman's delighted response, "he wanted plenty of time to find out the real reason for their visit. That boy of mine is pretty smart---those chips didn't fall very far from the stump if you ask me," to which the other women catcalled and laughed.

"But what were they up to?" Ethan asked. "Now you have me worried."

"Bawi heard them say that they were going to booby trap the walkway so that when you came along, the bridge would fall and their boss would be rid of a major problem."

"Yikes, now I really wonder who they were and for whom they were working."

"Let me get to that--we don't know exactly who they were, but we have some clues. By the way, you don't have to worry about them having sabotaged the canopy bridge," Orpa recounted, "because once Bawi learned their true mission, he made sure they suffered a lot on his roundabout route. By the time they arrived at the ironwood tree at the bottom of the valley, they were entirely knackered and all were complaining about dying of thirst. One of them had slid down a muddy slope right into a tangle of rattans from which it took a major effort to extract him. And better yet, it was that one with stinging ants. Must have been a terrible thing to witness," she said in mock horror.

The rattan species she mentioned was similar to the *Calamus jikaensis* that Ethan had recently described insofar as it also produced a hollow leaf sheath packed with ants that packed a wallop. If you fall on rattan like that, there's no chance to heed the warning of the staccato drumming of the head-banging members of the soldier caste. Canes from that group of species were not used for furniture, so they were often common even in areas frequented by rattan collectors.

The other women had heard the story before, probably more than once, but they made encouraging noises. They all liked Ethan and didn't want any harm to come to him, but they also shared in Orpa's pride about her son's quick thinking.

"Bawi scrambled up the ladder and encouraged the men to follow him."

"I climbed that ladder once," Ethan admitted, "and it was a terrible experience. The only thing amusing about ascending 125 feet straight up is the signs left by the Limey bastard who designed the walkway."

"What signs?" asked the women, few of whom had actually been on the walkway and certainly none of whom had climbed the emergency access ladder. It was much easier to walk out on the horizontal walkway from where it started on the hillside.

"One asks 'Are your knuckles white', which they obviously are because anyone with any sense grips the rungs for dear life. Another sign says 'Don't look down,' to which the natural response is to do exactly that, which is sure to cause vertigo. But the worst one is about two thirds of the way up—it falsely reports that 'You're not even half-way there yet,' which is totally discouraging. I almost started back down when I saw that one," Ethan admitted and then asked, "but did they make it up?"

"Ah, here comes Bawi now. Let's let him tell you the rest of the story."

After Bawi sat down and was caught up on the telling of the tale, he continued. "Climb? Those fat men? No, not even close. None of them wanted to climb at all, so they argued and finally forced the smallest of the trio to start up while the other two promised to follow closely behind. They were rough looking characters, but they certainly were all terrified of heights. That unfortunate climber hadn't even made it 20 feet when he froze in place--despite the taunts from his ground-based buddies, he wouldn't move. Finally, he climbed slowly down but refused to go up again. After arguing for a while, they finally gave up and shouted up to me that they were ready to go home. I was relaxing up on the walkway, watching and listening to them rant. I figured they hadn't quite learned enough of a lesson so I walked quietly to the end of the bridge and then came home via the trail along the ridgetop."

"You left them to find their way back on their own?" Ethan asked for clarification.

"Sure did, but they'd torn up the ground so much with their boots that anyone could have followed the trail back," Bawi responded and everyone laughed.

Ethan laughed along with the villagers, but quietly worried about this strange turn of affairs. Who would wish him harm? He wondered whether the men were the same thugs he'd heard about months before from Bernie Chan.

Still thinking about the strange events described by Bawi and Orpa, Ethan headed out to the walkway to collect his data. After carefully making monthly checks for flower, fruit, and new leaf production by each of the trees along the walkway for nearly a year, Ethan considered the trees as friends. He remained impressed by that fact that among those 312 trees were 138 species that, by his count, was more than grew in all of eastern North America.

As he walked along with his clipboard dangling from a string around his neck and binoculars in hand, Ethan swept off the boards with his feet; with all the rain, the fallen leaves could be slippery, especially where the various animals that used the walkway had defecated. Ethan was not surprised to see that his slow loris friend Petunia on her accustomed perch in a vine tangle that entwined the lower branches of a tree near the platform where he and Riska had spent the night. He assumed that slow lorises are territorial, but also knew that Petunia's home range centered on a live trap that had recently been removed by the medical research team. She was what mammologists called 'trap happy'; they caught her every time they baited the trap. Her appearance reaffirmed for Ethan the idea that hope springs eternal in the mind of a slow loris. With both hands on his binoculars and not bothering to hold onto the cables for stability, he walked slowly by the primitive primate who moved not at all, but Ethan knew he was being closely monitored. On the railing around the platform he left one of the bananas he'd brought from the village, expecting it to be gone by the time he passed back by. He still hoped to encounter a scaly pangolin, a tarsier, or a troop of leaf monkeys, but they were all much less dependable than the slow loris. He smiled broadly when a family of gibbons commenced duetting from a perch not far down the valley.

While Ethan enjoyed monitoring the behaviors of trees along the walkway, not much changed from month-to-month because most canopy trees in Borneo only reproduce during mast events, and virtually all are evergreen. Although mast fruiting is the rule, there were always a few scattered trees in flower and fruit. On a few trees in his study the same fruits had been hanging for months, apparently not much appreciated by local wildlife. On this visit he was surprised that all that fruit was gone. He noted to himself to ask what might have happened to them when he got back to the longhouse. Despite it being a lovely day, with a nice breeze blowing through the canopy, he was hungry so he decided to forgo his nap and return to the longhouse for lunch.

When he sat down to eat he asked the longhouse folks what had happened to all the fruit. He thought he detected some giggles in response to his question, but they were quickly suppressed. Ethan disregarded the reaction mostly because the promised curry was particularly meaty and quite tasty. After taking a few bites, he asked about the meat. In response to that simple question, everyone burst out laughing but then Orpa revealed that the secret ingredient was fruit bat. It took Ethan a few minutes to make the connection, but then realized that a flock of those huge bats must have passed by and ate all the fruit, but a few ended up in the stew pot. When the Bidayuh finally calmed down, they complained that the bats had also eaten most of their ripening mangoes and bananas.

Chapter 17. EVENING ON THE RIVERSIDE ROCKETS

Excerpt from an aerogram from Ethan Yarrow in Kuching, Sarawak, to his parents in Chevy Chase, Maryland:

10 January 1972
Dear Mom and Dad,
I spent an interesting evening earlier this week with a locally famous lady who lives on a houseboat here in Kuching. I could never get a "bead" on her—sometimes she seemed like a conservative Limey stockbroker, but then she'd say something bawdy and give quite a different impression. Mom, you'd be horrified to see that in a corner of her living room, which otherwise was like a Kasbah in Marrakech, a lava lamp sat pulsating. Just to mix it up more, on the table with the lamp were well-thumbed copies of Anna Karenina in both Russian and French. It was uncanny how much she knew about me—locals here are great gossips but she also quipped that the Yarrows had left a lasting impression on Sarawak. I intended to ask her to explain her comment, but she controlled the conversation and wanted to know more about the cultural and political happenings in the USA, about which she is surprisingly well informed. She wanted to hear about Woodstock, but mistakingly assumed that I was hanging out with Jimi, Janis, and the Grateful Dead. She also somehow knew that I'd participated in that failed attempt to levitate the Pentagon back in '67—I'm certain I never mentioned that escapade to anyone on this side of the Pacific—perhaps it was just a lucky guess.

"Why Bernice, aren't you looking especially lovely this evening," Ethan said smiling as he walked into Chan Motors.

"Why thank you young sir, I have a big date this evening," Bernice responded with an awkward curtsy, clearly tickled by Ethan's complement.

"Is that so? Who's the lucky gentleman?" Ethan teased.

"Ah, he's a prince," Bernice cheerily responded, "none other than our beloved Professor."

"Oh, I think I know the bloke—giant snout, looks a bit like a tapir, is that him?" Ethan asked.

In response to Ethan's question Bernice laughed with what almost resembled the tinkling sound of a young girl, and then the two walked arm-in-arm down towards the river. In her spike heels, Bernice was almost as tall as Ethan, which meant that they both towered over the people they passed on the street. With her decked out in a butt-hugging and very short pink skirt, a purple shirt, and a gold-lame vest, not to mention the rhinestone-studded tiara in her hair, they attracted not a little attention on their way through town, but mostly quick glances and furtive smiles.

After walking along and basking in the attention for a while, Bernice asked, "The Iban girls call you the Tiger of Sarawak but am I correct in my suspicion that you are actually afraid of women?"

Ethan laughed at the question, impressed by Bernice's perspicacity. "If you ever met my mother, you'd know the answer to that question---she can be absolutely terrifying." Ethan said, and then paused to consider what he recognized as a serious question. "So I guess my answer is that you are right."

"Don't worry, Mr. Tiger, I share your fear of women. Heaven knows why they're referred to as the 'weaker' sex—quite the contrary in my experience," Bernice opined.

They walked for a while in comfortable silence, enjoying a slight breeze coming up the river from the South China Sea, wafting with it the smell of the ocean with a layer of mangrove swamp topped with the reek of shrimp mixed with chili peppers and left to ferment in vats on riverside docks. *Belachang* was lovely to eat, but a nose full could still overwhelm Ethan.

"I also know from good sources," Bernice continued, "that you are also always a gentleman." After a slight pause, she added reassuringly, "Don't worry about this evening. Compared to those Iban girls you play with up in the *ulus*, the rocket ladies we are about to visit are all pussycats."

"Iban girls are indeed formidable," Ethan agreed, "and get more dangerous as they age. I'm still recovering from an encounter with an ancient medicine woman a few weeks back. I don't believe I've ever been so ravaged---verbally I mean—in my entire life...an intimidating person, to say the least."

Bernice laughed at that image and then said, "I'm looking forward to introducing you to some of my friends. At this time of day they will be prettying themselves up for their customers. I like being with them while they dress partially because they're always ready with beauty tips, which a girl like me appreciates."

"I really doubt that any of those working girls can hold a candle to you my dear," Ethan said while giving Bernice's arm a squeeze.

Bernice laughed at his obvious exaggeration and then said, "I guess it's true what they say about you."

Ethan looked at her for explanation, so she continued, "That you like big girls."

With that statement, Ethan stopped them both in their tracks, turned to Bernice and complained, "Oh that. Terrible misunderstanding. Cost me several night's sleep and nearly a broken back."

He suspected that Bernice already knew the true story, but he explained nonetheless in an exasperated voice. "My so-called friend Ian spread that rumor—I'm sure that all he knew that all I meant was that back in Wisconsin I grew fond of dancing the polka with large and strong farm women."

"No need to explain to me, I'd be the last person to question your taste. But I agree with you about Ian, he can be quite naughty," Bernice said somewhat wistfully and then looked off into the distance as they recommenced walking.

Ethan chose not to explore Ian's sex life, which he suspected was more colorful, or at least more diverse than his own.

As they approached the quay, Bernice's voice reverted to that of Bernie, and he said in a serious tone, "We're early, but if we run into any Aussie miners, let's give them a wide berth."

"Why, what's going on?" Ethan asked. "I usually like Australian blokes. Big fellas, but mostly friendly." After a few seconds he continued, "Other than the Vietnam vets, who can be a bit prickly with Yanks like me."

"I'm not sure if these fellows are prickly, but I know they're up to no good that whatever it is it somehow concerns you."

"Now you have piqued my curiosity, please explain," Ethan insisted.

"The girls have been pumping the miners for information. They reportedly work for a company called Icy Mountain Mining and Engineering. The girls figured that they'd found gold or something and want a piece of the action. But it turns out that they are interested in aluminum. What seems really odd, and I haven't been able to figure out, is that they aren't planning to mine bauxite here in Sarawak. Instead, they want to process ore here that they bring from Australia and New Caledonia. From what I know about aluminum, it must take a lot of energy to smelt it, but where could they get that sort of energy here in Sarawak?"

"One source would be a large hydroelectric dam. There are plenty of rivers here, but no dams," Ethan said, hesitated, and then added with a gulp, "yet."

Somehow Bernie effortlessly transitioned back into Bernice, who then said, "But we're on a date and shouldn't be discussing such serious matters. And anyway, here we are," she said brightly as they approached the first houseboat.

"Let me help you," Ethan said, offering her his hand as she walked across a rickety board that served as a gangplank.

The collection of gaily painted houseboats tied up along the riverside were in places lined up two or three wide. Each was 10-12 feet wide and 30-40 feet long, and outfitted with a small open deck and a large cabin. One of those decks was decorated to look like an ocean liner, another like a sport fishing boat, and all were strung with colorful lights. The brightly painted cabins had window boxes with flowers and colorful curtains. Many had large windows facing the gangways along which customers would walk and inspect the offered merchandise. This early in the evening the windows were not occupied because, as Bernice had explained, the ladies were still busily preparing themselves.

The houseboat onto which Bernice and Ethan first stepped hadn't stopped rocking before a half-dressed Chinese woman came rushing out to greet them. She gave Bernice a peck on the cheek, but never took her eyes off Ethan who, in turn, had trouble taking his eyes off her half-revealed splendors. Adjusting the neckline of her robe so as to be only slightly less provocative, she asked, "and who is your handsome date this evening?"

"Please allow me to introduce The Professor. Ethan, this is Florencia."

"Ah, I'm happy to finally meet you," Florencia gushed, "I've heard so much about you. Welcome to my humble home."

Ethan was taken aback by her familiarity but by no means was offended.

"The pleasure is all mine," Ethan responded politely.

"And that's our business. But I understand you're here on a serious anthropological expedition, not to indulge," she said with a sigh and a pout.

How Florencia knew this mystified Ethan, but he suspected that Bernice had long since broadcast their plans for the evening. His feelings about prostitution were convoluted, and he had actually never indulged, which few of his friends believed. In some ways he considered the world's oldest profession demeaning to both the women and the men involved, but also worried that his Puritan roots were showing.

"I am sorry to miss the chance to take you for a ride," she said with a lewd wink, "but perhaps some other time. Now I will let you get on your way. Do enjoy your visit. I know that Miss Jasmine is looking forward to meeting you."

Ethan had only a vague notion about this Jasmine person, and was increasingly aware that this evening's experience, like so many he had in Sarawak, was not going to be anything like he expected. As was his custom, when life seemed to be spinning out of control, his reaction was to get comfortable and go along for the ride. But more and more frequently of late he felt that his life was scripted and that he alone was denied prior access to the story.

"Nice to see you Florencia—and you do look lovely, but we do need to be moving along. I want to be sure that the Professor gets to enjoy the sunset," Bernice said and gently pulled Ethan by the arm to the gangplank leading to the next houseboat.

After they walked past a few houseboats where the proprietresses were presumably occupied indoors they stepped onto one where they were confronted by a small Ceylonese woman with nearly black skin and lovely European facial features. Bernice stepped in front of Ethan defensively and said with obviously feigned annoyance, "Bertrille, please push those black melons back into your bodice—your cups runneth over and the Professor isn't buying."

The woman laughed while she sighed and pulled up her shirt to cover her ample bosom. With a twinkle in her eye and a heavy Tamil accent, "But I know that these white men prefer dark meat."

In a haughty tone that was clearly assumed, Bernice responded, "I do believe that the Professor has better taste than you infer, but in any case we are on a mission and can't dawdle." With that, Bernice bent down and gave the woman a friendly kiss on her cheek and started to move on.

Ethan was unaccustomed to being short for words but this interchange had left him momentarily speechless. When he could finally speak he asked, "Are you Bertrille, as in Sister Bertrille?"

Hearing the question the woman smiled radiantly and responded, "One and the same, or at least I will be Sister Bertrille very soon. If the young gentleman would like to visit with the good sister, I'll go in and put on my habit right away."

Bernice made a frustrated sound and tugged on Ethan's arm to move him towards the gangplank, but Ethan resisted.

With a smile Ethan responded. "I'm apparently wanted elsewhere, but I do want to thank you for whacking my would-be adversary with your wimple."

"Oh that," Bertrille responded gleefully, remembering the encounter with the men who'd made threatening comments about Ethan, "he was being rude and really did seem to need some cooling off."

They all laughed and then over his shoulder as Bernice finally led him away Ethan repeated, "But I do thank you," and then they were gone.

They passed a dozen more houseboats and greeted an impressive array of ladies, or at least what appeared to be ladies. They came in all skin tones, more hair colors than the folks at Clairol ever imagined, sizes and ages that seemed to span orders-of-magnitude, and apparent personalities that ran the gamut. There were secretaries and sailors, nurses and geishas, more than one princess, and an impressive array of fantasy characters. Finally, after many introductions and a great deal of good-natured teasing they arrived on the deck of the river-most boat.

Ethan and Bernice had been standing at the railing for a few minutes, enjoying the breeze and admiring the sun setting over the river, when from the half shadows behind them came a voice with the timbre of a large feline. "What's a nice boy like you doing in a place like this?"

Ethan turned towards the voice and gasped in amazement at the most voluptuous woman he'd ever seen. In the flickering light of the setting sun reflecting on the water, it was hard to see her clearly, which was an entirely intended effect. That woman, Jasmine by name, had maintained her extraordinary good looks but she knew that on the far side of 40, strong light was not to her advantage.

While she was speaking Ethan thought he detected a Boston accent, but dismissed that possibility as highly unlikely. Imagine meeting a Bostonian whore on a Bornean houseboat.

Recognizing that the poor boy was still speechless, which was as she anticipated, Jasmine continued with a heavy Yorkshire accent accompanied by a subtle change in her facial expression that made her look a bit like a doughty English school mistress. "Can I offer you a cup of tea?" and then reverted to the docks of Boston and added, "or a cup of joe?" To Ethan's amazement, she then spoke with the tones and precise diction of the most pedantic of his professors at Harvard. "Don't worry, I know you're here for purely ethnographic purposes, but I would so like to talk with a countryman. I've been in exile for so long I have many questions that I hope you can answer."

Bernice then spoke up, having recognized Ethan's continued dazed and confused state. He'd seen Jasmine have that effect on men before, but still found it amusing, "Don't worry Professor, after your visit with Miss Jasmine, I'll escort you safely back to the straight and narrow, not to say, boring world."

"Thank you Bernice for taking such good care of my cousin," Jasmine said in flawless Hokkien, and then continued after a pause, "I'm not sure how your gallivanting around town with him in broad daylight is going to affect his reputation, but I am sure that yours will be much enhanced," and they both laughed. Ethan only partially understood what they'd said, but wondered about her use of the word for cousin; what was clear was the fondness the two had for each other.

With that, Jasmine swept Ethan into her houseboat. From the outside it looked like the rest in the fleet but inside it was lavish beyond imagination.

"Please, make yourself comfortable," Jasmine said, waving towards some large pillows that seemed to be casually strewn about on an expensive looking Persian rug. She continued with a voice that was pure San Francisco Bay area, "I can offer you tea or coffee, or, how about joining me in a glass of wine. I have a lovely merlot from a friend's vineyard up in Mendocino County."

"Wine would be nice," Ethan finally managed to say, "not a spirit I've encountered often of late." Ethan was trying not to stare, but the woman had captivated him and he was straining to see her in the soft light of her living room, or boudoir, or whatever it was.

Jasmine was rather enjoying the young man's confusion but at the same time endeavored to make him comfortable. "No, I suppose not, at least in the places that you frequent. I know it's culturally insensitive to say this, but I never could stomach *tuak*--knowing how it's prepared doesn't help," she said in reference to the practice in some Iban groups of partially chewing the manioc roots or rice to start the fermentation process.

"I totally agree," Ethan said more enthusiastically than he intended, but then continued in a steadier voice, "it's terrible when you can feel a hangover coming on while you're still drinking." Somehow this enticing and very exotic woman had a way of inspiring confidence, and her wiles were working well on Ethan. He'd just settled back on a pillow when she reappeared from an adjoining room with a bottle of wine, a corkscrew, and the mien of a highly valued courtesan waiting on her lord. In keeping with the unfolding charade, which was subtly rendered, Ethan jumped up and asked if he could do the honors—Jasmine handed him the bottle with an appreciative nod and then said softly enough that Ethan thought he might have misunderstood, "The famous Yarrow manners."

Ethan wondered about that comment but popped the cork and asked, "Shall we let it breathe?

Jasmine looked up at his face, for she was quite a bit shorter than Ethan, smiled, and then replied, "No, perhaps I'm being boorish, but life seems too short to postpone pleasure." Somehow the way she used the word 'pleasure' caused Ethan's already engorged member to jump—he realized that he was in the presence of seductress beyond his previous experience.

Ethan poured them each a glass—fortunately, Jasmine lowered her eyes demurely, which kept him from juggling that simple task. She seemed to know just how far to push him before he would reel out of control and she had other intensions for their first meeting. With glasses in hand, they settled back onto the cushions.

In the few minutes they'd been together, Ethan had the strong impression that his hostess could change visages as readily as she did accents and languages. The thought actually crossed his mind that perhaps he was mistaken and that one hallucinogen or another had shaken loose from his cerebral cortex and he was tripping. Whatever the explanation, he was fascinated.

After a sip of wine, Jasmine asked with the voice and off-hand manner of a fellow scientist, "How is your research going? Have you discovered new species that will save the world from cancers, or war, or perhaps greed?"

"Thank you for asking—little in the way of new species, and none with miraculous healing properties, but I do admit to being increasingly disillusioned with the focus of my studies. I do love the rattans, spines and all, but I find myself drawn away from plant taxonomy to the much more pressing cause of indigenous land rights and conservation," Ethan then hesitated, worried that he was boring the lady. He was also surprised that that after only a few minutes together, he was already bearing his soul. This switch from botany to political science was not yet settled in his own mind but here he was, revealing his inner turmoil to a stranger. He also realized that the questions she wanted to ask were most likely not about his work and that she'd merely been polite. He nevertheless continued, "Sorry, sometimes I bore even myself, but I'm bursting with curiosity about you...sorry, I know you have questions for me, but can I ask you one?"

"Certainly, and if I can answer I will. And my questions are not so pressing that they can't wait."

"Are you really American?"

"Why yes I am, blue passport and all." Jasmine hesitated, enjoying Ethan's surprise, and then continued, "But also French, Singaporean, Malaysian, and Australian."

Without thinking, Ethan asked how she managed to have so many nationalities, to which Jasmine responded with a lifted eyebrow, which spoke volumes and stopped that line of questioning. Ethan realized that he was dealing not only with a devastatingly attractive woman, actress, and linguist, but also an accomplished diplomat.

"I'm actually planning to move to the States fairly soon," Jasmine reported.

"Where do you have in mind?" Ethan asked, sipping his wine, mostly to calm himself with a familiar action.

"My American friend Ken is trying to convince me to buy some land in California near a place called Big Sur. Turns out that on the land there is a fancy old house that I could convert into a meditation center or something."

When she mentioned meditation, she somehow changed her posture and facial expression such that she needn't have even said the word—at the same instant, Ethan detected at trace of incense and the faint echo of chants. He had to shake his head to dispel what he was sure was an illusion.

"My neighbors would be a delightful tribe of people who call themselves the Pranksters."

Ethan was processing this information as fast as possible, but the surprises seemed to come one after another. He had to ask, "That Ken friend of yours, by any chance is that Ken Kesey?"

"That's him, lovely man. His books might not count as *haute literatur*, but they certainly are fun."

The look on Ethan's face said enough to prompt her to continue.

"Ken came to Singapore on a book signing tour right after Woodstock---I understand you were there too, remind me to ask you about that later—and we hit it off splendidly. We had plenty of time together because, after his first reading at a bookstore on Orchard Road, Lee Kuan Yu or one of his minions must have recognized the nature of Ken's writing and shut down the rest of the tour, including the stops in KL and Penang, so he stayed on my sailboat and we played for two weeks. We sure had fun," she said with a sigh, and then continued. "After what was admittedly not a carefully controlled experiment, but with a lot of replication, he was finally convinced of the superiority of our lovely mushrooms over his sometimes harsh chemicals. Haven't you come to the same decision?"

When she said this her countenance changed again. Suddenly, without moving perceptibly, she was a Haight Ashbury love child with a long braid, clad in a tie-die halter top and sandals. Ethan wondered if they were both experiencing flashbacks.

Ethan was beyond being surprised by what Jasmine knew about his life, so without being phased in the least about her question about psilocybin mushrooms and his preferred hallucinogens, he simply nodded in full support of her surmise. The two sat quietly for a few minutes, sipping their wine and smiling at each other, but then there was a gentle knocking at the door. After a few seconds a young woman appeared from the next room, dressed like many modern teenagers in Kuching in blue jeans and a somewhat ratty tee shirt. She was thinner of face and less full of figure than Jasmine, but the resemblance was clear. She was also familiar to Ethan.

"I hope I am not interrupting. Professor, it's so nice to see you." Ethan was clearly caught off guard and could only stare at the two women so she continued. "I thought you might like a bite to eat and hoped you'd try the new types of sushi that Kyoko taught me to make," she said as if his presence was a daily affair.

The teenager who had appeared in what Ethan found to be an extremely unusual place was Veronica from the Wacky Wednesday group. She'd impressed him with her penetrating intellect as well as by the ease with which she controlled Pagik, the son of his friend Jika, and Tommy Cheong, the two most obstreperous but also most fun members of the group. Ethan stood up to greet her and said, "Hello Veronica, it is nice to see you. I presume you two are sisters?"

In response to that question both women burst out laughing, the mom was the first to recover and addressed Ethan and then her daughter in quick succession. "Thank you sir, most kind of you, but this is my daughter. And you, Veronica, this is the sort of man I warned you about. He'll have your knickers around your knees before you can sneeze."

"Mom, please!" Veronica retorted with obviously feigned embarrassment—they were both enjoying Ethan's discomfort. "This is my professor. You should be on your best behavior around him."

"Fine, my love, I will continue to be the picture of propriety and a suitable role model for my young and innocent daughter." Turning to Ethan she continued with obvious pride, "Veronica is another reason for my planned move to California. In a few short months, she would otherwise abandon her aged mother to start her first degree in economics at Stanford."

Veronica harrumphed at her mother's comment about innocence and then reminded her, "But mother, I haven't been accepted yet." She then turned to Ethan and explained, "I'm finishing up my application now. Perhaps it's too much to ask, but might you have a look and give me some feedback on my essay."

"I'd be delighted," Ethan responded, "why not bring it to class a bit early on Wednesday and I'll go over it with you?"

"And while I am asking for favors, would you consider writing me a letter of recommendation?"

"I would be more than happy to, but perhaps due to my status as a lowly PhD student, my letter won't carry much weight with the selection committee," Ethan pointed out.

"Not lowly at all," Veronica said in a voice that had Ethan retained any rigidity in his character, it would have melted away, "I think your letter would carry a great deal of weight," and the matter was settled.

After a few minutes, Jasmine broke the comfortable silence by asking, "As the over-protective mother, is there anything I should get my little girl before she starts college in America?"

Ethan thought for a moment and then said, "If you're going to study economics, you might want to get a pocket calculator, perhaps one of those new programmable ones."

Veronica's responded with a laugh, "How very modern of you Professor, but I should tell you that I'm lightning fast with an abacus." As she deftly moved her hands in the air he could almost hear the clicking of beads on the imaginary abacus.

"I don't doubt it," Ethan responded, and then after a few moments of reflection, continued somewhat sheepishly but sincerely, "but what Veronica probably most needs is a plausible life story."

"What do you mean by that?" Veronica asked in a way that made Ethan wonder if she wasn't fully aware of his discomfort, and perhaps even enjoying it. Meanwhile, her mother looked on with a Mona Lisa smile.

Ethan considered the most appropriate way to address what seemed to him to be a rather delicate issue. American culture was changing and California was in the vanguard, but if she introduced herself as the daughter of a Singaporean whore with a presumably unknown father, she might ruffle some feathers.

"I'm not sure how to explain this, but Stanford is full of the snobbish sons and daughters of bankers, congressmen, and real estate tycoons, all rather unsavory professions in many ways but socially accepted in some circles," Ethan explained with a smile, and then faltered, not sure how to continue. After a pause he added, "As I recall from the application, oh, I applied to Stanford as well. That was a few years ago and perhaps the forms have changed, but they will certainly ask you to describe your parents' occupations."

Veronica looked at her mom and then around the room, obviously enjoying the effect the conversation was having on Ethan. "I've thought about that. I've read about your American sensibilities—you seem to take your Puritan ancestry pretty seriously." She glanced at Ethan to make sure that she had not offended him, but he nodded encouragingly so she continued. "How about if I say that my mother's occupation is," she hesitated and then said, "housewife?"

Jasmine laughed and then somehow it seemed to Ethan that her elegant silk outfit was transformed into a plain plaid housedress and she said with a clearly Midwestern accent, "How about houseboat wife?" and then laughed again.

Veronica paused to think and then in an almost stream of consciousness way continued, "No, that won't work. How about 'diplomat'? I'm afraid that 'courtesan' would be misunderstood." She paused and then continued, "But then people would ask questions about your nationality, which would be complicated to answer. I know, how about stockbroker? You are a stockbroker, aren't you Mom?"

"Indeed," was Jasmine's answer. It was obvious that she was also enjoying this repartee. "And what about your father? You can't say that he was a pirate."

"How about if he was 'in shipping,' which I gather is sort of true, but that he died when I was young."

With that the two women smiled at each other and then turned to their visitor.

"That all sounds quite plausible—I think it'll work," Ethan responded to Veronica, "do you think your mother will play along?" he said and looked over at his hostess who nodded in agreement. Ethan found it hard to believe that the voluptuous women in front of him could pull off being something as mundane as a stockbroker, but that apparently was one of her occupations.

"And what about your nationality and race?" Ethan asked, now more comfortable with the game they were playing.

"Race is easy, I just check all the boxes. As for nationality, what do you suggest?"

Ethan was still processing what Veronica's mother had told him about her own nationalities and on that basis suggested, "If you say 'Malaysian' I'm afraid you might be dismayed by the revealed geographical ignorance of many of my countrymen. What about British? If that's an option, I'd take it. Americans are ridiculously Anglophilic."

"That'll work. And I presume my accent should be more Oxbridge than Cockney?" she responded, miraculously employing both in just those few words.

"Indubitably," was Ethan's very English response.

With those issues settled, they turned to the elegantly constructed sushi that Veronica was still holding on a plate.

Nibbling on one of the beautifully wrapped treats her daughter had brought them, Jasmine said, "Veronica, I must say that you've outdone yourself...delicious, Kyoko is a good teacher."

Ethan was also enjoying the sushi, but kept himself from asking about its ingredients. He could detect sea urchin eggs, but there were other flavors so fleeting they were hard to identify.

After a few minutes, Veronica got up to leave. As she did so, her mother said, "If you see Bernice on your way out, why not let her try a few—I know that she's always hungry...don't let her tell you she's watching her figure," and laughed in a way that made Ethan smile.

As Jasmine walked her daughter to the beaded curtain that served as the door to the room, Ethan took the opportunity to gaze around. On the small table in front of him was an assortment of lovely Japanese silkscreen paintings of flowers; Ethan wondered if they were originals and displayed for his benefit. But what intrigued him more was that underneath the art, seemingly much out of place, was a copy of the Wall Street Journal. When he looked more closely, he was even more surprised by the publication date—only two days old. Seeing this made him wonder if Jasmine was indeed a stockbroker.

After Veronica left, Jasmine turned her full attention to Ethan in a way that somehow made him swell with pride, and then said, "I thank you for helping my daughter and the other children...your Wednesday evening sessions mean a lot to them. And now I believe you have some more questions for me?"

"Where to start? There's so much I don't seem to understand, the mysterious East and all that, sometimes I feel completely in the dark," Ethan said, thought a minute, took a sip of wine, and then continued. "How about telling me something about the Cheong family. Everywhere I turn, I encounter one of them—Tommy, your daughter's friend, is in my class, and his grandfather seems to be involved in everything that happens in Sarawak, even out in the *ulus*. He's always really friendly with me, almost more familiar than I would expect for an elderly Chinese business tycoon. And what about his sister, for an elderly woman with bound feet who can hardly walk, she turns up way more frequently than you can imagine."

"Oh, I can very well imagine. Yu Fang is quite a woman, one of my favorites. Her life would make a great novel or movie, but some of what she's told me seems too fantastic to be true," Jasmine recounted.

When Ethan looked at her with interest, she continued, "She must have been a beautiful woman when she was young...she's beautiful still, wouldn't you say?"

Ethan nodded in assent so she resumed her story. "She was born to a wealthy Hakka family and grew up in Guangzhou, Canton if you will, but when she was still a young girl, she was married off to a local warlord—as the second wife, which was worse. Her father must have been desperate to sell his young daughter into concubinage. That was back in the 20s. Reportedly she was abused by the first wife, disregarded by the servants, and suffered terribly from loneliness. After her husband disappeared for months and then was found dead, she was out in the street, penniless and disgraced. She wandered into the market district and she got a job selling flowers from a boat, an ignominious occupation for a high-born Chinese lady, but she had to eat." Jasmine paused again to collect her thoughts, "I don't exactly know how it happened, but at some point, it must have been in the late 20s, she came to the defense of a young boy who was being tormented because he was of mixed blood...tarred with a white brush," she said and laughed mirthlessly. "Well that young boy was none other than your man, Eddie Cheong."

Ethan nearly gasped at this revelation because to him, Cheong "Eddie" Hing Hong was as Chinese as Mao Tse-tung. The idea that he might carry some European blood did not jive with his impression of the Hokkien tycoon.

"Apparently when Eddie's father heard of the rescue," Jasmine continued, "he called for Yu Fang. To his father's credit, although the young woman was a 'sampan Hakka' and former concubine, he hired her to be, as far as I can figure out, Eddie's governess. She was only a few years older than the boy, but she'd 'gotten around' as you might say, was classically educated, and quite the civilized lady. Eddie's father was apparently ancient and his mother had died, so he needed the help. Anyway, that's when she became a Cheong, and they've been together ever since—he even introduces her as his older sister."

She paused for a minute but then continued reflectively, "Can you imagine, he went back to Kunming to fetch her soon after the Maoists took over—that must have been in 1950 or so. Imagine trying to get a woman who could hardly walk out of China right when all that 'cultural cleansing' was underway."

They both reflected on this image for a few minutes, sipped their wine, and then she continued. "But before that in 1937 when the Japanese invaded China, Eddie, Yu Fang, and many other merchants fled westwards from Canton and ended up in Kunming, which is where they stayed until the end of the war."

Ethan considered the coincidence of both his father and Eddie Cheong being in Kunming at the same time, but the connection was solidified when she said, "Because Eddie spoke some English and was a competent accountant, he was hired by the U.S. Army to help them deal with the Kuomintang."

She hesitated for just a moment but then continued, "I'm vague about how the Cheongs ended up in Sarawak, but for many years after the war, Eddie and his motherless son Billy along with Yu Fang ran an import-export business in Kapit. By the time I started working with him, he'd moved the business to Kuching."

"Eddie Cheong is certainly a complex character, not at all what he seems-- but his son Billy is another story...stick up his butt I'd say. Now the grandson, he's quite the handsome and pleasant young man," at which her eyes seemed to flicker, "and from what Veronica tells me, is quite bright, but then you know him from your reading group, isn't that right?"

"Actually, I know him better than that," Ethan responded. "He accompanied my colleague Jika and me on a collecting expedition to Ulu Batang. Handled himself quite well in the forest, I must say." Jasmine gave Ethan a look that encouraged him to continue. "Jika told me that a young man would come along to help us in the field, but I was surprised when Tommy and not his own son Pagik showed up at our base camp near Long Berawan. I knew from discussions in class that he was interested in nature and was trying to convince his father to let him major in science at university, but it was a surprise to me that he wants to be a field biologist."

Jasmine laughed and then said, "Yikes you really are clueless," and then laughed again in a way that made Ethan smile rather than take offence. "It appears that you focus so much on your spiny plants that you miss a lot of the human dynamics in this Peyton Place we call Sarawak."

Ethan was surprised by her reference to American television, but then politely requested "Please Madam, enlighten me."

"I would be happy to but it would take a Scherezade of nights to give you a full account, and I know that Bernice wants to parade her trophy around some more, but here's some of the basics. When Eddie lived in Kapit, he traded in rattan, dammar, bird nests, and *tengkawang* nuts that he bought from Iban collectors. Jika, your colleague, was his partner, field man, factotum, or some such—in any event, they worked closely together and became friends. I think it helped that up there they were both outsiders, Eddie a Hokkien surrounded by Foochows, and Jika a Second Division Iban surrounded by the Third Division Iban his grandfather, or perhaps it was his great grandfather, had so roundly trounced when in the employ of the first Rajah Brooke. I bet that Jika still has some of those heads."

Ethan nodded to affirm that last statement. On his first visit to Jika's longhouse, he'd been reverently shown those very trophies and heard their stories. They were well tended and displayed in places of pride each with its own woven rattan holder. Many of the other heads, in contrast, were disregarded and seemingly held in lower esteem. When Ethan asked about them he was told that the worst kept were from Japanese soldiers and represented the fruits of taking heads as an act of war, not the respectable ritual of headhunting (*ngayau*).

"Well the net tightens, as they say." Jasmine continued, "After about a decade in Kapit, Eddie and his son moved to Kuching. Eddie remained in the import-export business from which he earned his fortune, and he and Jika continued to be business partners and friends. Then in 1956 or thereabouts, Eddie's son Billy's wife gave birth to Tommy, your student, and Jika's wife gave birth to Pagik, their second child and another of your students. Unfortunately, Jika's wife tragically died soon after giving birth, and Tommy's mother couldn't, or perhaps wouldn't breast feed the infant, so both families needed a wet nurse. Enter Juus, daughter of the famous Ribut, Jika's protector and adopted father. Juus had also recently given birth but the baby was stillborn and she was loaded with milk. Problem solved. And now perhaps you have a somewhat better idea about a few of the many connections in this backwater of Sarawak.'"

All this information made Ethan's head spin and he wanted to ask a dozen questions, but before he could formulate the first one, a clock chimed in the next room and Jasmine stood up and said, "My, look at the time, here we've been gossiping away while your date awaits, how rude of us."

Ethan stood up, somewhat flustered—he couldn't recall ever suffering *coitus interuptus* in a conversation, but the woman had left him hanging in more ways than he could count.

"I do hope you return so we can continue our conversation, but next time I want to hear more about you and your work. Perhaps if you are a good boy," Jasmine said with a wink, "I can reveal some juicy secrets about your family---common knowledge here about which you seem blithely unaware. Things are not as they seem. Ah, here's Bernice, looking as radiant as ever—be off with you now."

Bernice had entered the room shyly through the portal through which Veronica had departed. As she stood there smiling, she asked Jasmine in Hakka, a dialect with which Ethan was even less familiar than Mandarin or Hokkien, "And how did you find my handsome friend. Was I right about his *chi*?"

Ethan was pretty sure that they were talking about him, but couldn't quite follow the exchange that followed, other than a few words, all verbs.

With a wide-eyed look and a radiant smile Jasmine responded in Hakka again, "glows with it."

Bernice responded, "Overflows with it." The two smiled at each other and then in a rapid-fire interchange in which various Chinese dialects were mixed, continued to comment on Ethan's abundance of that essence or force or energy. The two obviously enjoyed these verbal duels, at which both were remarkably adept.

"Drips."

"Flows."

"Streams."

"Gushes."

"Radiates."

"Beams", said Bernice. When Jasmine indicated that she didn't understand that word, which he'd spoken in Foochow, he provided the Mandarin synonym and they both laughed. At that, the game over by mutual consent and Jasmine rose from her cushion like a flower opening. After a moment, Ethan clambered to his feet in a daze.

"You young folks have fun this evening," she said, and then with a look that spoke volumes, "and don't do anything I wouldn't do." With that comment and a chuckle, she ushered Ethan out of the room with Bernice serving as his guide and guard.

As Bernice and Ethan made their way back to land, which required that they pass across several of the houseboats, the evening's activities were getting underway. They greeted various ladies along the way, and Ethan was once again impressed by their diversity and creativity. As the gangplank connecting the final rocket to the shore swayed beneath their combined weight, Ethan imagined that the motion was communicated to Miss Jasmine as a spider might sense movement on the periphery of her web. He was only starting to recognize the extents and intricacies of her connections, but was entirely comfortable about being thoroughly ensnared. He smiled when he realized that he probably shared this contented feeling with male spiders on the verge of mating, but hoped that she would delay a bit before chewing off his head.

Chapter 18. RESCUE BEFORE THE BORDER

Excerpt from an aerogram from Ethan Yarrow in Kuching, Sarawak, to his parents in Chevy Chase, Maryland:

22 January 1972
Dear Mom and Dad,
It's been great to get to know some Iban people well—I'm excited to learn more about how they think about land, and other property for that matter. I have no trouble speaking Iban, but often feel that I understand the words spoken but really miss what is said. They are MUCH more direct and forthcoming than other people here but it still sometimes seem like they say what I want to hear. That's odd given that they are often directly insulting---for example, they never lack for comments about my Yarrow nose...Interacting with young Iban here in Kuching is also fascinating, caught as they are between worlds and times—they sometimes seem modern and international, but then they reveal that they remain fundamentally Iban, whatever that means...

In the middle of the night, Isa came quietly into Ethan's bedroom in his apartment in Kuching. It was a familiar scene for her but this time was different. She'd first visited with her older sister, but since then she'd become a regular Wednesday night guest. On that first visit they'd taken turns exploring Ethan's apartment while the other chatted with him out on the porch. Isa didn't quite approve of the relationship between Singa and Ethan because she thought that her sister should marry again. She knew there were plenty of suitors for the young widow, whereas Ethan was just a diversion. At that time, and to some extent subsequently, she found Ethan physically repulsive, both his face and his smell, but once a week after the Wacky Wednesday Reading Group, she nevertheless found herself in his arms.

She sat on the edge of the bed, gently touched his shoulder, and said "Ethan, it's me, Isa."

During his time in the longhouses of Sarawak and otherwise, Ethan had grown accustomed to being woken up in the night and reacted in his habitual fashion by reaching out a comforting arm and pulling her towards him.

"No, no, no" was Isa's reaction, "this is important...there's an emergency."

That pronouncement woke Ethan from a deep sleep. He sat up and then asked groggily, "what is it Isa, it's not Wednesday is it?"

"Pagik is gone," she said in reference to Jika's teenaged son. Isa looked out for Pagik while he was at the boarding school in Kuching. Ethan knew him well from his reading club, and they'd spent time together in Long Awan when Pagik was home on school holidays and Ethan was working with Jika.

"Gone? Gone where?" Ethan asked when what she said finally registered.

"He's gone to join his cousins in their battle in Kalimantan." Ethan didn't know the full story of what was going on in Indonesia but had heard about race riots in Pontianak. "Some jerk delivered the red bowl to the school ....to the school," she repeated nearly shouting, "who would be so irresponsible as to get children involved in this ugliness?"

It took Ethan a few seconds to understand what she meant about the red bowl, but then remembered that Jika had told him that it was used as a symbol to assemble Ibans for battle.

News about the riots in West Kalimantan was sparse and confused, but it was clear that the disputes were fundamentally over land rights. The Iban, who were referred to as Dayaks in Indonesia, were rampaging against local Chinese farmers and shopkeepers as well as Javanese and Madurese immigrants. There had been numerous deaths on both sides, with the Dayaks taking some heads, which served to escalate the conflict.

Ethan was now wide awake and calculating the likelihood of his being able to intercept and then stop Pagik. He was reportedly with three Iban buddies who worked as laborers in town. Without traffic or delays at the border, Pontianak was only an 8-hour drive from Kuching.

"How are they travelling?" Ethan asked while checking the time...it was 1 AM.

"I heard that he and three others hitched a ride in a lorry; they left in the early evening," she explained with concern.

It was common for trucks to cross between Sarawak and Indonesia at night so as to avoid customs inspections and duties, but more so to minimize the illegal payments they would otherwise have to make to guards on both sides of the border. They carried manufactured goods from Kuching to Pontianak, and mostly brought back illegally harvested logs and rattan canes from Kalimantan.

"While I get dressed, please go make me a cup of coffee," Ethan requested.

Isa responded, "The water should already be boiling...I put the kettle on when I came in."

Once he'd bolted a scalding cup of bitter coffee, Ethan went down the steps two at a time, checked the gas in Roxanne, and pushed her out from beneath the house and down the hill. A few seconds later, Isa heard Roxanne roar to life. She then set about tidying up the apartment before quietly letting herself out.

Once out of town and on the main road to the border, Roxanne seemed to respond to the urgency of the situation and ran like a charm. With the dry road surface and sparse traffic, they were making good time. While he was tremendously concerned about Pagik, the steady thudding of the massive piston up and down in that single 633 cc cylinder was music to Ethan's ears. As they climbed into the hills, they took the corners at speed, which seemed to thrill them both. A little less than two hours up the road, Roxanne was still running well but Ethan's rush of adrenaline and caffeine rush was diminishing. He was planning to stop to purchase tax-free gas of dubious quality from a roadside shop when some freshly cut branches in the road warned him of was an obstruction ahead. Around the next bend he came upon a lorry pulled over on the narrow shoulder. Normally he would stop to see if the driver needed help, but tonight he was in a desperate hurry and he would not provide that courtesy. As he slowed to pass, he noticed a group of people standing around a campfire. Something about the group made him go back to see what was going on.

Ethan parked Roxanne in front of the lorry and then walked over to the fire. As he did so, he noticed that only one of the group stayed in the light of the fire while the others shifted back into the shadows where he couldn't see their faces. That behavior struck Ethan as more curious than threatening. He wasn't yet sure why he'd stopped, given the urgency of his mission. He nodded to the man, whom he presumed to be the driver, and then took off his leather gloves to warm his hands over the fire. He'd gotten chilled on the ride, despite his full leather suit. Night is indeed the winter of the tropics, and he'd climbed about a thousand feet in elevation from Kuching. The fire felt good.

The driver was surprised by the arrival of an *orang puteh* (white man), and then taken aback when he addressed him in Malay. "What seems to be the problem?" Ethan asked, increasingly curious about the three people in the shadows who were whispering to each other.

"Broken axle," the driver replied, you were lucky you avoided that pothole a few hundred feet back."

"I was lucky," Ethan replied, "In my country, we give holes that big names like the Grand Canyon," to which they both laughed.

The driver was intensely curious about Ethan's arrival, "And you, Tuan, where are you off to in the middle of the night?"

"Well that's kind of a sad story," Ethan explained, increasingly convinced that it was Pagik and his friends hovering just beyond the firelight. "A friend of mine, a young Iban man studying in Kuching, was convinced that he should go to Pontianak to kill Chinese people. I suppose you've heard about the riots?"

"I've heard a little, and plan to avoid Pontianak for that reason. Sounds like a bloodbath, and I don't want to get caught up in it," the driver explained, now understanding more about the motivation for the request from the young men for a lift. "I'm Iban too, at least on my mother's side, and I get angry about our land being taken away, but my father is Chinese and so are many of my friends. Killing them doesn't seem like the answer."

After listening to the conversation, the four boys shuffled slowly towards the fire, with Pagik in the lead. They all wore hangdog expressions but remained convinced of the nobility of their mission. They also still harbored the anger that comes easily to 17-year old boys struggling with the transition to manhood. For these boys this transition was complicated by the fact that manhood was traditionally marked by the taking of an enemy's head. Pagik finally spoke on behalf of all the boys, "We appreciate your effort, Professor, but you don't understand. We received the red bowl and it is our duty to help our brothers."

Ethan didn't react immediately to this obviously heartfelt response but then said, "You are absolutely right. I don't know what it's like to be an Iban. I can't possibly understand how it feels to have your land taken away, your forests destroyed, and your way of life threatened. I do understand that you need to do something in response, but don't think killing is the answer. I'm also worried that some Dayaks in Pontinanak are confusing the taking of heads with *ngayau* (traditional headhunting). Jika, your father and my teacher, made it very clear to me that these are completely different processes—one is an act of war or vengeance while the other is a pure, ritual act. Isn't that why the Japanese heads at your longhouse are so little valued?"

In response to what Ethan said the boys muttered but still seemed unconvinced, so he continued. "I see you have your parangs, I hope they are sharp so that when you kill people, they won't suffer too much." Ethan was now speaking mostly to Pagik, whom he knew to be a gentle character. "I suspect that it won't take much to catch the old ones. Just think about Eddie Cheong trying to avoid rough guys like you; he wouldn't stand a chance. Or, better yet, how about his older sister, the one with bound feet; she wouldn't be able to hobble two steps before you could be on her." The mention of Cheong Yu Fang was too much for Pagik. To most people in Kuching, that ancient woman was a mystery and suspected of both sorcery and senility, but the Cheong's had been extremely kind to Pagik, and Yu Fang was like a beloved great-aunt to the young boy. He'd also deduced that the Cheongs paid his school fees, but no one had ever told him that in so many words.

Ethan's little speech had the intended effect as first Pagik and then the other boys hung their heads to indicate their agreement. Rather than dwell on the topic, about which everyone present was distraught, Ethan simply said, "I'm sure you guys can catch a ride back to Kuching. Pagik, if we leave now, I can get you back in time for your first class with no one at school any the wiser. And you sir," Ethan said addressing the truck driver, "thank you for taking care of my friends. I hope that you get rolling again before too long."

With that, he and Pagik walked over to Roxanne. Although she virtually never kick started, Ethan gave it a try but to no avail. Since he had stopped on a flat stretch of road, there was no choice but to enlist help with a jump start, which relieved some of the tension and made the boys feel a bit less sheepish. With a hearty push, Roxanne roared to life with a big puff of black smoke, Pagik climbed on, and they headed back to Kuching.

In two hours they coasted up to the gate of Pagik's boarding school with the engine turned off. When the young man dismounted, Ethan could see that he was a bit shaken so he asked, "Are you okay?"

Pagik responded, "I'm okay, but do you always ride that way?"

Ethan was relieved that Pagik seemed to have taken his change of plans in stride and said, "No, I took it easy because I figured you weren't in a hurry to get back."

"Thanks for the ride," said the ashen-faced young Iban, "I better get back inside before the wakeup call." Ethan didn't know it yet, but that ride, which was nothing special for him or Roxanne, would soon be a legend, embellished more than a bit by Pagik's fertile imagination. Ethan knew, for example, that it was unlikely that the 400-pound motorcycle with two adult riders had spent any time at all airborne, but that's how the story went.

Chapter 19. TODDY, POLITICS, AND A WARNING

Excerpt from an aerogram from Ethan Yarrow in Kuching, Sarawak, to his parents in Chevy Chase, Maryland:

9 February 1972
Dear Mom and Dad,
Did I mention I play on a cricket team here in Kuching? They even let me bowl at which I make a spectacle of myself, which everyone enjoys. After the games we usually drink sundowners at the club, which only recently started admitting non-Europeans. Tomorrow's game is in the morning and afterwards we will retire for the afternoon to a toddy garden on the coast. Mom, you'll have to ask Dad about toddy, but it's basically fermented coconut sap. I hope I learned my lesson to drink the stuff in moderation, because the hangovers are monstrous. As for the taste, the first sip is rough, but after a bucket (it's served in small plastic buckets), it goes down too smoothly. My teammates are mostly Tamils who work for the Public Works Department—nice bunch of lads. No one cares much about winning and losing, but win or lose, they take post-game celebrations seriously.

After the cricket game, which Ethan's team had lost badly, he and Ian joined his teammates at their favorite toddy garden along the coast on the outskirts of Kuching. It was a typically hot day, but comfortable with a sea breeze in the shade of Australian pine (*Casuarina equisetifolia*) and coconut trees. It wasn't much of an establishment, just a grove of coconuts with a small shack in which coconut sap was fermented in huge open-topped ceramic jars that once contained eggs packed in briny mud and marketed as being one hundred years old. Log benches scattered around in the shade represented the only furniture. Ethan gazed out onto the beach and the numerous logs that had escaped from rafts on their way to sawmills. Many were badly eroded, encrusted with barnacles, and ridden with shipworm holes, but some looked sound and Ethan again wondered whether it would be cost effective to harvest them. Removing them would also benefit the sea turtles, whose egg-laying was impeded by their shifting presence.

The sap used to make toddy is collected by boys and young men who climb the palms every evening to shave a bit from the thick flower stalks they had previously lopped off. Into a bucket suspended from each stalk drips the sweet sap they climb back up to collect the next morning. From painful experience with other open-fermented alcoholic beverages, Ethan knew to avoid over-indulging. The whopping hangovers for which coconut, rice, and cassava wine are famous are at least partially due to their containing, in addition to ethanol, substantial amounts of methanol and, depending on which microbes happen to colonize the brew, ketones, esters, and aldehydes.

Toddy gardens resemble beer gardens in Europe, except for the clientele, which is all males and mostly of South Asian extraction. Instead of bratwurst and potatoes, the clientele is supplied with incredibly spicy and salty snacks to whet their thirst. Ethan enjoyed the laid-back atmosphere and, at least after the first bucket, rather liked the taste of toddy.

Ethan and Ian were sitting comfortably in the shade chatting with several teammates when Ramakrishnan, the police officer and principal wicket keeper on their team said, "*Thaipoosam* is coming, and we hope you and Doctor Ian will join us in the celebration. It's really something to experience before you leave." Ethan and Ian were both pleased with the invitation, which they accepted graciously. They'd heard a great deal about this important Hindu festival, and the way it was celebrated in Sarawak was world famous.

While pleased by the invitation, both Ian and Ethan were surprised by Ramakrishnan's suggestion that they would both soon leave Sarawak. After another drink of toddy, which was already starting to taste good, Ian asked, "But what makes you think we're not sticking around? I have another year on my contract and Ethan has a ways to go on his research and plenty of time left on his visa."

A cricket player who drove a truck for a cement company that had recently changed hands in what seemed to him like a hostile takeover said, "I suppose that story in the newspaper about the bloody bats in Fairy Cave sealed your bloody fate, Doctor Ian, but the effort is appreciated."

The man was referring to a nature essay about bats that Ian had published in the Borneo Times. The bats in question roosted in Fairy Cave, but in the essay he said nothing about conservation of the bats or of the cave system itself, which was reputedly but not publically threatened by being ground up to make concrete. Instead, the story focused on the relationship between the bats and the pollination of durian flowers. He'd discovered that relationship after mist-netting bats one pre-dawn morning as they returned to roost after a night out foraging. His boss at the Sarawak Museum had encouraged him to study the bats for alleged taxonomic purposes. When he removed the bats from the net and was admiring them in his hand, he noticed that the faces of many were lightly dusted with yellow pollen, about which he was curious. With pieces of tape, he collected some, which he later examined under a microscope. By checking against samples in the herbarium, he concluded that it was durian pollen. After setting his mistnets in several durian orchards and watching flower visitors for several nights, he confirmed that the bats were major pollinators.

The mood of the group was turning too dour for the occasion, so Ethan commented, "And what did I do wrong? You know, if you don't want me to bowl, all you have to do is ask."

"Oh, your bowling is indeed terrible—all speed and no spin—but you do keep the batters on their toes," Ramakrishnan said in reference to Ethan's frequent "bean balls." The batters wore some padding, but many had nevertheless been stung by his wild throws. That comment elicited guffaws of support from his other teammates who added, "and wicket keepers too," and then someone else shouted, "You even keep the umpires hopping, which they bloody well deserve."

When the group settled down, Ramakrishnan continued in a fashion that made Ethan think that someone had instructed him to make this statement. "All I know is that someone high up in the state government thinks you're stirring up trouble among the Ulu Belaga Iban." When Ethan's look revealed that he didn't understand his point, he continued to explain. "It seems that there are grand plans for that area, and your pesky Iban friends are in the way. The last thing the boss men want is resistance from locals, especially if fomented by an outside agitator, even one posing as a spin bowler."

"And do you have any idea what's planned?" Ethan replied, concerned by what Ramakrishnan had said but too far into his third bucket of toddy to take it too seriously.

"Probably more oil palm plantations," responded one of the other players. "If I had some money, that's certainly how I would invest it."

That comment led to a long discussion of the profit margins from oil palm farming as compared to rubber tapping and logging. Each land use had its advocates among the men, none of whom had the capital or political power to engage in any of these activities personally but nevertheless held strong opinions.

The conversation was far too serious for Ian, who was well into his cups, so he abruptly changed the subject by starting on a story about Ethan. As a great gossip himself, he was well aware that his American friend was the subject of a great deal of local interest, with rumors of his exploits circulated widely.

From Ian's preamble, Ethan felt a twinge of concern that the story might offend some of the listeners but then realized that after several pints of toddy, even he was having trouble understanding what his friend was saying. With drink, Ian typically lapsed into this native Yorkshire accent, in this case so much that it was unlikely that anyone else would be able to follow him. With that realization, Ethan sat back and listened in comfort.

"I figured out the secret to Ethan's success," he said with a glint in his eyes while he looked around for confirmation from the listening men, "it's referred to by evolutionary biologists as the Grover Cleveland Effect."

Ethan interrupted, "Cleveland, as in the massively fat former 22nd President of the U S of A?"

"22nd and 24th," Ian corrected, "one and the same."

With a puzzled look on his face, Ethan interrupted again. "I do believe you've mentioned him to me before, but I can't recall the circumstances." After saying this he did remember the circumstances, which caused him to grin sheepishly which Ian acknowledged with a knowing nod.

"Well," Ian continued, "as the story goes, one day the President and his much younger wife, Frances, I believe was her name, were touring a chicken farm. The two toured separately, each ably guided by a local farmer who was proud to show off the operation. After Frances watched one of the roosters mount a dozen hens in rapid succession, she coyly requested that her guide mention that performance to her husband. Later, after the guide did as he was bid, the President thought for a second and then requested that the guide please ask his wife whether it was always with the same hen."

Ethan and Ian both roared with laughter about the story, while the other men watched them with puzzled looks on their faces. As expected, the gist of Ian's story had been missed due to his accent and the many unexplained references.

As they sat in the shade enjoying their toddy, which they needed to squelch the mouth-fires ignited by the snacks on which they were munching, OfficerWong Swee Lee, out of uniform of course, came over to drink and chat with them. The mostly Tamil men from Ethan's cricket team happily made room on their bench for the off-duty policeman and they all talked about the game. After a while, Swee Lee turned to Ethan and, in a teasing voice said, "I lost some money on you today."

Ethan was only half listening and asked in a slightly slurred voice, "How's that?"

"I bet you'd be pulled after three overs, but you made it to five," Swee Lee explained ruefully.

That revelation prompted Ian to exclaim, "You should have bet on how many batters he would hit. I believe it was three today."

They all laughed at the good-natured teasing, but then Swee Lee continued, "But I found a way to win back my money."

"How's that?" Ethan asked.

"See that coconut tree over there?" Swee Lee said with a gesture, "I bet my friend that you can climb up to those nuts in less than 5 minutes."

Everyone was a bit slow-witted with drink and the heat, but excited by the wager. Finally, after studying the situation for a few minutes, Ethan asked, "And if I do climb it, what do I get?"

With seeming reluctance, Swee Lee considered the question for a minute and then said, "50 *ringgit*" (about US$20).

Ethan thought about it for a minute, and then responded, "I'll do it, but for 100."

Swee Lee hesitated for a few seconds and then agreed to the new payment, which indicated that he had quite a bit more than 100 *ringgit* riding on the bet.

Ethan then wondered about the source of Swee Lee's confidence in his climbing abilities, but he did have plenty of experience climbing coconuts from his high school days. In a fit of 'senioritis,' he and his studious-looking but wild friend Nat hitchhiked from Maryland down to south Florida for an extended Thanksgiving break. Their first stop was in Fort Lauderdale at Pan American Airline's School for Stewardesses where Nat's older sister was a trainee. The sister was also truant, having gone off sailing to Bimini with a pilot she'd met, but after being smuggled into the strictly chaperoned facility, the boys were well treated by the other trainees. After two days, they escaped and continued southwards.

After spending the morning on South Beach admiring the beautiful people and splashing in the tepid ocean, they caught a ride to Coconut Grove from a gay guy they'd met. Strolling through the wealthy neighborhoods where homeowners were preparing for an approaching hurricane, the boys realized that they were hungry and nearly out of money. They then hit on a way to earn enough money for food and the luxury of Greyhound tickets back to Maryland.

When they saw a fancy house with coconut palms in the yard, which was common in the days before Lethal Yellowing Disease killed most of them, Nat would go up and knock on the front door. When the door was answered, he would point out to the homeowner that their nut-laden trees were a menace to one and all but that he and his high school buddy, who were trying to earn money for a class trip to Kennedy Space Center, would be happy to deal with the threat. If the owner was still reluctant, he would pull out his slide rule, which for some reason he'd brought on the trip, and at least pretend to calculate the force exerted by a 3-pound coconut accelerated by a 100 mile-per-hour wind. That calculation was usually enough to convince the owners to shell out $20 per tree to have the nuts removed.

Once a homeowner agreed to the deal, Ethan scrambled up the trees and cut off the nuts. It was Nat's job to pile them on the roadside to be picked up by a fellow with a truck who was paying them 50 cents each. After just a few hours they'd earned enough for a massive dinner at a posh Cuban restaurant and the overnight bus back to D.C.

As Ethan prepared for the climb in the toddy garden, he slowly and ostentatiously removed his shirt and then folded it carefully on a bench, which caused laughter among the men. He then kicked off his sandals, and rolled up his pants. All fifty or so men in the toddy garden were now paying closeattention, and most were wagering with odds that changed by the minute. Ian, who'd heard Ethan's coconut story, bet everything he had, and then went into Ethan's wallet and bet all his friend's money as well. As the crowd awaited, Ethan requested a parang and a small knife.

After someone handed Ethan a parang, he walked over to a small hibiscus tree and banged up and down on its trunk with the side of the parang. Other than Ian, none of the assembled people knew what he was up to, so Ethan grandly explained, "Making an offering to the tree gods." After he had pounded the wrist-thick stem around its circumference, he lopped it off at head height and then again at ground level. He then peeled off the loosened bark, twisted it, tied it into a loop, tested his knot, walked over to the coconut tree, dropped the loop on the ground, and inserted his feet.

The crowd was silent while Ethan stared intently up the coconut tree's trunk at the nuts hanging high above. He put the small knife in his teeth, pirate style, reached as high as he could on the trunk with his hands, and then leapt up, grabbing it with the taught bark loop between his feet. Then, in a series of inchworm like motions, he was up the tree in less than a minute, pulled himself up into the corona and disappeared from view. The cheering and boos intensified when, after a few seconds, he hung down below the leaves and crowed like a rooster.

After resting for a few minutes and as the wagers were being settled among the drunks below, Ethan reached down with his knife and started harvesting coconuts, which he stored temporarily up amongst the bases of the leaves. After he'd assembled a substantial arsenal, he used them to pelt the crowd below to the tune of Camptown Raceway, which he sang at the top of his voice. The bombardment continued as the men dashed for cover, some diving under tables and others running flat out as the well-aimed missiles landed around them. When his supply of ammo was exhausted, Ethan swung down from the corona, adjusted his climbing loop, and descended quickly to the ground where he was met with shouts, slaps on the back, and a brimming bucket of toddy, which he quaffed with enthusiasm.

Chapter 20. THAIPOOSAM TRANCES AND DANCES

Excerpt from an aerogram from Ethan Yarrow in Kuching, Sarawak, to his parents in Chevy Chase, Maryland:

26 February 1972
Dear Mom and Dad,
Last week I had a nearly transformative experience at the Thaipoosam Festival. *Don't worry, I'm not going to shave my head, eat nothing but lentils, and become a Hindu, but my faith in science was definitely shaken. Admittedly it was after hours of dancing in the hot sun in a crowd of gaudily dressed Tamils, half of whom seemed to be in trances-- I definitely felt the pull myself. The people in deep trances were carrying "kavadis" or ceremonial burdens attached to their bodies with large hooks into their skin, rods inserted through their cheeks, and pokers through their tongues. Many* kavadis *featured full pitchers of milk, which will give you an idea of their weight. I came to my senses when we reached the stairs going up to their sacred cave. I watched in awe as* kavadi *carriers danced up the steps on the sharp edges of machetes held in place by dozens of helpers. But my belief in science was really shaken yesterday when one of the Indians at the herbarium came back to work. I saw him at the festival in a deep trance carrying a* kavadi *that rested on a pencil-thick metal dowel through his cheeks and was held erect with wires attached to his back and chest with large fishhooks. He'd invited me to the festival and said he was going to do the Kavai Attam (the Burden Dance) to petition Shiva for a loan to buy a Datsun (and his mother's continued good health, he added almost as an afterthought). His was not the most extreme example of self-mortification, but what I really can't explain is that only a week later, his cheeks were unblemished—no scab, no scar, nothing. I should add that he got the loan.*

It was mid-morning when Ethan arrived at the already over-flowing parking area for Fairy Caves. He parked Roxanne and was soon engulfed by a happy crowd of chanting, drumming, and dancing celebrants. Many of the mostly Tamil women were dressed in yellow saris and wore plentiful bracelets on their wrists and ankles as well as necklaces, earrings, nose rings, and other amulets. As the dancing crowd moved slowly towards the entrance to the cave complex, he was increasingly caught up in their euphoric mood. He knew the area, having spent several days exploring the impressive karstic limestone outcrop that housed the cave.

As the crowd flowed slowly around him, Ethan stopped to gaze up to where he, Jika, and Ahmad bin Mustafa, the newly hired Malay botanist, had rappelled down from the summit with their new-found palm species in hand. He felt proud, but just a bit deceitful about the minor role he was playing in protecting this lovely geological formation from being ground into cement. After Jika had successfully steered the young Malay to the plant and encouraged him to collect it, Ethan had guided him through the process of describing it as a new species. Ethan actually thought that it deserved only sub-species status insofar as it wasn't all that different from populations on other limestone outcrops, but for political purposes, he agreed to call it a new species. He smirked when he thought about Ahmad's description to the press of his single-handed discovery of this remarkable new species, to which the young *Bumiputra* botanist attributed both horticultural and pharmacological value. Even if the international botanical lawyers and taxonomic revisionists eventually sunk this new species, it and Ahmad had contributed to conservation, which Ethan figured was worth some rule bending.

Now even happier, he continued dancing along with the people around him. In this crowd there was little chance to respect personal space, but everyone was so happy that he gladly went with the flow. After a while he realized that the heat and the rhythmic drumming and dancing were serving to carry him aloft. It almost felt like the conditions were dislodging hallucinogenic compounds stored somewhere in his brain, but he felt very safe. He started to chant along with the crowd as they kept pace with the *kavadis* carriers who were wending their way towards the stairs leading up to the cave. After climbing those 108 steps to the cave mouth, they would be relieved of their burdens, blessed, and collapse into the arms of awaiting family and friends.

On the occasions when Ethan was fully aware of his surroundings, he marveled at the degree of gleeful self-mortification he was witnessing. He knew that the carriers of the *kavadis*, which looked like they weighed up to 50 pounds, felt nothing in their deep trances, but it was nevertheless remarkable to see all the hooks set into flesh and metal rods inserted under their skin and through their cheeks and even tongues. Those hooks and rods, together with various sorts of straps, supported the *kavadis*, which towered over the heads of the dancing penitents and petitioners. In a brief moment of lucidity, he realized that the concept of 'penitent' was probably incorrect, and that he was revealing his Christian cultural roots. Any concern he had passed quickly as he became fully immersed in the daze of dancing.

After what for Ethan was an undeterminable period of time, perhaps a few minutes or perhaps hours, he was gently lifted from his revelry by the realization that he was dancing against the flanks of a very friendly brown cow. The cow was resplendently decorated with flowers and ribbons and seemed quite comfortable in the crowd, which probably evoked some sort of herd instinct. For some reason it was much more of a shock to hear a familiar voice address him from his other side.

"Professor Yarrow, I presume," his student Veronica said into his ear, so she could be heard over the chanting crowd. "I see you've already made a friend," she said in reference to the cow. "It appears that my mother was right about you having a way with the fairer sex."

After Ethan shook himself from his revelry, he was stunned by the appearance of the young woman. She was dressed in a bright yellow sari, with yellow flowers in her hair and a dusting of yellow powder on her skin, but her heavily made up eyes were surprisingly bright and clear, given the circumstances.

It took a minute to register what she'd said, coming as he was out of trance-like state, but then he smiled and said, "Veronica, how lovely to see you." After a few seconds he continued, "Are you here alone?"

"No, I came with my mother. There she is, dancing amongst the *kavadi* carriers."

Jasmine was dressed the same as her daughter, but judging by her closed eyes and general mien, she was far gone in a deep trance. Ethan was again struck by the woman's phenomenal beauty to the extent that his knees started to buckle. Somehow Veronica had anticipated that reaction and moved closer to support him. "My mission now is to make sure that she's okay, but from the looks of you, perhaps I need to watch out for both of you," she said with a smile. She then offered him water from a canteen strapped over her shoulder. "First you need to drink."

With his thirst quenched, which Ethan had not realized was extreme, the two locked arms and walked along in the parade, keeping pace with Jasmine. Ethan's eyes never left the gyrating woman, whose trance seemed ecstatic. Before he too was drawn down into a similar state, he admitted to Veronica, "I think I'm in love with your mother."

Immediately after making that admission, Ethan jolted awake, aware that the daughter might take offense. Instead, Veronica laughingly responded, "Join the queue. She's entranced most of the men and half the women in Kuching. I'd say it's about time for us to move to California before her various suitors come to blows. Now don't you cause me any trouble," she said and laughed again and gave his arm a squeeze.

After another hour when the heat of midday and the fatigue of constant dancing was catching up with them, or at least with the fully conscious Veronica, the young woman gently steered Ethan and her mother into the shade of a large fig tree at the base of the limestone massif. She unwrapped a cloth from her sari, spread it on the ground, and made them both comfortable before going off to fill her water bottle.

As they sat away from the pulsating crowd, both Jasmine and Ethan slowly became aware of their surroundings and smiled at each other in total comfort. Eventually, Jasmine broke the silence by saying, "Someday I should prepare myself properly for this festival, eat only Satvik food for months, fast, forego most bodily pleasures, and shave my head. Maybe then I would grok this holiday."

Ethan wondered fleetingly whether she chose that verb from Stranger in a Strange Land for his benefit, but this woman had proved herself to be full of surprises and insights. He then responded by saying, "I admit that I too am confused. Here we are celebrating the birthday of the God of War, the embodiment of Shiva's light, with an incredible outpouring of love and peace. This is Woodstock but raised to some high power. But all these Hindu gods seem to embody their opposites. How is it that Shiva can be the god of both creation and destruction?"

"Exactly," Jasmine responded, and lay back with a sigh. "I believe you understand completely. I only hope that Murugan can successfully vanquish Soorapadman," she said in reference to a character in a famous Hindu legend. "I've had enough of that evil demon and prefer peacocks." With that she gently fell asleep. Ethan watched her breath for a while and then followed suit, entirely happy with his lot in life. His last thought before he slept was to remind himself to ask her later about her connection with Ganesha, Shiva's son. He remembered seeing several statues of that elephant-headed, pot-bellied, mouse-riding god in her houseboat. How could that one god be both the placer and remover of obstacles?

Chapter 21. GET OUT OF TOWN

Excerpt from an aerogram from Ethan Yarrow in Kuching, Sarawak, to his parents in Chevy Chase, Maryland:

23 March 1972
Dear Mom and Dad, Great news about the Bruins beating the Rangers—perhaps I'm the only one celebrating in Borneo. I also have good news about my research. I now have an almost entirely new PhD advisory committee, which reflects my switch plants to politics. I'll try to publish the taxonomic work I've already completed, but now dedicate my time to exploring how the Iban might defend their land rights. That tribe makes up more than half of the population of Sarawak but continues lose land to newcomers from elsewhere in Malaysia. I still find time to spend in the forest, but now I delve deeper into things Iban...

It was after dinner early on a quiet Sunday evening. Ethan was typing while Ian repeatedly tried to engage him in conversation. They both looked up when there was a tapping on the screen door.

Ethan went to the door and saw with some surprise that it was three of his students, none of whom had ever visited him at home before. He was happy to see them but curious about their visit. He suspected that they'd come to inform him about the results of their various university applications, for which they'd all ended up asking him to write letters of recommendation.

When invited in, Tommy, Pagik, and Veronica entered shyly but couldn't disguise their fascination with the clutter and piles of books in their teacher's apartment.

"I'm very happy to see you," Ian said in a welcoming voice, "this man is boring me to tears. All he does is work." They all stood around awkwardly for a few seconds and then Ian suggested, "Perhaps we should go out onto the porch where it's cooler."

"And to what do we owe the honor of this visit?" Ethan asked as they all moved out onto the porch. "Do you have news to share?"

The students glanced at one another and then Veronica started by reporting, "I was admitted to Stanford. I thank you Prof for your advice on my application and I'm sure your letter of recommendation made all the difference. I plan to dual major in economics and statistics."

"Sounds painful," Ian commented with a smile, "but California should be fun."

"Yes it should be, especially since my mother ended up buying that property at Big Sur, all 27 acres, complete with what is probably a ramshackle old hotel. She's pretty excited about the move, but her plans seem to change daily, sometimes hourly." Veronica hesitated for a minute, but then when she saw that everyone was interested in hearing more, she continued. "It's clear that she plans to open some sort of non-profit spiritual center that will make her a lot of money. I know, the idea of making money with a non-profit doesn't make sense, but she's been fanatically studying US tax laws and believes that something called a 501-C-3 will make it possible. Perhaps at Stanford I'll learn how non-profits can pocket big bucks, but for I have no idea. It's also not clear where she's getting her ideas, but the common refrain is that she wants to create a place where, and now I am quoting, I've heard it so many times---perhaps it's to be her mission statement—'where people can embark on vision quests while they deal with personal pain and unleash their latent potentials.' Yes, that's it, what do you think?"

"Yikes," Ian exclaimed, "your mother certainly has a great imagination and clearly some marketing skills. And what sort of spiritual assistance does she plan to provide?"

"That's where it gets even crazier. Sometimes she's all about meditation, then pyramid power, the other day it was acupuncture, this morning she was babbling at breakfast about deriving energy from crystals. Frankly I think that she's eaten too many of those funny mushrooms." She looked over at Ethan after mentioning the hallucinogens, but then continued after chuckling when he acted innocent. "And the people she talks about having on the advisory board of her institute are totally soup-to-nuts. She's mentioned some upstanding bankers and brokers with whom she's worked, but also Alan Ginsberg, Grace Slick, and of course her buddy Ken Kesey. Then there's Abbie Hoffman, with whom she's dangerously fascinated. I pointed out that Mr. Hoffman might draw undue attention from the authorities and might not work well with the Wall Street types, but she's being stubborn. I managed to talk her out of Timothy Leary, but she came up with another Harvard prof by the name of Ian Albert."

"Alpert," Ethan corrected, "but you should really address him by his new name, Baba Ram Das. Also note that Harvard canned him after he handed out psilocybin mushrooms to one of his classes---good shit, I might add. Woops, pardon my French."

"Professor, perhaps you could talk some sense to my mother," Veronica pleaded, half convinced that her mother's plan might work and not at all convinced that Ethan was the right person to advise her. Overall, she was enjoying his discomfort about her request.

"Err, it would be my great pleasure," Ethan assured her somewhat hesitantly, and then continued with more confidence. "I agree that Hoffman would be a pain, but I can recommend a local cartoonist and social commentator by the name of Robert Crumb. And how about Jerry Garcia, another local boy...be nice to have a Dead connection," Ethan said and waited while the others figured out what he meant.

After the group settled down, Ethan said, "And what about you, Tommy, do you have news?"

"Only that I accepted the bursary at Adelaide, and plan to study environmental law," Tommy reported.

"Going down the same path as our venerable future Chief Minister," Ian teased.

Tommy smiled and then with a glint in his eye said, "That's right, but I hope the path is dark when I meet him and that I'm well-armed or moving at a high speed--someone needs to stop him."

"Armed with the legal tools you intend to master, I presume you mean?" Ian asked while everyone laughed conspiratorially.

Having heard from the other two young people everyone turned to Pagik. "As you already know, I'm following you and Doctor Ian to Oxford. But just this morning I received the good news that I was admitted to Oriel College."

"Good show my man," Ian exclaimed, "now you need to select a mentor before all the good ones are taken."

"Please explain Doctor Ian," Pagik asked, "what sort of mentor?"

"An Oriel alum who can provide you guidance, generally from beyond the grave, but useful nonetheless. Mine was Samuel Wilberforce."

Veronica was the only one who recognized the name, which provoked her to exclaim, "Didn't he become the Bishop of Oxford and debate Thomas Huxley about Darwinism? But Doctor Ian, you're a staunch evolutionist."

"Spot on both counts," Ian exclaimed, "the good Bishop was wrong about evolution, but, like me, he struggled with internal demons but yet managed to function—somehow I've always found that inspirational."

They considered his answer for a minute or so and then Pagik asked Ethan, "And Professor, who was your mentor?"

"Mine was Uncle Walt Raleigh," Ethan responded.

Ian chuckled and then added, "To clarify, that's Sir Walter Raleigh, perhaps the biggest screw-up to ever graduate from Oxford."

"But he went on to great things," Ethan defended.

"Yea, like introducing sotweed from Virginia to the world, now that was a great move. And didn't he discover El Dorado? Oh, that's right, he failed at that one too."

"And ended up in the Tower of London for his trouble, which doesn't sound quite fair," Ethan added with mock defensiveness, "but he was released by the Queen."

"Didn't he end up back in the Tower again for bedding one of that same Queen's ladies-in-waiting?" Ian asked, already knowing the answer. This was a conversation with which both men were very familiar but which they nevertheless enjoyed. "Now she must have been a piece..." he said and then stopped himself, "apologies Veronica, I forgot that we were graced by the presence of a representative of the fairer sex," which caused Veronica to pout dramatically and everyone to laugh.

Ian continued, "Yea, he lost his head over that little dalliance."

"Wrong again," Ethan corrected in a supercilious manner, "he was actually beheaded for the seemingly minor infraction of massacring a bunch of Spaniards in some rinky-dink outpost on the Orinoco."

Turning to Pagik, Ian explained, "Now perhaps you understand the importance of selecting an appropriate mentor—Uncle Walt certainly led this unfortunate Yank down the wrong path."

Pagik thought for a minute and then suggested, "What about Beau Brummel, wasn't he an Oriel grad?"

Ian considered this option for a minute and then said, "Sorry my young sir, Ole Beau doesn't seem like a good choice for you, given that you seem to be sartorially challenged," he said, glancing at Pagik's too-baggy bellbottoms and raggedy shirt.

Everyone laughed at this teasing, and then Pagik continued, "What about Cecil Rhodes, he's another Oriel chap, right?"

"Right indeed," Ethan affirmed, "and a jolly good one at that. Not only did his money get me to Oxford, he's credited with inventing both apartheid and the concentration camp."

Laughing, Tommy teased his friend, "Great choice for a blackfella like you," at which everyone laughed again, "Mr. Rhodes will roll over in his grave."

The group sat comfortably for a while, basking in all their good news, but it soon became apparent to both Ethan and Ian that the three had something else on their minds. They waited for a while longer, and then Veronica started to explain the principal reason why they'd come to Ethan's apartment.

"Professor, we did want to tell you our news, but the principal reason for our visit is that our parents met earlier today and came to a decision that affects you," Veronica said in a rush.

"Wait, your parent know each other and they met together to talk about me?" was Ethan's immediate response.

"Well actually it was my grandfather," Tommy Cheong explained, "but yes, they're friends and business partners."

"And your father, Pagik, is he too involved?"

"Very," Pagik answered, "my dad and Mr. Cheong have been in business together since before I was born. More recently Veronica's mother joined them, and now serves as their investment broker. Instead of trading in just rubber and dammar, they are now into 'futures,' about which I need to learn more."

Ethan and Ian were both taken aback to learn of these linkages.

Noticing their looks, Tommy continued to explain, "You might also not know that Juus, the daughter of Jika's foster father Ribut, took care of both me and Pagik when we were young."

Veronica then chimed in with her portion of the story. "I'm not sure how, but somehow while we lived in Singapore, my mom became their shipping agent. She was forever dealing with manifests of rubber, incense wood, and whatnot—she plans to leave all that behind soon with her meditation center and 'futures,' but she still seems to enjoy complex export deals. When we came to Kuching after Lee Kuan Yew started to make Singapore too boring for her, which is my mother's interpretation of what was happening, she was already well connected here."

"Thanks for that interesting background, but what did they decide about my fate?" Ethan asked.

"That you need to leave Sarawak right away," Pagik answered gravely, his two friends nodded, and then he added, "And you too Doctor Ian, you should think about leaving soon."

While Ethan and Ian considered what the students had said, they all watched bats swooping around the roadside streetlight and listened to the *chechaks* (house geckos) call to each other. The much larger chimney gecko was also making its resonating call, which sounded like a bouncing ping pong ball being pushed down with a hand.

With some gravity, Ethan then spoke. "What you told me is a bit hard to process. Some of what you said makes sense, given what I've been hearing and seeing. While I certainly don't want to leave Sarawak, I'll take the warning seriously. And I would certainly be happy to meet with them."

"Unfortunately, my father already left for Ulu Balui," Pagik responded. "He's warning the people there about what the government has planned for their valley." When both Ethan and Ian looked at him for further explanation, he confirmed what they had begun to surmise. "A dam. They plan to dam the Balui River to generate electricity to smelt aluminum. If this goes through, Long Berawan will soon be under a hundred feet of water. I'm not sure what they can do to stop it, but they've gotta try," Pagik stated with determination.

"But my mom and Tommy's grandfather do want to see you very soon," Veronica added. "They want you would come by the store tomorrow morning."

"Tomorrow's Antonio's birthday," Ethan explained, referring to the young orphan orangutan he'd befriended, "so I'm heading up to the Rehabilitation Center to help him celebrate. I'm going to give him his first durian."

Since approaching the house they knew there was a durian around, but now there was an explanation. It wasn't durian season in Sarawak, but fruits imported from Thailand were available at a steep price in some of the fruit stalls.

"From there I'll head further up to Long Mongkos to check my trees along the canopy walkway. Given how dry it's been, I wouldn't be surprised if we aren't on the verge of a mast."

Despite the warning from the young people and others, Ethan remained hopeful that he would get to stay for the mast fruiting event that he and Jika both predicted was about to happen. They'd come to that conclusion mostly based on the fact that it had been relatively dry and sunny of late, and three years had elapsed since the last mast.

"But I'll be back early to see them—how about at 7?"

"Sure, that will work," said Tommy, and then somewhat sheepishly added, "They'll be happy to see you, but ask that you don't come thumping up on Roxanne. I think they want to avoid advertising that all of you are, what's the word, in cahoots?"

Ethan smiled at his word choice and then said, "I was unaware that we were in cahoots, but can't imagine better cahooters," at which Ian complained about the abuse of the Queen's English and everyone else chuckled.

The young people soon departed, leaving Ian and Ethan sitting on the porch. They were both thinking about what they'd just been told. It explained a great deal about recent goings on both up in the ulus and around Kuching. It also explained why there were again efforts to mine the limestone at Fairy Caves and why concrete factories were being bought up, presumably by shell companies run by the Chief Minister or his nephew.

Before retiring for the night, the two friends agreed that after his meeting at Cheong's store the next evening, Ethan would find Ian and bring him up to date. They wouldn't see each other in the morning because Ethan planned to leave at dawn so as to be back in plenty of time to get cleaned up and walk over to the store.

Chapter 22. MOTORCYCLES AND MORPHINE

Excerpt from an aerogram from Ethan Yarrow in Kuching, Sarawak, to his parents in Chevy Chase, Maryland:

15 April 1972
Dear Mom and Dad,
It appears that I'm approaching the end of my stay here in Sarawak. The good news is that I sent drafts of several chapters from my dissertation to my newly constituted advisory committee and they gave me provisional approval...still a lot of re-writing to do, but it sounds like I'm on the way to getting a Ph.D. in political science—quite a switch from botany, but I'm happy with what I'm doing. The other good news is that I can move back into my old room at 'Looney Lagoon,' that farm commune north of Lake Mendota where I lived during my last year in Madison—it'll be nice to see Suzy the Duck again. Meanwhile, I've gotten involved in investigating the government's plans for massive rural development schemes—my Iban friends are very worried. They keep losing land that was traditionally theirs, but the wave of logging followed by planting African oil palms seems unstoppable. My thesis should shed light on this land-grabbing.

When late on Monday night Ian's telephone rang it was Tommy Cheong on the line. After a cursory greeting he asked, "Doctor Ian, have you seen the Professor this evening."

"No, I figured that he was meeting with your grandfather and Veronica's mom."

"He was supposed to, but never showed up," Tommy explained with a worried tone and then continued without stopping, "and my grandfather just learned that two very suspicious characters from China arrived late last week but were initially missed because they travelled on Malaysian passports. From their description, he knows that they're from a really dangerous triad, the *Hung Fat Shan*—he tussled with them in China before the war. Now he thinks they're out to harm Ethan, or at least to chase him away."

Ian reflected for a minute on what he'd been told, but then responded to only the first part of the message, "Perhaps he decided to spend the night in Long Mongkos," but he was not completely convinced by that explanation for his friend's failure to arrive. While Ethan acted like he believed he was under no real threat, Ian could tell that his friend was worried by recent events combined with what they'd learned the previous evening.

"Yes, perhaps that's what happened. I will tell my grandfather. Good night," Tommy said and hung up.

As Ian was putting down the phone Hazel waltzed in and asked in her typically preemptive fashion, "Who was that?"

"Tommy Cheong. Apparently Ethan didn't make it back for their meeting," Ian explained, concerned about his missing friend but not at all upset about Hazel's arrival or surprised by her unabashed curiosity.

"What meeting?"

"Sorry, a lot's happened since yesterday. Let me explain." Ian outlined the previous evening's discussion with the three teenagers and then added his own corroborating, if circumstantial evidence for Ethan being in danger.

Hazel listened intently and then added a few bits of information she'd gleaned from overheard conversations in her office about the Chief Minister's nephew's plans to build a dam on the Balui River. Recognizing that Ian was genuinely concerned about his friend's safety, a concern that she was starting to share, she attempted to lighten his load by asking, "Don't you think he was waylaid by one of those Iban damsels he's always having to save?"

Ian tried to smile and corrected her, "Bidayuh. He was headed to Long Mongkos to collect his phenology data. But as I recall, he did mention a young lady. He also mentioned stopping at the orangutan rehabilitation center for Antonio's birthday party...he was bringing a durian as a present, can't you still smell it?"

"Oh, durian, I assumed it was just the reek of unwashed males and very dead socks," Hazel said chuckling as she pointed at a pile of dirty clothes in the corner of the room. "I do believe that Somerset Maugham had it right when he described that awful fruit as like 'eating raspberry blancmange in a public lavatory.' I can't understand how you can eat that terrible stuff, plus it makes me sweat."

She would have continued with her tirade but Ian interrupted by saying, "Let me call the rehabilitation center and see if he made it that far this morning. It's late but someone might answer."

The assistant director answered after the first ring and informed Ian that Ethan had in fact stopped by in the morning. He was in apparently in a talkative mood because he described without encouragement the glee with which Antonio accepted the durian. He went on to explain that although the young orangutan had most likely never seen that sort of fruit before, he knew exactly what to do with it. What shocked everyone was that whereas a human could only open a durian with the help of a *parang*, and even then it took some work, the young orangutan broke it open with his hands as if he were cracking an egg. That act made them realize the young animal's strength. He also said that as Antonio systematically ate the entire fruit, he seemed to go into a trance and that he ate the ripe flesh off the last few seeds while lying on his back with his feet in the air. The young man was obviously not very accustomed to telephones and was speaking so loudly that by holding the receiver up in the air, Hazel could follow the conversation.

After finally hanging up and reflecting on the information for a few seconds, Hazel asked, "Now what?"

"I'm going to bed, that's what. I'm sure he'll show up in the morning. Goodnight my dear," Ian said to which Hazel grumbled a response and left.

When Ethan had still not arrived the next morning, Ian called the Cheong's and spoke again with Tommy. The Cheongs already knew about Ethan's visit to the orangutan center, but had also learned that if he did go to Long Mongkos, he didn't stop at the sundries shop at the far side of the pass at Mile 47. It was his custom to stop there to buy treats to bring to the longhouse. Somewhat later they'd somehow been able to confirm that he never made it to the longhouse. Armed with that information, Tommy told Ian that his grandfather had explained the situation to one of Jika's cousins in the Sarawak Rangers.

When the Iban sergeant of the Rangers found out that Ribut's nephew was missing and that foul play by Paib's henchmen was suspected, he sprang into action. By side-stepping numerous protocols and clearly over-reaching his rank, by early afternoon he'd commandeered a helicopter and had two squads of crack Iban troops on their way to the mountainous terrain crossed by the road to West Kalimantan.

Late that afternoon one of the squads found Roxanne, smashed to pieces at the bottom of a cliff near the pass, but no Ethan. They radioed back that they were following what appeared to be a small group of mostly barefoot people. The tracks were small, like those of children, but the Iban soldiers suspected they were from adult Penan, even though members of that tribe seldom roamed as far as the First Division. They also found where poles had been cut and lashed together, which they presumed meant that they were carrying a body. Given the shape of motorcycle and the height of the cliff from which it had flown, they assumed that Ethan had not survived the crash.

The Rangers lost the trail during the night, but picked it up again in the morning. At midday they arrived at an Iban longhouse about 20 miles from where Roxanne was found. Just a few minutes after they arrived, a Ranger helicopter landed. Two hours before, the nurse assigned to the government health post at the longhouse had finally managed to get a message through to Kuching about needing help with an unconscious and badly injured European man. Somehow that message had been transmitted to Rangers back at their based in Kuching, who again flew into action.

The group of hunting and gathering Penan people brought Ethan to the longhouse rather than to the much closer Chinese settlement because one of the women recognized him as a relative of Ribut and his daughter Juus. After first believing that he was a ghost, they then concluded that he was a white Iban. Until they found the remains of Roxanne, which were some distance away from the unconscious man, they assumed that he'd fallen from the sky.

Even for the hardy forest-dwelling wanderers, the trek had been an arduous one. For one thing, Ethan weighed as much as two of them combined. The other problem was that whenever he regained consciousness, he trashed around terribly, which made him hard to keep on the stretcher they'd constructed. They finally resorted to tying him down, which must have been terribly painful because he had several broken ribs. After that, when he started to thrash around, the pain knocked him out again. Within seconds of delivering him to the outpost in the early evening, the Penan melted soundlessly back into the forest, happy to have delivered their burden.

Based on a sketchy description of Ethan's injuries, which included a compound fracture of his left femur, Eddie Cheong had already arranged to have a famous orthopedic surgeon flown over from Singapore to operate. When the helicopter carrying Ethan and the Rangers arrived at Sarawak General Hospital, the doctor was already Kuching-bound on a private jet hired for that purpose. He carried with him all the titanium alloy hardware he might need to put the patient together again, if he survived.

While his friend was missing, Ian was in frequent contact with Tommy Cheong, but held off contacting Ethan's parents until he had something definitive to tell them. Frank and Doris Yarrow were therefore taken by surprise when they received the following telegram from Eddie Cheong, which he sent a few minutes after receiving the news that their son had been located. "Ethan found, leg and rib broken, maybe you come." He signed it 'Eddie Jackass Cheong.' The 'Jackass' was one of Frank's nicknames for Eddie, derived from his given names, Hing Hong. After they received the telegram, Doris Yarrow immediately telephoned Ian, but he was at the hospital and missed her calls until Friday evening, by which time Ian had enough information to reassure them that Ethan was in good hands and would survive.

Ian comforted Ethan's parents as well as he could, but was actually relieved when his mother told him she'd already booked a ticket and would soon be on her way. The bad connection, the fact that parents were on extensions in different rooms and kept trying to talk at the same time, and the evident slur in Frank Yarrow's voice all made the conversation even more difficult than it might otherwise have been. Ian learned that Ethan's father had suffered a mild stroke and could not travel, but couldn't make sense of the link between the father and Eddie Cheong. Struggle as he might, he also could make no sense of the father's repeated questions about someone named 'Jade Flower.'

Meanwhile, back at the hospital, emergency room doctors and nurses cut off the shredded remains of Ethan's leather suit, which had served to hold him together. After four days in the forest, he was a complete mess, but they cleaned him up as well as they could, dressed his minor wounds, started intravenous fluids and antibiotics, wrapped his chest to keep his broken ribs from shifting, and otherwise did what they could to stabilize him. His vital signs were good, but even their best orthopedic surgeon was relieved he wouldn't have to deal with the leg fracture, which was a nasty one. In addition to the leg they were concerned that he'd apparently suffered a grade-three concussion. He was occasionally conscious but in such excruciating pain that the doctors chose to continue with the massive doses of morphine started by the nurse when he first arrived at the medical outpost.

Ethan caused considerable alarm when, during one of his period of apparent consciousness, what he said was incomprehensible to the doctors and nurses. They worried about brain damage and, in desperation, one of the nurses rushed out to the waiting room to ask whether any of his friends might be able to interpret. Ian volunteered and accompanied the nurse back into the room.

This was the first time Ian had seen his friend, and he was taken aback by his condition. Ethan's head was wrapped with gauze, his chest was strapped, his various cuts had been sutured or butterfly bandaged, his broken leg was held up in a sling, and he had I.V.s in both arms. He also wasn't fully conscious and his speech was mumbled to the point of being incomprehensible. Ian was on the verge of giving up when he realized that for some reason, Ethan was mumbling in bad French. When he put his ear right up to Ethan's mouth he could finally make out the chanted words. *"Chaussures marron, ne le faites pas, Quittez l'école, ne le fausse pas, Allez au travail et soyez fous, obtenez un emploi et faites-le bien. T.V. dinners aubord de la piscine, je suis tellement heureux d'avoir terminé l'école ?"* (Brown shoes don't make it. Quit school, don't fake it. Go to work and be a jerk, get a job and do it right. T.V. dinners by the pool, aren't you glad you finished school ?)

When Ian stood up laughing, the assembled medical staff were all shocked. Here he was, visiting a badly injured friend who was displaying symptoms of brain damage, and the man was laughing. When he saw their faces, Ian rapidly suppressed his mirth but then was hard-pressed to explain what he'd heard. He knew that it would make no sense to them if he told them about Frank Zappa and the Mothers of Invention or Ethan's job translating their album 'Absolutely Free' into French. He also recognized that it would be unwise to translate exactly what Ethan was saying, so instead he explained that their patient was reciting one of his favorite French poems. On the way out of the room he checked the doctors' shoes and, as he expected, they were brown.

Later that night, Eddie, Tommy, and Cheong Yu Fang, together with Ian and Hazel, were at the hospital when the surgeon from Singapore and the anesthesiologist came into the waiting room to inform them of their prognosis. The doctors, both Chinese, treated Eddie with more deference than Ian expected, but he was unaware of the roles Tommy's grandfather had played early in the careers of these two men. It was also apparent that the doctors knew each other and had worked together before, which was reassuring. They were both confident that Ethan could be patched together but that, as anticipated, setting his leg would require a fair quantity of hardware. What they were more concerned about was the quantities of morphine that he'd been receiving. They were loath to cut him off, but it was dangerous to administer a general anesthetic to a patient with such high titers of the opiate as well as a concussion, but they agreed they'd take that chance when they tried to pin and bolt his leg back together first thing in the morning.

The next morning as they prepared to administer the general anesthetic, the doctors were relieved when Ethan regained consciousness and spoke to them coherently. He asked about the procedure he was about to undergo and told them briefly that he had been forced off the road by a concrete truck that seemed to be waiting for him around a bend in the road.

After nearly three hours on the operating table, the surgeon emerged from the operating room and announced that they had successfully set the leg. Because they were still concerned about the anesthetic interacting with the morphine, the anesthesiologist had accompanied Ethan into the recovery room to monitor him until he awoke. An hour later the anesthesiologist emerged to reassure the assembled group that Ethan was awake, entirely disoriented, as might be expected, but quite conscious. He advised everyone that the patient would most likely sleep for the next few hours, but had asked for Ian, who was permitted to visit his friend for a few minutes. When the doctor told the group what Ethan had said about the concrete truck, Eddie Cheong asked immediately for more detail, but the doctor had none to offer.

When they'd received the good news about Ethan's operation, Eddie Cheong sent a telegram to the Yarrows that read, "Son okay. Leg fixed. Thick Yarrow head. Yu Fang cares. Afraid pillow will cut neck like you. *Hung Fat Shan* after him. Come take home."

When Ian went into the recovery room to see his friend, Cheong Yu Fang, bound feet and all, hobbled in behind him as if she owned the place. Once in the room she pulled up a chair next to the patient and sat down, not saying a word. Ian and Ethan chatted a bit, but as the doctor had warned, he was still in a post-operative fog but obviously pleased to see his friend. Ian promised to return in a few hours and went to leave, expecting Yu Fang to follow him. Instead, she gave him a look that sent him scurrying. The combined forces of the nurses and anesthesiologist were unable to dislodge her, but all efforts at doing stopped when Eddie Cheong suggested it would be best to leave her be.

Ian returned to his apartment and telephoned the Yarrows to give them the good news. They'd already received the elder Cheong's second telegram, but they appreciated hearing more details. Ian again had to contend with the two anxious parents bombarding him simultaneously with questions, most of which he couldn't answer. He hadn't seen the text of the telegram sent by Eddie Cheong, and so he didn't understand when Ethan's father asked him whether he was sure that the *Hung Fat Shan* triad was threatening his son. Ian admitted to not having any idea—actually, he was not quite sure what he meant by 'triad' and had never heard of *Hung Fat Shan*. Frank Yarrow then asked whether his son had been receiving sustained doses of morphine. When Ian answered in the affirmative, he heard sobbing and the father spoke no more. Ian was relieved to hear that Ethan's mother was leaving for the airport and would be in Kuching in 48 hours.

After another two days in the hospital during which Yu Fang took over many aspects of the patient's care, the medical staff agreed to have him transported by ambulance to the Cheong mansion. A nurse would visit several times per day to check on him, but the doctors had become convinced that the old woman was entirely competent. Their main concern now was about weaning him from morphine, which everyone knew was not going to be pleasant.

Floating happily a few feet above the bed in a drug-induced stupor, Ethan listened to a group of a half-dozen doctors and residents discuss his case amongst themselves. By that point everyone disregarded Yu Fang's presence, and would have assumed anyway, as did Ethan, that she didn't speak English. Hampering their treatment, the doctors explained to each other, were his multiple injuries, and especially the broken ribs. They suggested various strategies for dealing with what was clearly a raging morphine addiction. Yu Fang listened to them for a while and then, in a voice of authority she explained, in Hokkien, that she was in charge of the patient's drug rehabilitation. When one of the younger Hokkien-speaking doctors had the temerity to question her qualifications for this complex task, Ethan missed much of her response, but it sent the young doctor staggering backwards with his mouth opening and closing like a fish gulping air. After the group left, Yu Fang smiled at Ethan, patted his hand, and then said in halting English, "You trust me, but nice time over." After a moment's pause she added, "I help your father, now help you." With that, she busied herself making tea with her back turned and couldn't be persuaded to explain.

The next days at the Cheong house were a torture beyond anything Ethan could have imagined. The ordeal of cold-turkeying from a morphine addiction set new levels for suffering. The hallucinations were terrible. Feeling blood coursing down his back from cuts inflicted by pillow creases was bad, but it was worse when spikes emanating from Yu Fang's cheeks cut into his eyeballs. Perhaps it was fortunate that when he thrashed about in horror, the straps holding him to the bed bit into his chest and the pain from his broken ribs caused him to black out.

When Ethan finally fully awoke late on Wednesday afternoon after several days in-and-out of Hell, he was still groggy and in some pain. He remembered screaming, which accounted for his sore throat. His first sight was the now familiar face of Yu Fang, to whom he gave a wan smile. His memories of the past days were spotty, but he knew he owed that ancient Chinese woman a great deal, for which he felt a wave of gratitude and affection. She looked bedraggled and concerned, but he could see smiles in her eyes. He distinctly recalled her cheeks cutting his eyeballs, but now he could see that other than some wrinkles, her face was by no means threatening. He then recognized again just how beautiful she must have been as a young woman. He remembered her holding him down with her massively powerful hands, but when he looked at them now, they were the small, liver-spotted, and shriveled hands of an old woman. It was clear to him that her power was not of the brute sort.

When he opened his eyes again after a deep and restful sleep, the first thing he saw was again the face of Yu Fang, looking much more rested. He was still looking at her when he heard Tommy Cheong's voice which caused him to take in his surroundings for the first time. The room was sparely decorated with a high ceiling and plenty of light beaming in through large floor-to-ceiling windows that were open to admit a refreshing breeze. He figured it was still early morning. Also in the room was Eddie Cheong, sitting quietly next to his grandson.

After asking about how he felt and clarifying for Ethan the day of the week and his whereabouts, Tommy described his medical condition, including an explanation of his metal-reinforced leg. Ethan listened quietly, but then was startled into trying to sit up when Tommy mentioned that his mother was due to arrive in an hour; only the pain from his broken rib set him back gasping. After Ethan had recovered, Tommy announced somewhat abruptly, "In the meantime, my grandfather wants to tell you about his time together with your father in China."

"Wait, your grandfather knows my father?" Ethan said in shock. "Why didn't he tell me that before?"

After another rapid back-and-forth conversation in Hokkien, of which Ethan understood little, Tommy responded. "He didn't feel like it was his place to talk about your father." Then, with a perplexed look on his face because all of this was news to him as well, Tommy continued, "If there's time, he also wants to tell you about your grandfather, your great grandfather, and your great great grandfather. It appears that our families have been intertwined for many generations."

Eddie was perfectly capable of speaking for himself, but he wanted to be sure his grandson was totally attentive as he revealed aspects of his history as well as Ethan's. Despite his intention to communicate through his grandson, after a few more minutes Eddie Cheong took over and started to explain his relationship with Frank Yarrow, and the various other connections between the Cheongs and the Yarrows. He punctuated his account with questions to Ethan, trying to help the young man spin together what he already knew with what he was being told. He started with a question. "What did your father tell you about his war years?"

As Ethan responded, he was once again embarrassed about how little he knew about his father's life. He started by apologizing for his ignorance and then explaining that it had become abundantly clear when he was interrogated by Ibu Luni at Long Awan.

Eddie, nodded at the mention of Ibu Luni and then asked, "Is she still beautiful?"

Ethan nodded and then Eddie added, "And terrifying too I bet." He smiled as he remembered his own encounters with the medicine woman but then returned to the topic at hand. "But now tell me about your father."

"I know that he spent most of the war in southern China, in a place called Kunming."

Most of the unfolding story was new to Tommy, and he perked up with the mention of Kunming.

"He was in a group called the Flying Tigers, which always surprised me because my father hates to fly. Their mission was to ferry supplies from India over the Hump to China for the troops led by General Chiang Kai Shek."

With the mention of the Generalissimo Chiang, Eddie Cheong made a sour face and said with a vehemence that surprised both Ethan and Tommy, "Chancre Jack was and remains a thug and a thief." With that stark statement he stopped speaking, and waited for Ethan to continue, apparently approving the way the conversation was unfolding.

Tommy was enthralled by the story and its many revelations. He was even more intrigued by Ethan, the first European with whom he'd ever spent much time. Over the past year he'd also occasionally wondered why his grandfather seemed to take such an interest in the young American given that he was usually so wary of Westerners.

"My father was initially supposed to be a radio operator, which he said was only because he was a musician, but his skills as an accountant were needed and he spent most of the time on the ground, trying to keep the Chinese from stealing everything."

With a snort of laughter about the challenges of what was called the Lend-Lease Program, the elder Cheong said, "That was me. I was the chief thief and his Chinese counterpart. And the truth is that we were allies in trying to get the supplies to the soldiers who were actually fighting the Japanese. Chancre Jack certainly made that a challenge for both of us."

"I remember him saying that he enjoyed the food and playing with the children in the town near the base."

After Eddie turned to his grandson and said, "One of those children was your father," the teenager's face reflected his total surprise.

Ethan too was surprised by that information, but after a minute he continued. "I also remember him talking about playing the piano. As a kid, it seemed strange to me that there were pianos in China, but if there was one, he would have found it and banged away every chance he got. Oh, I remember, he said the piano was in a church."

In response to that final word, the elder Cheong started to laugh, caught himself, and then laughed even harder as Tommy and Ethan looked at him with questioning expressions on their faces. When he could finally speak, all he said was "church," which caused an additional paroxysm of laughter. After a few more minutes, he explained his mirth. "Your father was always a great tease. That church was the saloon that my wife and I ran."

That unexpected response from Eddie Cheong caused Ethan to remember his father being teased by some of his war buddies. The group of middle-aged veterans were in the Yarrow's living room comfortably drinking Ballantine beer and retelling familiar snippets of their war stories while their wives cooked and kibitzed in the kitchen. Ethan was lying unnoticed on the floor under the piano on which his father was intermittently playing. When his father's war wounds came up, he remembered the men teasing him about getting shot in the butt when fleeing from a brothel in China. His father laughed along with the familiar joke, but Ethan remembered that he did still carry some shrapnel in his lower back, too close to the spine to be removed---it bothered him sometimes, especially when it was cold.

"Did he tell you about saving my son, Tommy's father?" Eddie asked, which caused Tommy to turn to him in even more surprise and Ethan to shake his head. "No, I suppose he wouldn't. He never would brag, other than about his piano playing." With that the elder Cheong sat quietly in reflection as the two young men anxiously awaited continuation of the story. Finally, after what seemed to them to be an interminable delay, he continued. "One afternoon when I was off on an errand, your father was in the bar playing the piano and some of the girls were singing. Your grandmother was there as well," he said to Tommy. "Ethan's father really is a good piano player and the best accompanist ever--he could make any singer sound good---no, I take that back—he failed with my older sister."

Yu Fang had been sitting quietly in the corner of the room, but in response to this comment about her limitations as a singer, she barked something in Hakka at the elder Cheong, which made him look at her and smile.

In keeping with the mood, Ethan inserted, "He's also unsuccessful with my mother," and then laughed about the memory of his mother's dreadful singing in the early hours of the morning after his parents had partied most of the night with their musician friends. She and his godmother were famous for being the worst singers anyone had ever heard. Nevertheless, after what must have been some copious drinking, the two would each sing their signature songs. Their performances elicited hoots and howls of pain from the partiers, most of whom were musicians and presumably had sensitive ears. His godmother would sing 'Second Hand Rose' and then his mother would follow with her overly maudlin rendition of 'Love for Sale.' That song usually signaled the end of the party, at which point the parents go upstairs to fetch their peacefully sleeping children who, until the last missed note had been gleefully watching from the upper reaches of the stairway.

While Ethan and Eddie were both reflecting, Tommy was squirming, waiting for the rest of the story about his father's rescue. Finally, Eddie continued. "Reportedly they were having a great time when they heard a military truck come skidding to a stop outside. Someone looked out and saw that the truck was brimming with already drunk Kuomintang soldiers bristling with the M1 carbines your father and I had supplied them the week before." He hesitated for a few seconds, picturing that scene in his head for the millionth time. "The local warlord, who had of course become a Kuomintang officer, had been getting increasingly aggressive in his demands, and the girls and your father knew they were in for trouble. Before the soldiers could storm into the bar, your father picked up Billy, stuffed him inside the piano, closed the lid, and stood up defensively. He told me later that he thought about pulling out his service revolver, but then realized that by doing so he might escalate the situation. Yu Fang was there, and came over to stand next to Frankie."

"The soldiers were really angry that I wasn't there, and started busting up the bar while the girls huddled together in an effort at self-protection. When a soldier roughly grabbed one of the girls, your father went over to intercede, but another soldier cold-cocked him with the stock of his gun." Eddie stopped again, obviously still very much troubled by this story, while Tommy and Ethan sat in stunned silence.

"I heard later from one of the girls that Yu Fang then lunged at the soldier who hit Frankie, but she too was knocked to the ground. After that, the girls were herded outside and loaded onto the truck."

"With my grandmother?" Tommy asked in dismay.

Eddie nodded sadly, and then continued. "I returned about an hour later." To Ethan he said, "Frankie had regained consciousness and was raging mad. Your father," he said to Tommy, "wanted me to get guns and go after the soldiers. He was terrified and angry and sad all at the same time." Eddie was clearly overwhelmed by his recollections, and sat silently with his head hung. Yu Fang hobbled over and put her hand on his shoulder in support. After a while he said, "I don't think any of us ever recovered fully from that experience, even to this day."

Eddie Cheong was silent for quite a while but then Tommy asked, "What did you do next grandfather?"

Eddie took a deep breath and then responded. "I did what I always do, started to negotiate. Your father," he said to Ethan, "rushed off in his jeep and did the same." He then reflected, "He was still recovering from his wounds, and moving that fast and jumping into his jeep must have hurt like the dickens."

"It took several days, but we finally got all the women back. The girls were banged up but all recovered." After pausing for a few minutes, a suddenly very old seeming Eddie continued the story. "Unfortunately, the roughing up that your grandmother took was more than she could stand. She died several days later."

Tommy stared at the bowed head of his grandfather in disbelief mixed with anger, rage, and frustration. Out of respect he held off asking for more of the story, but after a few minutes during which no one spoke he finally asked, "But what happened to the soldiers?"

"Nothing. Of course, nothing," Eddie responded with spite and then continued. "That warlord I mentioned, he's now a respected government official in Taiwan."

As they all sat reflecting on this incredible story, one of the servants came in and whispered in Eddie's ear. In response to the message he shook his head as if to clear it of the terrible images and announced, "Enough of that ancient history. Ethan, your mother is here."

Before Ethan could do more than take a deep breath, Doris Yarrow burst into the room.

Chapter 23. FAREWELL PARTY WITH REVELATIONS

For Ethan's going away party the Golden Dragon, a private dinner club at a new golf course in the hills on the outskirts of Kuching, had been lavishly decorated. As Ethan and Ian watched from the head table, the large room was filling with their many friends and colleagues. People had travelled long and far to attend this send-off celebration and most came dressed in their traditional finest. Even for Sarawak, famous for its ethnic, cultural, and religious diversities, the group assembling more resembled an event at the United Nations than a dinner party at a golf club in a small tropical city on the north coast of Borneo.

Some of the guests were surprised by the other invitees, but all were impressed by the breadth of the young American's social network. Those who weren't chit-chatting about Ethan's various friends and the young man's purported exploits, about which there was always plenty of gossip, were speculating about the upcoming meal. A few wagers were flying about the number of courses that would be served, with equal odds about whether the soup would be birds' nest or shark fin.

The table where Ethan and Ian sat faced eastwards towards the wide glass doors of the entryway. A place was set on Ethan's right for his mother, with another for host Eddie Cheong to the left of Ian and towards the kitchen door. Cheong Yu Fang stood next to that door, unnoticed by the guests but much in the minds of the waiters, who bustled about industriously under her stern gaze. The head table was arranged to give Ethan space to prop his cast-encased leg on a stool. The rest of the room was encircled by round tables, each graced by a wooden Lazy Susan with a porcelain tea service and a bouquet of very non-traditional flowers. Although few guests likely noticed those unusual floral displays, Ethan recognized and appreciated the handiwork of Hong Tuck Liew, his colleague from the herbarium; it was a wonderful tribute for a departing botanist. Ethan was particularly pleased to see that the arrangement on the front table featured a towering palm inflorescence. As the guests arrived, they passed by the head table to greet Ethan and Ian before finding their marked places and sitting down or mingling nearby.

When Ethan commented on the challenge of seating such a diverse crowd, Ian explained that he'd been consulted on that topic by Tommy Cheong, who helped translate for Cheong Yu Fang. Ian also remarked with admiration about how much Yu Fang knew about the intricacies of Kuching society, a topic about which he too was fascinated.

Ethan noted with some surprise that most of his male guests were accompanied by their wives, many of whom he'd never met. At the few formal affairs Ethan previously attended in Malaysia, the men usually came unaccompanied. The young American found it especially odd that if there was an after-dinner dance, Filipina women were hired to serve as dance partners. In response to Ethan's observation about the presence of so many wives, Ian laughed and explained. "I gather that your friends were under a great deal of pressure to bring their wives, who absolutely refused to miss this show." He laughed again and then continued. "Based on the threats I heard, the poor fellows no chance. But aren't they all lovely?"

At one table sat Hong Tuck Liew, Ethan's rather rotund colleague from the herbarium, with his very slight wife. At the same table sat the three policemen and their wives. While Captain Abdullah sat looking a bit uncomfortable in a batik shirt of fine silk, his quite voluble wife, who was bedecked in a brilliant orange *baju kurang* (the traditional dress of Malay women) chatted amiably with the wife of his colleague, Wong Swee Ming. Ramakrishnan was dressed in a white *kurta* (a knee-length shirt) over loose linen trousers. Talking to the wife of Tuck Liew, Ramakrishnan's rather Rubenesque wife wore a *gagra choli* (a loose wrap that leaves some of the belly and back exposed) over a pleated *lehanga* (skirt) with traditional *gota patti* embroidery.

The table that attracted the most attention was occupied by an outlandish gaggle of young and not-so-young women. They ranged in skin tones from black to white and were garbed in an extraordinary diversity of outfits. Jasmine had done what she could to tone down the sartorial excesses of these ladies-of-the-night, but it was hard for them to fully disguise their profession. Ethan was particularly impressed by Sister Bertrille, who was flowing out of a Malaysian Airline stewardess *kabaya* (a two-piece dress) into which she'd been stuffed. He smiled to himself when he realized that if MAS stewardesses looked like her, Singapore Airlines would soon be out of business. Sitting among them and looking not a bit out of place was a white woman in a brightly colored off-the-shoulder sari. Neither Ethan nor Ian initially recognized that woman as their friend Hazel. She had spent what she would later describe as one of the best days of her life being "made over" by the girls on the rockets. Her initial reluctance to submit to the primping diminished after they convinced her that dressing up was not something one did necessarily to attract the attention of men, but rather to make oneself feel good inside. Somehow under the pancake makeup and that revealing bit of blue silk, Hazel's frumpiness had disappeared, which brought smiles to the faces of both young men.

When Ethan's mother made her grand entry on the arm of a beaming Eddie Cheong, a hush passed over the room. Standing nearly six feet tall in her bare feet, her height was accentuated by heels and her abundant auburn tresses arranged on top of her head and crowned with a silver tiara; she towered over Eddie and the rest of crowd. Her still statuesque frame was wrapped in a tight-fitting emerald green silk *cheongsam* abundantly embroidered with pearls. That her dress was split to mid-thigh was only partially compensated for by the decorous high collar that was elegantly adorned with silk frogs. This was the dress that Ethan's father had presented his then very young wife when he returned to the states after the war. Ethan remembered discovering the dress when as a small boy he explored the contents of the cedar chest in their attic at home, but he'd never seen his mother wear it. That he and everyone else in the room was accustomed to the facial features and statures of Asian women only served to accentuate the impression his mother made.

Soon after Eddie and Doris Yarrow sat down, the meal service started. It would be fully as sumptuous as expected, the winning number of courses was twelve, and the soup was birds' nest. They started with roast duck followed by shrimp in a red vinegar sauce, soup, sliced sea cucumbers with greens, shiitake mushrooms with noodles, fried squid, sliced beef with *belachang*, lobster with ginger and garlic, steamed fish, cold marinated jellyfish salad, Chinese dumplings, and red bean soup for desert. Between the courses, as if choreographed, different people came up to the head table to chat with the guests of honor. For those whom his mother hadn't met over the week since she arrived, Ethan or Ian provided quick briefings as they approached the table.

After the soup, about which Ethan and Ian had been challenged to explain to his mother, Hong Tuck Liew came to the table. After he greeted Eddie and Ian and was introduced to Doris Yarrow, he announced that for his going away present to Ethan he'd boxed up all of his herbarium specimens for shipment to the States. Given the sizes of many of the spine-beset samples, the packaging was a major task, for which Ethan's thanks were profuse. Although the principal focus of Ethan's research had shifted to the politics of indigenous land claims, he fully intended to finish with his studies of climbing palms, in which he had dedicated a great deal of time, sweat, and not a little blood. Ethan's thanks for both the packing job and the floral displays were profuse, which made Tuck Lee's wife beam with pride.

After the sea cucumber dish, Isa and Singa walked arm-in-arm up to the table. They'd coiled their raven hair atop their heads and held it in place with long black-and-white striped porcupine quills. On their shoulders and covering their breasts they both wore the traditional Iban *marik empang* adorned with detailed beadwork over colorfully striped *kain ikat* (tied cloth) sarongs. As they approached Ethan was hard-pressed to know what to tell his mother about these two young women, but her mother's intuition allowed her to interpret correctly the stuttering of her normally eloquent son. In any case, she bestowed on them a beaming smile of recognition as they approached. After Ethan introduced the girls to his mother, Isa asked, "Did your mother enjoy the addidas?" That seemingly polite and innocent question referred to Ethan's previous description of how eating sea cucumbers was like chewing on old sneakers. In response, Ian and Ethan both burst out laughing, which put everyone at ease even if his mother had no idea what had just transpired.

While Ethan found both women extremely attractive, his mother hadn't been in Borneo long enough to adjust fully to local senses of beauty. She did admire the poise with which they carried themselves, and recognized immediately that they were women of considerable power. Then over the course of their short conversation, which was more-or-less faithfully translated by Ethan, she recognized how much they resembled the Tahitian maidens in one of her favorite paintings by Paul Gauguin, except for their tattoos and distended earlobes.

After chit-chatting for a while, Singa presented Ethan with a beautifully crafted rattan bag of the dimensions of the one he always carried, which was a casualty of his motorcycle accident. As the guests-of-honor admired the handiwork, which was exquisite, Singa explained. "You should know that this bag was woven under the careful supervision of *Ibu* Luni herself. That great lady is sorry to not be here with us this evening, but wanted me to extend to your mother an invitation to visit her at Long Awan. She also asked me to thank you for not bestowing on us any more ugly offspring." With that last comment, for which she used an idiomatic phrase in Iban that Ethan took a few seconds to interpret, the young women looked at each other and laughed. Eddie Cheong also laughed, and then responded to the girls with a comment in mixed Iban and Hokkien that Ethan understood had something to do with bad weather. Up to that point Ethan had been faithfully translating for his mother, but he decided to skip this little interchange. Instead, he smiled at his friends with love and they made their ways back to their table.

Between the lobster and the fish courses when Jasmine and her daughter Veronica started to walk gracefully across the room towards the head table, Ethan's mother inhaled suddenly and Ethan too was struck by their beauty. They were not alone in their admiration; even Hong Tuck Liew had stopped talking. The two stunning women were resplendently attired in matching, bright purple Mysore silk saris trimmed with gold thread. Ethan had the distinct impression that their *bindis* (vermillion dot applied to the center of the forehead to indicate the sixth chakra) were actually functioning as third eyes. Their noses were adorned with small but precious looking gemstones that perfectly matched their saris. They smiled as they approached in a way that instantly disarmed the normally suspicious Doris Yarrow and had the identical effect on her son, who had long been smitten by them both.

Doris Yarrow was surprised when Jasmine welcomed her in English with a distinctly American accent but then sounded like an Indian when asked Ethan about his condition and apologized for not having visited him on his sick bed. Veronica then explained in her best valley girl accent that they'd been in Singapore for the past week, preparing for their imminent move to the states.

After chatting with mother and son for a few minutes, and extracting a promise that they'd meet again soon in California, Jasmine announced formally, "We come to you as delegates from the Table of Tarts," she said with a sweeping motion of her hand.

"Miss Jasmine," Ian interjected, "I simply must ask about some of the finery on display at your table."

"Well Doctor Ian, why don't you come and join us for a while, I'm sure the girls will be more than happy to tell you all about their dresses," Jasmine replied with a wink.

At this, Veronica spoke up, "But please don't provoke Sister Bertrille, she's still miffed that Mom wouldn't let her come in her habit," at which everyone within earshot burst out laughing.

"I will certainly come over after dessert," Ian replied when everyone had settled down, "but in the meantime, would you please tell the 'cream tart' that she looks absolutely luscious," to which Ethan concurred by nodding his head and smiling at the ladies, all of whom had their eyes on the front table (as did almost everyone in the room). Hazel realized that the smile was mostly for her, and blushed deeply but then smiled back shyly.

Jasmine then handed Ethan a book-sized package wrapped in a batik cloth and said, "The river girls wanted to present you with an example of their handicraft. Please open it so I can explain."

Ethan quickly unwrapped the package to reveal a stack of what looked like coasters used to keep glasses and cups from leaving marks on furniture. They were tastefully made and dyed in subtle earth tones, but it nevertheless seemed like a curious gift for a group of women to present to a young man on the eve of his departure for distant shores. When Ethan looked up with a puzzled look on his face Jasmine answered his unspoken question. "Yes, these are coasters, but of a very special nature. These are designed for travel."

When Ethan indicated that he still didn't understand, Jasmine continued. "The girls made these from the fruiting bodies of your favorite mushrooms. The dye is from gambier leaves, which I don't think you need but they do make a nice color," she said and they both smiled at the inside joke that pertained to the common use of gambier extracts to treat male sexual dysfunctions.

Finally, Ethan understood the nature of the gift but to confirm his suspicion, raised one to his nose to take a sniff. When it was clear that they were made from shredded, pressed, dried, and died psilocybe mushrooms, he smiled broadly.

As a parting comment Jasmine said, "Perhaps when you come visit us in Big Sur, we can share these with Ken and my Hogfarm neighbors. I suspect they enjoy handicrafts as much as we do."

Ethan and the other guests watched as the two women glided back to their seats. Doris Yarrow had no clue that the coasters were powerful hallucinogens, but thought that a handmade gift was sweet. She was also captivated by the two women and turned and told her son as much.

Because Ethan and his mother were talking to each other and examining the coasters, neither noticed the next visitor to the head table until she was standing directly in front of them. When they looked up into her face, they were both shocked.

For Ethan, peering into the face of Juus, daughter of Ribut and granddaughter of their shared grandfather was like seeing his reflection in the surface of a rippled pond. For Doris Yarrow, in the time it took to gasp in recognition of the familial resemblance, she ran through various explanations but then settled on Juus being Ethan's half-sister.

Seeing the shock and confusion on their faces, Juus did not delay in explaining her presence to Ethan in Iban, which he quickly translated for his mother.

"Hello cousin and auntie, I'm very pleased to make your acquaintance. Cousin Ethan, I'm especially sorry that it is only now that we meet. I came to Long Berawan to see you a few months back, but you'd already left with Uncle Jika."

As an Iban, she found it hard to accept that her American relatives were previously unaware of her existence or that of her late father, but when the two Americans still looked at her wide-eyed with confusion, she explained. "Ethan, we share a grandfather, Storm Yarrow. My father, bless his soul, even took his name."

"Ribut?" Ethan asked, already knowing the answer. Quick as lightning, he was making sense of many comments and conversations that he had previously only half understood. When he translated the revealed information to his mother, she sighed in relief and then smiled at the revelation of this other side of her late father-in-law, with whom her relationship was sometimes rocky.

Juus nodded, so Ethan asked one of the many questions that were popping into his head in rapid fire. "And you raised Tommy Cheong and Pagik?"

"Yes, and I understand that you too have taken them under your wing, for which I thank you."

"No need to thank me," Ethan responded. "They're wonderful young men."

Listening attentively to their conversation, Eddie Cheong realized that the reunited family had more to discuss than would be possible during the dinner, so he invited Juus to join them for breakfast the next morning at his house. She agreed and returned to her table where she had somehow previously sat unnoticed by Ethan and his mother.

With too many revelations to process at once, Ethan and his mother were chatting about matters of less consequence with Eddie Cheong and Ian as they awaited the final course. While the hubbub in the room continued, Ethan suddenly sat bolt upright and exclaimed to no one in particular, "That can't be!" When his mother looked at him for an explanation he continued, "Do you hear that thumping?" She initially strained to hear the sound he described over the noise of dozens of people in the room chatting and eating, but when the volume of the thumping increased, she nodded and Ethan whispered, "Roxanne." He said that word with such love in his voice and with such a big smile on his face that his mother finally put two-and-two together about her son's mysterious paramour about whom all questions had been deftly deflected since her arrival.

They watched as the big double doors of the restaurant were swung open and a gigantic, gleaming, smoke-belching motorcycle was driven into the center of the room by a tall and remarkably white young man, Ethan's friend Adam. Riding pillion, sidesaddle, in a bright blue, floor-length sequined dress with an impressive beehive hairdo decorated with a variety of shiny blue objects was Bernice. Both were smiling ear to ear, as was Ethan, but his mother watched the unfolding scene with some alarm.

Doris Yarrow had been introduced to many of her son's friends and colleagues, but Adam and Bernie/Bernice were new to her and both came as something of a shock.

Adam hit the kill switch and after a few loud sputters, the machine quieted and the two riders dismounted and approached the head table. While staring at the motorcycle with intensity, Ethan managed to ask "Can it really be Roxanne?"

Bernice answered in her man's voice, which startled Ethan's mother, "Well, mostly. Perhaps it would be fair to say that Roxanne and Lucille are now united."

Adam, nearly bursting with a combination of happiness, embarrassment about being the center of attention, and deep respect for his new friend Bernie/Bernice, added, "And a lot of new parts as well. I have never before witnessed such feats of artistry at a machine lathe. Your friend here," he smiled at Bernice, "is truly a genius," in response to which Bernice curtsied awkwardly.

Now fully cognizant that she'd been toyed with about Roxanne for over a year, Doris Yarrow shot her erstwhile ally Ian a scathing glance down the head table. In response, Ian held up his hands in mock surrender and as an admission of guilt, but then they both burst into laughter. Having seen the mangled wreck of Roxanne in pieces on the floor of Chan Motors, Ian too was surprised that she was again functional.

Without waiting to be asked, Ian and Adam helped Ethan over to his beloved Roxanne. As he caressed the big machine in a way that inspired jealousy in not a few of the women present, Ethan asked the triumphant Bernice about a few details of the repair. When Ethan made it back to his seat, he was greeted by a stern look from his mother who simply said, "You'll pay. I assure you, you'll pay." And then to Ian she said, "And you, Doctor Benedict Arnold, don't think you're getting away scot-free. Be assured that I will extract vengeance for your perfidious complicity." While both young men gazed at her in alarm, Ethan's mother could no longer contain herself and burst out in hearty laughter, which the young men soon joined.

As the story of what had transpired at the front table made its way around the room in both directions from the head table it caused everyone who heard it to smile and a few to laugh out loud. When it reached the Table of Tarts, Ethan glanced over to see Hazel shaking her finger at him in condemnation, but smiling broadly at the same time.

After the crowd had settled down, Eddie gestured to one of the waiters to bring in a large box, which he placed in front of Ethan.

Ethan looked at his benefactor and asked, "A present? After all you've done for me, you needn't have."

Eddie harrumphed and then encouraged him to open the package. Inside was a brand new leather suit, exactly like the one that had been shredded in the accident. "My tailor kept your measurements," Eddie explained, "so it was not a problem, unless you've been eating too many chapatis and gained weight."

Ethan was delighted with the present, which he held up for all to see, and then said, "I shall think of you whenever I wear this beautiful suit, but," he continued in a teasing voice, " it will also remind me of you setting me up in that scooter race a few months back. I might have won if you'd warned me about the Teochew boys' roller derby trick. I assume that you knew about it," he said and looked at Eddie Cheong for confirmation to which the older man responded with unconvincing shrug of innocence.

After the crowd quieted down again, Adam approached the head table with Pinai on his arm. He was as awkward as ever and looking down at his feet while Pinai beamed a triumphant smile. Ethan and his mother waited for one of them to speak. After Pinai poked him in the ribs gently with her elbow, Adam looked up and spoke.

"Mrs. Yarrow, we are happy to make your acquaintance. My apologies about the uproar Bernice and I caused.

After Ethan's mother gave him an encouraging smile he continued. "Please allow me to introduce my fiancé, Pinai. We are to be married next month and then move to Madagascar," Adam said in an almost deadpan voice.

"Yikes," Ethan exclaimed, "you got the job with Heifer International?"

"Yes, I wanted to tell you but you were laid up. They have a job waiting for me. I'll be helping rural people manage small animals—goats, sheep, ducks, and so forth."

"Now that sounds like the perfect job for you. And I understand that the Malagash language is derived from Iban, which will make it easy for you both to learn. Pinai, you may even have distant relatives there."

"I do come from a family of wanderers," Pinai responded, "so you never know." The young woman considered what she was going to say for a minute and then addressed Ethan's mother. "I want to thank you for raising such a dutiful son. He's been a great friend to both Adam and me." She hesitated again and then continued. "I don't know what he said to Adam, but I really doubt that this," she said holding up her left hand to display her engagement ring, "would have happened without his encouragement." With that she leaned over the table and kissed Ethan's cheek.

After the final course of sweet red bean soup, Ethan's mother stood up to make an announcement. To a completely quiet room she announced, "My husband, Ethan's father, is very sorry that he couldn't be here to celebrate with all of you, but he sent a cassette tape that I would now like to play." She handed the tape to Tommy Cheong, who went over to put it in the player that he'd connected with large speakers. "He asked me not to listen to it before now, so what he has to say will be as much a surprise to me as it is to you."

Tommy pushed the play button and after a few seconds, the voice of Frank Yarrow could be heard throughout the room. His voice came through clearly, but Ethan could notice a slight slur, which caused him to catch his breath. Ethan glanced quickly over at his mother, who gave him a reassuring look in response as his father's voice continued. "My dear son, I trust you're recovering from your wounds. I look forward to welcoming you home. I'm sorry I couldn't join your mother on this trip, but you know how I am about flying. Hopefully your mom is not enchanted by the exotic East and wants to stay—she cooked up and froze a bunch of meals for me, but if she's gone for more than a fortnight, I'm cooked."

After a slight pause, Frank Yarrow continued. "You can't imagine my surprise when I learned that you were in the care of my old buddy Eddie Cheong. Hi Eddie, you *Biǎo zi de érzi* (son of a whore). I thought I was shut of you 30 years ago and here you are, rearing your ugly puss again. But I was overjoyed to learn that Jade Flower is there with you—don't worry, I told Doris all about her—well, perhaps not all, but a lot." With that admission Frank Yarrow chuckled and then continued. "Hopefully she's the one taking care of my precious little boy and not you, you Old Donkey---your bedside manner still gives me the shivers. I don't know the details, but heard that Ethan suffered the same cold-turkey devils I did. And Doris, my darling wife, note this as further evidence that he is my biological son," he said and laughed again. His comment about parentage struck the assembled crowd as unusual, but was an old family joke. Perhaps because the son was the spitting image of the father and had been since birth, Ethan's mother was comfortable teasing him about something that in many families was a sensitive subject. For example, when the three of them were together and they were passed by a Rolls Royce or other luxury car--she would take the opportunity to shout 'come back, he's your son, come back for him,' which would make them all laugh.

"But Ethan, in all seriousness, when I heard about your suffering pillow cuts to your neck, my tears flowed. And now I'm getting choked up again...let me stop this damn machine and collect my thoughts a bit."

After some machine clicks he continued "Eddy, how did that handsome boy of yours turn out? The last time I saw him he was eight going on twenty, and already had more sense than you. I suspect that by now he's made you rich and him famous—at least I hope he's kept you out of prison." He laughed at his own joke, while most of the people in the banquet hall looked at each other somewhat sheepishly.

After some more machine noises Frank Yarrow continued. "Jade Flower, I have something special for you. I suspect that Doris told you that since my stroke I haven't been able to play the piano, but for you my young lovely, I will make an exception, as long as you promise not to sing," he said with a laugh. Since the tape first started, Yu Fang, the ancient woman with bound feet, had been moving quietly towards the head table from her station near the kitchen door from whence she supervised the staff. Of the 50 or so people in the room, only Eddie Cheong knew that she was the mysterious Jade Flower, and he was smiling broadly about the unfolding drama. Everyone else was looking around with perplexed expressions and whispering about possible candidates. In none of these whispered conversations was Cheong Yu

Fang mentioned—most people had long-since stopped even noticing when she came or went from a room. "And Ethan, please do what you can to keep your mother from singing. You know I have very sensitive ears and even from across the Pacific, a duet by the two of them would be extremely painful."

From the tape recording being broadcast into the room Frank Yarrow's voice was replaced by a piano rendition of a familiar big-band song from the 40s called 'I'll Be Seeing You.' It was played simply and with care, without the flourish with which Ethan's father was famous. Ethan looked over at his mother, who was equally affected. For a former piano virtuoso to have to plunk out a simple tune with his one good hand clearly reflected deep feelings for his Chinese friends and Jade Flower in particular. Doris knew but Ethan didn't quite understand that after his father was wounded during the War, it was this mysterious Jade Flower who nursed him back to health. Other than the now elderly Cheongs, she was also the only one to know that part of that nursing involved helping Frank kick the morphine addiction brought on by incompetent Army doctors.

It was only when Yu Fang began to sing in a high, almost screeching voice with tears rolling down her face that the assembled well-wishers realized that she was the mystery "Jade Flower."

Other than the recorded piano music and the woman singing, the room became entirely silent; even the staff stopped what they were doing to stare at the old woman and listen to her sing. After a minute, Ethan's mother went over and put her arms around Jade Flower and they both wept and sang. The sound of their voices together was as bad as his father had forewarned, but moving beyond words. This was a song of love from both of them and sung to both father and son. When the song came around to the refrain of "*I'll be seeing you / In every lovely summer's day / In everything that's light and gay / I'll always think of you that way,*" Ethan hobbled over to the two women on his crutches and joined them with his rich baritone as they hugged each other, crying and at the same time smiling in relief.

GLOSSARY OF NON-ENGLISH TERMS AND CONCEPTS

Amok: Malay for the killing madness

Chi: Chinese, literally "life energy"

Chi kung: Chinese for the traditional art of developing and controlling one's *chi*. Believed to provide invulnerability

Dammar: resin from trees in the Dipterocarpaceae native to Southeast Asia, used as incense and varnish

Face: as in, "saving face": a central and complex component of Chinese society, similar but not quite "self-esteem," but more based on how one is perceived

Gambier: ground leaves from a woody vine (*Uncaria gambir*) native to Asia; used for tanning leather, for brown dye, and as an herbal medicine; also known as pale catechu; peak trade (for tanning) 1830-1890

Guan-hsi: Chinese for a mutual aid relationship

Gutta percha: the sticky latex of *Palaquium gutta* trees that was used to insulate marine cables and is still used as by dentists as a temporary filling material

Ibu: Malay for mother; also a title of respect for women

Idli: a savory Indian cake made by steaming a batter consisting of fermented black lentils and rice

Kabaya: a modern tight-fitting two-piece dress worn by Malay women

Kancil: Malay for lesser mousedeer

Mangosteen: delicious purple fruit from *Garcinia mangostana,* a tree native to Southeast Asia

Ngayau: traditional and ritual-laden headhunting by Iban

Penghulu: Malay/Iban for regional chief

Rambutan: delicious fruit covered with hairy protuberances from *Nephelium lappaceum,* a tree native to Southeast Asia

Rattan: the stems of climbing palms; ascend to the canopy with the aid of long, hook-beset modified leaves or inflorescences; basis of a large furniture industry

Sepak takraw: Malay, known as 'kick volleyball'; traditionally played with a ball woven from rattan

Tokay: store-owner, boss, sometimes used as a term of respect, especially for Chinese men

Tong: Anglicized Mandarin word for hall or lodge (*tang*), used to refer to secret societies (e.g., Masonic Lodge, Elks Club, Republican Party, Italian Mafia, Black Hand Tong), see also "Triad"

Triad: used in reference to Chinese secret societies, derived from the common use of a triangle in their emblems, equivalent to trade unions or sworn brotherhoods, take oaths of allegiance

Tuai Rumah: Iban, head of house

Uyir moochu: Tamil for "life's breath," similar to the Chinese "chi"

Zhu-lian jiu-zu: Chinese for cousin nine-times removed

Zi-qu-qi-ren: Chinese for self-deception while deceiving others

CHRONOLOGY

1271-1368	Yuan Dynasty in China, Mongol, initially not considered Chinese
1368-1644	Ming Dynasty
1644-1911	Ching Dynasty in China, Manchu (also not Chinese), defeated in revolution led by Sun Yat-sen
1740	*Chinezenmoord*, killing of 10,000 ethnic Chinese in Indonesia by Dutch Colonial Government and native collaborators
1746-1801	**Francis Yarrow**, Harvard Class of 1767, American Revolution, Boston trader, whale oil
1780-1860	**Cheong Ming Tsia**, Cantonese merchant, met Joshua Yarrow in Singapore
1787-1839	**Joshua Yarrow**, Harvard Class of 1810, Anglican missionary, trader, Singapore in 1822 with Raffles, whale oil, nutmeg and pepper from Indonesia
1803-1868	**James Brooke,** first white rajah of Sarawak (1848-1868), went up the Rejang River to defeat renegade Iban with help from Iban from near Kuching
1809-1868	**Cheong Yow Pong,** Cantonese merchant, translator/scribe for Miles Yarrow
1828-1903	**Miles Yarrow**, Harvard Class of 1849, Yankee Trader in Canton, **Cheong Yow Pong** his agent, helped him escape Canton in 1850, traded with James Brooke for *gutta percha* used to insulate telegraph cables during the US Civil War, imported Chinese laborers for railroad work (1865-1870)
1839-1860	Opium War, Canton a 2000-year old walled city. Cheong's ancestors got to know the Fanquis.
1841	Hong Kong established by British
1845-1903	**Cheong Say Pink**, Storm Yarrow's clerk in Hong Kong
1823-1913	Alfred Russel Wallace in Sarawak in 1854 as guest of James Brooke
1857	Kuching sacked by 600 Hakka miners from Bau
1829-1917	**Charles Brooke** (son of the sister of James Brooke), reigned 1868-1917 as the second white rajah of Sarawak, established the Sarawak Museum in 1891
1870-1953	**Storm Yarrow**. Harvard Class of 1882, Hong Kong 1895-1898, Sarawak 1898-1910, trader in *gutta percha, gambier,* rubber, *dammar;* starts rubber plantation with Iban that fails but Foochow take over; fathers Ribut in 1903 (Iban wife died soon after), returns to USA in 1910 to run family import business, starts American family; trader through WWI and WWII; **Cheong Say Pink** his

	agent in Hong Kong, makes connections for him in Kuching
1874-1963	**Charles Vyner Brooke**, third white rajah of Sarawak (1917-1946), ceded government to Britain; oversaw rubber and oil booms; banned Christian missionaries
1884	Great Kuching fire
1898-	**Cheong Yu Fang** (Jade Flower), Hakka concubine then boat-girl nanny of Cheong Hing Hong in Canton, adopted by Cheong family
1900	Boxer Rebellion, failed coup by the secret society *Yi Ho Chuan* (Fists of Harmonious Righteousness), used martial arts and employed a fist in their emblem
1905-	**Cheong Hing Hong "Eddie"**, Cantonese merchant, flees Japanese to Kunming in 1939, handles Lend-Lease program for Kuomintang; flees to Kapit, Sarawak in 1948, rescues "older sister" (Cheong Yu Fang) in 1950
1911-1976	**Tom Harrisson**, Cambridge polymath, naturalist; inserted behind the lines in Sarawak with Iban Sarawak Rangers, reputedly paid for Japanese heads; Sarawak Museum Curator 1946-1966
1920-	**Frank Yarrow.** Harvard Class of 1946, degree interrupted by WWII—math and music major, New England Conservatory, 1942 July joins US Army Air Corps Flying Tigers, stationed in Kunming
1926-	**Jika**, Iban hunter, Sarawak Ranger during WWII, blowgun champion of Sarawak, trader in forest products, partner with Eddie Cheong, plant collector for the Sarawak Forest Department
1934-	**Juus**, daughter of Ribut, wet-nurse to Pagik (son of Jika) and Tommy Cheong, very recognizable resemblance to Yarrow family males, moves back to ulus after raising the boys
1936-	**Billy Cheong**, born in Kunming, moves to Sarawak with father in 1948
1936-	**Abdul Paib bin Mamud**, born in Sarawak, later became Chief Minister
1940-	**Jasmine,** born in Singapore before Japanese takeover, Eurasian beauty, mother might have known Evan Yarrow, or grandmother knew Miles Yarrow, but definitely connected with the Yarrows
1941	7 December Pearl Harbor, U.S. declares war on Japan
1942	January-February: Japanese take Singapore and Sarawak; July: American Voluntary Group becomes part

	of Army Air Force, "China Air Task Force", under Claire Chennault
1942	Jika's parents killed by Japanese
1945	September: Japan surrenders
1945-	**Ian**, British biologist, Oxford Class of 1966, Oriel College, Ph.D. 1970, Sarawak Museum 1971-?
1945-	**Pamela Wilson**, Harvard Class of 1967, Ph.D. pending completion of dissertation; Field operative for U.S.A.I.D.'s Alternatives to Slash-and-Burn Program
1946-	**Roxanne**, Norton Big Four 633 cc side valve, single cylinder.
1947-	**Ethan Yarrow,** Harvard Class of 1967, studied botany, lettered in ice hockey; 1968-1969 Rhodes Scholar at Oxford, Oriel College; Ph.D. program at University of Wisconsin 1969-?, Sarawak 1971-1972
1948-	**Lucille**, Norton Model 18, 490cc, single cylinder
1948-1968	**Paling**, Jika's first son, killed in Mitsubishi logging concession where he worked as a feller
1949-	**Singa**, Iban woman, briefly wife of Paling, former Dutch boyfriend, training as a healer
1951-	**Isa**, sister of Singa, *au pair* for child of American Consul
1956-	**Tommy Cheong**, son of Billy Cheong, born and raised in Kuching
1956-	**Pagik,** second son of Jika, born in Long Awan but raised partially in Kuching after the post-parturition death of his mother
1957	"Merdeka," what became Malaysia becomes independent from the U.K.
1963	Federation of Malaysia formed with peninsular Malaysia, Singapore, and North Borneo
1963-1966	"Confrontasi" President Sukarno of Indonesia claims Sarawak ("Kalimantan Utara"), some fighting
1965	Failed coup by reputed communists in Indonesia leads to the indiscriminant killing of perhaps millions of ethnic Chinese
1966	President Suharto replaces President Sukarno in Indonesia
1968	Dayaks rise against Chinese and Madurese transmigrants in West Kalimantan
1969	May: Chinese and Malays clash in Kuala Lumpur, estimated 600 Chinese killed, resulted in the New Economic Policy that favored Malays
1969-1974	Richard M. Nixon President of the USA
1970	**Antonio**, an orphaned orangutan being raised in a rehabilitation facility

1971 U.S. Table Tennis Team visits China: ping-pong
diplomacy starts

TELEPHONE INTERVIEW WITH JUAN CAMILO MORO

Rolling Rocks Magazine (RR): Mister or Madam Moro...
JCM: Please, call me JC.
RR: Sure, JC. First of all, why did you choose to set this novel in Borneo?
JCM: Can you think of a more storied place? When I say the word "Borneo," don't you immediately imagine immense forests, ferocious beasts, nubile jungle maidens, and, of course, headhunters?
RR: Sure, those images and more. But you seem intent to de-mystify the place, to put Borneo in a new light.
JCM: Spot on. My goal was to add dimensions to readers' impressions of Borneo and Bornean people. I've always loved jungle novels and movies, but get annoyed when tropical forests are portrayed as all evil or all good, and tropical people as simpletons, shallow, verbally constrained, and lacking the capacity for complex emotions.
RR: You've certainly done a lot to dash those stereotypes, and not just for the Iban but also Chinese of various sorts, Indians, and others. Ethan, your main character, seems to be quite a linguist. How about you? Readers may want to know just how many languages you speak.
JCM: Speak, not many, or perhaps I should say just one other than my native tongue. That extra one is my own version of Esperanto, or perhaps Papiamento, kind of a hodge-podge of words I fluently assemble into a language that is mostly nonsensical to anyone but me. I readily admit that I am not be much of a linguist, but I can claim to be a good listener to both verbal and non-verbal forms of communication.
RR: And what about all the science? <u>Borneo Dammed</u> is peppered with so many interesting detail about forest that readers might suspect you're an ecologist or botanist.
JCM: A fine compliment indeed. Unfortunately, like one of the characters in this story, I hold only an ABD in botany.
RR: ABD?
JCM: All-but-Dissertation. Isn't it ironic that someone who turned into a writer couldn't manage to write his dissertation? Ah well, that was a long time ago. And now I can just enjoy plants without having to study them.
RR: <u>Borneo Dammed</u> is set back in the early 1970s when most of Sarawak was still forested. What's happened to those forests since?
JCM: Mostly gone. Shocking and quite depressing. A quick peek at Google Earth will reveal that, aside from the real *ulus* and a few parks, the forest has been replaced by African oil palm plantations. And if you look more closely in the center of the state, you'll see a large reservoir behind Bakun Dam. That dam is a monument to corruption that set new global standards for cost overruns. It's a colossal financial and environmental disaster from which Paib and his family continue to profit. Really depressing. And don't get me started on the fates of all the Iban, Bidayuh, and other people displaced by plantations, dams, and what not. For all those reasons, I really have no desire to return to what was among my favorite places in the world.

RR: But I understand that you've been banned from Borneo, so perhaps you couldn't go back even if you wanted to.

JCM: You're right about that. The bloody Malaysian government has declared me *persona non grata* and banned my book.

RR: I'm really sorry to hear that.

JCM: Don't be. After the book was banned there was a tremendous spike in Amazon and Kindle sales globally, but especially in Malaysia.

RR: Go figure. I know you have a plane to catch, but perhaps you'll allow me one last question. What's next?

JCM: I'm glad you asked. I'm really excited about my current project, a dance-filled musical set in Papua. I don't want to spoil the story for you, but the characters include a rather sagacious tree kangaroo and a too-curious spiny echidna while the music runs from gamelan to reggae, with some polkas and a mamba. I'm really having fun with the choreography—if you can imagine a cassowary dancing with a wallaby, then you'll get an idea of what is coming.

86118967R00121

Made in the USA
Middletown, DE
29 August 2018